W9-ANU-121
9/2021

STARLIGHT
ENCLAVE

Also by R. A. Salvatore

FORGOTTEN REALMS®

STARLIGHT ENCLAVE

A NOVEL

R. A. Salvatore

HARPER Voyager
An Imprint of HarperCollins*Publishers*

STARLIGHT ENCLAVE. Copyright © 2021 by Wizards of the Coast LLC. All rights reserved. Printed in the United States of America. No part of this book may be used or reproduced in any manner whatsoever without written permission except in the case of brief quotations embodied in critical articles and reviews. For information, address HarperCollins Publishers, 195 Broadway, New York, NY 10007.

HarperCollins books may be purchased for educational, business, or sales promotional use. For information, please email the Special Markets Department at SPsales@harpercollins.com.

Harper Voyager and design are trademarks of HarperCollins Publishers LLC.

FIRST EDITION

Designed by Michelle Crowe
Maps courtesy of Wizards of the Coast
Frontispiece and opener art © Aleks Melnik / Shutterstock

Library of Congress Cataloging-in-Publication Data has been applied for.

ISBN 978-0-06-302977-4

21 22 23 24 25   LSC   10 9 8 7 6 5 4 3 2 1

I have to thank my agent, Paul Lucas,
my editors David Pomerico and Laura Cherkas,
and the rest of the team at Harper Voyager.
And of course the folks at Wizards of the Coast
for helping me and allowing me to continue this wonderful
journey.

A special shout-out to Evan Winter for answering my call
and spending the time to offer perspective, and to explain,
to teach,
some things I needed to learn.

And to my special six:
Julian, Milo, Nico, Charlie, Owen, and Riley.
May you find a place someday to match Callidae.
And may you find someone to share it with you as
wonderful as your Oma.

CONTENTS

STARLIGHT ENCLAVE

Icewind Dale

The Spine of the World

The Silver Marches

• Menzoberranzan

Gauntlgrym

Silverymoon

The Crags

Neverwinter

Sword
Mountains

The High
Forest

N

• Ched Nasad

Thornhold

Waterdeep

The Sword
Coast

Baldur's Gate   *River Chionthar*

Sea of
Swords

0   300

miles

To Memnon

PROLOGUE

The Year of the Nether Mountain Scrolls
DALERECKONING 1486

S leep seemed shorter and shorter. Why hadn't twilight come? Where was the night? Had she missed it during her many naps?

Had she lost track of time itself? It seemed to her as if most of the day had passed before the sun had reached its highest point in the sky—and why was that highest point so far to the side? Was the sun circling her? Why was it circling her?

She knew that she used to know that answer, but now it just confused her.

None of it made any sense because none of it mattered. A longer time awake just meant a longer time to be hungry, and more time to be ready to run away from whatever animal or monster saw her.

That had happened a lot until she had gotten down from the mountainside and out onto this frozen plain—going south, so she had thought, but now was not so sure.

The sun wasn't helping, but if she could just stay awake until the nighttime, she knew that she could navigate using the stars. It seemed, though, that no matter how long she tried to stay awake and moving, she couldn't quite make it to anything resembling twilight, and no matter how short her sleep seemed to her—even on one occasion when she thought she hadn't actually slept at all—the dawn's light had already become daylight before she emerged from her cave or snow shelter.

Or maybe it was just daylight still, and not again, but that made no sense, except that it did, and she didn't know where to go or how to go.

And now she was growing hungrier. Desperately so.

She had survived on the rich drow mushroom bread in her pack for a tenday, rationing it from the start as much as she could while still getting the nourishment she needed to trudge along barren terrain. She counted the meals to try to measure the passing days, and thus tried to estimate the distance she was covering, but those calculations, like everything else, had melted somewhere within the recesses of her thoughts, lost in the monotonous whistle of the chilly wind. More than chilly—it was cold. At first she had thought that was due to her elevation, but no, even with those mountain slopes far behind, it was still cold.

Now the bread was long gone. She had a bit of mistletoe, and used it to create magical goodberries each day or two, little orbs that nourished and replenished her and even healed any minor cuts or bruises she had suffered while trying to cross the brutal, seemingly lifeless landscape. But the mistletoe was not infinite, and she understood that it would not last much longer.

She was tired. She was confused. She was cold. She was lost.

She looked down at the crude spear she had fashioned, one of so many she had made in the days—or tendays . . . or months or *whatever* it might be—that she had been wandering this rugged, forsaken land. No, the sun hadn't set, so it had to be hours, but how could it be? How could she have come down from that now-distant mountain in mere hours?

But where was the twilight? Where was the night?

She remembered her sword, her friend, her protector, her mentor. *Khazid'hea.*

"Cutter," she whispered through her cracked lips, the nickname of the powerful weapon. "My Cutter."

But it wasn't on her hip. She had only this spear, which was barely effective as a walking staff.

Refusing to die, living with the single thought of exacting revenge on the wizard who had thrown her through a portal to the side of that snow-covered mountain, Doum'wielle Armgo put one foot stubbornly in front of the other. She had to keep moving, had to find some alternative to her primary food source.

Then what?

Why wasn't there anything to kill? Where were the animals? Where were the plants? She hadn't seen any plants in days and days, not since she had left the foothills. Every now and again she spotted a bird, but none had come close enough for her to take it from the sky with a magical spell or a spear throw.

It didn't matter. She had to keep moving, had to keep going the right way.

If there even was a right way.

She was almost certain she wasn't walking in circles. In perhaps the only glimpse of insight remaining for the battered young half moon elf, half drow, she remembered the towering mountains were far away now, replaced by patches of rock in a sea of snow, lined with stony ridges like motionless eternal waves, a frozen painting.

Was that it? She wondered with all seriousness. Was she stuck in a painting? A frozen scape of lifelessness? Or, more likely, had she been thrown through Archmage Gromph's portal to an unknown plane of existence, a place of frost and snow, of endless day where sleep couldn't latch on as that weirdly arcing ball of light in the sky ceaselessly watched over her, taunting her?

Always taunting her! This was the world of her drow father turned upside down. The blessed darkness replaced by infernal white. She stumbled across the empty expanse, with one thought plaguing her.

Would she ever again see the night sky?

And then it happened. Hungry, her stomach growling, her berries growing less effective as the mistletoe waned, Doum'wielle at last watched the sun dip to start its journey below the horizon. She had to dig her nightly cave, she thought, and so she set to the task with the enthusiasm of knowing a full day was going to be rewarded with deserved sleep.

But the sky didn't darken much at all, and she watched in blank amazement as the sun continued on its way, not lowering, not darkening, but rather, moving *along* the horizon.

And soon after, rising once more, the sun in the sky again! Or, not again.

Still.

She climbed into her hole. She tried to sleep, but knew she was doomed. This could not be her world.

"No," she decided. "This is eternal torment for Doum'wielle." It mocked her for her father's drow heritage, she decided. It was a taunt, a forever taunt, punishing her for the sins of her father.

And Doum'wielle screamed and screamed into the wind, until she could scream no more and fell limp with exhaustion.

And she lay there and shivered. And sometime later, she ate a berry and came forth into the daylight.

She trudged on because she had no choice.

But neither did she have any sense of direction. Or hope.

She cursed the sun with every step, and praised any clouds that crossed the sky to dim it, and cheered aloud under the storm clouds on those few occasions they appeared, as if they were her champion in the battle with a fiery orb that would not relent to night.

Yet she was losing the war. Her mistletoe died. She could not make berries. She had no bread. She could make flame, which she did to keep warm and to melt some of this endless sea of snow so that she could drink. But it was temporary. And soon that magic would fade, too.

And then so would she. Fade into this windswept plain of snow and frozen waves of rock and ice.

Everything was different from what she knew. Everything was the same.

She drank more meltwater. She sheltered in caves she dug in the snow.

At one point, at some time that was the same as any other time,

Doum'wielle came upon a crack in the ice, a chasm wide enough for her to descend. Weak and shaky, she removed her pack and climbed down, and down some more. A piece of ice broke off in her hand and bounced and tumbled far below.

She held her perch and held her breath, but began to wonder the point. Perhaps she should just let go and fall and die.

But then she heard a splash.

More curious than hopeful, Doum'wielle continued her descent and found some focus in her jumbled mind, enough to bring forth a magical light. With every movement down now, she cast another cantrip, a burst of shocking energy that cut the ice and made a solid handhold. She came at last to dark water, running as far as she could see along this narrow gorge.

It heaved and swelled, and Doum'wielle sensed that it was a wider body than the gorge, surely. She cupped her hand and took a sip, then spat it out, for it tasted of salt. She had traveled to the Sword Coast and the ocean before—this was not as salty, but neither was it potable.

But if this was indeed a sea . . .

Doum'wielle put her hand into the cold water and cast a minor spell of light to create a glowing area beneath her. Then another light, this time on a small coin, which she tossed into the water, watching the brightened area as it descended.

She waited.

She saw movement, just a flitter of a small form darting through the unnatural brightness.

Doum'wielle settled on a secure footing, digging holes with her lightning on either side of the narrow chasm where she could set her feet. She rolled up a sleeve, put light upon her hand, and bent low, then submerged her arm to the elbow, wincing at the sting of the cold water. She waited.

A distortion.

Lines of tiny lightning shot out from her fingers, a shocking grasp that became a small ball of stinging energy, and she yelped and retracted her hand. She was rubbing it and looking past it when she forgot all the pain, for a small stunned fish floated to the surface. She snatched it up and shoved it whole into her mouth, desperate for food, not caring about the bones or scales or that it wasn't cooked.

Only caring to find more!

Time didn't matter. Another fish, and a third, and she devoured both. Then another, and another, and she bashed them against the ice to stun them or kill them, stuffing them into her pockets.

And she waited for more, and thought that she might just stay here forever.

But no, how could she?

It took her a long time to sort that puzzle out, for she did not want to leave this place—how could she leave this place that offered food?

She lit and dropped another coin, then another after that. Then a large form moved through that lowering light. A much bigger fish. As long as her arm.

Doum'wielle pulled a fish from her pocket and bit out its belly, tugging out its entrails with her teeth, then tossed the squirming, dying mess into the water.

Up came the larger fish to feed, and down went Doum'wielle's hand, grasping it, shocking it (and shocking herself in the water yet again!). She accepted the pain and cast the spell once more, then lifted the thrashing steelhead from the sea, viciously and repeatedly slamming it against the ice until it went still.

She loosened the fine cord of her belt and tied the prize to her waist, and then Doum'wielle, beyond pain, beyond exhaustion, somehow climbed up the same side she'd come down. She knew not for how long, or how far, or how many times she had to cast a minor cantrip to secure her grip, but at last she crawled back up onto the sea of snow and ice beside her pack.

The sun was still there to mock her.

She dug a small hole in the snow and crawled in, as much to get out of the relentless light as for the shelter offered against the chill wind, and for the first time in days—months? Years? An eternity?—she slept.

She ate the small fish when she awakened, stuffed the large one in her pack, and walked on, staying near to the chasm.

She had to keep moving.
She had to keep eating.
She had to keep moving.
She had to keep eating.
Move.
Eat.
Sleep.
Drink.

Her thoughts reduced to only that. She forgot why.

And why wouldn't the night come? Where were the stars she had danced under in the . . . in the place before that now had no name in her memories?

Many times in that seemingly endless wander, Doum'wielle tried to recall her more powerful spells, but to no avail. At some point, she finished the last of the large fish, but was too weary to go back into the chasm, or perhaps she just forgot, and so she moved along, step after step in the glaring, unrelenting sunlight and the incessant cold wind.

She knew not how long after—she had slept four times, but that meant little—her belly began to growl again from hunger and her arms began to hang heavily at her sides. She ignored it for a long while, but then realized, to her horror, that she was no longer walking beside the large crack in the immensely thick ice pack.

She spun all around, trying to get her bearings, the shock of her suddenly more dire situation bringing a moment of clarity. She tried to retrace her steps, but already they were disappearing behind her in the constant swirl of blowing snow. She rushed about for as long as she could manage, but could not find again that chasm, that conduit down to the sea so far below her feet, to the fish that had sustained her.

She had no idea what she should do. She looked to the horizon, to the distant mountains, though she couldn't tell if those were even the same mountains she had first landed upon. It didn't matter, as any way was as good as another, so she locked the image of a distinctive peak in her thoughts.

"A straight line," she told herself, though she wasn't really sure why that might be a good thing.

And she walked on, and on, then slept and walked and slept some more.

Doum'wielle had come to understand beyond any doubts that many of the pieces of time that she used to call a day had passed when she realized that she was out of time and out of strength. The water from the melted snow was not enough anymore.

She fell to her knees and screamed at the sun, cursing it, demanding the night.

She wanted to die at night.

She didn't even dig a hole to sleep in. She just fell down and the darkness of sleep came over her.

Then a deeper darkness.

Doum'wielle didn't know how much time had passed when she opened her eyes once more, only to find herself *in* darkness. Cold, cold darkness.

She tried to get up, or roll over, but her cheek was stuck to the ice.

For the first time since she had walked from that mountain where Archmage Gromph had thrown her, Doum'wielle Armgo cried. She cried for her misery, for this miserable end. She cried for her betrayed mother, who had been left for the orcs by her father when he had chosen to walk with Doum'wielle into the darkness.

She cried for Teirflin, her murdered brother. What had she done? She pulled a hand up to her eyes, expecting to see his blood still upon it.

She tried to tell herself that Khazid'hea had made her do it, that the sword had selected a champion, and so she had been given no choice. But no, she couldn't quite bring herself to blame the sword, or hate the sword, no. Never that. In the end, she wept, too, for Khazid'hea.

It should be in her arms, clutched to her as she left this world.

This dark world.

That last thought caught her by surprise. She tried again to lift her face, to turn her face, then, when that failed, she set her hand against the cold ice and pushed suddenly with all the strength she could muster, tearing herself free. The pain was excruciating, but the liberation was worth it. She stumbled and thrashed, winding up on her back and looking up at the sky, at the clouds and the stars.

The stars! A million, million stars!

The day had ended, at last.

With great effort, she pulled herself up to a sitting position, and felt the bite of the freezing wind more distinctly.

As a deeper cold crept in, she believed that she had awakened only to witness her own death, that her mind had somehow decided that she must be alert in these last moments.

She would lie down now and once again let the cold take her, she decided, for what choice did she have? But as she started to roll back, Doum'wielle noted a curious light low in the sky far to her left, a diffused yellow glow. Her first thought was that the sky was swallowing the sun, and that the night was winning some celestial battle here.

But then she realized that the glow was below the silhouette of the mountain range.

That could not be.

Somewhere deep in her thoughts, the word "campfire" whispered, and with it a memory that a campfire meant other people.

With the last strength within her emaciated, broken form, Doum'wielle crawled for that light. On and on, so long that she expected the sun to rise, and thought that there should be some predawn glow. But no.

Then the firelight flickered out before her, and she redoubled her pace, fighting, thinking every movement would be her last, feeling a coldness within her beyond anything she had ever known, so cold that she thought her hands and feet were on fire.

Head down, the withering, dying half elf almost crawled right into a mound of snow, and startled, she looked up and started to move around it—except that her mind couldn't quite grasp what she was seeing. This was no natural mound, but a nearly perfect dome, and one with a low awning of sorts made of snow, creating an entrance tunnel.

Not even thinking of anything more than getting out of the wind, Doum'wielle crawled in. She froze when she felt fur, thick and soft, but after a moment of terror, realized that it was not a living animal but a thick blanket.

It was warm in here, warmer than it should be, she thought, for the walls, too, were of snow.

She didn't understand.

She also didn't care. She crushed her face into the fur and cried and let herself fall away from the world.

Until she heard a growl.

Her eyes popped open to see the pointy fangs of a snarling canine creature barely a finger's breadth from her face.

She screamed and the creature half barked, half yelped at her, while another nipped at her from the other side. Doum'wielle screamed again and rolled, slapping desperately, turning about for the doorway . . . to find two forms blocking the entrance. Humans, she thought, and one holding a small lamp.

"Help me," she started to say, until the larger of the two pulled back the furry hood of his heavy coat.

Definitely not humans.

Orcs.

Reflexively, Doum'wielle reached out a hand to grab at each and brought forth her lightning magic, shocking them both. She pushed them aside as they lurched in pain, and crawled for the tunnel and her very life.

Sharp teeth latched down on her foot, so she kicked at the beast with her free leg, but when she tried to bring that foot back, a powerful hand clamped down upon her ankle, grabbing and holding fast. Doum'wielle clawed with all of her strength. She dug her fingers into the ice and snow, crying and screaming, desperate to get away.

But she had no strength, and the orc tugged her back in so easily. She tried to turn, but the pair were on her, pulling at her, pinning her, their fierce pets yipping and growling, snarling and snapping at her feet.

The orcs were talking at her or to her or to each other—she didn't care and just kept thrashing.

It was no use; she could not fight them. They had her held fast against the floor. They pulled at her clothes. They pulled *off* her clothes. They pushed her down on the fur where she had first collapsed.

Disgust filled Doum'wielle when she felt them come against her on either side, their filthy orc flesh against her own. She tried to resist, sobbing, until she could fight no more.

This was worse than the empty plain. Worse than the cold and hunger. She wanted to escape her body, expecting horrors.

But they just held her and pressed against her, and pulled another fur over them all, and the orc woman—for one of them certainly was female—began to sing softly in Doum'wielle's ear, and the sounds were shocking.

Because they were gentle and melodious.

IT WAS STILL DARK OUTSIDE WHEN DOUM'WIELLE WOKE up, but a small candle burned not far away, offering some light. She was warm under the thick fur, and alone.

Almost alone, she realized as she struggled to sit up, for the exit to the small dome structure was blocked by one of the pets, a short but thick wolf, or not a wolf, she realized as she leaned forward, but more like a huge badger, but one with too many legs, four on each side! Its thick fur glistened golden in the candlelight, but all Doum'wielle could really see were its long and pointy fangs, bared at her.

Doum'wielle fell back and the badger creature did likewise, curling into a ball, its middle two legs on one side scratching at its thick fur.

She tried to make sense of it all. Where was she? What had happened to her? Feeling strange, she looked down and kicked the fur off her bare legs, then shuddered to see that her feet were black and swollen, but smudged with some white lotion she did not recognize.

It was on her hands, too, and she rubbed them together, then smelled them. Her fingers were also blackened, but like her feet, they didn't hurt. What was this stuff? What was this place?

She looked around for her clothes, but did not find them. She did, however, see a bowl set beside her bedroll, filled with some mushy substance. Keeping one eye on the fierce and strange badger creature, she picked up the bowl and noted a wooden spoon beside it. An aroma filled her nostrils, a bit pungent and quite fishy, but not off-putting.

Doum'wielle didn't know if this was for her, or if it was food at all, but she wasn't waiting for permission. She scooped up the spoon and shoveled the food into her mouth, only to wince in pain as the large spoon stretched her cracked and broken lips. She tossed the implement down and lifted the bowl like a wide cup, licking at it, swiping her fingers across the bottom and then sticking them in her mouth to get every drop. In that effort, she tasted, too, the lotion on her hand, and it felt wonderful against her lips.

A healing balm?

"*Won abo, a bik tiknik tu gahta bo*," she heard from the entryway, and she snapped her head around to see the larger orc, the male, crawling into the dome.

Doum'wielle spoke a bit of Orcish, but she hadn't a clue what this one was saying to her. She stared at him for just a moment, before realizing that the blanket had fallen, revealing most of her naked torso. She gathered up the covering defensively and set her glare on the orc, silently vowing to fight it to the death if it came at her.

But that didn't happen. The orc smiled and nodded, and averted his gaze, then held up a bundle, nodded again, and tossed it to her lap.

Her clothes.

He went out and the eight-legged guard followed. Doum'wielle grabbed up her clothing, pausing only in surprise that it was so warm. She moved quickly to dress herself, then fumbled about her breeches and realized that the orcs had apparently discovered and taken the small knife she carried in her pocket. All she had were those breeches, her undersmock, and her shirt.

No overcoat or cloak or hose or shoes.

She heard talking outside and the female orc crawled in. She began speaking gruffly and pointing to Doum'wielle's feet, and when the elf paused to try to decipher any of it, the orc grabbed her ankle and tugged her left leg out straight.

Doum'wielle kicked at her with her right foot, retracted it, and moved to kick again, but held her leg cocked when the orc brought up her left hand, lifting a very thick spear, with a very long white and decorated tip, up before Doum'wielle's face.

"*Meenago foto fo!*" the orc snapped at her. Behind her, the hulking male entered the dome.

Doum'wielle let her leg sink back down to the floor. She winced as the female inspected her foot, roughly rolling the leg from side to side. Nodding, apparently satisfied, she then placed the foot down on some smaller furs she had carried in, and began gently but tightly wrapping it.

The male tossed Doum'wielle a pair of large mittens and motioned for her to put them on.

She put on the left, but then motioned her right hand to the empty bowl and tapped the same hand against her lips.

The orcs both shook their heads. "*Tu gahta bo,*" the male said.

Disappointed, Doum'wielle put on the other mitten.

The female orc finished wrapping both feet, tying the furs tightly in place, then nodded to her partner, who dropped down and grabbed Doum'wielle by the ankles.

"What?" she cried. "No!" She tried to wriggle free, but hadn't a chance against those powerful grips. She struggled to roll over, but again, the orc held her feet steady—while his partner tied her legs together with a heavy cord.

"No!" Doum'wielle demanded again. She grabbed the bowl and threw it at them to little effect. She fell back and tried to bring forth a spell, tried to shake off the mittens so that she could make the proper movements.

But then she was sliding, being hauled through the short tunnel and out into the cold, cold dark.

Before she could even make sense of it, the female orc was beside her, hoisting her upright and wrapping her in the fur blanket upon which she had slept—upon which they all had slept, Doum'wielle only then remembered. She shuddered and gasped as it occurred to her what they might have done to her . . .

No, she realized. They hadn't hurt her at all in any way. They had just come in and slept against her. Kept her warm. Healed her feet and hands.

It made no sense.

Too confused to sort it out or even begin to think of any spells, too weak to have any hope of fighting back, the elf had no choice but to let whatever might happen, happen. Wrapped tight, she couldn't begin to resist anyway as the large male hoisted her up in his arms and carried her for a bit before plopping her down on a small sled. She was sitting up, her back against the vertical back of the carriage, and a large rope went over her, the orc binding her tightly in place.

His partner came over and placed hot stones all around her, then dropped other items, including Doum'wielle's pack, which now appeared stuffed, on the front length of the low sled, securing them. The male returned, leading four of those badger-wolf creatures tethered together, and soon, tethered to the front of the sled.

He walked back around Doum'wielle and she could feel his weight when he stood upon the back of the sled, right behind her.

His companion rushed past her then, startling her, driving her own sled and a similar scrabbling team.

"Hike!" the male shouted, startling her once more, and away they went, sprinting across the snowy and icy plain.

Hours passed.

They stopped and rested, throwing large chunks of blubbery meat to the eight strange badger-wolves, or whatever they were.

Formidable was what they were, Doum'wielle quickly understood as the pack went at the meat, shredding it with ease, ripping it apart with one tear in what seemed like hardly an effort.

The female orc kneeled beside Doum'wielle, bowl in hand, and began giving her small bites of the fishy mush, while the male inspected and tightened her bindings.

It occurred to Doum'wielle that they weren't keeping her alive so much as fattening her up. She wasn't about to refuse the food, though.

Off they went again, rushing across the snowpack and coming to another small dome of snow. They didn't strip her down that night— her clothes weren't wet, she understood—but they did share the blankets, all three, and they did keep her legs tied, and they did keep one of their pets at Doum'wielle's feet.

While she thought about escaping the two orcs, Doum'wielle

wasn't about to do anything to spark the ire of that fearsome and powerful beast.

It was still dark when she fell asleep, and still dark when she woke up, when they ate again, when they put her back on the sled and started off once more.

Eternal sunshine, and now eternal darkness.

Doum'wielle knew that she was lost, that her mind was gone, at least in regard to the passing of time. This was the night that wouldn't come for what seemed like many tendays, and now . . . it wouldn't leave.

They repeated the cycle over and over, moving to more domes set in a line. The mountains loomed much closer now—or was it even a mountain before her? The silhouette against the night sky was level, though high. After the fifth rest—or maybe it was the sixth; Doum'wielle couldn't be sure—they started off again, but pulled to an abrupt stop soon after. The two orcs moved between the sleds, right beside her, jabbering at each other, and again, Doum'wielle couldn't make out a word of it.

She got the feeling, however, that they had sensed something or someone out there.

The female orc lit a candle, which seemed like quite a stupid thing to do.

The male took it from her and held it up high above his head, which seemed stupider still.

She understood, though, as a group of humanoids approached. Allies, clearly, for the female orc rushed out to meet them and converse with them.

Doum'wielle couldn't quite make out who or what they might be. They weren't built with the sturdy frame of an orc, but were lithe, elflike. But too thin for this freezing weather, she thought. Were they even wearing clothes?

The male orc began untying her from the sled as a pair of the newcomers approached. Yes, they were dressed, Doum'wielle saw, but in a weird, dark, thin material, a single piece of clothing, booted and gloved and with a coif as one might see on a suit of fine chain mail, and with a full face mask as well.

Red eyes peeked out from the slit in one, glowing amber orbs from the other.

They looked at each other and shrugged, then nodded and drew out handcrossbows, bringing them up as the orc unwrapped Doum'wielle from the blanket.

"No, no!" she cried, realizing her fate. She tried to turn and pull away, getting so far as to plant one foot and try to leap off the sled. Then she heard a pair of clicks, and felt the burn as two quarrels burrowed into her.

"Why?" she asked, turning back to the two slender newcomers.

The strength left her legs and she fell back upon the sled. She felt the cold wind, but then it seemed to go away.

All of her senses receded.

Doum'wielle fell in on herself.

Why won't the sun come up? she wondered, her last thought on the frozen plane.

PART 1

FINDING PURPOSE

My little Brie.

For most of my life, I have been blessed with friends and with a sense of, and clear direction of, purpose. I see the world around me and all I ever hoped to do was leave it a bit smoother in my wake than the choppy waters through which I traveled. I gained strength in the hope of some future community, and then indeed, in that community when at long last I found it. Found it, and now embrace it as my world expands wonderfully.

It's been a good life. Not one without tragedy, not one without pain, but one with direction, even if so many times that perceived road seemed as if it would lead to an ethereal goal, a tantalizing ring of glittering diamonds so close and yet just outside of my extended grasp. But yes, a good life, even if so many times I looked at the world around me and had to consciously strive to ward off despair, for dark clouds so often sweep across the sky above me, the murky fields about me, and the fears within me.

I weathered change—poorly and nearly to self-destruction—when my friends were lost to me, and never were the clouds, the fields, or my thoughts darker. During that midnight period of my life, I lost my purpose because I lost my hope.

But I found it again in the end, or what I thought the end, even before the twists of fate or the whims of a goddess manifested my hope in the return of my lost friends. I might have died alone with Guenhwyvar on that dark night atop Kelvin's Cairn.

So be it. I would have died contented because I was once more true to that which I demanded I be, and was satisfied that I had indeed calmed many waters in my long and winding current.

But then there came more, so unexpectedly. A return of companions, of love and of friendship, of bonds that had been forged through long years of walking side by side into the darkness and into the sunlight.

And now, more still.

My little Brie.

When I burst through that door to first glimpse her, when I saw her there, so tiny, in the midst of my dearest friends, in the midst of those who had taught me and comforted me and walked with me, so many emotions poured through my heart. I thought of the sacrifice of Brother Afafrenfere— never will I forget what he did for me.

Never, too, did I expect that I would understand why he did it, but the moment I passed that threshold and saw my little Brie, it all came clear to me.

I was overwhelmed—by joy, of course, and by the promise of what might be. More than that, however, I was overwhelmed by a sense I did not expect. Not to this degree. For the first time in my life, I knew that I could be truly destroyed. In that room, looking at my child, the product of a love true and lasting, I was, most of all, vulnerable.

Yet I cannot let that feeling change my course.

I cannot hide from my responsibilities to that which I believe—nay, quite the opposite!

For my little Brie, for other children I might have, for their children, for any children Regis and Donnola might have, for the heirs of King Bruenor, and Wulfgar, and for all who need calmer waters, I will continue to walk forward, with purpose.

It is a good life.

That is my choice.

Fly away on swift winds, clouds of darkness!

Take root, green grass, and blanket the murky fields!
Be gone from my thoughts, doubts and fears!

It is a good life because that is my choice, and it is a better life because I will stride with purpose and determination and without fear to calm the turbulent waters.

—Drizzt Do'Urden

CHAPTER 1

The Year of the Star Walker's Return
DALERECKONING 1490

Stirring the Pain

He sensed the cold, just the cold, like a tomb of ice tightly wrapped about him, squeezing and freezing. He felt her fear, her lament, frozen it seemed, like the physical world about her, as if she was stuck and held in the moment of her death.

Kimmuriel gripped the feline-shaped hilt of the weapon tighter, physically trying to strengthen the telepathic connection.

Startled by the returned image, the same image, the same sensation of simple cessation of . . . everything, the drow fell back a trio of steps, then looked at the blade for just a moment before placing it down on the table before him.

"You seem shaken," came an unexpected voice across the small and dimly lit chamber. Kimmuriel glanced over to see his host, Gromph Baenre, the archmage of Luskan's Hosttower of the Arcane. "I am not quite used to such a sight as that."

"I do not fully grasp the enchantment on this weapon," Kimmuriel explained.

"It is a minor dweomer in the grand scheme of Mystra's Weave and

Lolth's Web, surely," Gromph answered. "The sword seeks bloodletting, and will manipulate its wielder to that end."

Kimmuriel was shaking his head through the explanation. "It is more than that," he answered. "It is . . . pride. This enchanted sword, above all, wishes to be the instrument of the greatest wielder."

"For more blood."

"I think it more than that."

"And this quibble has Kimmuriel Oblodra, who dines with illithids—what do they eat, after all? And how do they eat it?" Gromph paused and shuddered as if his train of thought had been derailed by the image he had conjured in his mind. "You dine with illithids and are flummoxed by a mere sentient weapon? I could more greatly enchant a dozen such blades within a month, if that will keep you so entranced and pleased."

"It is not Khazid'hea," Kimmuriel explained. "It is the connection to those the sword has truly dominated."

Gromph's flippant expression changed at that explanation and he walked over.

"It senses Catti-brie," Kimmuriel explained. "When I am holding it, and when I force myself into it, I can feel that which she is feeling. Or perhaps it is what she was once feeling. I cannot be sure."

"Now, that could be interesting," Gromph said with a wicked smile, and Kimmuriel glared at him. "She is human, and so weak," Gromph needled against that disparaging stare.

"Not just Catti-brie," Kimmuriel said. "Another, too. Elven and drow."

Gromph arched an eyebrow.

"Doum'wielle Armgo," Kimmuriel explained.

"Not that wretched creature," the archmage replied with a heavy sigh. "She lives?" He snorted and sighed again, shaking his head.

"If you had wanted her dead, why did you merely banish her? Why didn't you just do it yourself, then and there?"

"Because that would not have been painful enough."

"Your anger seems misplaced." Kimmuriel reached for Khazid'hea again, lifting it before his eyes. "I believe she was more victim than perpetrator in whatever it was that elicits such rage from you."

"She was half elf and half drow," Gromph dryly replied. "That is sin enough."

Kimmuriel shrugged and let it go. Gromph was making some progress these last months in Luskan. He was beginning to see the wider picture here, with a civil war quietly simmering throughout Menzoberranzan as his sisters and House Baenre did battle with much of the city, aided by a force now being called the Blaspheme: nearly eight hundred resurrected drow, returned to their previous forms after centuries of servitude in the Abyss as horrid driders. Menzoberranzan was on the verge of a war for its heart and soul, and it appeared that the devotees of Lolth were in a losing position, though the fight would likely last years if not decades.

"She lives, though?" Gromph asked, taking Kimmuriel from his thoughts.

"I don't know," Kimmuriel answered after considering it for a few moments. "So it would seem, unless these are the final memories of Doum'wielle somehow stored within Khazid'hea. Still, I do not believe that to be the case, so likely, yes, she lives."

"Who else does this sword sense?"

"There are others, but they are faint. Perhaps they held the sword long ago, or it never gained such control over them as it clearly held over Catti-brie and Doum'wielle, or . . ."

"Or the others are dead now."

Kimmuriel nodded. He understood that Khazid'hea was an old, old creation, and figured that it had likely been held by many hands over the centuries, and that it had surely dominated most of them. No, those who had been overcome by Khazid'hea and were now dead were not lurking here in the sensations of the sword.

Gromph gave a laugh.

"What is it?" Kimmuriel asked.

"Catti-brie," the archmage explained. "The sword fully dominated Catti-brie."

"That was long ago, when she was barely more than a girl."

"I know," said Gromph. "I find it humorous, of course, for now, were she to grasp that blade and Khazid'hea tried to dominate her, she would laugh it away. She would likely twist that sentience so far about itself that it would never unwind."

"You just said she was human, and thus weak," Kimmuriel reminded him, and he grinned at the cloud that passed across Gromph's amber eyes. The truth of Catti-brie clearly pained the wizard. She was not supposed to be as powerful as she obviously was. She was human, just human, and yet she was no minor warrior, no minor priestess, and no minor wizard. Gromph hated admitting it—even to himself, it seemed—but he truly respected her.

"Where is the Armgo whelp, then?" Gromph asked, unsurprisingly shifting the conversation away from the source of his present consternation.

Kimmuriel shrugged. "I do not know. Only that it was bright, the sun shining on white snow. And cold . . . so very cold."

"I threw her into the far north," said Gromph. "That she has survived at all is surprising. Was that your thought when I entered?"

"She was terrified," Kimmuriel said. "She was afraid and perhaps in the moment of death."

"The north is full of large animals, I am told." Gromph's voice trailed off as Kimmuriel began to shake his head.

"She was not running from animals," he explained.

Gromph stared at him curiously.

"It was a memory," Kimmuriel said then, and he was talking as much to himself as to his host. "Likely one from the same time period when her father was killed in the dragon duel above Mithral Hall."

Gromph started to respond, but bit it back and just nodded and departed.

Gromph knew that he didn't believe his last explanation, Kimmuriel realized. Still shaken, Kimmuriel wasn't sure what he believed.

He placed Khazid'hea back on the table.

Maybe it was time to give the sword back to Jarlaxle.

"IS IT YOUR HOPE GUIDING YOUR SUSPICION?" DAB'NAY said to Jarlaxle. They walked along the merry streets of Silverymoon, the most enchanting surface city Jarlaxle had ever seen. There weren't many drow here, but neither were the two Bregan D'aerthe rogues unique in the place, and no suspicious eyes followed them as they made their way toward the bridge that would take them over the River Rauvin to Northbank, the older half of this city that straddled the large river. From the bridge they would go to the north gate, for their business here had concluded and Jarlaxle was anxious to get on with the second part of their information-gathering quest.

He was going to miss this place, though, and he told himself resolutely that he would one day return for a leisurely visit.

"Why would you ask me that?" he asked the priestess. "You heard the old elf."

"The very old elf," Dab'nay corrected. She tapped the side of her head and gave an expression and a shake that showed she wasn't very impressed with that one's mental faculties.

"Yes, we were fortunate to hear the whispers regarding Freewindle when we did."

"Or perhaps it was already too late."

Jarlaxle stopped and turned to the woman. "Why are you playing the role of such a naysayer?"

"He said it was just a dream."

"He said that *perhaps* it was just a dream."

"And you hold on to that because you don't want to believe that it was just a dream."

"I believe his story more than he does, it would seem."

"You know what I mean," Dab'nay replied. "Freewindle was confused, clearly. He is old, ancient, and the tale he told was that of a young elf. Centuries ago, Jarlaxle. How many memories can you recall of your earliest days—without the help of Kimmuriel or his squidheaded friends, I mean?"

"I can recall the ones that mattered. And perhaps many of those, too, seem more of a dream to me."

"Or perhaps it was just a dream with Freewindle. Even if not, how much did he say to us that is of any value, other than the notion that such a place exists?"

Jarlaxle considered that for a while, a smile growing as he heard in his mind the shaky voice of the old elf describing the city of drow. Not Menzoberranzan, not Ched Nasad, not in the Underdark at all.

And one not devoted to the Demon Queen of Spiders.

"Perhaps it's nothing," Jarlaxle agreed. "Just a dream."

"You don't need to do that," Dab'nay said.

Jarlaxle glanced over at her, to see her nodding and a bit choked up. She wanted it to be more than a dream as much as he, he realized.

"Come," he said. "If we hurry, we can make the castle and the southernmost boughs of the Moonwood before nightfall. If we're lucky, we'll conclude our business here in the next couple of days and we can ride back to Mithral Hall and fly the stone portals to Luskan."

"And then?"

"That's what I'm trying to figure out. But you won't be coming with me if there is a second journey."

Dab'nay stiffened.

"I need you in Luskan," Jarlaxle explained. "I need eyes on the happenings in Menzoberranzan, and I prefer it to be a priestess who can keep the score and measure regarding the power of Lolth. Whatever may come of this trip or a second one, the fate of Bregan D'aerthe itself rests on us picking the correct side when the war begins."

"I think we already have," Dab'nay said. "Are we not friends to the two heretics? Lady Lolth is not merciful."

"But no one knows the truth behind her machinations. Not even you, a priestess who garners her divine spells from a goddess she loathes."

They left Silverymoon soon after, using their obsidian figurines to summon magical hellsteeds that ran tirelessly along the road to the northwest, toward the castle of Lord Harthos Zymorven, who had offered the information about Freewindle to a Bregan D'aerthe associate in exchange for a new breastplate, forged in Gauntlgrym, which Jarlaxle had delivered two days previous.

"YOU ASK ME TO TELL YOU OF SOMETHING THAT DE-stroyed my life," the elf quietly replied.

"Lady Sinnafein, I mean no harm," Jarlaxle assured her. He silently reminded himself that the Lady of the Moonwood had done him a great favor, traveling many hours at the request of Lord Harthos in order to meet with Jarlaxle here in the forest, not five miles from Zymorven Hall, which was still visible on the hill in the distance. "Quite the opposite."

"My daughter meant no harm, either, but that sword of which you inquire led her to great harm. Now you wish me to help point you in the direction of that vile item? You would make me a party to more misery?"

"Khazid'hea—" Jarlaxle began.

"Speak not that name!" Sinnafein sharply retorted, and the mercenary rocked back in his chair. Behind him, outside the beautiful tree dwelling that had been put up the previous night in this southern-most stretch of the Moonwood, he heard the elven guards stirring. He turned to look at them, even flashed them a wink, then swung back to find Sinnafein waving them away.

"The sword exists whether we know its location or not," he said. "It may even now be in the hands of one who cannot control it."

"It cannot be controlled."

"You know better than that," Jarlaxle said. "Were it in the hands of Drizzt, would you fear it?"

"Yes."

"It is just a magical toy, lady. It is no demon, though its hunger is demonic—"

"It is imbued with a demon spirit," the Lady of the Moonwood interrupted.

"No, lady," Jarlaxle calmly replied. "I understand that from your perspective that may seem so, but you may have heard of the war along the northern Sword Coast, in Gauntlgrym and Luskan, in the Crags and Port Llast, even touching into Waterdeep. That war was one pre-cipitated by true demon-possessed jewelry, which in turn possessed those who wore the jewels. Khazid— your pardon, the sword, is not demon possessed. It is simply hungry, and will play upon a wielder who cannot control that hunger in whatever manner it can find to sate its bloodlust."

Lady Sinnafein put a smile on her angular and beautiful elven face that set Jarlaxle back in his chair yet again.

"You don't know, do you?" she asked.

Jarlaxle shrugged and cocked his head, trying to make out the source of her grin—one unexpected given the discussion of a great tragedy for her, and one that revealed to him that she did indeed know something he did not begin to fathom.

"You know of the war that was fought in the Silver Marches, dwarf against the orc Kingdom of Many-Arrows before your friend King Bruenor went to reclaim Gauntlgrym in the east?"

"Of course."

"Do you know how it started? How it really started?"

Jarlaxle's thoughts swirled as he tried to recall all the events of that conflict, one that seemed quite straightforward, after all, since it involved dwarves and orcs doing battle.

Sinnafein called to the elves standing outside her chamber. "Pray, bring us some food," she told them. "My friend Jarlaxle and I will be in here for a long time, I expect."

She relaxed back in her chair, and Jarlaxle could see from her eyes that she was trying to sort through what had been a great tragedy in her life. He knew only part of the story: that her daughter, Doum'wielle, had run off from the Moonwood elves, and that Doum'wielle and her father had returned to Menzoberranzan.

"You know Tos'un Armgo?" she asked.

"For many years. Before he left Menzoberranzan. House Barrison Del'Armgo is one of the most formidable, second in the city."

"Our sages were studying the sword and gave it back to Tos'un in the early days when he came to live with us here in the Moonwood," Sinnafein said. "He had it under full control, we believed. Of course I believed that! There were many things I believed about Tos'un, and now I know only that I know nothing where he is concerned. Maybe it was the sword, or perhaps I simply did not understand the foul truth of that man."

"Because he was drow?" Jarlaxle whispered, and regretted the words as soon as they left his mouth—certainly the elf, Lady Sinnafein, didn't deserve that.

"I fell in love with him because of who I believed him to be, not because of his background," Sinnafein returned rather sharply. "And I was betrayed by him because of who he was, or perhaps because of that vile sword, and not because he was drow. Do you think so little of me that—"

"Lady, my pardon," Jarlaxle said. "I was out of my proper place. I have lived a lifetime of unacceptance because of my heritage, or worse, of feigned acceptance by those who wish to prove something of themselves to the world by accepting one of my heritage." Jarlaxle shook his head and gave a self-deprecating smile. Rarely was he so careless as to say those quiet thoughts out loud.

To his surprise, Sinnafein laughed, and he knew as soon as he looked up at her that she was not mocking him or his feelings. Rather, she was nodding.

"You sound like Tos'un," she replied. "The good man I married. The good father to my children. Not the Tos'un who . . ." She paused and took a deep breath, her tone, indeed her whole aspect, changing.

"If Tos'un had control of the sword, our children did not," she explained. "When Tos'un told them that one of them would inherit the blade, it began a contest between them, an escalating battle promoted strongly by my son, Teirflin. Too strongly. It became an obsession with him that he would win the sword. Somehow and sometime in the ensuing days, the sword and not my husband chose its wielder, and corrupted my Little Doe, quickly and fully. Doum'wielle killed her brother with that sword, then ran off. Tos'un and I tracked and pursued her into the orc kingdom, and there, beset by a horde, Tos'un betrayed me.

"You noted that I did not stand when you entered," she said. "It was no disrespect to you, friend of Drizzt. Nay, the simple act of standing pains me now, for in that dark moment those years ago, Tos'un crippled me and left me for the orcs, while he ran off down a tunnel—back to the Underdark, I later learned, and with Doum'wielle by his side. I cannot tell you how I felt when I learned that he had died riding a white dragon in a battle above Mithral Hall. I cannot tell you because I still am not sure how I feel. I do not believe he was an evil man when we married, but rather that the sword corrupted him." She looked plaintively at Jarlaxle. "But of that, I can no longer be certain."

"Perhaps it was a bit of both," Jarlaxle offered. "But no doubt the sword had a role in Tos'un's fall.

"The orcs found me quite helpless, as Tos'un intended, but they did not kill me," Sinnafein explained. "Despite the fighting all along the chase that ended with my capture, they did not torture me, either. They did not harm me in any way. They gave me back to my people, a ploy by the orc Lorgru, heir of Many-Arrows, to continue the vision of King Obould of a peaceful alliance in the region. For this action, one the zealots considered a great betrayal of their wicked god, Lorgru was chased away and Many-Arrows went to war. So you see, Jarlaxle, the War of the Silver Marches was, in no small way, caused by that very sword you now seek."

"I do not seek the sword, Lady Sinnafein," Jarlaxle admitted. He rose a bit from his chair and slowly drew a blade, laying it on the table before a startled Sinnafein.

Sinnafein did rise then, and couldn't catch her breath for many moments, for the blade was unmistakable to her, with its keen edge and a barely perceptible line of red light, almost like the formulation of a mist of desired blood.

The elf's expression changed when she shifted her gaze to the pommel, shaped like a great black cat, a displacer beast, its twin tentacles arching back to front to form a basket about the grip.

"What is—" she started to ask, but shook her head. "A sister blade?"

"That is Khazid'hea," Jarlaxle replied. "I have had it for years now, though mostly it's been kept hidden away, in the hands of a friend, a psionicist, who sought its secrets."

"Then why did you say you had come to speak with me of a sword you wished to find?" she asked sharply.

"That is not what I said," Jarlaxle replied. He took the sword from the table and slid it away, hoping to distance Sinnafein from the source of her obvious tension, and he was glad when she sat back down. "That is what you heard because I was indeed cryptic in the way I phrased my purpose. I had to know first if there would be approval on your part."

"Approval? I approve of nothing short of the destruction of that foul blade."

"Approval of me going to find your daughter," Jarlaxle said, and if he had slapped Sinnafein across the face, she would have looked no different. "My friend is convinced from his examinations of the sword that Doum'wielle, your Little Doe, might well still be alive. Once this sword has dominated a person, it knows of that person, no matter the distance between them."

"Where is she?" Sinnafein demanded.

"That, I fear, is a more complicated issue, for I do not know," Jarlaxle admitted. "But I believe that I can find out, and intend to do so. Because I am not convinced your daughter deserved the fate delivered to her." The mercenary gave a helpless little laugh. "Of course, she did some foul deeds, including the murder of her brother, your son . . ." He sighed.

"Then why is it your place to go find her?"

Jarlaxle shrugged. "I come from Menzoberranzan. I know the influences an overpowering demon—or demonic bent of a magical item—can hold over people. Over otherwise good people. It is the story of my city, after all, of my kin."

"I still don't understand. I know nothing of where she is," Sinnafein snapped, biting off every word. "Why come to me?"

"Because when I find her—and I will—I want her to know that her mother will forgive her," Jarlaxle said, and yet again, Sinnafein sucked in her breath.

"Many times, you have said it was the sword, or at least you have made it clear that you want it to have been the sword," Jarlaxle explained. "It was. I tell you that it was, and that your daughter did not deserve her magical banishment."

For many moments, Sinnafein held silent, her eyes darting all about as if she was looking for an escape, or for someone to rush in and help her.

"This is not your affair," she said at length. "Why are you making it your business?"

Now it was Jarlaxle's turn to settle back and let that simple question truly sink in. "I do not know," he admitted. "Perhaps it is just my wanderlust now that things in the far west have at last quieted. Perhaps it is the test I put before he whom I intend to present with this sword."

Sinnafein sat up straighter, a scowl quickly flashing.

He put his hand up. "I assure you that this person will never be dominated by the likes of Khazid'hea or any other magical weapon," Jarlaxle said with a disarming grin. "He is a warrior with few peers in skill and experience, and fewer still in terms of determination and heart—perhaps rivaled only by his own son, whom you know well."

The elf didn't seem convinced.

"And perhaps it is because I believe that Doum'wielle can earn her redemption," Jarlaxle at last admitted. "She is of House Barrison Del'Armgo, the Second House of Menzoberranzan, the house that may prove decisive in a coming civil war."

"You seek a spy," Sinnafein cleverly deduced.

"I seek an ally," Jarlaxle said. "If Doum'wielle can help to avert a war and to turn the drow away from Lolth, would that not be a good thing? Would that not be recompense for the trouble that she—under the influence of Khazid'hea, of course—caused?"

Sinnafein's expression shifted repeatedly, finally settling on a look of understanding. News of the war in the west had long since reached the Moonwood, including the unexpected ending that spoke of a great heresy by powerful drow against Lady Lolth. "I know not where Little Doe is," the elf quietly repeated. "I thought her long dead, or residing in the city of Menzoberranzan with her father."

"I do not know, either," Jarlaxle said again, and rose from his chair. "But I will. Now that I know what I can tell Doum'wielle of the Moonwood when again I see her, I assure you that if she is indeed alive, I will. And if she is not alive, I will report that to you."

He couldn't read Sinnafein's expression in that moment, and understood that a great turmoil roiled within her heart and soul. The tragedy visited on this woman, her family, this community, was no small thing.

Jarlaxle took some comfort in her lack of reaction. He was determined to find Doum'wielle Armgo for power and gain, as was his way. Perhaps the young elf would prove to be a key component in his greater hopes.

But now, looking at Sinnafein and thinking that maybe, just maybe, the return of a healed Doum'wielle who was freed of the influence of Khazid'hea might bring some comfort here made the rogue all the more determined. More than he had imagined, even. He thought of Brienne Do'Urden. The comparisons to Doum'wielle Armgo were fairly obvious, and if Brienne was to be Jarlaxle's hope of the future, was Doum'wielle truly to be his fear?

Those unsettling thoughts stayed with Jarlaxle as he moved out of the treehouse, down the tree, and out of the Moonwood altogether, back to Zymorven Hall, where Dab'nay waited. The thoughts stayed with him all the way back to Mithral Hall and the magical gate that would transport him back to Gauntlgrym and Zaknafein—more than stayed with him. They haunted him. All of his life, Jarlaxle had done the pragmatic thing, trying to simply survive. He had always tried not to do the wrong thing regarding those around him who didn't deserve it, and mostly he succeeded, but rarely had he tried to do the *right* thing for anyone else above himself and his immediate needs.

It was a small needle, but Jarlaxle had threaded it pretty well over the centuries, he believed.

Now, though, somewhere inside him, he couldn't deny that he was beginning to place the needs of others at least at the level of his own needs, and if his feelings at this very moment were to be believed, perhaps even *above* his own needs. He tried to shake that unsettling notion away by reminding himself that he had stayed alive precisely because of the previous balance.

But no, he could not, and when he exited the portal back in Gauntlgrym, he offered only a nod and not a word to the dwarven guards. He made his way to his own chamber, the ghosts of Brienne-inspired hopes and Doum'wielle-inspired fears close behind.

CHAPTER 2

The Word of a Goddess

I t would be a visit, nothing more," Drizzt answered Catti-brie's scowl. His wife hadn't been happy with his suggestion that he take Brienne to the east, to Damara and the Monastery of the Yellow Rose, to meet Grandmaster Kane. "I owe them the full recounting of Brother Afafrenfere."

"She only started walking a season ago, and now you want her to learn how to kick through a board?" Catti-brie countered.

Drizzt started to reply, but just chuckled instead and shook his head. "Come with us," he simply suggested again.

"This isn't just a visit, Drizzt. I know what you want," she said. "You want her to go there and train there and learn there."

"Eventually," Drizzt admitted. "I cannot tell you how much those months with Grandmaster Kane have done for me in the way I see the world around me. And after my . . . 'transcendence' is what the monks call it, but I find that word insufficient."

"I'm not concerned about what words you use to describe that experience."

"Fair enough. After my departure from this world, this life and existence, I have come to see so much more. How could I not wish to share that with my child?"

"The same way that I wish to share with Brienne my love of Mielikki?" Catti-brie asked rather sharply, which brought a wince from Drizzt.

He knew the stubbornness behind her refusal here, for she and Drizzt had been quite at odds regarding the goddess Mielikki since Drizzt's companions had returned from the enchanted forest years ago. The argument had started over a discussion that seemed more theoretical than of material or practical importance, a dispute regarding the nature of orcs and goblins and the like. Drizzt had come to believe that these goblinkin races were not evil by nature, as the drow were not, but were bent to such acts and practices by the influence of powerful godlike forces, as were so many of the races of Toril.

But no, Mielikki had denied such a theory to Catti-brie. His wife knew that drow were not evil creatures by nature, of course. She had married Drizzt, after all, and he knew with confidence that she loved him with all of her heart and soul. So how could she hold such a prejudice? No, that idea was impossible.

But goblinkin were different, she had insisted, both in her opinion and according to the edicts of her goddess. Mielikki had told the priestess, indeed a *chosen* priestess, that goblinkin were evil incarnate, brought to the world to cause misery. Nothing more. Yes, she had conceded, Drizzt had met an exception once long ago in a small town called Pengallen, but while Catti-brie hadn't doubted his memory or his sincerity, she had relayed that she thought his judgment in that particular situation regarding a goblin named Nojheim to be skewed. He hadn't seen the full picture, perhaps, she had gently offered.

Drizzt wasn't sure of his convictions on this matter, but what he was certain of was that he would not be guided against his conscience by a supposed goddess, any goddess. Once, he too had followed Mielikki, but he had always thought of her, of all the gods, as manifestations of that which was in the hearts of their respective followers—they were just names given to conscience—or if more, no matter, for following them meant following that which you believed to be true, not the words relayed. Or in this case, not even the words directly conveyed.

This debate hadn't come up much over the last few years, but the implications had clearly persisted and resurfaced now that they had a child to raise, with all the questions such a daunting task entailed. They were to guide the life of another sentient, independent, growing being. They were to shape Brienne's earliest understanding of the world, and such influence, both Drizzt and Catti-brie understood, could be a guiding beacon or a stifling anchor to Brienne's journey.

Drizzt started to respond several times, but faltered with each attempt. He had to take care with his words here, for he was speaking to the very soul of himself and of Catti-brie. They didn't have to align on every issue, of course, but this was a fundamental belief that went even beyond the nature of goblinkin and to the very concept of god and creation and the purpose of life itself.

"She *will* know of the goddess," Catti-brie said.

"I know."

"Can you say with all of your heart that you feel equally strongly that she will know Grandmaster Kane and the Order of Saint Sollars?"

"I am not of the Order of Saint Sollars," Drizzt reminded her.

"Aren't you, though? You ably performed their most spiritual and accomplished act in leaving the Material Plane of your own volition."

"The philosophy of Grandmaster Kane is one of self-discovery through meditation and perfection of the body through repetition. This is the teaching of the man they call Saint Sollars, yes."

"Saint," Catti-brie echoed, making clear the implication.

"Philosopher-warrior," Drizzt corrected. "These teachings are showing me a way in the manner of Melee-Magthere, and before it, the training of my father, Zaknafein. Yet I do not deify him."

"You do not deify anyone or anything anymore, it would seem."

Drizzt let that sink in for several long breaths. "Am I any different in that regard than when I left Menzoberranzan?"

"Did you not lead me to Mielikki?"

Drizzt had to pause on that. "I told you what was in my heart, and the name I had given it was Mielikki."

"Because she was the embodiment of your ethical beliefs," Catti-brie replied.

"Yes."

"But she is a living goddess, and so when she speaks in communion, are not those declarations commandments you must follow?"

"No." It actually surprised Drizzt how quickly the answer left his mouth, and the conviction behind the response. "I don't know that I can call her a goddess, or the divine beings of Toril gods at all," he said, speaking as much to clarify the thoughts in his own mind as in explanation to Catti-brie. "Perhaps they are no more than caretakers of destinations that might best fit their followers. Perhaps they are illusions, or self-deceptions, because of our fears of what is next, if anything."

"You have died and returned!" Catti-brie reminded him. "Am I deluded in that?"

"Did I? Or did I find some magic of the mind that transcended my physical form and would thus leave me in a temporary state as I dissipated into nothingness?"

"Or everythingness?"

"That, my love, is my hope," Drizzt admitted with a smile.

"You said that you felt the joy of true peace. Yet still you doubt."

"Perhaps that was my own deception to ease the transition."

Catti-brie's chuckle wasn't meant to mock him, but it did. "My doubting husband. It is real. There is more. I have seen it. I have lived it in Iruladoon, though that was merely a place of holding. But I was there, with Wulfgar, Bruenor, and Regis, after we had died. And Zaknafein, lost for scores of years and now is returned."

"I know," Drizzt said. "There remain so many things beyond my ability to truly understand."

"That's why it is called faith."

Drizzt conceded the point with a shrug.

"Yet you doubt the word of Mielikki," Catti-brie said. "She has told me the nature of goblinkin, and that nature is one of evil."

"I hold true to that which is in my heart," Drizzt countered. "I hold faith that my conscience guides me—"

"You put yourself above Mielikki." Catti-brie's voice took on a sharper edge, but she softened it immediately, Drizzt noted, as weary of this recurring argument as he.

"And so you would not wish me to introduce our daughter to Mie-likki?" she asked at length.

"Of course I would. If you do not, then I would. I would give her the whole world to see and devour, so she may pick those morsels that are within her heart."

"And if she chose Mielikki, to become a priestess, above your training with Grandmaster Kane?"

"Why are they exclusionary?"

After a long sigh, Catti-brie admitted, "They probably aren't, though the latter has led you further from the former."

"Perhaps you alone should take Brienne to the Monastery of the Yellow Rose and hear the lessons of Grandmaster Kane," Drizzt offered with a smirk. "You were once formidable with the blade, and deadly with the bow, I recall."

"Deadlier now," his wife replied, narrowing her eyes and turning them just enough to the side to emphasize the quiet, lighthearted threat.

Drizzt leaped over to her and wrapped her in a hug, kissing her cheek, then whispering in her ear, "I find that quite alluring."

"It is a dance, after all," Catti-brie whispered back, turning within his grasp to kiss him fully.

"Want Genn!" came a tiny voice from the door.

"Perhaps we should have Kimmuriel take her to the illithids," Drizzt said through his helpless smile. "For the child can read minds."

"I'm not so sure reading your mind is that difficult at this point," Catti-brie teased, swaying against him just a bit. "Call the panther. Let her play with her *Genn* for a while."

"While we finish our discussion?"

Catti-brie widened a smile and chuckled, but her expression changed suddenly into a feigned stern look. "Don't ruin it," she warned.

"YOU SEEM A BIT . . . DISHEVELED TODAY?" JARLAXLE SLYLY remarked, and he tried too obviously to hide his grin, telling Catti-brie that she was blushing.

"Every day is a trial with a toddler," she said.

"Very busy, I imagine."

"A constant chase, yes."

"I do hope you have found some time for yourself," the mercenary quipped. "That is always important."

"Yes, Jarlaxle, I've examined your fiery whip," an exasperated Catti-brie finally said in an attempt to end this one's endless games of cryptic remarks and even double entendre. Yes, it was obvious that she had just come from Drizzt's bed, she knew, and so she would expect nothing less from this cavalier drow so dedicated to the pleasures of life.

She moved across the dais of the small chapel she had consecrated not far from the suite she, Drizzt, and Brienne shared in Gauntlgrym and reached behind a bench to produce the marvelous whip Jarlaxle had given her.

"Did your ring offer any insights?" Jarlaxle asked.

"Not really. It does cut into the Plane of Fire, yes. The magic is true, but we already knew that."

"Do you understand the dweomer? Is it a form of extraplanar gate spell, perhaps?"

Catti-brie shrugged. "I expect there is something of that sort, yes. But there is nothing I can detect, or understand. This is an old weapon, of that I am sure. And I doubt it was created by human or elven or dwarven hands."

"Or even on this plane?"

"Probably. More likely it was fashioned in the Abyss or the Nine Hells, and by a being of greater magical knowledge than I."

"You speak of the lower planes. Did you sense any malevolence within the whip?"

"No. It is just a bullwhip, with a marvelous magical edge that can cut lines into the Plane of Fire."

Jarlaxle blew a long sigh.

"What?"

"Will it work, I wonder? Or will I be destroying a most marvelous tool?"

"I do not know."

"But you have used the Great Forge in such a way before," the mercenary said. "With Drizzt's broken scimitar and Vidrinath. You combined the powers of the two. And again with Bruenor's shield and the magical web shield called Orbbcress."

"Combined, perhaps, but it was not strictly additive. Some powers remained in the products of the magical items; some disappeared."

"In both cases, however, the returned item was greater than either of the two you put to the flames of the Great Forge."

Catti-brie nodded. "The combination of Vidrinath and Twinkle is formidable, and the only drawback to Bruenor's shield is that he spends more time conjuring mugs of ale and lager and mead for his forces than he does in planning the next fight."

That brought a smile to Jarlaxle's face. "Why, then, do you hesitate now regarding my proposition?" he asked. "They are my toys and so the risk is all mine. Do I not have your trust?"

"Of course you do," the woman replied. "It is just that . . . when I forged Drizzt's scimitar and King Bruenor's shield, it was almost as if it was not me doing it. I was more the conduit for powers I do not understand."

"Your goddess?"

"Maybe, or more likely it involves Maegera, the primordial who powers all the forges of Gauntlgrym. It is a creature of the Plane of Fire, a veritable god of that plane trapped here in this place. And you ask me to feed into its flames . . ."

"Ah, the whip!" Jarlaxle said, catching on. "You fear that it will somehow—"

"Would you throw a bag of holding into your portable hole?" Catti-brie interrupted.

"Of course not. Or at least, I would not have before . . ."

"What?"

"It does not matter," Jarlaxle replied. He had paid Gromph Baenre a small fortune to shift the magic of his portable hole so that it could accept such other extradimensional pockets without the terrible side effect, but she didn't need to know that now.

"Why wouldn't you?" Catti-brie pressed.

"Because it would tear a rift into the Astral Plane and suck me in and throw me free, untethered. But this is different," he insisted. "Neither the primordial nor the whip is an extradimensional pocket."

"But the potential for some unforeseen catastrophe remains," Catti-brie replied. "And not just one for me or those around me. If I give the primordial a passage out of this place, the magic of Gauntlgrym goes with it."

Jarlaxle paused and rubbed his chin, staring at the woman carefully, not dismissing a word of her warning. "Do you truly believe that placing the whip within the Great Forge will prove disastrous?" he asked with disappointment thick in his voice.

Catti-brie recognized the tone and the look on his face. Jarlaxle had been planning this for a long time, and not for any gain for himself. Or not too much—it was Jarlaxle, after all.

"I do not expect that it will, but neither do I know what the primordial flames will do. I knew what I wanted when I forged Twinkle and Vidrinath, but the weapon I got wasn't quite that. The same was true regarding Bruenor's shield. I can know the various dweomers of an item, but how they combine is beyond me."

"You have an idea, though."

"I do."

"Will you try?"

"Do you have the other item?"

"Not yet. And getting it will be no easy task, nor a cheap one. But I will get it, and soon, and when I do, if you will help me in this, if you will join it with this whip through the power of the Great Forge, I promise you a treasure you will think worth the effort."

"So you said. I am the daughter of King Bruenor, the wife of Drizzt Do'Urden, a friend to the Ivy Mansion, and the chosen of Mielikki. What might Jarlaxle offer that I do not already have?"

"Adventure," he whispered, and Catti-brie was sure that her blue eyes were twinkling despite her desire to remain aloof.

"One whose completion you will find most worth your time," Jarlaxle added. "I know you well, good lady. I know your heart. You will be glad for the reward."

"If it is so worthy an adventure, then why must I perform a trick for you to undertake it?"

Jarlaxle laughed aloud. "This is why I am so endeared to you," he said, and he pulled his enormous wide-brimmed hat off his bald head and swept a low bow.

"You didn't answer my question."

"Because it is all connected," Jarlaxle replied. "The forging, the adventure, the gifts to all involved. I will need this whip, or the result of your efforts, to better ensure the success of the journey that awaits me—that awaits us."

Catti-brie paused a moment to consider that, and to consider again why and for whom Jarlaxle had asked her to consider utilizing the Great Forge of Gauntlgrym. "So, the whip and this other item combined for Zaknafein, and adventure for me. And what for Jarlaxle?" she asked.

"Relief from the tedium of governing and counting pieces of gold, and the security of strengthening the bonds with friends I hold dear."

"And?"

"Nothing more," he said, but Catti-brie didn't believe him, and her expression showed that quite clearly.

"What I, what *we*, seek, may turn the tide of Menzoberranzan's swirling waters," the rogue explained. "Even if not, it is an adventure, a quest, worth undertaking. I am more than confident that you will agree with that when the time comes for us to begin."

"After the forging," she replied. "How soon after?"

"There are other things in motion," Jarlaxle answered.

"Aren't there always? With you, I mean."

"Why, yes, lady, that's why I win."

"But this time, it is why we all win?"

"I hope so," Jarlaxle answered, his voice suddenly sober and full of weight. "I have Gromph hard at his study, trying to find us the proper starting point. By the time I can return with the other item for the forge, and you can finish your work here, I expect he will be finished, and we can truly begin."

"Your words always seem to bring more questions than answers."

"Because, my dear Catti-brie, the world is so full of wonderful puzzles."

"I will see what I can further learn," she said, surrendering with a sigh. "If I determine that the risk is small enough, I will do this forging for you. But I'll not be responsible if the result is not to your liking."

"I live for such games of chance," he said. "And I live to make sure that I have done all that I can to ensure that I have placed the bet correctly."

That, too, Catti-brie knew not to doubt.

CHAPTER 3

A Confluence of Interests

They've already left?" a surprised Jarlaxle asked when he stepped out of the teleporter to enter the small chamber in the bowels of the Hosttower of the Arcane in Luskan, to find Beniago waiting for him, pacing anxiously and holding the small item Jarlaxle would need to catch them if his suspicion was accurate.

Beniago confirmed the departure with a nod. "The *Pelican* was spied sailing south past Auckney yesterday at dawn," he explained.

"She'll come in, then."

Beniago shook his head. "Captain Arrongo knows that his last acts of piracy went beyond the edicts of the Five Captains, and that he's coming here with a price on his shaggy head. They'll sail right by us until the outrage has diminished."

Jarlaxle sighed. "Civilizing these humans is more difficult than I would have thought. They have an amazing capacity for ignoring their own reflections. We are surrounded by Captain Arrongos, yet the majority of these humans remain so convinced that we drow are the evil ones."

"True enough, but Captain Arrongo has got more than human blood in him," Beniago reminded him. "*Pelican's* far out and at full sail. She'll glide right past Luskan, beyond the horizon, and probably stay out wide of the coast all the way to Baldur's Gate."

"That might be Arrongo's intent, but I expect he'll fall far short of his goals," Jarlaxle said, walking past and taking the magical sculpture Beniago held up for him.

"High seas out there," Beniago warned. "Expect to get wet."

"You don't have to smile when you say that," Jarlaxle muttered.

"Oh, but I do," the high captain replied with a laugh.

Jarlaxle respected that.

The pair left the Hosttower moments later, crossing to the northwest coast of the island, the lights of the famed City of Sails behind them. This was where the highest surf hit the island and thus the most remote part, and also, as Beniago reminded him, the most likely place along the city's coast to find a large shark.

"I know, I know," Beniago said, holding up his hands against Jarlaxle's scowl. "I don't need to smile when I say it."

Jarlaxle could only laugh and remind himself that Beniago's fine mood was not unexpected. In the nearly two years since the defeat of the demon hordes, the northern Sword Coast had found peace once more, and was settling into a fine place. Luskan was back under Bregan D'aerthe's full control, and even though the folk of the city now understood the true nature of the power behind the high captain to be a gang of drow (although Beniago continued to wear his human disguise), complaints were few and far between. Beniago served as a benevolent leader, and with the new relationship to Waterdhavian House Margaster and their connections, the goods were flowing and Luskan was thriving once more.

It helped that Bregan D'aerthe had driven the gnolls and demons from the city. That Bregan D'aerthe had saved the lives of so many of Luskan's folk—human, dwarf, halfling, elf, and all other sorts.

The people of Luskan were living well, surrounded by allies and with as formidable a fleet as any city on the Sword Coast, albeit one particularly disorganized.

Life had gotten easier.

Maybe too easy, Jarlaxle thought as he set the sculpture, a small sailing vessel, into the water and whispered a command word, "Bauble." Immediately the craft began to glow and to grow, becoming a small square-sailed sailboat, suitable for only a couple of passengers. Emblazoned on its side was the name Jarlaxle had given it, the very command word that brought forth the magical craft.

Jarlaxle stepped onto *Bauble* and took a seat, motioning to the bench beside him.

Beniago considered it for a moment, but shook his head.

"It's been a long time since you've put a blade to good use," Jarlaxle said.

"It's been a longer time since I've wanted to."

Jarlaxle tipped his great hat to that and turned his focus seaward. Jarlaxle whispered, "Beacon," and a glass set on the prow became a light, rotating slowly left to right, then back again. The movement tightened back and forth, just right of center, then narrowed some more.

Finding its target.

A magical wind arose from the taffrail, filling the sail, and the boat slid out from the shore. Jarlaxle overrode the guiding magic of the beacon at first to keep her straight through the breakers. Splashing and bouncing, taking air more than once, *Bauble* proved up to the task, though the mercenary captaining her was soaked when the little craft had at last settled beyond Luskan's surf. There in the calmer seas, Jarlaxle gave over the steering to the magic, and instead took up the single pole rising from the middle of the bench seat. Slowly, he pushed it to lean forward, and every finger's breadth of movement increased the wind at his back.

Soon wake sprayed high at the sides of the prow. "Following winds and fair seas," Jarlaxle said, reversing the adjectives in the sailor's typical blessing.

What a marvelous little item this was! A most superb gift from a lord of Waterdeep upon the signing of a trade agreement between his house and King Bruenor of Gauntlgrym.

The lights of Luskan receded behind the fast-gliding boat, the clear sky above showing Jarlaxle a vision of pure tranquility and peace. For a long time, he just basked in that sensation, the ocean smell and the rhythm of the swells beneath him, the water spraying from the prow becoming almost a chant, a mantra of meditation.

Only the lights of a ship far ahead broke that welcome trance, a reminder to the rogue that the peace wouldn't last.

Deudermont's Revenge was likely the fastest schooner on the Sword Coast and was running at full sail now, her cloth fore and aft billowing in the strong southwestern breeze. Supplemented by her magical winds, though, Jarlaxle's small magical craft had no problem gaining on her. The beacon on the prow kept the small boat running straight for a point on the *Revenge*'s port side, and as she neared, Jarlaxle lifted a whistle and blew.

He saw the veteran crewmembers scurrying about almost immediately—they had seen him coming even with his meager single running light—and several appeared at the taffrail, pointing down and waving. Others showed at the port rail, some working a crank to unwind a plank that had been secured up tight against the hull, a diagonal walkway running from the deck down to water level. As the plank went perpendicular to the hull, a landing board freed up, flipped over, and fell down against the water with a splash.

Jarlaxle's guiding beacon steered him right to the landing, where he gracefully stepped from the boat, holding his small craft by that high prow. He spoke quiet commands and his boat shrank suddenly, becoming a miniature replica once more, and he tucked it into his pouch as he made his way up to the deck. Before he even crested the deck level, he heard the distant sound of retching, and, guessing the source, spread a wide grin.

"We thought you would miss all the fun," said Bonnie Charlee, Captain of *Deudermont's Revenge*, who stood just beyond the rail to greet him.

"Never," Jarlaxle assured her. He stepped past her, heading for the starboard rail further aft and the sounds of seasickness, but Bonnie Charlee grabbed his arm, turning him about. She didn't say anything at first, but her grave expression spoke for her.

"You still fear the mission," Jarlaxle remarked.

"Captain Arrongo's a smart one," Bonnie Charlee replied. "He's gobbled up the best crew of scalawags cut loose by the Margaster invasion."

"You mean the most vicious."

"Pirates," Bonnie Charlee said. "Luskan was and's still full o' them. And Arrongo got the toughest. *Pelican* sailed all the way to the Sea of Moving Ice. Arrongo's crew goes to Ten Towns in Icewind Dale for scrimshaw, and take more than they pay for. There're thousands up there in the dale, all tough folk living on the edge of disaster every day, but they bend the knee and trim the coins to Arrongo."

"The legend is greater than the truth," Jarlaxle told her. "That's almost always the case with the powerful. When you strip the armor, there's more fat to be seen than muscle."

After a moment of consideration, Bonnie Charlee replied, "As with Bregan D'aerthe?"

"*Almost* always the case," Jarlaxle pointedly returned.

"Don't you start thinking *Pelican* an easy picking," Bonnie Charlee warned. "She's got a dozen wizards and priests, all skilled in sea fighting. She's got a crew full of brawlers, murderers, gnolls, half ogres, and every other mix of danger a mind can imagine."

"Yes, she's the strongest corsair, captained by the most notorious and feared pirate in the north now," the mercenary agreed. "And that's exactly why *Pelican* must be stopped and put to the deeps. Right now."

The serious tone of Jarlaxle's voice had the woman back on her heels. Her reaction told Jarlaxle just how much this coming fight meant to him and his hopes for Luskan, even beyond the more personal gain of gathering a certain weapon for his warrior friend.

"Luskan is bleeding still," he went on. "Luskan has been bleeding for decades."

"Luskan's been yer own for years," Bonnie Charlee said.

Jarlaxle shook his head. "Not really. We've pulled the strings from the shadows, indeed, but that's not enough. No more."

"Jarlaxle the king?" Bonnie Charlee said slyly, tilting back her head to eye the drow suspiciously.

He scoffed. "I don't want to be the king."

"Then what? Why're ye caring for *Pelican* and Captain Arrongo one way or th'other?"

"Because I want the people of Luskan to *want* me to be their king."

"Ye just said ye didn't want to be that."

"I don't. But when they come to see what Bregan D'aerthe is really offering them, I expect that they will demand no less from any who would deign to lead them."

Another long pause from the woman. "Ye're a strange fellow, Jarlaxle. What is it ye think ye're offering them?"

"Freedom from men like Captain Arrongo."

Jarlaxle noted that if he tapped Bonnie Charlee's forehead in that moment, she'd likely topple over backward.

"Aye, I'll not argue that Arrongo is a dangerous one," he said. "Too dangerous."

"Dangerous enough to take Luskan from Jarlaxle," the woman replied.

"Which of us do you think the people of Luskan would prefer?"

"Ye're a drow," she said, as if that were answer enough.

"Yes, they know that now, and they know that High Captain Kurth is backed by drow power. But they've known that power for years, even if they didn't know the true identity of it. So I ask again, which of us—Jarlaxle or Arrongo—do you think the people of Luskan would prefer?"

"Old beliefs die hard."

"Then let me ask it differently," Jarlaxle said. "Which of us— Jarlaxle or Arrongo—does Bonnie Charlee believe better for the City of Sails?"

The woman didn't answer other than to nod. She knew, of course, Jarlaxle could see. She had been behind the curtain for months now and understood well the designs of Bregan D'aerthe, and that those designs benefited the people of Luskan most of all.

A moment later, Bonnie Charlee nodded again, more confidently.

"It's your ship, Captain Bonnie Charlee," Jarlaxle said then. "You know what we face out there on the dark waters, and you know now the stakes. If you wish to return to Luskan at once, give your orders. *Deudermont's Revenge* is Bonnie Charlee's ship to command. Bonnie Charlee plots her course."

"Are ye talking to me or talking to Luskan?"

"Yes."

"Then good for Luskan, I say, when we put into her long wharf carrying *Pelican's* black and Captain Arrongo's head."

Jarlaxle tipped his hat and bowed to the captain. He tossed her an approving wink when he stood straight and turned again for starboard.

"You completed your business, then?" she asked, stopping him before he took his first step.

Jarlaxle nodded, confused for only a moment before he guessed her next question even as she asked it.

"Was Wulfgar there? In Gauntlgrym."

"I didn't see him," he admitted. "I heard that he was out of the tunnels and into Bleeding Vines."

"Very well, then," she said, disappointment thick in her voice and clear on her sea-weathered face.

"Deliver the *Pelican* to me and when we return to Luskan, I'll get you a ride through the magical gates so you can go and visit Wulfgar yourself," Jarlaxle promised.

A smile betrayed the woman, but was quickly replaced by a shake of her head, one rooted, quite obviously, in nervousness.

"Why do you underestimate the man?" Jarlaxle asked. "Or is it yourself that you find inadequate for the moment?"

"I'm not wishing to intrude. He has his life, I've me own."

"You've your own because of him," Jarlaxle reminded her.

"Because of you."

"No, because of Wulfgar. I trust him—more than he trusts me, I am sure—and I am more fond of him than he is of me. He came to trust Bonnie Charlee, and thus, so do I. He is quite impressed with you and would be happy to see you."

The woman shrugged, and even in the starlight, Jarlaxle could see her blush.

He pulled her from that moment with a pointed sigh. "I wish I could go back through the years and find that which brought you to this place in your own heart," he said. "Do you truly value yourself so little that you are afraid to go and see the man?"

"He has his life and I have mine," she repeated.

"You fear he'll reject you."

"He has his life and I have mine."

Jarlaxle laughed. "So you reject the rejection before it can be offered. It is such silliness—and I say that with all respect, Captain Bonnie Charlee. I see this in so many around me, elves and drow and dwarves and folk of all ilk, men and women alike. I find it most silly in humans, who live so short a time. Why would you waste what could be good days and instead sit miserable and chewing your lips in the fear that those good days won't be good?"

"Ye're babbling."

"Far from it! Go and see him, and likely find a grand memory in your too-short life, instead of sitting here and forfeiting the possibility."

"He has Penelope Harpell," she reminded him.

"Penelope?" Jarlaxle said and snickered. "She's likely at the Ivy Mansion and is not about to be jealous in any case, I assure you."

"And if she's not, and is in Gauntlgrym?"

"She'd probably join you, if you had the mind for it," Jarlaxle said with a great laugh. "And even if not in that way, we all would do well to spend more time with Penelope Harpell. Aye, but we'd all learn a lot from her, particularly in how to enjoy life more." He paused, noting her expression, and added, "Yes, even Jarlaxle!"

That brought a wide grin to Bonnie Charlee, and a nod, and Jarlaxle hoped that she would take his advice. "Now, I must go to my friend," he said after another round of vomiting sounded. "How long has he been sick?"

"Since we breached the second wave out of Luskan," Bonnie Charlee said with a genuinely grateful smile and a nod.

"How long to the *Pelican*?"

"Before dawn if we find her sails. So aye, go to Master Zaknafein. If you want him ready for a fight, you'd best be getting him up from the rail."

Jarlaxle tipped his hat again to the captain, and like every time he dealt with Bonnie Charlee, he was very glad that Wulfgar had stood up for her in those early moments when the demon and gnoll fleet led by Brevindon Margaster had overrun Luskan. She was a valuable member of Jarlaxle's team now, an able captain, a scrappy fighter, and with so much critical knowledge and insight into the region and the city itself. And Jarlaxle hadn't lied to her. More than anything else, he wanted the people of Luskan to *want* the leadership of Bregan D'aerthe, and Bonnie Charlee was one of the people who might well get him there.

He moved across the deck and around some barrels and sacks to spot a figure resting against the low rail, propped up with his arm over it, but seeming very much like he was about to slide down flat on the deck.

"Prebattle jitters?" he asked, moving over to stand above Zak.

"What form of hell is this?" Zak replied, trying but not quite managing to lift his gaze high enough to look Jarlaxle in the eye.

"I warned you that the rolling waves are unsettling to one who has known only the solidity of land."

"Shut up."

"It would be just like the bobbing webways of Ched Nasad, I believe was your answer. It's hard for me to recall the exact words, as you were saying them while chewing undercooked eggs, if I'm remembering correctly."

The mere mention of the runny eggs had Zak rolling back to get his face out over the rail, where he began to throw up some more.

"Captain Arrongo will prove a formidable foe, by all accounts," Jarlaxle said. "Would you have me serve as your champion and defeat him? I would respectfully refuse, for in that instance, how would you properly claim his sword as your own?"

Zaknafein leaned a bit and lifted his scowl at the mercenary leader, unable to hide his intrigue at this new motivation.

"Come, come," Jarlaxle said, offering a hand. "Let's get you up and walking, at least."

Zak didn't take the hand and looked away. "I need more time."

Jarlaxle heaved a great sigh and pulled the magical eyepatch off his face, then bent low and set it over Zak's head, adjusting it to cover the weapon master's left eye. He grabbed Zak by the shoulder and began to hoist, and now Zak did come up, and stood straight and not wobbly before Jarlaxle. His expression went from uncertainty to befuddlement in fast order.

"The truesight dweomer of the eyepatch is a great aid," Jarlaxle said. "I was the same as you when I first sailed these rough waters."

"But now you don't need it?"

"Oh, no."

"Then why didn't you give me the eye—" Zak stopped short and scowled mightily.

"You'll never grow accustomed to the roll of the seas without the discomfort."

"I'm never coming out here again."

Jarlaxle snorted but didn't argue. "Take heart, my friend; you will find the reward worth the vomit."

Zak turned his head to the side and spat out over the rail. "You need associates on the land. I'm better serving there."

"I'm only out here for you," Jarlaxle said.

"Why?" Zak asked skeptically, and he tilted his head to the side and studied Jarlaxle through the eyepatch, using another of its marvelous enchantments to recognize honesty in the rogue's words. "Thank you?"

"Consider this part of your journey a growing experience," Jarlaxle explained. "You don't have your son's scimitars anymore. Do you think I would allow my second—"

"Kimmuriel is your second."

"He's the other half of my first. In my part of Bregan D'aerthe, in my, shall we say, personal journeys, you are my partner."

"You called me your second. Now I'm your partner? And does Artemis Entreri know of this new arrangement?"

"We've a fight coming. Are you going to argue about everything?"

"Titles matter."

"What would you prefer?"

"Your better," Zak said, and he pulled the eyepatch from his head and tossed it back to Jarlaxle. Both his claim and his action would have carried more weight if Zak hadn't chosen the very next moment to relieve himself of the rest of the contents of his stomach as he slumped down once more against the rail.

"Keep chummin' and ye'll bring a host o' sharks up on our side!" Bonnie Charlee called out.

"Why is she still alive?" Zak asked.

"More alive than you, which won't bode well when we catch the *Pelican*," Jarlaxle told him.

"You don't need me to catch the *Pelican*."

"A warrior should earn his sword."

"I have a sword. Two!"

"You have a pair of sharp sticks. Captain Arrongo of the *Pelican*, he has a sword."

"Do you think he would beat me with his sword against my sticks?"

"That's the challenge, isn't it?"

"Is it?"

Jarlaxle shrugged. "If you care, Arrongo also has a hold full of innocent prisoners, including children, all of whom will be put to a horrible death or sold into slavery." He held out the eyepatch.

Zaknafein stared at it for a moment, then pulled himself to his feet and refused the offer. He closed his eyes and wasn't trembling, and Jarlaxle could see him physically steeling himself against the seasickness—yet another reminder to Jarlaxle of the force of Zak's willpower.

He was so glad to have this one by his side again.

Zak opened his eyes. "You owe me some eggs."

"It will be our victory meal," Jarlaxle promised.

HOURS LATER, JARLAXLE EMERGED FROM CAPTAIN BONNIE Charlee's quarters, where he had realized some much-needed rest, to find a growing commotion along the starboard rail. Several sailors were gathered about a pair of men wielding gaff hooks, taking turns reaching low over the rail as if trying to recover something from the sea.

"From *Pelican*," Bonnie Charlee told Jarlaxle as he neared. She nodded her chin to the pile of retrieved items: clothing, mostly, including a shredded dress that seemed to be tangled about something. As he neared, Jarlaxle winced and turned, realizing the tangle to be a severed arm still caught in what was left of the gown's sleeve.

One of the gaffers yelped and fell back from the rail, losing his grip on the long pole. A woman caught the handle and held it tight, bringing it over to reveal that the end of it was broken away.

"White shark," Bonnie Charlee told Jarlaxle. "They're following *Pelican* and Arrongo's crew's having fun with it."

"Fun," Jarlaxle echoed with disgust. He shook his head. "How far?"

"We'd see her sails if the sun was up."

"Every moment we waste might cost another her life."

Bonnie Charlee nodded. "Fill the sails with wind," she told her chief mate. "Douse all lights, not a candle burning, and shut 'em up, every one. Not a sound from *Revenge*. Arrongo and his dogs'll see us before they hear us, and when they see us, it'll be too late for them."

The woman nodded and ran off, relaying the orders.

"They'll use their captives against us before the fighting starts," Bonnie Charlee told Jarlaxle.

The drow rogue shook his head. "I have a plan."

"Ye might want to be tellin' the captain."

"I won't be on your ship, captain," Jarlaxle replied with a grin, and he tapped the pouch holding his magical boat.

"Ye're going out?"

Jarlaxle nodded, the plan only then formulating in his thoughts. "I'll leave you with all my forces, to deploy as you will. The opening fight is Bonnie Charlee's to command."

"And then?"

"And then I'll help" was all that Jarlaxle would offer at that time, and with a tip of his hat, he took his leave, going belowdecks to the back corner of the main hold, where he had left Zaknafein and Entreri with several other Bregan D'aerthe associates.

He hadn't even stepped from the ladder when he felt *Deudermont's Revenge* lifting her prow a bit higher, the full sails catching the wind and racing along. Yes, he thought, he was glad indeed that he had listened to Wulfgar regarding Bonnie Charlee.

Captain Bonnie Charlee.

THEY HEARD A COMMOTION FAR AHEAD IN THE DARKNESS, a scream, some splashes. Then more screams, increasing in both number and intensity.

Jarlaxle leaned on the pole, trying to get as much out of the windy magic as he could. Beside him on *Bauble*, the priestess Dab'nay whispered to herself, gathering magical energy for the fast-approaching trial. Up forward, beyond the mast, Zaknafein and Artemis Entreri leaned out on either side of the small boat's high prow, straining their eyes to peer into the darkness.

"A running light," Zak whispered, pointing ahead.

"Trick of the starlight on the water?" Jarlaxle asked.

"No, more," Entreri put in. His dark cloak billowed out behind him in a strong wind gust, and he popped his hand atop his new hat, a stylish black affair with a five-finger crown, pinched in front, and a three-finger brim bent low in front, lying flat on the sides, and curling slightly up in the back. Dressed less for battle than for a night on the town.

But no less deadly for it.

"Lanterns," Zaknafein quietly declared. "A torch."

"They want to watch the sharks tearing at those they've thrown in the water," Entreri said. He leaned to the side and low, peering back at Jarlaxle under the bouncing bottom seam of the single square sail. "You still think any of these pirates are worth sparing?"

"Some have asked the same of Artemis Entreri in the past," Jarlaxle reminded him.

"When you were a younger man, you would have done this?" Dab'nay asked.

"No," Entreri answered with conviction. "Not to prisoners whose only crime was to get caught by the pirates." He turned away and looked ahead and added grimly and softly, "But I'll do it to pirates."

"Dab'nay, silence us, and darken *Bauble*," Jarlaxle said. He reached into his belt pouch and lifted a cylindrical item, then kept lifting until the long scope came free of the bag of holding. He set it on a notch on *Bauble*'s prow, extending it far forward of the craft, and though Dab'nay's globe of darkness covered the small boat stern to prow, sail to water, Jarlaxle could still view their destination through the far end of the scope, which was beyond the globe and enchanted to work in exactly this situation.

The lights of the *Pelican* came clearer to Jarlaxle as the small boat raced across the open sea.

Jarlaxle reached back and tapped Dab'nay, signaling her to remove the magical darkness and as soon as it was gone, he motioned for the others to be quiet and for Dab'nay to also lift the silence spell. "Slow us," Jarlaxle whispered, and Entreri pulled back the lever.

"They'll soon see the *Revenge*," Zaknafein remarked.

"Good. They'll be looking at her and not at our own low profile," Entreri added.

Jarlaxle nodded and was pleased by Entreri's exchange with Dab'nay. He seemed a different man now, right down to his choice of hat. Releasing the souls from his vampiric dagger appeared to have lifted a great weight from his shoulders, as if now—and only now—he was believing in his own chance of redemption.

"You all know your places?" Jarlaxle whispered, and to Dab'nay, he added, "You've the proper spells ready?"

"We'll be as silent as shadows," she promised.

"Slow! Slow!" Jarlaxle harshly whispered, waving his arm frantically.

Entreri reacted immediately, pulling the throttle all the way back, ceasing the magical wind, and *Bauble* slowed so dramatically that they all had to catch themselves or pitch forward to the deck or the sea. It took Entreri only a moment after Dab'nay released the magical darkness to understand Jarlaxle's urgency, for just ahead and off to starboard, something floated in the dark water. As they neared, the shape became that of a woman, bobbing in the sea.

Zaknafein turned the boat to come up beside her, and Entreri leaned out to grab at the unresponsive form.

But the man pulled back in horror, and the woman overturned.

Or, rather, half the woman overturned.

Entreri pushed the pole, the wind kicked up, and *Bauble* leaped away. And not a moment too soon, as the huge shark broke the surface right behind them, claiming the other half of its meal.

The four shaken sailors collected themselves as the small craft raced toward the large ship, not another word of mercy for the pirates spoken between them.

Not another word at all.

Silent as death, they slid up alongside their target. Jarlaxle brought a dagger into each of his hands with his magical bracers, and with a word to *Bauble*, he dropped the mast. He stabbed the daggers to catch on to *Pelican*, hand-walking the small boat back under the steep curving hull by the high stern, securing them up tight out of sight of the deck near to her rudder. He handed off the stuck daggers to Entreri, stepped back, and used his favorite wand, gluing the crafts together with a glob of viscous goo, and there the four sat, waiting.

Very soon after, they heard the commotion above, pirates running about, mates barking orders.

Deudermont's Revenge was still far away, but the dark silhouette of her sail was in sight of the four in the small boat soon after, and coming up fast.

"Patience, patience," Jarlaxle whispered when Zak drew his swords. Jarlaxle was speaking as much to himself as to the others, he realized when he took off his great hat and reached inside.

Suddenly, the sky lit up between the two ships, a barrage of small flames leaping out from *Pelican*, and then a larger missile of burning pitch, the shudder of *Pelican's* catapult nearly swamping *Bauble*.

Peas of magical flame exploded into huge fireballs, one after another—though they really couldn't be described as balls, or anything spherical, as they ignited against *Revenge's* magical shields, which fended off their flames. The catapult missile hit a wall of wind, sparks and embers flying harmlessly aside, and conjured water rained down on it, stealing most of its fire. Still, much of its payload got through, plunging down across the deck, and the flames of several fireballs also found their targets.

One of *Revenge*'s sails was burning. Jarlaxle and the others could hear the screams of more than one sailor caught by the fires or splattered by burning pitch.

But *Deudermont's Revenge* came on, her crack crew reacting as Jarlaxle demanded, as Captain Bonnie Charlee had trained them.

Now a volley of fireballs responded from the prow of *Revenge*, crashing against similar defenses from *Pelican*.

Back and forth it went, and what became quite clear to all was that *Pelican* had no chance of outrunning the magnificent schooner. *Deudermont's Revenge* had been built according to the secret plans of *Sea Sprite*, the legendary Sword Coast pirate hunter captained by the famous Deudermont. No ship along the Sword Coast could outmaneuver *Sea Sprite* in her day, and the same was true of Deudermont's namesake, especially with such an excellent crew.

And her excellent captain, Jarlaxle was beginning to understand, to his great satisfaction.

More shudders rocked *Pelican*, both from the firing catapult and from some hits scored by *Revenge*'s many wizards.

Lightning bolts replaced fireballs as *Revenge* came up fast on *Pelican*'s stern, and predictably, *Pelican* began a hard port turn, wanting to give her archers and spellcasters a proper bow rake.

"Hold fast," Jarlaxle warned, and almost as soon as he issued the words, *Pelican* shuddered and lurched violently.

"Ice storm," Entreri quietly explained to Zak and Dab'nay. *Revenge*'s main wizards had waited for the turn, then had sent a torrent of ice and cones of magical freezing into the water before her left-sliding, turning prow. The jolt and the grind hadn't stopped the turn, of course, but it had sent a shock of force creaking through *Pelican*'s decks. More than one pirate had gone flying into the water on the port side, the four could hear, and by the time *Pelican* had recovered from the shock and surprise, *Revenge* was too close and was herself turning too hard for the bow rake to prove of any consequence.

"Count," Jarlaxle told his friends, and Dab'nay began casting her spell, lifting one hand to offer a countdown to the others.

"Five," Jarlaxle said quietly, and he pulled a circular piece of cloth from inside the crown of his great hat.

"Four," he said, and he whispered and threw the cloth out, spinning fast.

"Three, two," he said quickly, catching up to Dab'nay's count as his magical cloth, a portable hole, struck the *Pelican's* hull, opening a wide passage into the ship's lower deck.

Before he even finished the count, Artemis Entreri dove through the portable hole, Zaknafein right behind. A scream greeted them, but one cut very short as Dab'nay cast her magical silence into the hold.

Jarlaxle rolled in through the hole, coming to his feet gracefully to stand at the ready. He called to the bracer on his right wrist, creating another dagger in his hand, bringing it back behind his shoulder, ready to throw.

The sight gave him pause, for across this long and narrow room were prisoners, battered, emaciated, chained by shackles affixed to the ceiling. Men and women, children, even, hanging by bloody wrists, most slumped. A couple of the poor group somehow maintained an upright posture on their tiptoes, but the children and the shorter adults simply dangled in the air, swinging about with every sway of the ship.

Only when Zaknafein rushed across from left to right did Jarlaxle spot a pirate, a hulking gnoll, who met Zak's charge with a sweeping strike of its spiked club.

How clumsy and slow it appeared against the enraged weapon master, whose blades worked in perfect coordination to tap and redirect the club, once and again. Zak's left hand stabbed out with blinding speed right behind the sweep, aimed true for the gnoll's gripping hands.

The ensuing yelp went unheard in the magical silence, but Jarlaxle understood the agony behind it well as he watched several gnoll fingers go spinning down to the floor.

Zaknafein quick-stepped straight ahead, stabbing left, right, left in rapid succession, filling the pirate with deep wounds and sending it crashing back to the floor and wall.

Zak took one step in apparent pursuit, but broke away suddenly to his right, back toward Jarlaxle and Dab'nay, who was crawling in. He threw himself into a roll, sword coming up at the last moment to knock aside a hurled axe.

Jarlaxle leaped ahead and let fly his dagger, then a second almost as soon as the first had left his hand. Then a third and a fourth, all in the air even as the first struck that second pirate, a human this time, plunging into her upraised hand. Then the chest, the shoulder, and the throat met the other three.

Both drow fighters were moving then, side by side, and both skidded to an abrupt stop as they noted the third and fourth pirate guards, both gnolls, both with long knives against the throats of hanging prisoners, warding back the attackers.

Jarlaxle let his dagger fall and lifted his empty hands high.

Zaknafein hesitated, looking to his companion with surprise. Jarlaxle's grin reassured him that all was under control.

A red blade flashed.

A wall of ash hung in the air.

A severed gnoll head went spinning into the air.

And the second pirate gnoll got pushed out to the side, all strength leaving its knife arm, as the sword of Artemis Entreri sprouted through its shoulder, armpit to collar.

"Impressive," Zaknafein said, though his voice could not be heard.

Jarlaxle understood anyway, for the salute was shared. Entreri had somehow navigated the narrow chamber to get behind those two without being noticed, and his horizontal swing had turned fast into a dipping blade even as its dipping and turning wielder put himself into the second uppercut strike. It was executed as perfectly as any master of Melee-Magthere could teach, and better than most drow could possibly learn.

It was a move worthy of Zaknafein, worthy of Drizzt.

Jarlaxle set his gaze on Zak and was pleased by the expression he saw there. It was good that Zak's first real introduction to Artemis Entreri the fighter had happened in this manner.

Respect was important between these two—

The thought was interrupted when all four went flying as the ships collided, *Deudermont's Revenge* slamming and sliding hard against *Pelican's* side. The prisoners swung wildly out and back as Jarlaxle's team quickly recovered. He noted how strange it was to see the mouths opened in shocked screams, to see barrels and crates flying and smashing, to feel the tremendous impact, the ceiling beams cracking, almost collapsing, as the boom from *Pelican's* mainmast fell free.

And all of it without a whisper of sound.

BONNIE CHARLEE UNDERSTOOD THE STRENGTH OF HER ship. *Revenge* had been built with redundancy, designed to take a beating and keep on sailing. Her hull was magically sealed and would not split apart under a collision or a barrage of catapult or ballistae, her planking magically warded from fire, where even the scorch of a lightning bolt would leave no more than a black scar. Her sails, too, were magically protected from fire. They might catch in the flames of a fireball, but they wouldn't burn long or fully.

And *Deudermont's Revenge's* mainmast was designed to break free in a collision, and not just fall, but fall in a controlled manner that would turn the boom into a plank onto the deck of the enemy ship when she came in hard broadside.

The captain didn't hesitate when the ice storm and freezing cones solidified the water before *Pelican's* turn. She signaled the pilot and the strong giantess leaned hard into *Revenge's* wheel, putting the ship into a hard port turn.

"Drop 'em!" Bonnie Charlee roared when they had just enough momentum and the proper angle for the strike, and her crew let free the sails. They fell with a great whomping sound, furling perfectly to smother the remaining wisps of fires.

"Brace!"

She didn't need to yell that, for this crew knew well enough what was to come and where to grab a handhold.

The two ships came together side-to-side with cracking beams and smashing timbers, shuddering and screeching. Down fell the main boom, perfectly as designed, tangling in the rigging of *Pelican* and driving it crashing down as well. The ice slamming *Pelican's* hull had abruptly halted her turn, giving *Revenge* the initiative here, and Bonnie Charlee wasn't about to let that advantage pass.

The battle heated before the ships had even settled, archers and crossbowmen letting fly—and mostly missing wildly under the shaking and rocking. *Pelican's* wizards waved their arms to hurl fire and lightning, but they had to start over, for the crashing ice had interrupted all of their castings. *Revenge's* wizards slowed them more, disrupting their somatic movements by throwing a unified and mighty gust of wind, blowing about anything loose on *Pelican's* deck, including the pirates themselves.

The greater advantage came next, with a score of Bregan D'aerthe drow reaching into their innate magics to cover *Pelican's* deck in magical darkness.

The ships settled together. The pirates of the *Pelican* shot blind as her priests and wizards frantically tried to counter the unexpected, impenetrable shadows. Whenever a lightning bolt came forth from that blackness, a dozen handcrossbow bolts traced it back to its source, and the lightning became no more.

Determined that the fight would be on *Pelican's* decks alone, the attackers flung their grapnels high to tangle in *Pelican's* remaining rigging, and warriors—led by Bonnie Charlee and the drow—leaped onto those ropes and swung across, while more ran across along the dropped beam, and others set boarding planks. By the time *Pelican's* spellcasters had much of the darkness dispelled, they found *Revenge's* fighters massing all about them.

Archers became swordsmen, priests on both sides turned to healing their comrades, and *Pelican's* wizards spent more time hiding and casting defensive spells than throwing forth punishing evocations.

Wizards were truly deadly in the early moments of ship-to-ship combat, but now with swords crossing all along *Pelican's* deck, her lightly armored mages were out of their element.

Bonnie Charlee found herself in a fight even before the darkness was gone, a gnoll leaping from the gloom to meet her charge. She truly appreciated the strength of the magical sword Jarlaxle had given her, for her parry of the truncheon swinging her way did more than deflect the club, it sheared it in half. A twist of her wrist and a swift thrust sent the gnoll yelping back into the darkness.

Except now the darkness was no more, and all around Bonnie Charlee, the fighting began in earnest.

She had executed the first phases of the attack perfectly. They had crippled *Pelican's* rigging and masts, had prevented any serious range assault from her before they could get up close, and had scored heavy gains against her fighting force in the beginning moments. But the veteran sailor held no illusions that this would be an easy victory.

Pelican had become notorious up and down the Sword Coast because *Pelican* was capable, her crew seasoned and brutal, her combat tactics practiced and effective.

Still, she realized as the fight ensued and the enemy ranks quickly thinned, the crew of *Pelican* had never faced the warriors of Bregan D'aerthe.

JARLAXLE CAUGHT A POOR WOMAN SWINGING WILDLY AT the end of her shackles. He signaled to Dab'nay and she ended her magical silence. Immediately came the sounds of terror from the prisoners, as well as the noises of fighting on the deck, the shouting and the scraping of metal against metal, sometimes punctuated by the thundering boom of a lightning bolt.

From the side, Entreri threw a ring of keys to Jarlaxle, who redirected them more than caught them, launching them at Dab'nay. "Tend to them," Jarlaxle told the priestess. He looked into the wide-eyed stare on the face of the woman he had steadied, and told her, "We've come to get you out of here and to safety."

She screamed, her face a mask of horror as she stared at the drow. Jarlaxle sighed and shrugged and moved for the stairs that led to the hatch, Entreri and Zaknafein coming up on either side of him. They even started past him, but he held out his arms to impede them. "Captain Bonnie knows the plan," he explained. "Let her execute her part."

"They'd have an easier time of it with the three of us up there fighting with them," Zaknafein said, though he had to shout to be heard as the clomping of boots sounded right above them.

Jarlaxle nodded, but said, "A bit longer. Let it settle and let Captain Arrongo be isolated."

"I'll wade through his whole crew to get to him," Zak replied. "Unless, of course, you still think my two sticks would be no match for his grand sword."

"They're not, but I trust you'll make up the disadvantage, and if not, I still have Artemis Entreri here."

Entreri snorted, and then again even louder when Zak scowled.

"You could have at least given me that whip," Zak said.

"It is being studied by someone important," Jarlaxle answered.

He held up his hands and paused, tilting his head to better hear. The fighting seemed less intense in that moment, or perhaps the skirmish had simply moved aside.

"We go," Jarlaxle decided, but he still held back his companions.

"After you, then," Entreri said, but Jarlaxle shook his head.

He plucked the feather from his hat and threw it to the deck before him, where it transformed almost immediately into a giant flightless bird, one with thick legs and huge claws that could rake a man into four parts with one well-aimed strike.

"After him," Jarlaxle corrected, and he ordered the diatryma forward. It went up the stairs in one stride and blew out the bulkhead with a powerful peck of its deadly beak. Small wings flapping wildly to help boost it, the bird rushed up and out onto the deck.

"How will it know friend from foe?" Zak asked.

"Oh, good point," said Jarlaxle, and he rushed up the stairs to direct his monster.

"Has he always been this insufferable?" Entreri asked Zak as they ascended the stairs side by side.

"You've known him as long as I, from what I can tell," Zak answered.

"Then yes, he has," said Entreri, and Jarlaxle's champions leaped out onto the deck and immediately into the fray.

Jarlaxle stopped at the top of the stairs, directing his bird, which was doing more chasing than fighting, as none of the pirates, not even the vicious gnolls, wanted anything to do with it. Of course, that might have been due to the fact that it had come up onto the deck right into a pirate and was still carrying half of that victim's body around on one of its great talons, blood flying with every running stomp. Whatever the reason, more than the bird demanded the mercenary's attention, as he watched Zaknafein and Entreri roll immediately into their deadly dance. Not two dances, but one, the expert warriors finding harmony before they had taken their third step into the tumult.

Jarlaxle had fought beside both. Both had fought beside Drizzt. And it seemed as if that was all they needed to fight side by side now.

He had never doubted that together they would be beautiful to watch, working around each other, swapping targets seamlessly. Yet this was something even he had to admire. Entreri spun the brilliant red blade of Charon's Claw before his every turn, his left hand clutching the dagger Jarlaxle had given him to replace the infamous weapon he had once carried. Zaknafein worked a pair of swords as fluidly as he might his own hands, always holding them ready to block, to parry, to thrust, to sweep—whatever situation arose.

At one point, Zak fled a pair of gnolls, both chasing right behind. Up the mast he ran, inverting as he caught his footholds, throwing himself backward in a reverse somersault—and parrying the swords of the pursuing gnolls once, twice, a dozen times, it seemed, as he turned upside down above them.

The gnolls managed to stay alive, and Zak was left vulnerable on the descent, as he certainly had known he would be.

But he wasn't in any danger, and he hadn't expected to be, because he already had come to trust Artemis Entreri in combat.

A red blade flashed between the gnolls and the falling Zak as Entreri sprinted through, using Charon's Claw's magic to trail an opaque barrier of ash.

As the human ran by, immediately falling into a fight with another pirate, the gnolls stabbed their swords ahead through the wall of floating ash, too slow to hit Entreri, too blindly to come near to Zaknafein.

And through that wall came Zak, touching down, dropping low, rolling through the magical cloud beneath the stabs, then coming up too fast for a counter, blades angled perfectly to get under the dog-faced demon creatures' ribs and slide up into their lungs.

They tried to fight on, gasping and spewing blood, but Zaknafein had no more interest in the dying things, and spun away to rejoin his partner.

"A thing of beauty," Jarlaxle whispered.

Even before Zak, Entreri, and the diatryma had entered the fighting, *Revenge*'s crew had gained most of *Pelican*'s deck, pushing the majority of the remaining pirates to the higher ground of the sizable poop deck. Magical darkness engulfed the stairs and the front of that upper level, effectively sealing those pirates from the main fighting. Occasionally a stray arrow or even a lightning bolt flashed out of the veritable wall of lightlessness, but fired blindly and usually ineffectively.

Jarlaxle nodded his approval to Bonnie Charlee as the fighting thinned and she cleverly arranged a battery of archers and wizards, ready to blast clear the poop deck if the pirates countered the magical darkness. Bonnie Charlee returned the nod as she batted aside a saber and countered with a quick overhand chop against the man's forearm. His sword went flying and he dropped to his knees, begging for mercy.

The captain looked to Jarlaxle, who shrugged, giving her the choice. With another nod, Bonnie Charlee walked around the kneeling pirate and kicked him flat to the deck, standing over him, ready to finish him if he made a threatening move.

Some other pirates—human, elf, and dwarf—similarly surrendered, and following Bonnie Charlee's example, those *Revenge* fighters secured them with less than lethal force.

No such quarter was offered to any gnolls, however, with every one taken down or, if caught alone, quickly swarmed and overwhelmed and thrown into the shark-filled sea.

The deck quieted in short order, save for the chanting of *Revenge*'s priests' healing spells and the heavy steps of Jarlaxle's diatryma as he launched it for the captain's door, which was still visible between the globes of darkness that hid the stairs to the poop deck. The avian beast hardly slowed, plowing through the portal, then rushing about inside.

"Well, unless *Pelican* is set with secret holds, all remaining are up on that poop deck," Jarlaxle said loudly. "What say you, Captain Arrongo? Are you ready to surrender yet?" As he finished, he nodded to a group of Bregan D'aerthe fighters, and a score of crossbows clicked, sending a swarm of quarrels tipped in sleeping poison through the wall of darkness.

"A dozen fireballs could follow, Arrongo," Jarlaxle called a moment later. "You've nowhere to run and nowhere to hide."

When all of the prisoners were dragged together near the prow, secured and guarded, Jarlaxle gave Bonnie Charlee a signal, and on her ensuing call, the darkness disappeared, revealing the holdouts. A few wizards, a pair of priests, a handful of human pirates, and a dozen gnolls crowded together on that higher deck.

"Come on, then!" challenged one large, black-bearded man with a great hat and so much jewelry that even Jarlaxle thought it gaudy. "Ye got the bones for the fight?"

"It won't be much of a fight," Jarlaxle answered him, stating the obvious.

The man, who was surely Captain Arrongo, spat and glared. He looked to a nearby wizard and nodded.

"Wait!" Jarlaxle added, fearing some magical retreat to be imminent. "For I do prefer a challenge . . . and a wager. Your reputation precedes you, mighty Captain Arrongo. It would be a great shame to so unceremoniously send you and this fine vessel to the depths. Your ship is beaten—that much is obvious—and we have what we came for, the prisoners in your hold. So I offer you this: single combat between you and one of my choosing. If he wins, you'll get the end you richly deserve, the only one you ever thought you'd get, of course. And if you win . . . I'll let you take your remaining crew and sail away on *Pelican*, but only on the condition that you never darken Luskan's horizon again."

"What?" Entreri, and several others, all said, some more quietly than others.

"He knows the outcome already," Zak assured him.

"Now," Jarlaxle continued, "I find that most charitable, and more so than you deserve. So what say you?"

The large man looked all about, seeming confused, as did the others of his crew, with many of them also flashing expressions of hope, fleeting though they were.

"Pick yourself, then," Arrongo countered.

"I would, but I don't like to get blood on me, yours or mine," Jarlaxle answered. "Do you think your wizards will get you away before mine cut them down? Do you think they'll put you far enough away that I won't find you again, and with more ships than this? So fight my champion and I'll promise you that Luskan will never again hunt for you, no matter your crimes, as long as they are not committed in Luskan waters or against ships flying her flag."

Arrongo spat again.

"No matter my pick, you must agree these are better odds than what you now face," Jarlaxle told him. "Decide."

Arrongo put his hand on his sword hilt, a most beautiful orange and gold design of an avian creature. He came forward smiling, to the rail and down.

Bonnie Charlee pulled her crew back. Jarlaxle dismissed his diatryma as it came out the cabin door, startling Arrongo.

"Go earn it," Jarlaxle said to Zaknafein, who stepped forward to face the brutish pirate captain.

"I knew it'd be a damned drow," Arrongo said. "Killed many o' yer kind. One more for good luck, eh?"

"There isn't enough good luck in the world for you right now," Zak assured him, the two locking stares, barely three strides apart on the starlit deck.

"So they all thought," Arrongo replied, suddenly drawing forth a blade that seemed perfectly plain, given the beauty of the hilt.

Quicker than Arrongo's attempted thrust, Zak's blades came into his hands, his right slapping across to deflect the attack, left ready to stab in over the lowered sword.

To Zak's surprise, the blade of Arrongo's sword simply went flying away. Zak was too strong in balance to stumble in the absence of resistance, but he did hesitate, just for an eye blink, and in that fleeting moment, another blade—a shaft of light, brilliant and blinding—shot up from Arrongo's now empty hilt.

Eyes stinging, Zak could only retreat, falling off to his right, cutting his left-hand blade behind to barely parry Arrongo's stab. The drow felt the heat of the blade as it came within a finger's breadth of his chin.

"Ha!" Arrongo bellowed, pursuing with a cunning series of thrusts and sweeps, some one-handed, some two. He bore on, obviously confident that he had the drow half-blinded and unprepared.

Zaknafein knew it, too.

Gasps arose all about as Zaknafein dove and rolled, leaped up and threw himself aside, then came back in at the closely pursuing captain with a desperate flourish, swords waving to block and to try to get him back to even ground. He didn't quite succeed, but he did slap a cleverly thrown dagger out of the air before it could reach him.

Captain Arrongo was full of tricks indeed.

ACROSS THE WAY, ARTEMIS ENTRERI MOVED UP BESIDE Jarlaxle. All about them, humans and drow reacted with every movement of the duel, thinking Arrongo would finish the weapon master.

"Easy," Jarlaxle told his friend, holding up his hand to keep Entreri back—for indeed, the man was leaning forward, hands clutching his sword and dagger hilts tightly. "Faith, my friend."

"Darkness, Zak!" one drow called, and others quickly joined in, for the obvious move by Zaknafein then would be to create a darkness globe about himself and the captain, negating the advantage of the brilliant sword light.

"Why doesn't he?" Entreri asked after a few more attacks and counters, Arrongo keeping Zak on his heels, not surrendering the advantage at all.

"Because you wouldn't, either," Jarlaxle said.

"I cannot," Entreri reminded.

Jarlaxle looked at him and smirked. "You wouldn't if you could, whether it be stupid pride or confidence."

Entreri wanted to disagree, but he couldn't. He looked back to the fight, which seemed dire for Zaknafein as the weapon master was being pressed toward the rail by the huge captain, with only the sea behind him.

When Entreri looked lower at Zaknafein's feet, though, he found himself nodding approvingly.

CAPTAIN ARRONGO'S GLEEFUL EXPRESSION SILENTLY screamed *Over the rail ye go!* as he pressed in those last two strides, his powerful attacks forcing Zaknafein back.

And Zak was gone, and Arrongo's shout started out as one of glee. He cut it short and wildly spun right, however, cutting his blade across at waist height—for somehow, this clever drow had not fallen over the rail, but had back-hopped up against it and sprung away to the side in the space of an eye blink.

Now Zak was coming back in.

Now the initiative was his.

Now he had acclimated to the unexpected brightness.

He leaped above the captain's slicing sword, even managing to put the sole of his boot against it and kick it down and out. And his swords came in hard and fast.

To his great credit, Captain Arrongo managed to quick-step away to minimize the bite, and to his armor's credit, his resulting wounds were not significant.

But magnificent Zaknafein was hardly done. He landed leaning forward and threw himself in that same direction, and now it was Arrongo working his sword frantically, trying to keep the weapon master's nipping blades at bay.

Jarlaxle watched it all with a growing smile.

"Zaknafein is toying with him," Entreri whispered at his side.

Only an expert swordsman would recognize that, Jarlaxle knew, and Entreri, of course, was as fine as any.

Zaknafein's swords worked as if they were wielded by two different warriors, independent and yet still in perfect coordination. The blades came at Arrongo from so many different angles, all working to make him move his own sword, or turn his substantial body, with maximum effort.

Arrongo, too, was a fine warrior, a veteran of a hundred battles at sea and on land, but even those onlookers not so skilled could see that he had to greatly change the new equation of the fight here, and quickly.

Zaknafein's movements were fluid and easy, while Arrongo had to jerk and leap. The brilliant light of his blade showed the sweat gathering about his face, droplets shining on his wild and huge black beard. His breath came faster and harder.

Zaknafein had him cornered in the angle where the rail met the wall of the captain's cabin. Arrongo had nowhere to run.

Arrongo had to change the flow of the battle.

He knew it.

Everyone watching knew it.

And Zaknafein knew it.

Zak's right-hand sword swept out over the rail and came in from the side. Arrongo blocked it hard with a two-hand parry, then sent his sword back the other way and up high to deflect Zak's second blade.

Arrongo had his opening!

As his arms came across, he dropped his upper hand—his right hand—to his right hip, still having enough control and strength to surely push aside the drow's descending blade with his left. That freed right hand went for a dagger on his belt, thinking to throw it fast, which should at least break him out of the corner.

Only his parrying sword did not connect with any meaningful weight, which meant this wasn't an opening at all. The clever drow warrior had led him into a trap.

For Zaknafein was turning to his left even as Arrongo began the parry, turning and rolling his right elbow to bring that blade stabbing in again, and for the spot where he knew Arrongo's right hand would go.

The captain howled in agony as Zak's sword plunged between Arrongo's thumb and pointer finger, then into his hip between the seams in his leather waistcoat.

Zaknafein rolled to his left some more, toward the middle of the deck, leaving the sword stuck right there, pinning Arrongo.

The captain staggered out from the corner, left hand coming down, still holding his sword as he tried to gingerly brush Zak's out of his hip and his hand.

But Zak was already moving, leaping forward to the captain's side, running up the cabin wall and springing away, inverting and twisting right above the captain, landing in a spin and coming around fast and hard, both hands on his remaining blade.

Arrongo's severed sword arm fell to the deck, hand still grasping his blade of light.

The man staggered.

Zak stabbed him in the belly, retracted, and sent his sword tip up, cutting beard, splitting chin. The drow tugged his second sword free as his right-hand blade descended to scrape against the shoulder of Arrongo's stubbed arm.

In stabbed the left blade, once and again, and Zaknafein went into a great swirling spin, dipping low, then coming up diagonally with both swords, forcing Arrongo to turn and stagger to his left.

Zak rolled with the cut, and took another circuit to leap and circle-kick Arrongo square in the back, pitching the bleeding captain headlong over the rail and into the shark-infested waters.

The deck was perfectly silent, a great hush of shock, admiration, and confusion.

"Really?" Jarlaxle asked, holding his hand out toward the water, his expression one of disgust. "He had some fine jewelry."

Zak shrugged, wiped his swords with a quick crisscross along the sleeve of the severed arm, and sheathed them in an easy and impossibly fast movement. He stood straight and held his hand out toward the deck.

"I didn't lose the sword."

Jarlaxle shrugged and snorted. "True."

CHAPTER 4

The Unacceptable
Consequence of Trust

Y e understand what ye're askin' of me, do ye?" King Bruenor said to the two drow priestesses sitting across the table from him. "Ye saw the looks on the faces o' me boys when ye walked up from the low gate."

The drow who had introduced herself as High Priestess Minolin Fey Baenre leaned forward and replied, "Those looks were no less suspicious and angry than those Matron Mother Quenthel Baenre encountered on our journey back to Menzoberranzan, I assure you, good King Bruenor. I hope you appreciate the courage of the matron mother and of Priestess Yvonnel. Their action on the field of battle was a high sacrilege against Lady Lolth, and the Spider Queen is not a merciful goddess."

Bruenor looked around at his advisors: Regis and Donnola Topolino of Bleeding Vines; his queens, Mallabritches and Tannabritches Battlehammer; his three captains of the newly established Grymguard, Ivan Bouldershoulder, Athrogate, and Thibbledorf Pwent; and his adopted daughter, Catti-brie. He let his look linger on Catti-brie, for he had been both surprised and saddened when she had come to the meeting, late, without Drizzt by her side.

He meant to speak with her about that, certainly.

"Yer own—their own—fealty and devotion to the cursed Spider Face isn't me concern," he said, rather harshly and purposely rudely.

Neither drow blinked at that, nor seemed put off at all, which pleased Bruenor.

"The consequences of their actions will reach back to Gauntlgrym, of course," said the other drow, First Priestess Saribel Xorlarrin Do'Urden. "Of course, you see that. Are we to be partners in trade, or enemies?"

"Got to be one or th'other, eh?"

"If our side wins, we hope for the former," Saribel continued. "If Matrons Mez'Barris Armgo and Zhindia Melarn prevail, you can be certain that it will be the latter. Perhaps far in the future, but without doubt, at some point, they will march on Gauntlgrym again."

"Wins what?" Bruenor asked. "Been hearing about yer intended civil war for two years. Ain't heared a thing about drow blood in the streets o' Menzoberranzan, though."

"There have been many skirmishes, King Bruenor," said Saribel.

"There're always small fights in yer town, so I been telled. Yer skirmishes tell me nothing new."

"Are you so eager to have the smell of spilled drow blood wafting up the corridors to fill your long and crooked nose, dwarf king?" Minolin Fey Baenre said, eliciting a chorus of gasps from Bruenor's side of the table.

Not from Bruenor, though. Not even a scowl from Bruenor, just a knowing, sly grin. He looked at Catti-brie, whose face was a mask of surprise at least, perhaps even angry shock, but instead of matching it, Bruenor diffused it all with a sudden and boisterous laugh. "This one's got spunk!" he told his daughter. He turned back to Minolin Fey. "Ye'd make a good dwarf, elf!"

"We need the weapons and the armor," Minolin Fey replied. "Armaments forged in Gauntlgrym would secure House Baenre as Matron Mother Quenthel leads us to a better future—for us and for you."

"It's been two years," Bruenor reiterated.

"The houses have not all aligned," Saribel explained. "Will it be House Baenre and House Do'Urden against Houses Melarn and, quite likely, Barrison Del'Armgo? Will the other major houses side with Baenre and so break the will of our enemies? Or will they side with our foes, and leave things uncertain?"

"It is difficult, King Bruenor," Minolin Fey added, her voice calmer now. "We are asking our kin to repudiate all that they have learned throughout their lives, to repudiate the church of Lolth itself. To accept as allies the other peoples of Toril we have known only as enemies beyond the memories of the longest living drow. This is no easy thing, and the courage of Matron Mother Quenthel and Yvonnel cannot be understated. They crossed a line that cannot be backtracked. Outside your halls, in the sunlight of the forest, they enacted the greatest of all heresies. It is forbidden without exception to reverse the curse of the fallen spider, to revert a drider to her drow form."

"I know, and I'm not for understating that," Bruenor answered. "But ye're askin' me to fire up me forges and put me smithies to work to make a pile o' mail and weapons that might come marching back against us."

"They won't," Saribel said. "With your help, we will start the war. And with your help, we'll end it. We have eight hundred former driders, large and strong drow from another era."

"From an era when they hated dwarfs," Bruenor reminded her.

"Better than any, they know the truth of Lolth, and that truth is a lie, always a lie," Saribel continued. "They will sooner die opposing her than live in comfort worshiping her. To a one. Wearing the mail from the Great Forge of Gauntlgrym, carrying the weapons forged in primordial fire, and with both arms and armor enchanted in the Underdark by great Baenre priestesses and great Xorlarrin wizards, they will shake the walls of Menzoberranzan's cavern and bring the other houses to the side of Baenre, and to the side of truth: the enmity of Lolth."

It was a pretty speech, and an even prettier vision of the future, Bruenor had to admit. He leaned back in his chair and put his red-bearded chin in his palm, studying the two drow visitors.

"Aye, and then when ye're done with your rivals, might that ye'll march to get back that what ye paid for them armaments and more, aye?" a sour Athrogate chimed in, drawing all eyes his way. "I been a friend o' Jarlaxle for a long time. I'm knowing the ways o' the drow."

"You have witnesses to the events on the field," Minolin Fey protested. "They saw the enchanted web. They saw the heresy to Lolth. You!" she said, pointing to Thibbledorf Pwent. "I am told you were there, were you not?"

"Aye," Pwent replied.

"Course!" Athrogate boomed. "And it proves nothin'."

"How can you say that?" Minolin Fey countered. "Before the action of the Matron Mother and Yvonnel, Gauntlgrym was doomed, and you know it."

"Ye might take care with yer words there, drow lady," Queen Mallabritches interrupted.

"Do you doubt it?" Minolin Fey asked, not backing down. "Had we joined with Matron Zhindia and her demon army, and with eight hundred huge driders still in her ranks, do you really believe that Gauntlgrym would have remained in the control of King Bruenor and his clan? You were pinned above and below, with nowhere to run. Your magnificent portals were not fired then, and they wouldn't have been in time, and would not have been at all had not a drow, Gromph Baenre, realized the gravity of that which was happening here and himself taken a great risk." She turned back to Bruenor. "You know this, surely. King Bruenor is a veteran general."

"One what's gotten out o' tougher spots than that," Athrogate insisted.

"Bluster as you will," said the drow. "Behind your voice, you know that I speak truly. Gauntlgrym was doomed except that Matron Mother Quenthel chose a different path."

"Even if ye're speakin' true, I've seen enough o' Menzoberranzan to know that some things don't last," Bruenor remarked.

"Aye!" Athrogate agreed, hopping up from his seat and thumping his palms down flat on the table so that he could lean forward toward the two drow priestesses. "So what's to say that ye didn't play the clever ones, eh? Ye play yer tricks out there and Matron Quenthel—"

"Matron Mother," Saribel corrected, and Athrogate snorted.

"And she gets rid of that crazy Melarni witch—aye, I know all about that one. Heared about me friend's visit to her that should've put her away then and there and forevermore, excepting that yer Lolth don't much like to lose. So ye get rid o' her and ye put the Second House, Armgo or whate'er, in its place, and now ye come marching back altogether and put our own works against us."

"There could be no better opportunity to take Gauntlgrym than that we found when we came to your lower gate," Minolin Fey argued.

"Tweren't Lolth," Thibbledorf Pwent unexpectedly interrupted.

All looked at him curiously, Bruenor most of all. Athrogate's words here had been prearranged, of course, by Bruenor, who had tasked him with challenging the emissaries hard and long. Pwent didn't have a role, least of all at this critical moment. And while it annoyed the king for his plan to be disrupted, he was curious about what Pwent had to say.

"I watched it," Pwent said solemnly. "I watched them eight-legged abominations rushing through for all their lives—aye, even if it cost them their lives. They didn't care. They had a chance of freedom and they leaped in with both . . . err, eight feet. And tweren't Lolth, me King," he told Bruenor, shaking his hairy head. "I felt it when I threw meself through that web. Tweren't evil, tweren't Lolth."

Athrogate, clearly flummoxed, looked to Bruenor for some direction here.

"She is a deceiver," the dwarf king reminded Thibbledorf Pwent.

Pwent considered it, but shook his head, unconvinced, and muttered, "Tweren't Lolth," under his breath.

"Your general describes a remarkable and intricate scheme," Minolin Fey said to Bruenor, "when a straightforward attack on Gauntlgrym would have secured the prize."

"Ain't that the way o' the drow, then?" Bruenor asked.

Minolin Fey leaned back in her seat, as did Saribel, the two exchanging grim looks. "Do we have your answer, then?" Minolin Fey asked.

"No," Bruenor replied. "Ye have me word that me and mine'll talk of it, and get ye an answer. Ye're asking a lot, priestess."

"There is a lot at stake," Minolin Fey came back. "More for us than for you."

"Not sure o' that, and that's me problem." Bruenor nodded toward the room's double doors and the sentries stationed there opened them wide.

The drow priestesses rose and bowed, then went out with their dwarf escorts.

As soon as the doors were closed, the chatter began, a great argument between Pwent and Athrogate, with Ivan Bouldershoulder trying to play intermediary. Fist and Fury sat and whispered together, the sisters shaking their heads with every word as if they were too confused by it all to agree with anyone.

Even Regis and Donnola came down on opposite sides, with Regis advising them to throw in with House Baenre, to fight for a future of the northern Sword Coast that meant something more for all the folk, and Donnola, who had spent most of her life in a guild of thieves and assassins in a faraway land, shaking her head in strong disagreement with his every word and interrupting him with countering arguments whenever he paused to draw breath.

Above the din, Bruenor looked to Catti-brie. "He couldn't even be bothered to come to this?" he said.

"He's with Brie."

"Don't ye go there," Bruenor scolded her. "I'm dealin' with his people here, and his voice'd be worth hearing."

"What would ye have me tell ye, then, Da?" the woman said, reverting to her dwarven brogue—because her words always carried more weight with him when spoken in that dialect, Bruenor suspected. "Might that it's Brie, might that it's his meetin' with the Spider Queen in the tunnel in Damara, might that it's his time with Grandmaster Kane. Might be his time spread out across the lands, not dead, but aye, not alive. He's not the same man, Da. He's seeing things in ways I've not witnessed."

Bruenor had heard it all before, and he, too, had seen this change in Drizzt. It wasn't a melancholy, but more a passivity, and that in a time when Bruenor most needed the ranger in a fighting spirit! He looked at Catti-brie sharply, but forced away his sneer, not ready to have this fight at this time.

"When's Jarlaxle back?" Bruenor asked.

"He was in the east with Dab'nay, is all I'm knowing," Catti-brie replied. "Might be back already."

Bruenor huffed, then slammed his hands on the sturdy table, commanding attention. "I'm off to eat and to fill me beard with the foam of a shaken gutbuster. Ye're all here and stayin', and fightin' it out, and when I come back, I'll be hearing one voice."

"We've got a chance to change the world," Regis said.

"And I've got the task of telling more of my people that we're going to bury their sisters and brothers and parents and children," Donnola countered. "When have we known the drow to keep a treaty or keep any peace?"

Regis sat back and didn't reply.

"Bah!" Bruenor boomed. "*One voice.*"

And he stormed out of the room.

"But it'll be the voice o' the last one standin', I'm guessing," Athrogate muttered.

"You should get Drizzt," Queen Tannabritches told Catti-brie.

"Aye," her sister agreed. "He should be here."

Catti-brie wasn't so sure of that. Not now.

"YE DIDN'T SPEAK YER MIND," BRUENOR SAID TO CATTI-brie when she entered the small room where he sat with a beer. His helm, the Crown of Gauntlgrym, battered and with one horn broken away, rested on the table beside his drink.

Catti-brie sat down across from him.

"Pull me one, eh?" she said when he didn't move.

With a laugh, Bruenor lifted his shield, called upon the magic, and pulled out a perfect glass of golden beer, two-thirds liquid and capped with a perfect head of foam.

Catti-brie scooped it up, drained half of it, and forced a burp to make a dwarf da proud.

"That loosen yer lips?" Bruenor asked.

"If I had something to say, I'd've said it in there."

"Ask yer god or something."

"She's no dwarf god. Probably not even fond o' dwarf gods, or them that follow them."

"Bah! She bringed me back, eh?"

"To join in the fight to save Drizzt from Lolth," Catti-brie said. "Now we got others going to war on Lolth, so it seems."

"So ye're thinkin' I should help 'em?"

"So I'm thinkin', so it seems," Catti-brie repeated.

"So ye don't trust 'em."

Catti-brie finished the beer and motioned for another. "Strange, me da, but I do. I seen enough o' Jarlaxle and Zaknafein and Braelin Janquay and Beniago—even o' Gromph Baenre!—to tell me that there's good reason to think Yvonnel and Quenthel mean what they say and that it's not all a ruse to kill us with our own weapons. Many in that city loathe Lolth, so to speak."

"Could've fooled me, given the three wars that come fast to me thoughts."

Catti-brie nodded and scooped up the second beer. "Where're they to go, Da? Lolth's got the matrons, the matrons've got the nobles, the nobles've got all others. Ye speak against Lolth in the City o' Spiders, ye die. Or worse, aye?"

"Driders," Bruenor muttered.

"Drizzt wasn't th'only one, Da," she said. "He was just th'only one brave enough, or stupid enough, or angry enough, or whate'er it was enough, to walk out into the Underdark and somehow survive to find another life and way. Ye know this. Ye're trading with Luskan, and Luskan is Bregan D'aerthe's."

"This is different," Bruenor said.

"It is," Catti-brie agreed. "And that's why I didn't speak me mind, because I'm not really knowing me mind."

"Well then," Bruenor decided, and he slammed his palms down on the table and stood up quickly, the chair sliding out behind him.

"And now ye know yer own?" Catti-brie asked.

"Nope."

"Then what?"

"Might that I'll cut the baby in half," he said with a wink. He called to the guards and told them to fetch the drow priestesses, then finished his beer with a great swallow, gathered up his distinctive crown and wonderful buckler, and led his daughter back to the throne room.

A BEDRAGGLED AND THOROUGHLY FRUSTRATED CATTI-BRIE entered her chambers much later to find her husband dancing with their little girl. Or maybe they were training.

Drizzt did a broad jump.

Brie hopped, both feet off the ground. She touched down lightly and sprang again, and a third time, which put her up beside her father.

"You," Drizzt said.

Brie laughed. She jumped up as high as she could and turned in midair. She got about a quarter of the way around before she ran out of air beneath her, thumping down and holding her balance.

Drizzt leaped up gracefully and spun about, a full spin, landing and dropping into a squat that put his face right before that of his giggling daughter.

"You!" she said.

Up sprang Drizzt, executing a backflip that landed him on his feet, but only momentarily, as he plopped down on his butt before Brie with a surprised look on his face.

Brie laughed and went up as if to jump, but didn't leave the ground at all, and instead just fell back to a sitting position facing her father.

The two broke out in laughter.

"Boom!" said Drizzt.

"Boo boo!" said Brie.

Catti-brie rushed over and slid on the floor to stop beside the two, bringing a squeal of happiness and a big hug from Brie, and a warm smile from this man she loved.

"You're up so late," she said to Brie. "Up and playing with Da." She smirked at Drizzt as she said that.

"She had a fine supper," Drizzt said. "She wanted to stay awake to get a kiss and a story from her mum."

"Come then, my little love," Catti-brie whispered to the girl. She pulled herself up to her feet, one arm wrapped around her daughter, and carried the child into a circular side chamber they had set up as Brie's bedroom, complete with brilliantly carved reliefs of war-pig guards running about the base of the wall, some on four legs, some on two, some dancing, most laughing.

DRIZZT NODDED AS HE WATCHED THEM GO, THEN CROSSED the floor to what remained of his own dinner, growing cold on the table. For all of Catti-brie's love in that encounter, he hadn't missed the indications that she was mentally and physically drained. Bruenor was leaning on her—of course he was—and the tensions swirling about Mithral Hall couldn't be denied.

They had averted disaster, but very possibly only for the present.

Perhaps he should have gone to the meeting with the representatives from House Baenre, as Bruenor had asked and Catti-brie had begged. To him, though, it had seemed like a continuation of a cycle that could not be broken—what a stunning intellectual paradox transcendence had inflicted upon him! While he recognized and understood the importance of the contentious meetings now being fought out in Bruenor's audience hall, he was having a difficult time even feeling that urgency.

Transcendence had pushed him to a place where he viewed all of this as temporary, and so had twisted his priorities to such an extent that . . .

That he had ignored a meeting his friends and his wife had begged him to attend.

He knew that he was out of balance, in the same way that he knew that he was hungry, but couldn't quite find the energy to move his fork to lift the food to his mouth with any real purpose.

This was a melancholy he had not expected.

He was still absently picking at his meal, lost in that conflict of perspective, when Catti-brie exited Brie's room and closed the wooden door behind her.

"Are you hungry?" Drizzt asked.

"Bruenor saw to it before I left him," she answered.

"And what was the decision?"

Catti-brie stopped in her approach, put her hands on her hips, and sighed. "Bruenor set the smiths to work. A hundred suits of heavy chain sized for elves and two hundred fine and slender swords."

"Then they convinced him that their war is imminent," Drizzt presumed, but his voice faltered when he noted that Catti-brie was shaking her head.

"He's giving the Baenres nothing as of now," she said. "But if they convince him, he's promised that what they want will be ready for the journey to Menzoberranzan. He cut the baby in half, so he decided."

Drizzt considered it for a moment, then nodded. "Delaying," he reasoned. "Perhaps that's his best choice. I hope he holds no illusions of waiting out the drow. They'll play their hand on their own terms and times."

"He knows," Catti-brie assured Drizzt. "He's hoping to find some better answers from some better spies before he arms those who have come against him on three occasions."

"Jarlaxle?" Drizzt said with a laugh.

"Or Kimmuriel. Or Gromph. There are possibilities here."

Drizzt considered it and gave a little nod.

"You should have been there," Catti-brie said, her voice growing sharper.

Drizzt shrugged. "I have no insights about Menzoberranzan that I haven't already shared, and I know little of the priestesses who came as Baenre's ambassadors."

"You know Yvonnel."

"I know some things about her, but nothing I would trust with the lives of my friends. I find her quite beyond my understanding."

"You know more about Menzoberranzan than anyone in Gauntlgrym other than those two visiting priestesses. Just the way they looked at you across the table might have provided some hints as to their veracity, or the depth of their commitment. That war they're insisting will soon begin was in truth begun by you on the day you walked out of Menzoberranzan."

She stopped short and Drizzt realized that she had noted his wince.

"What?" Catti-brie asked, clearly caught off guard by the reaction. "Is that it? Do you think this a bad thing?"

"I think that there will be slaughter unlike anything we can imagine," he answered quietly. "More than twenty thousand drow in a holy civil war? Armies of demons in support? The whole of the cavern will be painted in gore."

Catti-brie's sympathetic expression didn't last and she gave a little snort. "Sounds like what we would have faced right here, and baby Brie, too, if Yvonnel and Quenthel Baenre had taken the easier path and joined with Zhindia Melarn."

"But we didn't. Do you not care that more than half the city will likely be murdered, or worse?"

"Should I?" she replied, rather unconvincing in her indifference.

"Perhaps not," he sarcastically countered. "They are just drow, after all, and thus deserving of their doom."

As soon as the words left his mouth, Drizzt wanted them back.

Catti-brie glared at him.

"Don't you ever say that to me," Catti-brie quietly replied. "I do not deserve that from you."

"No," he agreed, and took a deep breath. "I didn't mean it for you. But that is the common feeling among those who live on the surface and know the drow by reputation alone. And that is what Bruenor is working against when he has to decide whether or not to help."

"The drow have attacked him in his home."

"*His* home? For how long has it been his home?"

"Wha . . ." She lost her voice and just shook her head in obvious shock.

"What I have seen across centuries, my love, is the judgment of impact without any consideration of the intent. And not just for the drow and by the drow."

"Drizzt?"

"I am guilty of it as well," he admitted. "We all do it, foolishly, and extrapolate grand truths about our enemies that bring us to places where our disagreements cannot be reconciled."

"They also attacked Mithral Hall," Catti-brie reminded him.

"And Bruenor attacked Q'Xorlarrin," Drizzt countered.

"Q'Xorlarrin?" the flustered woman stuttered. "Gauntlgrym?"

"So he calls it."

"This is the ancient homeland of the Delzoun dwarves."

"And probably a place called home by a hundred other groups in the thousand years before Bruenor rediscovered it."

"You cannot be serious."

"I've never been more serious," Drizzt answered firmly. "When I walk among the humans, I am drow, and so many think me evil. And yes, the folk of Menzoberranzan have done some evil things, and wars between them and the cultures of the surface world are real and plentiful."

"And raids that kill families of elves and humans and dwarves?" Catti-brie said.

"Do you think a group of drow would fare any better if they met a superior force of elves, or humans, or dwarves, in a high cavern of the Underdark? Do you think that superior force of elves would stop and ask that drow family their intent or purpose?"

Now it was Catti-brie's turn not to answer.

"How might the duergar feel about Bruenor and his kin evicting them from Mithral Hall all those years ago?"

Catti-brie heaved a great sigh.

"Yes, the drow are evil," Drizzt said with a grand flourish. "Let us presume that to be the truth."

"Let us presume whatever you want without your condescension," Catti-brie returned.

Drizzt rubbed his face and silently reminded himself that his actions and tone were wrought from his own frustrations, and not anything to do with this generous person standing before him.

"Then what of Prisoner's Carnival in Luskan, where the magistrates torture helpless victims to a death they welcome as an escape from the agony, and all to the cheers of the massive crowds?" he asked calmly and seriously.

"The magistrates are evil," Catti-brie said.

"They follow the law," Drizzt argued.

"Then the law is wrong."

"Yes! And what of the pirates who catch a merchant ship unguarded off the Sword Coast and walk their victims off the planks into the jaws of waiting sharks?"

"We hunted them together with Deudermont. How many found mercy?"

"Exactly! We hunted them and put them to the depths, as we should have. Because they committed and would continue to commit evil deeds."

"Yes."

"And most were human, so humans are evil."

"What? No!"

"Of course not. And that is my point, and that is my frustration."

Catti-brie stared at him hard for a short while before slowly shaking her head in confusion.

"Good and evil," Drizzt said. "Or better, kindness and meanness, mercy and brutality. We were brutal to the pirates, but what was our intent?"

"To stop them from continuing their way of terror and murder."

"And that mattered. Don't you see?"

"Of course I see it!"

"That mattered," Drizzt said again, because he had to play this out for his own sake. "Determining goodness and evil can't be simply an issue of perception based solely upon the identity of the perpetrator—a drow? A moon elf? A halfling? A dwarf? A human?—or the alliance of the perpetrator's people. The judgment lies in intent. So, yes, the drow have done evil. The raid I was taken upon when I was still a young man was evil. But what of the raid that Wulfgar's people waged on Ten Towns on that occasion when Bruenor captured Wulfgar? How many would have been slaughtered if Wulfgar's Uthgardt kin had proven victorious?"

"I assure you that I have considered that point."

"But we—and Ten Towns—were living on the ancient land of those tribes, and taking scarce resources as our own." When Catti-brie didn't answer, he continued, "We thought it a great act of mercy that Bruenor saved Wulfgar—a boy then, but a man you came to love, a man I came to love. But what of the hundreds of his people dead on the field? What of the dwarves who could have shown such mercy but did not? None of us would have judged Bruenor ill if he had chosen differently that day, but Wulfgar would have become just another notch on his old axe."

"I don't know where you're going with this," Catti-brie admitted, and she didn't seem very happy.

"We're never to see peace—none of us—until we come to recognize that a child of a culture that is not our own is as precious as one who is. And I don't know if that will ever be possible. No peace, not for humans or dwarves or halflings or drow or elves."

Catti-brie cocked her head a bit and Drizzt detected a hint of a sly grin. "Or orcs?" she asked when he paused to look at her.

"I do not know," he admitted.

"Is this about orcs again?"

"No, this is about . . . everything. It is about the arc of justice and peace," he replied, his voice heavy. "What purpose, I wonder, has the road I have walked and the road I walk now—or that you would have me walk now—if any steps forward are fleeting, if at the end, there can be no peace?"

"You can't believe that," Catti-brie said, and she stepped forward and stared at him, her hands going up to his shoulders. She kept staring, and he locked that gaze, the two studying each other and moving back from their ledges. Drizzt was relieved indeed when Catti-brie gave him a much-needed hug.

"I don't know what I believe because of what I have seen." He pulled her back to arm's length and stared again into those deep blue eyes that had so fully captured his heart and had never let it go. "I think this is part of what Grandmaster Kane warned me about when he and I spoke of transcendence of the physical body and the physical world. So much of that which motivates us here becomes . . ."

"Trite?" she whispered to him.

He could only shrug.

Catti-brie stepped back, her expression going distinctly colder. "They would have conquered Gauntlgrym if not for the actions of Yvonnel and Quenthel Baenre," she said. "Brie was in here. You can well imagine what would have happened to her, particularly if they realized she was the daughter of Drizzt the heretic. Is that trite to you?"

"Of course not."

"They would have killed her, or worse. They would have killed all of us, or worse. Had not Yvonnel and Quenthel turned on Zhindia Melarn—"

"I know," Drizzt interrupted, "and maybe that's Bruenor's answer."

Catti-brie looked at him with obvious anticipation.

"Maybe that truth makes it worth the risk," Drizzt explained.

"And what is Drizzt's answer? When this war starts, if it does, what will Drizzt do?"

"I don't know," he said without the slightest hesitation. "And that is my pain."

"I would have thought that you would lead the revolution," Catti-brie told him, putting her hand on his shoulder. "You and Jarlaxle, with your father by your side, fighting to free your people from the grip of Lolth. Or is that what scares you most of all?"

Drizzt looked up at her curiously, and for a long while, the two just held each other's gaze.

"Because this isn't about the houses. It is about Lolth. And that's what you believe, what you have believed for many decades, right?"

Catti-brie elaborated. "That these foul deeds are the result of Lolth's influence and machinations and not the truth of the drow people. And now perhaps that question will be answered, and that answer scares you."

He didn't respond, other than to firm his jaw.

"Is it that you've been living among those who would blame you for so long that you fear that there might be more truth than simple ignorance to the source of their hatred?" Catti-brie was clearly surprised by her own words.

"No," Drizzt answered her, but haltingly.

"Good," she answered. "Because you shouldn't."

"Doubt is not the source of my melancholy—not doubt about the people of Menzoberranzan, at least. There, it is Lolth. The story Kimmuriel and Yvonnel told us of the founding and the corruption by the Spider Queen makes sense to me with all that I saw in my decades in Menzoberranzan before I managed to escape. It makes sense to me when I look at Jarlaxle and what he has accomplished away from the influences of Lolth's corrupting priestesses—Luskan is a better place under Jarlaxle's leadership. A fairer place, and one better for all who live there. And this makes sense to me when I consider Jarlaxle, and when I remember my sister Vierna."

"Whom you killed," Catti-brie reminded him, and Drizzt grimaced.

And Catti-brie grimaced in response.

"She denied Lolth with her last breaths," he said grimly, and he took a deep breath, blew it out, and continued. "Even in what I have seen from Gromph Baenre—did you not tell me that it was Gromph who pulled the lever at the Hosttower to return the magical energy to control the fire primordial?"

"So you have faith in your people. Then what?" she pleaded, grabbing his arms. "What is it? You have to talk to me."

Drizzt took another necessary deep breath, trying to find the words to explain it all—even to himself. Everything seemed too small to him at that time, and at the same time too overwhelming. So many of the endless wars and ridiculous prejudices rang to him as trite—yes, that word was exactly right!—and yet, that ran against everything he had striven to accomplish all of his life.

"It's the road," he said again. "And the point of it all if that road winds into nothing but a circle." He paused. "I know in my head that I should have been at the meeting, supporting those who deserve nothing less from me. But I also know that my heart was not in it. I'm not ready to reconcile what I recently learned with that which has carried me through all the steps of my journey to the point before my transcendence."

"You *should* have been at the meeting," Catti-brie flatly replied. "Because you think you've seen a better future beyond this life doesn't mean that what you've done in this life was without meaning. If you believe that, then you're not the man I married, and not the father Brie deserves."

Her words hit him like a punch. He even staggered back a step.

"You know that I'm right," she said sternly, not blinking, not backing down an inch.

He knew her.

He saw it.

Unlike his earlier flippancy, yes, even condescension, Catti-brie had been deadly serious. She had meant every word and there was no second-guessing that last admonishment. And that's when it rang true to Drizzt, a bell so clear that he could hardly believe he hadn't heard it all along. This was the friend who had traveled alone into the Underdark to rescue him from the dungeons of House Baenre. These were the friends all around him, the Companions of the Hall, who had come back from death itself to support him in his trials, indeed, who had saved him when he kneeled broken, physically and emotionally, atop Kelvin's Cairn.

He felt the warm blush of shame flush his cheeks. Of course he should have been at that meeting.

Catti-brie's stern stare made clear that she wasn't going to let him off the hook here when she and those they both loved needed him to find clarity.

And purpose.

Yes, he needed to rediscover his purpose, and not just for those around him, not just for his daughter.

For himself.

"This is why you are so anxious to go see Grandmaster Kane," Catti-brie stated, not asked. She paused for a long while, staring into Drizzt's lavender eyes.

Yes, he thought, for Kane had transcended, many times, and yet the old monk's life remained one of earthly purpose.

"This is why you must go to the monastery," she whispered, and kissed him, then turned and walked for the door.

"And eat yer durned dinner, ye damned pointy-eared, stubborn elf," she called from the door in her best Bruenor's-daughter voice.

Drizzt returned a much-needed chuckle.

CHAPTER 5

Shark Delight

Pelican's crew stood nervously before the rail, the shark-infested waters at their backs—waters bloody red once more as *Pelican's* gnolls had been summarily thrown overboard. The remaining pirates had no weapons, their wizards had their fingers tied together, and a crew of drow stood before them, hand-crossbows and swords at the ready.

And among those armed guards stood the drow warrior who had destroyed their powerful Captain Arrongo, a leader who had held them in thrall and in fear for a long time.

They shuffled nervously as the drow leader in the outrageous hat began his review, accompanied by a drow woman dressed in the formal robes of a priestess.

"This is my friend, one I trust dearly," Jarlaxle told them. "She is not young, certainly not so by the reckoning of a human, and she has spent more years than any among you have been alive studying the divine domain of knowledge. Part of that . . . well, you will see."

He looked to Dab'nay, and she nodded. Jarlaxle's claim about her was no false boast, for though she had been raised as a priestess in the service of Lolth, her studies had always been more along the lines of the domain of knowledge. She had been the eyes of her old house. And while other priestesses around her were focusing on the magic of duplicity and disguise, the divine domains of trickery or tempest or war, Dab'nay's most important duties had been to uncover such subterfuge from potential rivals or enemies. So that's what she was going to do now. She lifted her holy symbol and began to chant under her breath, bringing forth her magic, opening the minds of these prisoners that they could not hide behind false words.

Jarlaxle began to slowly walk the line of prisoners.

"I ask you all," he told them, "to consider which among you tortured prisoners on behalf of Captain Arrongo."

He stopped at the first, a panicked young man, and glanced back at Dab'nay.

She studied the young man for just a moment, then shook her head.

Jarlaxle clutched the man by the front of his shirt and tugged him away from the rail, sending him scrabbling to the middle of the deck. A pair of drow grabbed him there and brought him to the far rail.

So it went down the line, Jarlaxle repeating his request—they couldn't help but hear it and react to it. They needn't speak an answer aloud, for just hearing the question in their minds brought forth the memories and thoughts, the nonverbal tics and other physical indications.

Observing them and in their minds was Dab'nay, not like Kimmuriel might have done, but enough to confidently nod or shake her head to Jarlaxle's questioning gaze.

Those she believed less guilty got the head shake, and were dispatched to the guarding drow. Those whose thoughts made Dab'nay know that they partook in the torture with relish remained where they were.

All but five of the *Pelican*'s two dozen captured pirates remained at the rail.

When he was done, Jarlaxle tipped his hat to Dab'nay, who went to the hatch and lifted the door, helping the pirates' captives out onto the deck. She led them to Jarlaxle.

"Any in particular?" he asked them.

For a bit, none of the poor souls dared to answer, but finally one young man, barely more than a boy, lifted a shaking arm and pointed to a filthy fellow standing halfway down the line.

Jarlaxle walked up to him and paused, looked back at the boy, and pointed to the pirate.

The boy nodded. Two other victims did as well.

Jarlaxle pushed the man over the rail.

He was still screaming and thrashing when the next torturer was identified, then a third, then two more.

Over they went, all five, to the delight of the sharks.

"It's not so much fun when it's someone you know, is it?" Jarlaxle said to the remaining pirates. "And less still when you know that you might well be next. And you might, any of you. I make no promises, except to tell you that I am of an open mind on letting you live. You will work, untangling the ships and making *Pelican* seaworthy that we can sail her back to Luskan. And you will be judged from now until we arrive. One mistake, one threat, one attack, and you will join Captain Arrongo and the others in the bellies of sharks."

He stepped to the rail and looked over. "Although I would guess that Captain Arrongo has found several new homes, at least, within which he can . . . digest what he has done."

He spun back with the pun, staring at Zaknafein and Entreri, holding his hands up in surprise that they were not laughing.

"What?" he said innocently.

The other two just walked away.

THE SHIPS WERE SEPARATED IN SHORT ORDER—IT HELPED that *Deudermont's Revenge* was designed and built for ramming, tangling, and quickly extracting. And for fast repair. So by the time the captured pirates laboring under the watchful eyes and commands of

Bregan D'aerthe and a *Revenge* engineer had untangled the lines of the fallen mast on *Pelican*, *Revenge's* sails were back in place and ready to catch the wind.

It took another two days to get *Pelican* able to sail, and even then, it would be with a noticeable limp, as Jarlaxle put it. But sail they did, straight back to the east, *Deudermont's Revenge* nearby, both running protection from other pirates that might be about and reminding those captured *Pelican* crew that any resistance would be met with an overwhelming—and now merciless—response.

Jarlaxle, Zak, and Entreri all remained on *Pelican*, something surely not lost on the captured pirates. They would never regain this ship, let alone manage to somehow outrun and evade *Revenge*.

"You are a crew, my crew now," Jarlaxle told them repeatedly as he walked the deck. "I'll feed you well and keep you well, as long as you do as I say. Those sharks following us? They are my sharks, my pets, and I promised them that I would feed them well if you don't."

"He's the blustering one," Zak said to Entreri, the two sitting against the rail, inspecting their weapons and taking a meal.

"The conqueror, ever adding to his collection of assets," Entreri replied.

"'Assets'?" Zak asked, shaking his head. "I don't know this word."

"His treasure, don't you see?" said Entreri. "They, we two, Bregan D'aerthe, Luskan itself—we are all Jarlaxle's treasure. He's like a dragon, but he hoards people and power instead of gold and gems."

"And dragons themselves," Zak quipped. "Two of the strangest wyrms I've ever heard tell of. Where are Tazmikella and Ilnezhara, I wonder? They'd make this pirate hunting a lot easier, on my stomach at least."

"They flew back to Vaasa, I was told, but I'm sure that we'll see them again. Jarlaxle's not one to let that kind of power evade him for long."

He noticed that Zak was looking at him with some suspicion then, so Entreri lowered Charon's Claw across his lap and turned to meet the weapon master's gaze.

"You speak of him as a villain, yet you remain by his side."

"Hardly a villain," Entreri replied.

"He hoards people?"

"Aye, because they want to be there," said Entreri, following Zak's gaze to Jarlaxle, who was approaching. "That's his charm, don't you see? He understands the concept of creating situations that both sides will appreciate, understanding the mutual benefit. That's why he'll have Luskan fully for as long as he wants it. Because the folk of Luskan will *want* him to have the city. If the kings and queens of the world spent as much time and gold on caring for those they rule as they do on armies and weapons they keep ready in case those people rise up against them, they'd be richer and more secure by far."

Zak snorted. "You would have a hard time convincing the matrons of Menzoberranzan of that, I fear."

"Do you think the dwarves would ever rise up against King Bruenor?" Entreri finished the conversation as Jarlaxle arrived, and Zaknafein knew it to be a rhetorical question anyway, or at least one with an obvious answer.

"I'm losing my voice from so much talking and assurances," Jarlaxle said. "Do you think, perhaps, that either of you might muster the strength to walk the deck and coax the crew?"

"I could, but I don't want to," Zak replied.

"You bluff, Jarlaxle," Entreri added. "Both of us know you well enough to know that the one thing you could never lose is your voice."

That brought a smile to Jarlaxle's face, and he bowed in surrender and swept his arm gracefully. Entreri noted that Jarlaxle was wearing a couple of rings that he had seen on the hand of Captain Arrongo— and not the hand Zaknafein had severed and left on the deck.

He looked from the rings to Jarlaxle's waiting and knowing smile.

"I took what I could find," the drow rogue explained. "Fortunately, the giant shark was no longer hungry, but less fortunately, it is almost certain that greater treasures were among the contents of its belly."

"You disappoint me," Zak told him. "I would have thought you the type to follow the beastly shark until it shat out the rest of Arrongo."

"It was a thought," Jarlaxle replied, walking away.

Zak looked to Entreri, who could only shrug and admit, "I didn't even see him get wet."

Soon after, the lookout called down, "Land!" and as the sun set behind *Pelican*, it shone past them to the tips of tall, snow-covered mountains far ahead and to the left, and when it went into hiding behind the sea, the stars came twinkling to life above them, and so too did the lights of Luskan sparkle, far away and straight ahead.

"HAVE YOU DISCOVERED MORE?" JARLAXLE ASKED CATTI-brie a few days later in Gauntlgrym.

"I believe that I know as much about the whip as I'll ever learn," she replied. "I have spoken with great wizards, even creatures of other planes—even with Maegera, to a degree, if our communions can be considered a dialogue." She shrugged and admitted, "Though I'm not sure how much of the full story or power that may be, nor even where fact ends and supposition begins."

"But you're comfortable with the attempt?"

The woman shrugged again. "I have little idea of how the flames of the primordial will treat the weapons, though I am more confident now that Maegera will not be able to use the powers of the whip to somehow escape its chasm. The only loss I foresee would be that of the whip and whatever else we feed to the Great Forge."

"Splendid!" Jarlaxle said, and clapped his hands, then reached toward his left hip.

Catti-brie fully took note of the sword hanging there for the first time, and though the pommel was different, she surely recognized the hilt and cross-guard. She gasped and grabbed Jarlaxle by the forearm.

"No. Never."

Jarlaxle turned a perplexed look her way.

"I will not add magic to that sword," she explained. "Never. I'll not feed it into the Great Forge, but I would gladly, no payment needed, throw it into the primordial chasm to be destroyed, or otherwise removed from the hands of its next victim."

"Ah, you recognize Khazid'hea," Jarlaxle replied.

"And our conversation is at an end," she said, and started away.

"No, lady, no," Jarlaxle said, stopping her before she had fully turned from him. "I do not wish you to feed Khazid'hea in with the whip. The sword is magnificent on its own, of course."

"You're a fool for even wielding it."

"I carry it," Jarlaxle told her. "Sheathed. I do not wield it."

"Destroy it, then, and make the world a better place."

"It is a powerful tool, and in the right hands—"

Her narrow-eyed look stopped him for a moment, but only a moment. "Khazid'hea allowed Drizzt to fight Obould to a draw," he reminded her. "It is just a sword."

"I know all about that . . . sword."

"You do, and my apologies for bringing it here this day," the drow said with a bow. "But I repeat: it is not Khazid'hea I wish you to feed to the forge beside the whip." He reached to his hip again, but under Khazid'hea, bringing forth a beautiful small sculpture of a yellow-and-orange fiery bird, which she recognized as a phoenix. After a moment, she realized that it was more than a sculpture; it was a long sword hilt, but one missing a blade. The wings of the bird were out to its sides, serving as a cross guard, and with the outer feathers bending back toward the pommel to form a solid guard. The long neck snaked up higher, and Catti-brie thought that it was blocking the butt to which a blade might be attached.

But no, she realized, there was no attachment prong, nor a hollow into which a blade might be fed and secured.

She looked at the tiny rubies that served as eyes for the bird, and a third, larger red gem, set in the pommel, which seemed to be formed of the bird's tail feathers curled up into a ball.

"That?" she asked. "Why that? The whip has a handle."

"And the hilt has a blade," Jarlaxle explained, and he lifted it and tightened his grip. The three rubies flared with inner magic and the blade of light suddenly appeared, accompanied by a momentary low hum.

"A sun blade," Catti-brie said. "I have heard of this. It is said to be a marvelous weapon."

"It is indeed, and one worthy of all but the greatest of warriors. We— well, Zaknafein took it from Captain Arrongo and is anxious for it back. But I promised him that I would return to him something even more wondrous than Arrongo's sword alone."

"You wish to risk that prize in the primordial's fires?" she asked, her doubts showing.

"I wish to make this weapon worthy of the greatest of warriors," Jarlaxle reminded her. He rolled his wrist as he dismissed the blade of light, then handed the phoenix pommel over to Catti-brie.

She took it and held it out before her gingerly for a while, staring blankly, trying to let it all properly register.

"Do it, I beg," Jarlaxle pleaded. "I believe this will complement well the whip of flames."

"Just give this to Zaknafein along with the whip," Catti-brie suggested. "He will be as powerfully armed as almost any warrior along the Sword Coast."

"I seek more than that. I wish it to be truly worthy of Zak. Do it."

"And if the result disappoints?"

"Then I have an excuse to find another adventure to replace what I have lost."

"You'll not find another whip like this," she warned.

"It is marvelous, but situational," Jarlaxle answered. "And next to useless when an enemy is close."

"Then Zak uses the sun blade."

"I wish him to have more options."

"You risk a lot."

"I like to bet," he said, and held his hand out toward the door that led toward the forge room of Gauntlgrym. "But there's a difference between gambling and taking a risk. I rarely gamble."

Catti-brie took up the whip in one hand, the phoenix hilt in the other, and paused, but only for a moment. She shrugged and started off, glad that Jarlaxle was behind her, for she didn't want him to see that she was truly intrigued.

They said nothing until they got to the Great Forge. The forge room was mostly empty at that late hour, though one fellow worked at a small oven across the way, hammering at some tool.

Catti-brie fast approached and unintentionally startled him when she called to him, so much so that he nearly dropped his tongs and the hot metal he held with them.

"Aye, Princess!" he replied, setting down his instruments and pulling off his protective mask. "What might I be doing for ye?"

"Festus, yes?" Catti-brie asked, recognizing the dwarf as one of the Adbar boys who had stayed on after the retaking of Gauntlgrym.

"Aye, Festus Grymforge at yer service," he said with a bow.

Catti-brie looked at him curiously, trying to place the name. "I'm not for knowing Clan Grymforge," she admitted.

"Was O'Maul, lady," he explained. "O' the Adbar O'Mauls."

"Ambergris," Jarlaxle said.

"Fourth cousin," Festus said.

"Then why Grymforge?" asked Catti-brie.

"New clan under Battlehammer," Festus announced. "More and more joining. Ragged Dain started it, with the queens' own sister, Hannabritches Fellhammer. Aye, she and Ragged Dain'll be taking Grymforge as their clan name when they marry later in the year. And they'll have a fine clan around them, what. Boys from Felbarr and Adbar, from Mirabar, too."

"Just boys?" Jarlaxle quipped. "Sounds like a short-lived clan."

"Every dwarf is called that," Catti-brie replied. "Always their 'boys.' And that's meaning all o' them. It's a term of endearment and camaraderie, nothing more.

"Grymforge," she repeated, looking back at Festus. "I like it. Like the new Grymguard. Seems fitting."

"Aye, that's what we were thinkin'."

"Ye chose well," Catti-brie said. "Might I ask ye the favor of firing up the oven of the Great Forge, Festus Grymforge?"

The dwarf looked at her curiously. "Are ye doin' it again?" he whispered after glancing all around to make sure they were alone.

Catti-brie knew what he meant, for the whispering hadn't stopped

since she had combined Twinkle and Vidrinath, and combined Bruenor's shield with Orbbcress, and her bow Taulmaril with the marvelous
buckle that magically concealed weapons.

"Fire the forge and ye'll see," Catti-brie promised.

It didn't take long before the oven of the Great Forge blazed
white-hot. They didn't have to feed it wood or coal or anything else,
of course. All that they were doing was opening the appropriate valves
enough to let the primordial send forth a furious tendril of flame. The
ovens were the real engineering and magical marvels here, strong and
secure, with countering enchantments to prevent the beast's escape—
and the largest and most impressive of all was that of the Great Forge.
A wizard or priest detecting magic on it would be blinded as surely as
if they stared into the white-hot flame within.

"You are sure?" Catti-brie asked one last time when she stood beside Jarlaxle at the feed to the oven.

Jarlaxle nodded and the woman lifted the beautiful hilt, examining its magic with her spells, and then the bullwhip, which she had
already studied intently.

"Is it all up to the oven?" Jarlaxle asked.

Catti-brie shook her head, but was too deep in her thoughts to
break them by answering aloud. She put the whip on the tray. She cast
a spell of protection upon herself, bade Jarlaxle and Festus to back up,
then opened the oven gate.

She started to push the whip in closer, but even with her protective enchantment, the heat was too much for her. She turned to Festus
and pointed and the dwarf tossed her his gloves. She donned them and
took up long-handled tongs.

In went the whip, the flames roiling about it almost hungrily, then
dancing about it as if joyously, as if they had found a long-lost cousin.
The whip itself shed wisps of smoke in the heat, and threw shots of its
own flame to dance with the primordial tendril.

"That doesn't look good," Jarlaxle remarked, but Catti-brie held up
her hand to silence the drow, urging patience.

She lifted the blade of light, admiring the beautiful phoenix hilt and hoping that this artwork would not be melted to an ugly lump. She put it on the tray, but picked it back up immediately on a notion, and called forth its blade.

"Well, lookie there," she heard Festus say.

Onto the tray it went, and Catti-brie grabbed it with the tongs and placed it into the oven beside the whip. Then she shut the grate and began to chant, calling through her magical ring to Maegera, asking the primordial to reveal its beautiful power of creation once more.

"Open the valves wider," she bade Festus.

"Lady," he said slowly and with obvious concern.

"Do it. It is okay."

It went on for a long while before Catti-brie at last bade Festus to shut down the oven.

When she opened the grate, she saw only the small flame that never extinguished within, and it was dancing mesmerizingly, as if telling her to go ahead and remove the items and witness again the beauty and power of Maegera.

Catti-brie swallowed hard. The whip was gone, the blade of light was closed, but the phoenix hilt remained, apparently unscathed.

She pulled it forth and lifted it. Feeling no heat, she removed a glove and gingerly brought her bare hand close, then grasped it and closed her eyes.

A smile spread upon her face, and she nodded approvingly, then turned to Jarlaxle.

"I think you'll be pleased," she said, and tossed him the hilt.

He, too, closed his eyes, and Catti-brie knew that the new weapon was revealing to him its powers, as it had just done to her.

"Very," Jarlaxle said a moment later, his eyes widening. "And so will the wielder."

"Ye goin' to tell me, then?" Festus asked. "What happened to that whip?"

"It's in there."

Festus leaned over and looked curiously into the open oven.

"Not in there, in the hilt," Catti-brie explained.

"Huh?"

"Do yourself a favor, friend," Catti-brie said. "Do not ever anger Zaknafein to the point of battle."

"Ne'er occurred to me," the dwarf assured her.

"Would you leave us, good dwarf?" Jarlaxle then asked.

"Aye, but not for long, I've plenty the work to do."

"It won't take long," Jarlaxle promised.

Festus bobbed his head and scurried along. He was barely out of the room when Jarlaxle again drew Khazid'hea.

"I already told you," Catti-brie scolded, "I'll not put that infernal blade into the Great Forge."

"Of course not, and Festus is gone and the oven is closed, in any case. But I wonder, would Catti-brie be interested in forever defeating the threat of Khazid'hea so that the sword will never again do to another what it did to her?"

"I will happily throw it into the chasm with Maegera to be devoured."

"No, no, there is a better way," Jarlaxle assured her. "And in this way that I have discovered, you might well save another of the sword's victims, and might well help me prevent the grand slaughter that will soon befall Menzoberranzan."

Catti-brie cocked her head, her blue eyes unblinking.

"Take it," Jarlaxle bade her. "Hold it, dominate it, demand of Khazid'hea that it tell you of another victim, and point the way."

"What madness is this?"

"No madness, good lady, never that. You know there is no risk here, for you are far beyond the willpower of Khazid'hea. Do as I ask and I will explain. Or more likely, do as I ask, and you will come to understand all on your own."

Catti-brie hesitated. She wiped her hand on the side of her breeches, then slowly lifted it toward Jarlaxle, toward Khazid'hea, flinching.

CHAPTER 6

The Unlikely Band of Merry Friends

I n the training room of Ship Kurth in Luskan, Zaknafein twirled the phoenix-shaped hilt in his left hand, expertly rolling his fingers to keep it moving end over end. A blade erupted from the hilt, a shaft of brilliant light shifting from orange to yellow to white and spitting flames along its length.

Now Zak went into a more engaged routine, widening his stance, rolling the blade along one side, across before him where he let it go in a spin, caught the hilt in his right hand, and snapped it across and out wide, cutting a line of fire into the air, surely a rift to the fiery plane.

Zak sent it rolling again, easy and smooth, the deadly magical blade moving in a balanced and mesmerizing dance. It went behind his back, then into his left hand, and in a circuit once and again on his left side.

On that second turn, the blade elongated, drawing a gasp from the onlookers (except Jarlaxle, who appeared quite pleased, most likely with himself), and when it came up over his shoulder, it wasn't a sword, but a whip, which Zaknafein snapped out straight ahead, again cutting a rift in the air, from which dripped a ball of flame.

Both fiery rifts sizzled out at the same time, with a hiss and a pop.

Zaknafein's whip became a sword, and then just a beautiful hilt once more.

"You are pleased?" Jarlaxle asked.

Next to him, Artemis Entreri snorted at the absurdity of the question. What he had just seen was a weapon of power and of deception, which seemed a perfectly deadly combination.

"It makes my other blade seem . . . inadequate," Zak answered.

"Because it is," Jarlaxle agreed. "You prefer your left hand with the whip?"

"Perhaps I will fight with this weapon alone. I have much training ahead with it to better disguise its tricks from my enemies."

"In your left hand, though?" Jarlaxle pressed.

"Both hands," Zak replied. "But yes, I prefer my left hand for the whip. Are you seeking weaknesses, Jarlaxle?"

"Then perhaps this in your right hand?" Jarlaxle said, drawing out a gleaming silver sword with a dark hilt shaped in the likeness of a displacer beast, and with a slight angry red glow along its fine edge.

"Cutter," Entreri remarked.

"Ah, so you planned that one for me," Zak said. "I had thought you meant to keep that treasure for yourself."

"I promised you weapons fit for your talents. You have one, and this one will compliment it, for you'll not find a sharper edge than that of Khazid'hea in all of Faerun. You can have it now, but I will need it from time to time."

That brought curious looks from both Zak and Entreri.

"You mean to have Catti-brie put this blade, too, through the Great Forge?" Entreri asked. "I warn—"

"No, no," Jarlaxle assured them both. "She would more likely destroy it than heighten its enchantment, for she has no love of this sword. I do hope to make a change to Khazid'hea in the journey we will find before us, but the Great Forge of Gauntlgrym will not be needed."

"What are you talking about?" Entreri asked.

"Our friend Kimmuriel has spent many long hours with the sword," Jarlaxle answered. "Let us just say that he has learned many secrets contained within, including a way that I might break the sword's will, once and for all. That I might excise the demonic magic within it."

"That magic has guided many a hand to great heights of sword-play," the man reminded him.

"Novice hands. But that is nothing that Zaknafein Do'Urden would ever need," Jarlaxle explained. "Ah, to have Cutter's fine edge and sentient wariness, but without its malignant bent!"

"I have no idea what you're talking about," Entreri surrendered. "Enjoy your journey."

"*Our* journey," Jarlaxle corrected. "Khazid'hea ruined a previous wielder and brought great harm upon her family and great turmoil in the land. I have recently learned that in no small way, this sword's malignant sentience was responsible for the War of the Silver Marches. I intend to make sure that can never happen again, and at the same time, to bring peace to one who did not deserve her fate."

"Doum'wielle Armgo?" Zak asked.

"She is alive, and lost, and I believe that using this very cursed weapon to save her will help us to break the spirit of the sword and so remove the demonic magic."

"When you're done speaking in riddles, let me know what you're talking about," Zak replied.

"No riddle," Jarlaxle promised. "The sword can lead us to Doum'wielle—I believe she is alive. Saving her would be an act of great heroism, and more than that, Doum'wielle would almost certainly prove a potent ally for us, for House Baenre in their struggle against the Melarni and the other Lolthians. She is Armgo, of the Second House. She will be our ears and eyes."

"I thought Gromph threw her to the far north?" Entreri asked.

"Indeed, and there she likely remains."

"Likely?"

"We can know. Kimmuriel has found a way that we can know. And so we can get to her and bring her back. Pick up the sword. Hold it tightly, send your thoughts into it, and demand answers."

"Take great care," Entreri warned as Zak reached for Cutter. "The sword is thick with pride, powerful of will, and clever."

"Not clever," Jarlaxle insisted. "It manipulates with emotion, but not with concocted, thought-out falsehoods."

His expression showing that he wasn't sure what either of the two might be talking about, Zaknafein grabbed the sword and pulled it in close against his chest. He put it through some sudden and unexpected maneuvers, and Jarlaxle nodded and smiled, understanding that what Zak was doing here was putting the proud sword off its guard, for now Khazid'hea was where it always longed to be: in the hands of a true weapon master.

When Zak smiled, Jarlaxle knew that the sword was smiling, too, in its own way.

Finally, Zak lowered the blade. "So you once wielded it," he said to Entreri.

"It learned to hate me," the former assassin dryly replied, "because it could never control me."

"Perhaps because you were already vicious enough without its help," Jarlaxle said with a laugh, and Entreri tapped his brow in salute.

"It knows my daughter, too, I have heard," Zak said. "Catti-brie wielded the blade and it got the best of her, to near calamity."

"That was a long time ago," Jarlaxle said. "She was young and inexperienced in the way of the warrior, and trained not at all as a wizard or priestess."

"And Doum'wielle?" Jarlaxle asked.

"Little Doe?" Zak returned after concentrating on the sentient weapon.

"Yes, that is what her father called her."

"Tos'un Armgo," Zak said, nodding.

"He, too, wielded the sword."

"I do not sense that," said Zak. He closed his eyes and brought the sword close, but then shook his head. "Not at all."

"Yet he did. So tell me, who else does Khazid'hea know?" Jarlaxle asked.

"You," Zak replied. "And my son."

"And?"

Zak shrugged.

"But not Tos'un, because Tos'un is dead, and no others, because all others who have wielded the sword are dead," Jarlaxle explained. "Which means that Doum'wielle, Little Doe, is not. She was thrown through a portal into the northern wastes by Gromph years ago, but she lives, it would seem. And I intend to go get her, with the two of you by my side."

Entreri and Zaknafein exchanged curious looks, but neither argued.

"The northern wastes is a large area, yes?" Entreri said at length.

"We'll find her," Jarlaxle said. "The sword holds a strong bond with those who have wielded it and been overcome by its influence. Kimmuriel believes that any so dominated for any length of time will forever carry a bit of Khazid'hea's magic within them. A bond of those enslaved by it, so to speak."

"So the sword will find Doum'wielle?" Entreri asked doubtfully.

"Khazid'hea would not even desire such a thing, not when it can be in the hands of a warrior of Zaknafein's caliber."

"Then what are you babbling about?"

"As I said, Kimmuriel insisted to me that the bond likely extends to others who have been similarly coerced, possessed even, by the will of the sword," Jarlaxle explained. "Khazid'hea won't lead us to Doum'wielle, but one who was similarly dominated by the sword might well be able to do so."

"That sword never held me in thrall," Entreri was quick to say.

"Not you."

"If you think I'm going to submit to a wizard's trick in a sword—" Zak started, but Jarlaxle interrupted him.

"Not you."

"No," Entreri said suddenly. "She won't do it."

"She will."

"Who?" Zak asked.

"Catti-brie."

Artemis Entreri shook his head, but Zak asked, "So we three and Catti-brie are going into the wastelands of the frozen north?"

"Why not?" Jarlaxle said. "Whatever might happen in Menzoberranzan is a long time off, it would seem. Luskan is secured, Gauntlgrym is secured, Bleeding Vines is mostly rebuilt. Beniago and Bruenor do not need me to intervene in their dealings any longer and Lord Neverember is no more a threat. Nor are the Margasters. Are we to sit here and watch the world turn about us when a grand adventure awaits?"

"The last time you told me such a tale, I wound up in the company of dragons and in the prison of a Damaran king," Entreri reminded.

"And you are a better man for it! And so was King Gareth, for that matter. And Kane the Grandmaster of Flowers. Did you get a chance to speak with him when last—"

"Shut up, Jarlaxle," Entreri grumbled.

"I think the adventurous woman would love the chance to see the road again," Jarlaxle said, getting the conversation back on track.

"She has a young child," said Zak.

"And a husband more than capable of taking care of that child, to say nothing of Bruenor and his queens, who spend more time with Brie than they do at governing," Jarlaxle said.

"So, Drizzt will not join us on this journey, then?" Zak asked.

Jarlaxle chuckled. "He is in no mood for such follies. Perhaps you've noticed."

Zak nodded, for he had indeed.

"Besides, we will need a mighty priestess or a powerful wizard, and I tend to trust a priestess more," Jarlaxle explained. "I do not intend to walk all the way back from wherever Gromph sends us."

"You presume an awful lot," said Entreri.

"Of course I do. That is my charm. And you know that you will both agree! So then, let me get these adventurers prepared for the road," Jarlaxle said, and held out his hand.

Shaking his head, Zak handed over the sentient sword.

"Do practice with your whip and sun blade," Jarlaxle told him. "I had it specially crafted because I expect that it, too, will prove invaluable when we are in the frozen north, surrounded by the monsters that thrive in those extremes and will not be pleased by the opposite extreme." He smiled, tipped his hat, and turned away.

"I doubt Catti-brie will join us," Entreri remarked, "even if you can convince her to hold that sword." When Jarlaxle looked back at him, he only added, "She and I have a history on the road, from long ago."

Jarlaxle only shrugged and turned away once more. But he paused again, smiled widely at Entreri, and produced a familiar jeweled dagger, tossing it to the floor before the man.

Entreri recoiled.

"The souls within it were cleansed," Jarlaxle reminded him. "And this weapon, too, was deeply inspected by my friends at the Hosttower of the Arcane. It is still brilliant, still vampiric—"

"Then I want nothing to do with it! Throw it to the primordial."

"But the true curse of it is gone," Jarlaxle continued. "Its taste remains for the physical health of the victim, but that alone. No more will it take the souls."

"It doesn't matter."

"Of course it matters," Jarlaxle countered. "That was your sin—you said it yourself. Sharon showed it to you clearly in that wasp-filled cocoon. Now that curse is gone, but what remains is worthy of who Artemis Entreri has become. Take it, for it far exceeds the dagger you now wear on your hip, in its beauty, in its deadliness, and in its ability to heal you as it defeats your foes. You cannot deny the utility."

Entreri stared long and hard at the dagger lying on the floor right before his foot.

"It is just a weapon now, and nowhere near as malignant as that sword you so easily dominate." The drow rogue grinned as he noted Entreri's expression. He wanted to pick up the dagger, that much was clear.

He looked up at Jarlaxle. "You are sure?"

"As sure as I am that Thibbledorf Pwent is no longer a vampire," Jarlaxle answered. "Wondrous and glorious was the web of Yvonnel and Quenthel. You witnessed its work on this very dagger on that field, and now you know that the curse is forever gone. Take it."

Entreri licked his lips.

He took the dagger.

Quite pleased, Jarlaxle nodded at that and went on his way to

Catti-brie, confident that he could persuade the powerful priestess to join them, and that she would be able to use the bond of Khazid'hea like a divining rod to point them toward Doum'wielle Armgo. If only Gromph could get them somewhere near to where he had dumped the poor woman.

But Jarlaxle was confident he could make that happen, too.

"Yes, the poor Doum'wielle," Jarlaxle whispered to himself, and he meant it. He wanted to save her, just for the sake of doing so, for her and for her family. More than that, he truly believed that he would show Doum'wielle a way to make amends for all that she had done, and in doing so, perhaps prevent utter catastrophe in Menzo-berranzan, and facilitate an end to the domination of Lolth over his kin and kind.

Even if not, Jarlaxle would still go, and that truth sang sweetly in his heart. For this was not merely self-serving. He was sincere about his desire to rescue Doum'wielle from the injustice, indignity, and terrible wrongs that had been precipitated upon her. For her, and for lovely Sinnafein, who had been played such a cruel trick by the malignant sword.

Even that, he now understood, was for a perfectly selfish reason, he finally admitted to himself, as with his freeing the prisoners from Captain Arrongo's hold.

It felt good.

It felt really good.

A reward greater than baubles and magical toys.

"You've cursed me, Drizzt Do'Urden," Jarlaxle said when he came out of Ship Kurth onto the streets of Closeguard Island, heading for the Hosttower of the Arcane and a meeting he had arranged with Kimmuriel and Gromph. "And I love you all the more for it."

"WE SHOULD SPEAK ABOUT BREVINDON MARGASTER," ZAK said to Jarlaxle when the mercenary leader had returned to Ship Kurth.

"What about him?"

"We'll be gone for tendays?"

"Months, more likely," Jarlaxle replied. "It will be no easy task, finding Doum'wielle, even with Catti-brie's help."

"Worse, then," said Zak. "I don't trust him."

"You'd be a fool to trust him," Jarlaxle agreed.

"He's vile to his bones," Zak went on. "Aye, a demon had hold of him from that phylactery he wore, as with the other Margasters and their associates, but he embraced that demon."

"He desired what the fiend offered, and he was not the head of his family, in any case," Jarlaxle explained. "If he had stood against Inkeri and Lord Neverember, even if he'd survived, what would have been left for him? Was he really unlike so many of our kin in Menzoberranzan in that regard? We embrace a demon, too, because not embracing her is—or was, before this time of revelation—too terrible to imagine. I don't think our own lives all that different from the choice of many of those who joined with the demon horde in the Luskan war, and who are we to judge them?"

"Brevindon cooperates with us now only because of the power that affiliation offers."

Jarlaxle shrugged.

"Is that enough?" Zak asked.

"Isn't it?" Jarlaxle retorted. "Isn't that enough for the folk of Luskan? Having Brevindon seated beside Beniago as a second captain in thrall to Bregan D'aerthe strengthens our play here. It was his house, House Margaster of Waterdeep and Luskan and not Ship Kurth, which commissioned *Revenge,* yes?"

"He likes the power. With us gone, there will be more for him to take, particularly if he is successful in opening any other trade agreements with Waterdeep," Zak warned.

"True enough."

"Take him with us?"

"No, he will stay here. But so will Kimmuriel be here," said Jarlaxle. "I'll advise him to visit Brevindon often, right there in the man's thoughts. I don't disagree with you that Luskan will face some trials in the coming months, but understand this, as I have come to understand it over these long decades: to build anything—any organization, any city, any ship and crew—worth having, one must bring it to a point where it can operate without the builder. I do not yet trust Captain Bonnie Charlee on *Revenge* without some trusted informant among her crew. That ship offers her great power and great opportunity to abuse that power far from Luskan's lights. But I do trust that I will be able to trust her soon enough, you see? And in that event, when *Revenge* can run the waves and do that which is good for Luskan, and therefore good for me, without my oversight, then, only then, will I have created something good.

"I don't doubt your assessment of Brevindon Margaster's heart," Jarlaxle went on. "I don't know him enough to trust him and don't like him enough to want to get to know him well enough to trust him! And I expect that if we took him with us, somewhere along the way, I'd discard him. For now, though, the play is his, and when he moves his piece, be it a knight or a pawn or his queen itself, we will counter if necessary, in a most appropriate way. *If* necessary, though, and I hope it will not be."

"But we'll likely be gone, far away on the road in the north."

"As you've noted. And as I've said, Kimmuriel will be here. You don't know Kimmuriel well enough, my friend, even though you worked together in the Underdark. Trust me on this: if Brevindon Margaster makes a move against Beniago and Bregan D'aerthe while we are on the road and Kimmuriel holds Luskan, then Brevindon will wish that he had waited for my return. Yes, I am not above killing my enemies. Kimmuriel does much worse than that. He'll serve the fool to a hive of illithids for their dining pleasure."

Zak smiled, and shuddered—he couldn't help it. He knew that Jarlaxle wasn't lying. He also wasn't overly sad about the prospect Jarlaxle had just painted, as he truly despised that particular man.

"Now, come along," Jarlaxle said. "Let us find Artemis and gather our gear. We'll be going to Gromph in the morning, I expect. Summer is running long and we'll want to be done with our business in the far north and back before autumn sets in."

"Catti-brie is really coming?"

Jarlaxle shrugged. "I do believe so. She understands all that is at stake, and while our own concerns for Menzoberranzan likely weigh more heavily upon us, the idea of both saving Doum'wielle and forever removing such dominating powers from the sword you carry that she so hates weigh more heavily upon her. If not, if she decides against the adventure, we'll take Dab'nay, since we'll need a priestess. But then our journey may prove much longer still, since our link to Doum'wielle through Khazid'hea will be lost to us."

"I HELD THE SWORD AGAIN," CATTI-BRIE TOLD DRIZZT. "I asked Khazid'hea about her. I believe that Jarlaxle is correct. Doum'wielle is alive."

"It would have to be an elaborate ruse to fool both you and Jarlaxle, I expect," Drizzt said, nodding. He lowered his eyes, reflecting on Doum'wielle and her tragic tale. He knew Sinnafein quite well, and had known Tos'un Armgo in those days when Tos'un lived in the Moonwood with the elves. He had watched their family grow from afar, thinking it a good thing, a hopeful joining and perhaps a vision of a better future.

And then, so abruptly, it had all ended in tragedy, with a son murdered by the runaway daughter and Sinnafein betrayed.

"So she is alive, perhaps," Drizzt said. "Why is that a concern for Jarlaxle?"

"Because she is of House Barrison Del'Armgo and will want a chance at redemption. Jarlaxle thinks her a critical ally in working his will upon Menzoberranzan."

"Hmm," Drizzt replied, pondering the possibilities. He knew well that Jarlaxle survived and thrived through information and informants.

"It would be a good thing, would it not?" Catti-brie asked him. "If Doum'wielle so terribly sinned because of Khazid'hea, is she not worth saving?"

"Of course she is. But could you not spend your days instead wandering the alleyways of Luskan and healing the sick and the poor?"

"This could avert a war."

"If Jarlaxle believes that, who am I to disagree? This is his area of expertise, after all."

"And there is something else, something personal," Catti-brie admitted. "Jarlaxle has had the sword's mysteries studied extensively. He sees the rescue of Doum'wielle as a way to defeat the malice within Khazid'hea."

"So it is personal to you?"

"I can't deny . . ."

"Throwing it into the primordial pit seems an easier course."

"Jarlaxle wishes the sword for your father."

"Jarlaxle has an answer for everything," Drizzt warned. "He has found a benefit for you, a benefit for Zaknafein, a benefit for Doum'wielle, obviously, and—"

"And a great benefit for Menzoberranzan, in the hopes that Lolth is at last pushed aside."

Drizzt nodded. "Again, I am not one to argue with Jarlaxle about something such as that."

"But you don't seem convinced."

Drizzt shrugged and held his hands out helplessly. "Even for all of that, it seems a long and difficult journey. Do you believe that this is the full story of why Jarlaxle would go to such lengths?"

Catti-brie laughed at that. "I do not, or at least, I would not be surprised if there is more. I've been looking about for ulterior reasons. This is, after all, Jarlaxle we are talking about. Is there ever only one reason for him? Or only three reasons, as you have outlined, and particularly when they are so obvious and openly stated by that ever-mysterious rogue? Do you have any thoughts on that?"

"Who can say? As you said, it is Jarlaxle."

"He means to go and find her," Catti-brie explained. "Tomorrow to Luskan to prepare, and then to the far north a few days hence. And he thinks I am the living rod of divination who can locate her, and so he has begged me to accompany him."

"That could be an extended journey. What would we do with Brie?"

"Not 'we,'" Catti-brie replied. "He asked *me* to accompany him."

"Ah," Drizzt said. "Just you two in the wilds of the north, or Zaknafein, too, perhaps?"

"Your father, yes, and one other." She paused, then added, "Artemis Entreri."

"Another who has wielded Khazid'hea, as have I," Drizzt remarked. "That's a formidable group of four. What of Wulfgar, who knows the north as well as any?"

"I can only magically recall a small group back to the south, should we find Doum'wielle, who is, perhaps, not alone. Jarlaxle prefers to keep the party within those limits."

Drizzt nodded. It made sense. "Are you going?"

"I am here to discuss that very thing, obviously."

"The choice is yours."

"But how do you feel about it?"

Drizzt shrugged. "I'll be terribly lonely, but Brie and I are surrounded by friends." He gave a little laugh. "You were absent for most of the excitement of the Demon War as you cared for the unborn Brie. Could it be that my dear wife misses the road of adventure? Are you bored, my love?"

Catti-brie's smile was so complete that her eyes seemed to be laughing. "You don't bore me," she said.

"But . . ."

She laughed aloud. "Yes!" she admitted. "I miss the road. I miss the adventure. I miss the danger. Does that make sense? Does that make me a terrible parent?"

"Haven't we had this conversation the other way?" Drizzt said, laughing, too. He opened his arms and let Catti-brie fall into them. "And this seems a noble cause for Sinnafein and her daughter and for Menzoberranzan, perhaps. That, I cannot deny. Besides," he added, pushing her back a bit and giving a wry smile, "Khazid'hea is well-deserving of your revenge." He pulled her back in tight and kissed the side of her head.

"Your mood is much improved," she said, returning the hug.

"Someone reminded me."

"Of what?" Catti-brie asked.

"Of why," Drizzt corrected. And he grinned and crushed her in a tighter hug still.

"Do you have any advice to me regarding my companions?" she whispered in the midst of the great hug.

"Trust them as you would trust the Companions of the Hall."

"Even Artemis Entreri?"

Drizzt pushed her back to arm's length. "You tell me."

Catti-brie nodded. "It is strange to me that I know I can trust that man. Strange and . . . hopeful. In the wider sense."

"A belief in redemption is the most important spice in hoping to cook a better tomorrow," Drizzt told her. "Maybe that's why Jarlaxle really wants to go to the north. Even beyond the hopes for Menzoberranzan, maybe Jarlaxle desires to offer such a chance to Doum'wielle Armgo."

"But not just for her," Catti-brie said, catching on, and Drizzt nodded. "For Jarlaxle, because he wants to see such a thing. He wants to feel such hope."

"So, tomorrow?"

She nodded. "I leave for Luskan tomorrow, but Jarlaxle thinks we will be several days there preparing for our journey."

Drizzt spent a moment composing himself, then said, "Go and tell Brie, and take your time saying goodbye. And then, my love, we'll spend the rest of the night saying farewell to each other."

She grabbed Drizzt by the cheeks and stared into his lavender eyes. "I will come back," she promised.

"I know."

"And you will be here, or at the Monastery of the Yellow Rose?"

"There, I think. I'm going to leave right after you are gone, through the gates, but to Mithral Hall and then Adbar, and the road to the east. With Brie. I'm not sure I need to speak with Kane now, but I find that I want to."

"And you want him and the others to meet Brie."

"There is that," he admitted. "Do we agree?"

Catti-brie nodded and kissed him, then whispered in his ear,

"And when I return, I will take her to magical gardens dedicated to Mielikki."

"THAT WAS FOUR YEARS AGO," GROMPH REMINDED JARL- axle and the others.

"But it was your portal," Jarlaxle replied.

"Yes, created only to be rid of that troublesome *darthiir*!"

"Half elf, half drow," Jarlaxle reminded him, for Doum'wielle wasn't only *darthiir*, the pejorative the dark elves used for their surface cousins.

"I don't care. And I didn't care then, which is why I cast her out."

"To the north?"

"Yes."

"A mile? Ten? A hundred? Have you gathered any thoughts on the matter as I implored you?"

"She landed on the slopes of the northernmost mountains in the Spine of the World," the former archmage of Menzoberranzan replied. "That is my best recollection of the scene on the other side of the portal."

Jarlaxle looked at his traveling companions. "That will have to do, then," he said to nods.

"Four years," Gromph reiterated. "She is likely dead, but if not, then she could be anywhere. In the Underdark? In Waterdeep? In Calimport in the far south, even."

"I don't believe so," Jarlaxle said. "My investigations with Khazid'hea make me believe that she's still up there somewhere."

"To what end? Why do you care?"

"To cleanse the sword."

"Enough of your lies," said Gromph. "Throw the thing into the primordial pit in Gauntlgrym and be done with it, then hire the proper wizards and blacksmiths to make another just like it but without the demonic sentience. There, a far easier course."

"But not the one we've chosen. Will you replicate the portal for us as you agreed?"

"Why do you care?" the wizard demanded again.

Jarlaxle stood with hands on hips, staring at him.

"Because she is Armgo," Gromph finally realized. "You think to make her a spy for us in Menzoberranzan."

"More than a spy, likely. Doum'wielle will have the ear of the Barrison Del'Armgo nobles, and they will have no idea that she is not who they believe her to be, for it was the sword and not her heart driving her. Through her, we can manipulate the information filtering to Matron Mez'Barris."

"If you believe that, you're a bigger fool than I already suspected, and that is a high hurdle indeed."

"You deny that she would be useful?"

"I doubt that her use would be worth all of this trouble."

"Trouble for us, though, and not for Gromph. Not really."

Gromph scoffed at him and shook his head, but after a few snorts of derision aimed Jarlaxle's way, he did begin his spellcasting. A few minutes later, a swirling cloud appeared at the side of the room, framing a distant vista as if it were a picture. A mountainside, thick with snow.

Jarlaxle tossed the final payment, a bag of expensive and hard-to-find spell components, to Gromph. With a tip of his hat to the mighty archmage, Jarlaxle then led the way, stepping into that "picture," passing through the image and onto the mountainside, to find himself standing atop deep snow beneath a crisp blue sky, with a line of fast-streaming dark clouds creating a stark and beautiful contrast.

He didn't see an animal, not even a bird in the sky, and not a tree or a plant.

And didn't hear a sound, except the threatening whisper of the very cold wind.

Had Khazid'hea deceived him, he wondered, and wondered, too, if he should ask Catti-brie to immediately cast her magical recall and return them to the south.

PART 2

JOURNEYS

As I have come to understand the greatest gift afforded me by my training with the monks of the Monastery of the Yellow Rose, the realization has both shocked and enlightened me.

One might think that greatest gift to be the strengthened connection between my mind and my body, a truer understanding of that which I want to perform and the deeper interactions of my physical form required to more easily and more completely execute the movement. I could always jump up in the air, for example, spin about and kick out my trailing foot as I turned. Almost any warrior, certainly any drow warrior, could do such a thing. But now my mind is speaking to the finer parts of my body, coordinating better the turn of my hips, the angle of my foot, the coil of the muscles on the back of my thigh, and the timing of the release of the kick. Where before, I might force back an opponent with such a maneuver, now I can end the fight with that single heavy blow if my opponent has not properly balanced and blocked to defend.

I do not understate the beauty of this gift. I can even manipulate my muscles to push poison from a wound! But this is not the greatest of the treasures I have gained.

One might think that greatest gift to be the understanding of ki, of life energy. Of being able to reach within and pull forth power beyond that of muscle and bone. The addition of this inner energy allows me to throw an opponent several strides away when I strike with my open hand. It allows me to find my wounds and turn my blood and muscles and all that is physically within me into some mediation of those injuries. With ki and the understanding of my physical form, I now run faster and jump higher. I make my scimitar strikes follow quicker and in perfect balance.

I am a finer warrior, but no, this is not the greatest of Grandmaster Kane's imparted treasures.

And then there is transcendence. I escaped the retriever with this act, melting my physical body into everythingness, becoming a part of all that was around me, the elemental starstuff that is the one eternal in the multiverse. That of which we and all we see about us is made. The sheer, unspeakable beauty of transcending the limitations of the physical form so fully would have left me forever there, a better place—a truer and fuller existence and understanding—than anything I have ever known or could ever know in this physical life.

But even this transcendence is not that which I now consider, in this moment of my existence, the greatest gift of all.

That pinnacle is reserved for the quietest of Grandmaster Kane's teachings, for meditation, true meditation, has freed me of the most common curse of the reasoning beings, be they drow, human, halfling, dwarf, elf, or perhaps even the goblinkin and giantkind, perhaps even others I do not begin to understand:

An unconscious bent toward some determined level of tension.

This is the gift that I am even now most determinedly trying to impart upon my dear little Brie, for it is the remedy to a curse that I have come to believe is imparted in the earliest years of life.

That curse cannot be understated, and I suspect it a universal affliction determined by degrees, not by its presence or absence.

We all have within us a level of tumult, a vibration in our hearts, our minds, our very souls, which we are most comfortable with as "normal." Like a pebble dropped into still water, that tumult is a result of drama, of conflict in mind or body or both. This sense of normalcy is taught very young, and refined as we become fully reasoning beings.

The curse lies in not understanding it.

In its most extreme circumstances, I have seen it in myself, or in King Bruenor, surely, when we both grew uneasy, itchy even, as we created about us an environment of peace and comfort.

"Ah, to the road!" was our common call to action, even when action wasn't needed.

Because the vibrations, the inner conflict, was needed for us to feel normal.

Bruenor hates being king when all the world about him is settled. It bores him profoundly (though now, with his wives, perhaps he finds suitable replacements of excitement and conflict!). He needs that sense of normalcy, and so he will achieve the needed tension no matter the situation around him. He will grump and moan about one thing or another, often minute, but never would he say a word or care about the small details of the more mundane issues flitting about him when threatened by a horde of demons. In that event, the tension is real and pressing, and thus the little problems no longer matter.

The curse, I now see, is that those littler problems do matter without that demon horde, and so they are unconsciously elevated to a place of distraction.

I have often wondered if this peace I seek in the world around me isn't really a lie I tell myself, given my own desire for adventure, and yes, even danger.

But those are extreme examples of the inner vibrations. Extreme and rare and of urges more easily defeated because they are so obvious, and possibly, so destructive or self-destructive. The lesser examples, the smaller pebbles, are ever-present in all of us and all about us. They manifest in gossip, in senseless arguments over unimportant actions or debates, in unreasonable fears about things over which we have no control, in silly worries about inadequacies or perceptions that have no place beyond the present in terms of importance . . . yet they are magnified within each of us into vibrations and tumult.

Of the mind, of the heart, of the very soul.

And thus, the greatest gift I have been granted by my time in the Monastery of the Yellow Rose is the true stilling of all three, of making the pond that is Drizzt Do'Urden so glassy and calm that the reflection of the world around me becomes an accurate representation of that which is, instead of that which is perceived through the ripples of inner tumult and inner vibration.

I am free of the itch. I am content in the present, every present, any present.

That does not mean that I have surrendered the love of adventure—far from it!

Nay, the gift is that now I can choose the adventure, now I can diffuse the drama, now I can throw away the fears and the worries to see the picture most clearly and to embrace the best course to repaint that picture or enjoy it without the unsummoned urge.

And conversely, what I know now is that I can bring forth that itch more perfectly when it is needed.

This blessing of clarity is indeed freedom.

All people have long periods of true trial, but their times of true ease seem less so. These moments of peace are often sabotaged, so I now believe, by our own insistence on worrying about things that aren't worth the worry.

To create ripples in the stillness creates for them the proper normal.

To one who has learned the way of Kane, those ripples are external alone, and when they come, they are seen with perfect clarity.

—Drizzt Do'Urden

CHAPTER 7

Mutual Benefit

D rizzy daddy," Brie said happily, bouncing along in front of Drizzt on Andahar's broad back as they rode the trail southwest out of Citadel Adbar. In a couple of hours, moving through the magical gates from Gauntlgrym, where they had said farewell to Catti-brie, to the common portal shared by the three dwarven kingdoms of the Silver Marches, and then to Citadel Adbar, the father and daughter had covered nearly eight hundred miles. But they had a thousand more to go now, and without the help of magic.

Except, of course, for the magic of Andahar, the wonderful unicorn companion summoned from Drizzt's whistle, who could run tirelessly throughout the day.

Even with the unicorn's long strides, Drizzt figured it would take them a month to get to the Galena Mountains and the Monastery of the Yellow Rose. Alone he could do it in a tenday, but with Brie along, the breaks would come often, perhaps quite often, and the day's rides would surely be much shorter.

He could have chosen a magical journey, of course. He could have ridden a portal to Longsaddle and had Penelope arrange for a teleportation to Grandmaster Kane's front door. But he wanted to undertake this journey, just him and his Brie, to see the wide world and enjoy the vistas and the many peoples and cultures they would find along the way. Still, it was not without a sizable amount of trepidation that Drizzt had ridden out of Citadel Adbar's gates that afternoon. The world was not always a welcoming place; the lands they would cross were not without monsters of all shapes and sizes. He could take care of himself as well as anyone, he knew.

But could he take care of Brie?

He set Andahar at an easy but determined canter through the forest, and the land rolled up and down about them, one tree-covered ridge after another, the shadows protecting them from the summer sun, the sun-speckled ground before them giving Brie endless entertainment.

In the early afternoon on the fourth day out of Adbar, they came to a wide stream and pulled up for a rest. As always, Drizzt didn't dismiss Andahar, wanting the steed about in case of the need for a fast retreat.

He watched Brie splashing in a small side pool while he filled his waterskins. He marveled at the simple joy in her eyes. He wanted to keep that joy of life itself there forever. More than anything, he wanted his daughter to grow up strong and clever and full of confidence, and full even more with happiness. He never wanted her to lose her delight at the simplest things: the sun-dappled earth, the splash of water over stones, the sounds of the forest about her, the shapes of the clouds.

"What's my name?" he called to her.

"Drizzy daddy!" she enthusiastically called back.

"What's my name?" he repeated in his scary voice, coming toward her, his arms up and rocking like the arms of a rearing bear.

"Drizzy daddy!" Brie cried out, and laughed, and splashed away with a squeal.

"Drizzy daddy!" she repeated again and again during the chase, finally ending in a laughing squeak when Drizzt caught her and scooped her up into his arms, turning her horizontal and bringing her up high.

He put his lips against her exposed belly and blew hard, and Brie laughed riotously at the tickle and the sound.

"Drizzy daddy farted," she declared after Drizzt put her back down.

"I ate your belly," he corrected.

"No," she insisted, and stuck out her tongue and blew a raspberry of her own.

Drizzt chuckled, but felt a pang within that honest laughter. This was the childhood he had never experienced, the carefree creation of giggles that too few got to enjoy. He wished he had played this game with Zaknafein, though he couldn't even imagine the possibility of any such playfulness with his mother, Malice.

Such a waste of life itself, he thought, given what he knew now, what Kimmuriel had helped the priestess Yvonnel and Matron Mother Quenthel Baenre reveal of the hopeful beginnings of Menzoberranzan before it had descended into its current, joyless reality.

Before the way of Lolth, where the tension and excitement of chaos swirled away the pleasures of simplicity and love.

They ate a meal beside the flowing stream, watching the dance of sunlight on the rushing water, making up silly songs about Bruenor and Zaknafein and, mostly, Catti-brie. Drizzt trusted his wife and her skill, but he couldn't help the fears within that perhaps she would never return, that Brie would grow up without that beautiful influence in her life. This was the first time in many years that Catti-brie had set out on such a dangerous mission without him, though danger had always been a part of their lives. Now though, with Brie, were they bound to change that? Should he have talked Catti-brie out of going? Would she have tried to talk him out of it had their opportunities been reversed?

Because he would have wanted to go, he knew, and that realization made him dismiss his doubts and fears as his own selfishness. He thought, too, of the time this wonderful partner had gone alone into the Underdark, all the way to Menzoberranzan and House Baenre itself, to rescue him.

"Moomooma?" Brie asked, as if reading his mind, the silly name she used for her mother. He looked down at her with surprise, and realized that, no, it wasn't that. Brie was looking across the stream, where the branches of a tree still rustled from something, or someone, moving through them.

Drizzt calmly and slowly slid his hand out to his bow. He gave a little wince, thinking that perhaps he should not have given Taulmaril back to Catti-brie for her adventure, that maybe he'd be better off now if he had with him the readily accessible bow that could shoot small bolts of lightning. He wished, too, that he could bring Guenhwyvar to his side now, to leap off across the stream and find out what had moved through that bush.

The sound stopped.

It was likely a squirrel, he told himself. He thought back to the first time he had seen Brie, to the feelings of vulnerability that had filled him like never before.

To lose her . . .

Drizzt shook that dark thought away, but also shook away their happy moments here by the stream. He gathered up his items and his daughter and set them in place on Andahar, then walked the unicorn across the water. Up he went and off they went, slowly at first, but gathering speed.

Then more, as Drizzt noticed some scorched grass not far in, wisps of smoke still rising from it, and the faint scent of foulness, demonic foulness, in the air.

The trail was less defined here, the trees more tightly packed, and Drizzt had to pay attention to the way directly ahead, while still glancing to the sides, watching for pursuit.

Through the trees to the left, he saw the form of a rider, galloping hard, clad in black on a black mount that snorted demon flames.

Then it was gone, behind a hillock, but he heard more hoofbeats over on the left, and then on the right.

Doubts whispered about him.

He brought his arm tighter about Brie and urged Andahar ahead, thinking of Taulmaril, thinking of Guenhwyvar, thinking of . . . the unthinkable.

"Forgive me," he whispered to the breeze, as if hoping that it would somehow send the message all the way to Catti-brie, wherever she might be.

"THAT CAN'T BE THE WAY," ARTEMIS ENTRERI INSISTED, his teeth beginning to chatter.

"North face," Catti-brie replied, and she shuddered as a gust of wind swept down from above, carrying snow dust and a bite as ferocious as an Icewind Dale winter night. But it was not night, and it was not winter. The sun hung pale and meager before them, more to the left and much lower toward the horizon than it had been when they had left Luskan, but the sun nevertheless.

"Too cold," she added, looking to Jarlaxle, who was bent over. A moment later, he casually stepped up onto the deep snow, barely leaving a footprint, seeming unbothered by the wind. Only then did Catti-brie notice that the rogue had changed his shoes and was no longer wearing his signature high black boots, but instead a pair of mid-calf boots, furred and thick, and very out of place with the rest of his sleek outfit, the same clothes he would wear on a Calimport street in the heat of the desert summer. Catti-brie didn't have to cast a spell to determine whether those boots were magical, and it was pretty easy for her to guess the enchantment upon them.

"I didn't expect it would be this cold. Have you a spell to counter it?" Jarlaxle asked her.

Catti-brie nodded. "It is not a minor dweomer and I don't know if it will last long enough to get us off the mountain. You have our heavier cloaks in your magical pouch." She motioned for him to retrieve the winter clothing.

"Cast your spell anyway," Entreri bade her.

"We'll be fine," Jarlaxle assured them, and he drew their eyes to Zaknafein, who was crouching low much as Jarlaxle had done, half-buried in the snow. Apparently noticing their glances, Zak looked up, then tugged his shoulders back, and Catti-brie understood him to be pulling on a similar pair of boots before he even stepped up atop the snowpack, confirming her suspicion.

"It's like sitting in the mouth of a white dragon," Zak remarked as he pulled a pack off his back, fumbling with the drawstrings.

"Soon enough, likely," Entreri replied, his teeth violently chattering now.

Zaknafein pulled out a thick blanket and tossed it to him, then another to Catti-brie. He kept fishing about as the two wrapped themselves in the coverings.

Catti-brie cast her protection spell upon herself, then upon Entreri, who immediately took a deep breath and shuddered just one more time before steadying.

"We've an hour to get down to shelter before the dweomer expires," she warned the others.

Jarlaxle held up his hand and stared at Zak, who finally pulled his head and hand out of his large backpack and brought forth a small coffer. He bit the glove off his hand before gingerly opening the container, then walked lightly across the snow and produced a ring for his daughter-in-law and another for Entreri.

"Put them on and let the magic find its way to you," Jarlaxle explained. "They should provide the protection you'll need."

"Ready for anything," Catti-brie dryly noted.

"I saw the snow on the other side of Gromph's gate," Jarlaxle replied with a shrug.

"Then why didn't you give us the damned rings before we left?" Entreri complained.

"I knew it would be cold, but I didn't think it would be *this* cold," Jarlaxle admitted. "But yes, always prepared. I did acquire some magical assistance from the more industrious wizards of the Hosttower in preparation. The same trinkets they use for journeys to Icewind Dale, I expect."

"Better your boots, then," Catti-brie remarked, pointing her finger to note that while Jarlaxle and Zaknafein were standing atop the deep and powdery snow, she and Entreri most certainly were not.

"Why didn't you just give us the damned rings back in Luskan?" Entreri asked again.

"You need to attune to them—"

"Which could have been done in Luskan!"

"Yes, but I do not own them, you see?" Jarlaxle replied. "They are on loan from Caecilia."

"The cloud giant?" Catti-brie asked.

"Yes, and she is very particular about her magical toys. She'll know every attunement when I return them to her."

"And so you'll have to pay more," said Entreri, shaking his head.

"Another spell, then?" Jarlaxle asked, changing the subject. "A floating disk so that you two can drift down the mountainside—perhaps one for each of us? A levitation spell and a pair of ropes, so that Zak and I can fly you two like children's kites as we skip our way down?"

"Or maybe I just make you carry me on your back," Entreri groused. "Or beat you senseless and swap your boots for this ring, or maybe keep both for myself."

Jarlaxle clapped his bare hands together. "You see, Zaknafein, my old friend. This is what I so dearly missed of the road. The camaraderie!"

Artemis Entreri grunted, or perhaps it was a growl.

"You two embrace the protective magic of the bands while Zak and I scout about," Jarlaxle said.

"That can't be the way," Entreri said, bringing them back to the original topic.

"Gromph said that we'd land on the face of the northernmost mountains," Catti-brie answered him, waving her arm out at the land spreading wide below them, down the mountainside and through small, rocky foothills before flattening out in a vast white plain.

"But we left in late morning and the sun is low to our left, and if north is before us, then left is west."

Catti-brie took his point with a curious "Hmm," and noted the perplexed look on Jarlaxle's face, though Zaknafein seemed not to fully comprehend the point.

"And it's too low, in any case," Entreri went on. "Does that much time pass when traveling through a magical portal? I've never seen such . . ."

"No, we just stepped through," Jarlaxle assured him.

"The sun was higher in the Luskan sky than that," Entreri insisted, and none could argue. "But lower in the sky than it would have been in Calimport," he went on, thinking it through, and holding up a finger, tap-tapping it in the air as he pondered. "The sun was always higher in Calimport than in Luskan, and even more so than in Icewind Dale."

"And the days are shorter in Icewind Dale than in Calimport?" Jarlaxle asked more than stated.

"In the winter, not in the summer," Entreri replied. "Not by much, at least."

"But we're still in summer, so you said," Zak put in.

The others exchanged glances. "How far north did we go?" Entreri asked.

"Gromph didn't say," Jarlaxle replied.

"Is there a limit on how far he might have thrown us?"

Jarlaxle shrugged. "With that one, probably the outer reaches of the Astral Plane."

"Are we still on Toril?" an agitated Entreri asked.

"Gromph said we would be," said Jarlaxle.

"But even if the days are shorter here, and they shouldn't be in summer," Catti-brie put in, stammering for an answer as more questions popped into her head. "It's not yet even noon, at least, not in Luskan. So why is the sun so low in the west?"

"Are we on top of the world?" Entreri asked.

"Or over the top and on the other side?" Jarlaxle asked.

"Wouldn't left, looking north, still be west?" Entreri asked.

"But then it would be night," Catti-brie hesitantly remarked.

"The Underdark is a much simpler place," Zak dryly put in.

"Aye, because if we stood about bantering this long, we'd already be dead," Jarlaxle replied.

"I don't understand it," Catti-brie said, staring out to the left. Her eyes widened as she noted that the sun had moved, but not so much in its proximity to the horizon as farther to the right. "But wouldn't that be to the east?" she whispered, more to herself than to the others.

"Zaknafein," Jarlaxle said deliberately, "the milky-white orb, please."

Zak fished in his pack again and produced a small bag, then rolled a perfect orb, like a giant dull pearl, into his hand and tossed it to Jarlaxle. Jarlaxle closed his eyes and held it out and up before him, and the ball began to slowly rotate in the palm of his open hand.

"Interesting," Jarlaxle said a moment later, staring at the orb. "Yes, we are on Toril. We haven't stepped through the planes of existence, for I was assured by Caecilia that the orb wouldn't work anywhere but in our own plane and world." He pointed down the snowy slope and a bit to the right. "It appears to be working, and that way is north."

"The giantess told you that?" Catti-brie asked.

"And loaned me the item."

"Loaned?"

"Is she charging you gold for each usage?" Entreri quipped.

"Quite a hefty price," Jarlaxle replied. "I suppose that when you're flying castles about the world, direction is important."

"Doum'wielle wouldn't have known the way, if this is anywhere near where Gromph dropped her," Entreri said.

"It was just a guess by Gromph when he re-created the portal," Jarlaxle admitted.

"Wonderful."

"She wouldn't have known that, but would it have mattered?" Catti-brie said. "All she would have known was that she needed to find shelter and warmth." She looked back over her shoulder, the mountain towering above them, and that only one in a great range of jagged, high peaks. "And she would have had no more choice in where to go than we do, because we aren't getting over these mountains unless we find a proper pass."

"We have a choice," Entreri reminded them, and looked to Catti-brie.

"Where's your sense of adventure, old man?" Jarlaxle quipped. "We know she's alive."

"And likely half a world away," Entreri interrupted, but Jarlaxle just scoffed and continued. "Let us find some proper shelter and we can begin our search using the sword. If Doum'wielle is near to us, I guess that Khazid'hea will sense it."

"So Catti-brie will sense it," Entreri reasoned.

"I feel like one of Jarlaxle's toys," the woman remarked.

"We'd have to get rid of Drizzt first," Jarlaxle quipped.

Zaknafein punched him in the shoulder, or tried to, but missed and lost his balance as the snow collapsed a bit beneath his lead foot, sending him down to one knee.

"Displacer cloak," Jarlaxle explained. "But good try, my friend."

"Always prepared," Entreri muttered, echoing the thoughts of both Catti-brie and Zaknafein, and drawing an even wider grin from the irascible Jarlaxle.

HE HAD TIED BRIE TO HIM WITH A CORD AND NOW HELD A bow in hand, arrow nocked. Drizzt quietly urged Andahar on even faster, trusting the unicorn to navigate the woods while he cast his gaze all about, looking for enemies.

He could hear them now, the running hooves left and right, and caught occasional glimpses through the thick summer canopy, but nothing more than black-clad riders on black mounts—he thought them hellsteeds, nightmares, the demon horses used by the cavalry of the lower planes. Drizzt knew them well from the magical figurines that both Jarlaxle and Entreri used.

And just like Andahar, these mounts flanking him wouldn't tire. And they were just as fast.

He could only hope they were carrying minor fiends, and that he could encounter them a few at a time, that he might dispatch them before they got near to Brie.

And, and, and . . .

He lifted his bow, seeing movement behind some brush not far to the left, but then jerked and nearly dislodged the arrow as Andahar came over a sudden ridge, slowing as it moved down the steep decline. The unicorn deftly jumped a group of large stones at the small ravine's nadir, only to struggle in the soft and sandy ground on the climb out the other side.

Easy, my friend, take care of your child, Drizzt heard in his mind, and he thought he recognized the intruder even before he looked up to see a trio of drow, two astride nightmares, at the top of the climb before him.

Drizzt lowered his bow and tugged Andahar's mane to stop the unicorn.

The center drow pulled back the cowl of his hood, revealing himself as Braelin Janquay, and motioned for Drizzt to come up.

Knowing Braelin well, Drizzt did so, pacing Andahar easily up the hill while untying poor Brie, who was crying from the shaking of the gallop. By the time he reached Braelin, he had Brie up on one shoulder and was whispering into her ear.

"You could have announced yourselves earlier," Drizzt scolded the Bregan D'aerthe scout. "I don't appreciate being shadowed for miles through a forest."

"We are but forward scouts, and were instructed not to approach you," Braelin apologized.

"What are these?" Drizzt asked, waving his free hand to indicate the hellsteeds that Braelin and one of the others sat astride. "Has Luskan begun trading with the Nine Hells?"

"A few of the more clever wizards at the Hosttower have spent great effort in creating obsidian steed figurines," Braelin explained. "And Jarlaxle has spent quite a fortune in trading for them with Waterdeep's noble families. He is determined to make of Bregan D'aerthe a cavalry force, I am sure."

Somehow, Drizzt wasn't surprised. "Where is he?"

"Jarlaxle?"

"No, the one who brought you out here." *The one who was just in my mind,* he thought, but didn't say.

Braelin looked back over his shoulder toward a thick stand of trees and a few moments later, Kimmuriel came out of the shadows, riding yet another magical mount, this one translucent, save for flashes and sparkles of light that gave it equine form, more resembling a constellation in a night sky than anything solid. The psionicist waved away the drow flanking Braelin—and likely sent them telepathic instructions—before pacing his celestial mount up before Drizzt.

Recovered from the shock of it all, Drizzt felt his relief turn to trepidation, for something had to be amiss here, surely.

"No, nothing like that," Kimmuriel answered his thoughts.

"Stop it," Drizzt warned, and the psionicist bowed respectfully. "What are you doing here?"

"Archmage Gromph told us of your intended journey. I tried to catch up to you in Gauntlgrym, but you were already gone."

"So you followed me through the portals to Adbar?"

"It was worth the trouble just to see the looks on the faces of the dwarves of Adbar," Braelin put in. "In Mithral Hall, too, though they were more willing to accept our presence since King Bruenor was with us for that part of the journey."

"You still haven't answered my question."

"Because I have much I'd like to discuss with you," Kimmuriel explained. "And with Grandmaster Kane, if you would be willing to offer me an introduction."

"You couldn't have just had Gromph teleport you to the monastery and met me there?"

Kimmuriel shrugged.

"Jarlaxle," Drizzt reasoned. "He told you I was coming out here with Brie and bade you to escort me."

"These are dangerous lands."

"I've ridden them before."

"With a child?"

Drizzt didn't answer.

"If we caught you, why couldn't others?"

"To be fair, you hadn't exactly caught me. You found me, but I'm not so easily caught. Besides, I don't know many other bands of highwaymen riding around on magical hellsteeds."

Kimmuriel smiled widely—and that seemed to Drizzt the most disconcerting thing of all. "Nor will you, now. I have a score of drow with me, including wizards and priests."

"If I had wanted an escort, I would have asked King Bruenor. Or Regis, perhaps, with his band of halfling friends, the Grinning Ponies."

"Should we be insulted?" Braelin Janquay said lightheartedly.

"You won't even see us, then," Kimmuriel promised. "Nor any enemies that might come against you. We'll dispatch them beyond your child's vision and hearing. Except for me, I hope. I would like to ride with you, for a while at least, that we can converse and I can, perhaps, convince you that I am worthy of an audience with the great Grandmaster Kane."

"I'll introduce you without reservation."

"I'm humbled by your trust."

"What trust?" Drizzt said. "If you threaten Kane, he will finish you before you know that he has sensed the threat."

"As you will," Kimmuriel replied. "Are my terms acceptable?"

"As you will," Drizzt replied.

Kimmuriel dismissed Braelin then, and Drizzt led the way. Brie was calm again and Andahar wouldn't tire, so there was no need to pause.

For a long while, Kimmuriel said nothing, just paced his celestial steed easily beside the unicorn, and true to the psionicist's promise, Drizzt noted no sign of the escorting drow brigade.

Not a whisper of noise or a shuffle of leaves.

He wasn't surprised.

CONFIDENT THAT CATTI-BRIE AND ENTRERI HAD ATTUNED themselves to the rings, the group began to move, though it became immediately apparent that this would be no easy task. The snow was deep and unpacked, and while Jarlaxle and Zak could effortlessly walk atop it, both because they were elves and because of the boots they wore, the two humans could not.

"Maybe you could swap boots for rings," Entreri grumbled after only a few plowing steps. "You skinny elves won't sink in as far, even without them."

"That would mean another long delay," Jarlaxle said, "for such items have to be acclimated to a new host."

"Of course," Entreri grumbled back. "And then you'd have to pay Caecelia more for the second attunement on the rings."

"You see?" Jarlaxle returned. "I will teach you yet what it is to be a proper merchant."

"I haven't the spells to protect us all while we wait for that," Catti-brie put in. She looked from the man to Jarlaxle, who was nodding solemnly—too much so, she thought. She knew that he almost certainly had scrolls that could be read to protect them all from the cold, or other wondrous items that could move them easily down the hill.

But Jarlaxle never showed his hand. And never used up his magical items when he didn't have to.

One trudging step at a time, Catti-brie pressed on, thousands of feet of snow-blanketed mountain before them. Entreri came past her suddenly, driving hard and spitting curses. When he finally ran out of momentum, he stopped very abruptly—at least, his lower half did. He lurched forward at the waist, getting a face full of snow.

Jarlaxle tried to ask if he was all right, but all Catti-brie heard through the howling wind was a snicker.

But then something else. Something lower-pitched. Something beneath her.

Entreri straightened and didn't even bother to wipe the snow from his head and shoulders, just grumbled and started forward.

"Wait," Catti-brie bade him, quietly but insistently.

Entreri kept going as if not hearing her.

"Wait!" she said louder and with urgency. "Hold, all of you."

"What do you know?" Jarlaxle asked.

Catti-brie shook her head and held up her hand to keep them quiet. She was no stranger to this type of terrain, having grown up in the frozen wastes of Icewind Dale. That barely perceptible rumble below her foreboded great danger, she realized, and she could only hope that it was just a warning and not the beginning of the inevitable catastrophe.

"Well?" Entreri demanded, quite loudly.

"Shh!" she insisted. "Quietly. The snowpack is loose. The top levels, at least."

"Top levels?" asked Zaknafein, who had no experience with anything like this environment.

"The snow grows deeper with every storm, and what was there before melts under the sun, hardens to ice, and thus grows more slippery," she explained. "This deep snowpack is not stable, layer to layer, and if we cause too much tumult, the entire side of this mountain covering will break free and slide down."

"Avalanche," Entreri said. "Are you sure?"

"I feel it," Catti-brie said.

"Wonderful."

"What do you suggest?" Jarlaxle asked.

"Going home," said Entreri.

"I don't think we can get down like this," Catti-brie replied. "Especially where it gets steeper just ahead."

"Then we move laterally, perhaps? And find a different route."

"Every step could bring half the mountain down on top of us."

"Give them our boots and we can levitate much of the way," Zak offered, a suggestion that didn't seem to sit well with Jarlaxle.

"Wait," Catti-brie said.

"Please don't recall us to Luskan," Jarlaxle begged. "I have gone to such trouble—this is too important."

Catti-brie looked at him curiously, for his sudden intensity seemed too great for the stated mission. She heard Drizzt's words in her head again—*Do you believe that this is the full story of why Jarlaxle would go to such lengths?*—and couldn't deny her agreement.

But no, she wasn't planning to send them home. Not yet. She had a different idea. She wasn't sure it would work, but thought herself quite clever as she began spellcasting. Moments later, a wide ball of flame appeared on the snow immediately before her. It seemed to sink in, and rivulets of water shed from its base, weaving paths downward but freezing again almost immediately when they got past the heat of the moving flaming sphere.

Catti-brie willed her creation forward, straight down the mountainside. A semicircular depression appeared in its wake, almost as wide as Catti-brie was tall, and glistening more spectacularly than the shining snow.

Catti-brie pressed forward to the upper lip of the newly formed ice chute and bent over it, pulling herself up. She took an arrow from her quiver and jabbed it against the ice as she sat up, then used it to control the speed of her sliding descent. As she went, she kept the ball of flame moving far before her.

"Wait here," she told the others.

A minute later, the flame winked out, but Catti-brie cast another one right at that spot and sent this one, too, straight down the mountainside. She was hundreds of feet below her friends now, and held up her hand to beg for a bit more patience.

A third ball of flame replaced the second, then a fourth, and by the time its magic expired, the icy slide extended over a thousand feet from where they had begun. Catti-brie paused there and surveyed the mountain, looking for a path. One seemed promising, off to her left and down to a ridge of black rock protruding from the snow. It was also risky, for she couldn't see beyond that jutting stone and she had the energy to cast only one more ball of flame for the day.

She heard Zaknafein shout out to her from far above. She just held her hand up in response and continued to consider the rocky ridge.

She was still pondering the possibility when she felt another, more insistent rumble beneath her.

One that didn't stop, like a vibration deep inside, a yawn and a growl from a waking mountain beast.

Catti-brie cast her spell and sent the ball rolling away for the stone ridge. She looked back and waved to her friends frantically, and saw that they needed no prompt from her.

For above them, the avalanche had begun, a great wave of snow sliding down the empty mountainside.

Entreri dove onto the slide, Jarlaxle right behind, and Zaknafein right behind him.

Catti-brie tossed her arrow brake aside and sped away down the last run, angling straight for the jutting stone ridge. It would have been exhilarating if not for the terror driving her. She dismissed her ball of flame short of it, and a good thing that was, for she plowed headlong and hard, but into the remaining snow and not the stone. She pulled herself out and scrambled to the ridge, then to the top.

She heard Entreri's approach and turned to see him, the other two sliding fast close behind, and the avalanche wall of snow gathering speed and nearly overtaking them.

Catti-brie peeked over. A substantial drop loomed, but at least the bottom showed snow and not rock, though she knew not how deep. The ground began to shake wildly.

She didn't have a choice, and so she rolled over the crest and fell.

She landed hard, twisted, and everything went dark, and the ground about her shook with the violence of a wounded dragon.

CHAPTER 8

Probing, Probing

ay we join you?

Do come in, Drizzt responded in his thoughts, knowing they would be heard. *Quietly, please. Do not wake my daughter.*

Drizzt chuckled as he considered that last request. When had he ever thought his biggest concern in communicating telepathically with Kimmuriel Oblodra would be that the drow might wake up his daughter?

A few moments later, Kimmuriel came out of the thick tree line to the left of the hilltop clearing Drizzt had decided upon for his camp. He had not seen the psionicist or any of the other accompanying drow more than once or twice over the four days since he had first met them in the forest not far from Citadel Adbar. True to their word, Kimmuriel and Braelin had kept the Bregan D'aerthe escort far afield from Drizzt and his daughter, affording them their privacy and quiet moments.

Quieter moments, Drizzt thought, and was appreciative, for he did indeed feel more secure with Brie out here in the wild knowing that those drow soldiers were looking out for him, and mostly, for Brie.

A second form exited the copse of trees behind Kimmuriel. At first, Drizzt thought it to be Braelin, but no, it was a woman.

Kimmuriel walked right past Brie as he approached, giving her just a quick, expressionless sidelong glance, but the woman behind him stopped to admire the child, her smile spreading wide. Her face was beaming as she turned back to Drizzt, approaching near enough to the fire for him to recognize her.

"She's beautiful," the priestess Dab'nay said. "So innocent."

"How often did you think that about drow children in Menzoberranzan?" Drizzt asked, despite his desire to be gracious here.

"Always," Dab'nay answered, seemingly taking no offense. "Although, by the time they were your darling Brie's age, many had already lost that aura." She moved to the side and sat down on the ground, as did Kimmuriel, right before Drizzt.

"You know priestess Dab'nay?" the psionicist asked, and Drizzt nodded. "I trust that we have not ruined the time for you and your daughter. We would not steal these moments from you."

"I'm grateful for that, and, in retrospect, for the escort."

"Good. I can tell you that your wife and our acquaintances have stepped through Gromph's portal, wherever it might have landed them."

"Are you in contact with them with your mind magic?"

"No, Gromph informed me."

Drizzt nodded and took a deep breath. The realization that Catti-brie was now out on the wild road hit him harder than he expected, which surprised him since he had known it was coming.

"I have much I would like to discuss with you, if you would oblige me," Kimmuriel requested.

Drizzt shrugged. "Why?"

"Why?"

"Why have you come out here?"

"I was about to tell you that," Kimmuriel replied.

"No, not what do you wish to discuss with me, but why have you come out here at all?" Drizzt clarified, and in his thoughts, he didn't try to hide his suspicions here, or confusion at least, about the seemingly sudden turn from this one and so many others. "And why did you stand with Yvonnel and House Baenre—you hate House Baenre above all others!—on the field outside of Gauntlgrym?"

"I do admit resentment for the fate that befell my house," said Kimmuriel. "I hold no love for Quenthel Baenre, of course, or any of the others."

"Then why?"

"Because I saw the other side. Behind their curtains, I saw the other side of this war, and only then did I realize that this was the fight that so many of us have been hoping for over the course of many centuries. Firsthand, under the guise of imprisonment, I saw Matron Zhindia in her house plotting the demise of . . . well, you, and your father, and of Bregan D'aerthe."

"So it is simply self-serving."

"No, no, not at all," said Kimmuriel. "Zhindia Melarn wasn't determined to be rid of Bregan D'aerthe simply to advance her own fortunes. She was doing so because we were daring to change the paradigm that Zhindia, and so perhaps Lolth, demanded. One of arrogance and isolation, of pure, foolish racism, and of endless cruelty. I saw her, Drizzt Do'Urden, her feelings unguarded, her words flowing free, for she believed at the time that I was fully caught, enslaved to her at the end of an illithid's tentacles."

"Illithids. Always with you, the mind flayers are somehow involved," Drizzt mumbled.

"They are to me a vast library," Kimmuriel said. "A guiding repository of near-limitless knowledge."

Drizzt eyed him carefully. He had heard from Jarlaxle that long ago Kimmuriel had been missing for a bit, but really, Drizzt knew nothing more than what Kimmuriel had just told him. Was that even true? Or was this all an elaborate ruse?

"Tell me, Drizzt Do'Urden, what do you think of the gods?" Kimmuriel asked.

Drizzt rocked back, taken off his guard by the blunt, personal, and surprising inquiry.

"I am no priest," he replied after a moment of collecting himself. "Shouldn't you be asking Dab'nay about that?"

"Oh, we've spoken about it at length, for years now," said Kimmuriel. "I assure you, she is as curious about your answer as I am."

"The broadness of your question makes me wonder what answers you're seeking."

"About the gods," Kimmuriel explained. "You rejected Lolth, obviously."

"Rejected her? She never had me, not a bit. I ignored the lessons she taught more than I rejected her in those early years in Menzoberranzan. I always thought of her as more of a demon than a goddess. And yes, when she came to me in that corridor and demanded my fealty, I did reject her offer, whatever the cost."

"But it would have been easier to acquiesce," Dab'nay said.

"Easier? To just give her my loyalty? My soul? How could I? How can anyone? A person's beliefs might change, but you cannot change something that fundamental to your heart and soul upon request. I could profess fealty to Lolth superficially, but she could never hold my faith and loyalty truly, and if she were actually a god, she would know that."

"But you did find a god. Mielikki, yes?" asked Kimmuriel, and again Drizzt shrugged. "I have heard from your father that she has become a matter of debate between you and your wife, who worships her."

"Maybe Zaknafein should speak less," Drizzt answered.

"Oh, I assure you that it was quite pertinent to our discussions of late in Luskan, which is why, I am sure, the information came to him in his mind. And though I can't properly recall the conversation, I'm not sure the words ever found their way to his lips."

"It must be difficult keeping such things straight when you spend so much time in the minds of other people. Where you do not belong."

"Yes, it is a curse," came the dry response.

"For all of us," Drizzt replied, and Dab'nay chuckled.

"But Mielikki," Kimmuriel prompted. "Tell me. You found her and chose her as your deity."

"Not really," Drizzt replied after considering the question for a few moments. "It was more that I found a name to connect with that which I felt in my heart. I didn't worship her. I didn't ask her for guidance or divine intervention, or even magical spells. I was comfortable with the goddess Mielikki because to me, it was just a name. I didn't need her to tell me right from wrong, Kimmuriel. I had seen enough of that overlord game in my younger days in Menzoberranzan."

To Drizzt's surprise, that answer seemed to please both of the people seated before him. Kimmuriel even turned to Dab'nay and smiled and nodded, and she returned the gesture, whispering Drizzt's words "overlord game" as if they pleased her very much.

When he turned back, Kimmuriel leaned forward eagerly. "You left this world," he said. "Tell me. What was there? What do you know?"

Drizzt stared hard, caught off guard once more.

"Please?" Kimmuriel begged.

"Know? Sensations of calm and beauty and harmony, at least then. Regarding the longer-term destination of that journey, I know nothing," Drizzt answered, and this was a question he had asked of himself a thousand times since he had left this existence. "In the moments of transcendence, or for however long it was, I felt . . . brotherhood. Oneness with everything, and a peace I had never known before or since."

"Did you go somewhere?" Dab'nay pressed. "To the Grove of the Unicorns?"

"I went nowhere and everywhere all at once. I cannot explain it more than that—even to myself, and I assure you, I have tried.

"Why are you asking this?" Drizzt went on, his tone changing. "And why would you be discussing such things with Zaknafein?"

"Zaknafein was dead for many decades," Kimmuriel answered. "I wanted . . . I want, to know where he went and how he found that experience."

"Kimmuriel is obsessed with death?"

Drizzt was surprised that the psionicist didn't answer or argue.

"You don't seem to me to be one who was ever much concerned with Lolth, or any other god, for that matter," Drizzt said.

"I am guilty of your accusation."

"I always assumed you believed you would just meld into the hive mind of the illithids, and there reside for eternity."

"The thought has occurred to me. And perhaps I'm not even curious about such things as this for myself. But you know of the happenings in Menzoberranzan."

"Only that there aren't any."

"Yet," Dab'nay said before Kimmuriel got the word out.

"The reasoning peoples of Faerun are not monolithic in thought or behavior, even within their own cultures and ways, even within their own religions," Kimmuriel explained. "Are they choosing their gods because of their family traditions? Are they choosing based on what they will experience when death calls upon them, picking a heaven as one might find a wonderful patch of ground upon which to build a home?"

"It seems rather shallow when you speak of it that way," said Drizzt.

"And it always has seemed rather shallow to Drizzt Do'Urden, is my guess."

"Good guess."

"Then what?" Dab'nay asked bluntly. "Who is your god? Or are you so proud that you think yourself a god?"

"Hardly that."

"Then who?"

"I don't know."

"That is a dangerous admission, don't you think? If you have no god, then what will you know when you die?"

"I don't know."

"But you're not afraid?" she asked.

"No. Because whatever god I might name to you, whatever afterlife I would choose as my patch of ground upon which to build my forever-after home, seems irrelevant."

"Because that which is in your heart should determine the place and experience, not any outward profession of faith and fealty," Kimmuriel reasoned. Again, he looked to Dab'nay, and the two smiled and nodded.

"Why do I get the feeling that you're merely confirming that which you already knew about me?" Drizzt asked.

"Or perhaps we're just happy to have found a kindred soul," Dab'nay said.

"I thought you were a priestess of Lolth."

"So did I, for many years," she replied. "And so, perhaps, I still am. I know that when I call for spells, I receive them, though I am pointedly not calling upon her, or anyone else. I understand your difficulty in explaining your experience, Drizzt. For me it is no less. Have I transcended spiritually, as you did both spiritually and physically? Am I now beyond the call to any particular god and, rather, accessing the divine magics from some being I do not even know, and yet one I seem to understand all the more clearly?"

"An over-god? A god of gods?" Kimmuriel threw out there.

"I don't know about that," Drizzt admitted again. "I know right from wrong, at least most of the time, and I recognize goodness versus evil, and I follow the path of one and reject the other. Maybe that is the course of divinity. It gives me enough purpose that I don't worry about the names attached to it, one god or demon or celestial overlord, or whatever they might be."

"And that's the truth of it, of you," Kimmuriel decided. "Have you ever wondered if these gods promising power or peace or love or freedom to exercise eternal cruelty are nothing more than selfish overlords, greater beings than we, who use us to their ends and not our own?"

"Yes." Drizzt didn't elaborate. He knew that he didn't have to. He felt calm opening up like this, strangely so considering that the audience was a pair of Bregan D'aerthe associates—the unreadable Kimmuriel and, most of all, a priestess of the Spider Queen! But while it surprised him, he didn't doubt the truth of his composure.

"You know that many priestesses and priests of many religions, not just Lolthian, would condemn you, perhaps even cruelly torture you until you recanted or begged for death, for uttering that admission?" Kimmuriel asked.

"I have witnessed as much, both in Menzoberranzan and in Luskan, where Prisoner's Carnival holds their cruelest executions for such crimes as questioning an accepted god. Which makes me even more confident that I am right in my convictions."

"Because a goodly god should never wish such cruelty," Kimmuriel said.

Drizzt nodded. "You surprise me here, Kimmuriel."

"Trust me when I tell you that I surprise no one more than I have surprised myself since I went into the memories of Yvonnel the Eternal through the vessels of her daughter and her namesake granddaughter, to the earlies days of Menzoberranzan."

"The corruption of Lolth," Dab'nay added.

Drizzt tapped his fingers together and grinned widely. It was his turn to lead this discussion, he thought. "Yes, those tales—Zaknafein and Jarlaxle have told me the revelations in detail. But let's discuss them more, shall we?"

No sooner had he said that than Brie began to fuss. "I'll need a few moments," Drizzt told them, rising.

"Perhaps that is a good thing," Kimmuriel replied. "It will give us all a while to consider what I expect will be an important discussion, and so let us enter it with clear purpose."

"That sounds more like an argument."

Kimmuriel shook his head. "We cannot know what we cannot know, and so an argument over such things would be futile."

Drizzt moved across the camp to fetch Brie, staring up at the stars coming to life in a clear sky above, letting his heart and soul lift him to the peaceful heavens.

CHAPTER 9

Lands Unwelcoming
and Unkind

Catti-brie couldn't see anything and she was twisted pain-fully at the waist. She kept enough of her wits about her to realize that she had landed in soft snow, mostly, but had badly clipped her left hip against rock that wasn't buried deeply enough to pad her fall.

Then she felt an impact on her lower back. Dull waves of dis-comfort swept through her body, and she heard the grunt of Artemis Entreri, who had obviously come over the rocky ridge soon after her.

She tried to begin a spell of healing, but the ground was shaking more violently by the syllable, and reaching a thunderous crescendo so clearly that Catti-brie wasn't the least bit surprised when the snow began to drop upon her. More and more, packing her tightly, burying her. Instinctively, she got a hand up in front of her face before such a movement became impossible, and had her fingers working franti-cally to dig out a bit of an air pocket, at least, to try to keep herself breathing.

Which would matter little if the snow simply crushed her.

Terror filled her as she thought of Drizzt and little Brie. She couldn't manage a spell, but still she prayed for Mielikki to find her and save her. She could not be done with this life, not now! Not with her daughter so young . . .

WHEN DRIZZT RETURNED TO THE CAMPFIRE, HE FOUND that Braelin Janquay had joined the two guests, bearing with him a fine stew Braelin had thrown together from his foraging, and a loaf of bread Dab'nay had magically conjured, along with a bottle of Feywine.

They invited Drizzt to share in the meal, of course, and held off the conversation until Brie had fully settled back down in her bed. Kimmuriel took them right back into the previous discussion, pressing Drizzt yet again on the coming storm in Menzoberranzan and its broader ramifications, and on the point and purpose of it all.

"I don't doubt the power of the web Yvonnel and Quenthel spun," Drizzt answered to Dab'nay's mention of the great heresy.

"There could be no greater act of defiance of Lolth," Dab'nay said.

"Yet there are some who consider the altering of the driders, the reversion of Lolth's abominations, to be no more than a devious trick," Kimmuriel was quick to add. "One done in the hopes of shaking the faith of Matron Zhindia's zealous followers. Even to this day, the argument over the web, whether it was sacrilege or an inspired and temporary illusion, or merely a temporary transformation even, is a heated and confused topic in many of the houses and along all the streets of Menzoberranzan."

"Whether the drider transformation was a trick, I cannot say," Drizzt conceded. "But I do know that there was power in that web. Great power to remove curses. For Thibbledorf Pwent is very much alive, and the vampire that was Pwent is no more. I have never before heard of a cure for vampirism, nor had any of Bruenor's clerics, nor the wizards of Longsaddle. But Pwent is cured."

"Divine intervention?" Dab'nay offered.

Drizzt shrugged, having no answer.

"But you don't believe in the gods," Dab'nay returned.

"I believe in the beings some call gods," Drizzt corrected. "Of course I do. I have met Lolth face-to-face. I do not doubt for a heartbeat that she could have reduced me to ash in that encounter, or could have made of me a drider, or, were I drider, returned me to my life as a drow."

"Maybe it was Lolth who gave the powers to Yvonnel and Matron Mother Quenthel to revert the driders to drow through that web," Braelin Janquay remarked, and all eyes went to him, all expressions doubtful—but only for a moment.

"It has long been whispered that Drizzt was no heretic in the eyes of the Spider Queen," Kimmuriel reminded them. "Would that not be much the same thing?"

"How so?" asked Dab'nay, as Drizzt nodded his agreement.

"Because her goal is chaos," Kimmuriel explained. "Drizzt was chaos in Menzoberranzan, even long after he had left. And so this reordering of the city now, with a war approaching, surely will bring great chaos and confusion, and thus great joy and power to Lady Lolth."

"Fleeting power, if House Baenre prevails, though," said Drizzt.

"Possibly," the psionicist admitted.

"But if Lolth was the one who reverted the driders to drow, could she not just reverse that and re-curse the damned beings?" Dab'nay asked.

"I do not think it would be that easy, but who can know?" said Kimmuriel.

"Sometimes I wonder what we can really know, and what we can only think we know," Braelin Janquay said.

"Like the true history of Menzoberranzan?" Drizzt asked somewhat slyly, bringing the conversation back to where they had left it earlier. He turned his gaze to Kimmuriel, but the psionicist just shrugged.

"The history told by Yvonnel and Quenthel, informed by the memories of Yvonnel the Eternal, is not the history taught to us in my youth," Drizzt reminded. "We were taught that even Yvonnel the Eternal was not nearly old enough, not by millennia, to have witnessed the true founding of the city."

Again a noncommittal shrug from the psionicist.

"There are no witnesses, just legends and lore," said Drizzt.

"The ones who told the newer tale have the memories of a witness," Kimmuriel reminded him. "The actual memories of Yvonnel the Eternal, and not mere stories she or someone else told them."

"Perhaps, or perhaps these really are nothing more than stories someone told them, disguised as memories. Have you been around illithids too long, Kimmuriel? Do you really think them reliable and truthful? Without ends of their own? Or is it just that you prefer the story they have told?"

"The story of the true founding of Menzoberranzan was told by Yvonnel and Matron Mother Quenthel," Kimmuriel insisted. "They know of it as direct witnesses, for Matron Mother Yvonnel the Eternal was a witness."

"Because it was given to them by an illithid, an intermediary, if you will, between the physical remains of the brain of Matron Mother Baenre and that which it imparted to Baenre's daughter and granddaughter."

"Ah, yes," Kimmuriel replied. "I see that you've been speaking with Jarlaxle."

"Often."

JARLAXLE CAME TO THE END OF THE SLIDE, THE AVALanche roaring close behind, and quickly scrambled to the top of the ridge. There, like the two humans before him, he jumped, but unlike Catti-brie and Entreri, he didn't plummet down into the snow some twenty to thirty feet below, but instead continued upward, propelled by his momentum in the weightlessness of drow levitation.

Zaknafein floated beside him as the avalanche overran the rocky ridge below them, tons and tons of snow swirling up like a great white wave and rushing over the peak to tumble below and continue to pour down the mountainside.

Clouds of powder flew up into the air, obscuring the vision of the two drow for some time, until the tumult finally subsided.

Jarlaxle looked down and found his breath taken away. The bulk of the avalanche had rolled past the ridge and was far down the mountain, still moving, but it had left nothing but a blanket of white behind it. How deep, he wasn't sure, but the front of the rocky ridge was gone now, and the drop on the other side had been reduced at least in half. As the mercenary leader tried to digest that dramatic and terrible change, he saw Zak fall beside him, dropping down to the snow. The weapon master pulled the hilt from his belt and called upon the magic, enacting a flaming blade of bright light.

Zak plunged it into the snow, where it hissed, and he frantically began scraping and plowing it all about, a cloud of steam rising around him.

Jarlaxle, too, dropped down, and began digging and clawing with his hands, throwing the snow aside. When it seemed like he had worked himself wildly and barely made any progress, he took a different tack and summoned his hellsteed. He moved to the side, trying to stay clear of where Catti-brie and Entreri had fallen—or, at least, where he thought they'd fallen—and urged the mount to begin pawing furiously, its fiery hooves melting and spraying snow and steam with every movement.

"Don't stab them!" he called to Zak.

"Don't trample them!" came the response.

Furiously, the two dug for their buried friends, but every handful came harder, for the melted snow was already freezing atop the remaining mound, and their progress proved painfully slow.

"YOU TRULY DON'T BELIEVE THAT THE ILLITHIDS COULD be manipulating this?" Drizzt said. "That the memories given to Yvonnel and Quenthel might be fabrications for the designs of the fabricators?"

"Matron Mother Quenthel," Dab'nay corrected.

Drizzt laughed at her. "Quenthel," he said again. "You do not believe, Kimmuriel, that those memories could be faulty, even purposefully fraudulent, or not the entire story, or just a piece of the story of the founding of Menzoberranzan?"

"Even Jarlaxle doesn't believe that," Kimmuriel replied. "He feared it, at first, but he has—"

"Jarlaxle doesn't want to believe it," Drizzt reminded him.

Kimmuriel gave Drizzt a perfectly somber look, and fully flummoxed the ranger when he simply replied, "Does it matter?"

"Of course!" Drizzt reflexively began, but the words stuck in his throat.

"Drizzt Do'Urden," Kimmuriel said evenly, "history is told by the victors, and is related from person to person, and the tellers change the story to exaggerate their own role or own selfish hopes with every retelling."

"There is no objective truth, then?" Drizzt said doubtfully.

"Of course there is . . . somewhere."

"We have writings . . ."

"No, we have copies of writings, and in lost languages that were transcribed from other, more fully lost languages. The tales we were taught in the Academy of the founding of Menzoberranzan go back more than five thousand years. Do you realize how long that is?"

"Drow live a long time," Drizzt reminded him.

"Longer than they remember," Kimmuriel countered, drawing a curious look from Drizzt. "Think of yourself," the psionicist prodded. "You are not a young drow anymore, but likely not halfway to a natural death. How much do you truly recall of your younger days? How much do you truly recall of the early edicts of the Ruling Council or of your studies at the Academy unrelated to the fighting training which you have continued for all of your life?"

"Yet *you* rely on the memories of Yvonnel the Eternal?"

"No, that is quite different. With my help, you could access more memories than you can recall separately, throughout your life. Memory is not a reliable thing, but what the illithids did with Yvonnel the Eternal's brain was extract the memories of events *as they happened*."

"Or did they alter those events for their own purposes?"

"Again, does it matter?"

"Of course the truth matters!"

"A truth that cannot be known," Kimmuriel declared. "And in

this moment, when our kin might at last shrug off the poison that is Lolth, is that truly your biggest concern? The histories sung by bards are unreliable—have you not heard songs of your own legend, often attributing things to you that never occurred, or embellishing others?"

Drizzt couldn't argue against that point.

"Like death?" he asked. "For the living, I mean. A truth that cannot be known."

"Or the gods," Dab'nay interjected.

"And the histories taught by those in command most often serve their privileged status," Kimmuriel explained. "Do you believe that if what Yvonnel and Matron Mother Quenthel learned from the memories of Yvonnel the Eternal was the truth of Menzoberranzan, the leaders of the city, even Yvonnel the Eternal herself, would ever let that be taught at the Academy, a place designed to subjugate free will to the will of Lolth as expressed by the Matron Mother and the Ruling Council? Of course not. They use history like a snake-headed scourge, flashing it to their own benefit."

"But you know better?"

"My family knew better," Kimmuriel stated. "For we long communed with the hive mind, and the hive mind knows better. That is probably the single greatest library in the multiverse, Drizzt Do'Urden."

"So it serves the illithids to make you believe."

Kimmuriel held up his hands in surrender. "We all have our own truths, I fear," he said. "Perhaps someday, I will take you there."

"I've been there," Drizzt sourly reminded him.

"As my guest and not a prisoner," Kimmuriel assured him.

Now Drizzt held up his own hands.

"Let us assume that the memories are true, that Menzoberranzan was founded based on the concept of common good and a desire to be away from the whims and wars of kings and queens," Kimmuriel suggested. "What, then, is Drizzt Do'Urden's play?"

"My play?"

"Do you really have no responsibility here? Do you not understand how your example, the drow who escaped and thrived, has brought so many to this cause? Do you think Jarlaxle would manage Luskan now without the example of Drizzt? Or that he ever would have thought to go on grand adventures with Artemis Entreri across the surface of Toril? Do you think Gromph Baenre would be satisfied with his position in the Hosttower of the Arcane had he not learned that another drow refugee had come to true acceptance on the surface?"

Drizzt pondered that for a bit, letting it sink in. He didn't know if this was his greatest victory or his greatest catastrophe, given the rumblings of a civil war in Menzoberranzan that had been growing louder of late.

"Now you claim that I am a catalyst for the ejection of Lolth from the drow," he said at length. "Did you not earlier claim that I am no heretic in her eyes? Am I her golem then that grew beyond her control?"

"Perhaps, or maybe she just doesn't care as much who wins in Menzoberranzan as we do. Consider, the cult of Lolth will not be fully erased from the families of Menzoberranzan no matter the outcome. There will be glorious chaos in a war that will likely span decades, and even when settled, it won't be settled. It will never be settled."

"Then why fight it?"

"You tell me, Drizzt. You have been fighting it—fighting Lolth— all of your life. Does that weary you?"

"No." The quickness with which he answered surprised Drizzt, but the answer was obvious to him. He had never once regretted turning away from the Spider Queen. He had never once thought her deserving of his fealty or love or obedience.

"Neither shall we regret it," Kimmuriel promised, with Dab'nay and Braelin Janquay nodding in agreement. "Neither shall we."

"THE SNOW IS GETTING THICKER AND HARDER," ZAK cried. "We shouldn't have brought her!"

Jarlaxle and his hellsteed had made more progress than Zak and his sword, but they still seemed far away from reaching their trapped companions, who were likely suffocating if they were even still alive. He couldn't deny Zak's words, either, for the snow had indeed grown denser under the weight.

But they had to try. Jarlaxle jumped down from his hellsteed and ordered it to keep pawing. He threw the feather from his great hat, summoning the huge flightless bird, and ordered it to peck and claw at the mound. He summoned daggers from his magical bracers, one in each hand, and went at the snow furiously, throwing it aside.

He knew, though, that they wouldn't make it, a point driven home when he looked at the rocky ridge and realized that he wasn't even sure if they were digging in the right place.

"Use the magical hole," Zak told him.

"It doesn't work like that. It's an extradimensional space."

"I've seen you use it to go through wall, or into rock. Surely it can do the same with snow."

Jarlaxle thought about that for a moment. It might work. If he just created a hole, like the opening he had put in walls, they would be much closer.

Still, doubts spun about him as he reached for his hat. What if he put the hole in the wrong place? They would dig right by their friends and never know it. What if he put the hole onto one of his friends? Would it disappear flesh, an outstretched arm or leg perhaps, as it vanished stone? Even if so, Jarlaxle couldn't imagine a good outcome when that vanished limb returned with the dismissal of the hole!

Still, he decided to try, and pulled off his hat. A cry from Zaknafein stopped him short, however, and Jarlaxle jumped about and yelped out in shock and fear.

Until he recognized the monster standing before him, a giant black panther digging furiously at the snowpack.

"Get her, Guenhwyvar," he whispered. "For all that is good in the world, get them both."

THE DROW WERE GONE IN THE MORNING, BUT DRIZZT WAS not alone with Brie as Andahar trotted along the open road. Questions followed him and spoke to him, prodding him as much as the little girl sitting before him was arguing against their urgency. Drizzt didn't know what he was going to do. The prospect of joining a war in Menzoberranzan was certainly not appealing, but how might he live with his choice if he ignored the call of his people in this great conflict that seemed to be coming to a climax, and one that might well determine the security not only of Menzoberranzan, but of Gauntlgrym and the northlands as well?

He repeatedly tried to remind himself that this decision was for another day, that he was riding a road in an untamed region of a dangerous and strife-ridden land, and that his daughter's future was the purpose of this journey. And yet, that very future seemed to be the purpose of his thoughts . . .

The forests had given way to vast fields and copses of trees, or lonely trees beside the road, used as waypoints for travelers. Sometimes in the distance Drizzt noted thin streams of smoke. Cooking fires, likely. And every now and again, he saw a distant cluster of cottages. They were crossing Netheril, a land of great empires and great falls. This was a very different place than the one Drizzt had known only a few years before, for the great Netherese Empire, with its massive floating cities, had crashed once more, both figuratively and literally.

Drizzt knew the land fairly well, both because he had crossed it before and because of long conversation with Netherese lord Parise Ulfbinder and the sorceress Lady Avelyere. He had memorized their maps, and knew the mountains and features to guide him true.

He slowed Andahar's pace when he came over a rise to see the land spreading wide below him, the road curving and forking about a large and ancient oak. He shielded his eyes as he studied that tree. Something seemed amiss.

He went down slowly, walking the unicorn, and secured Brie tightly before him. He nocked an arrow, lifted and leveled, when he spotted a large humanoid form hanging upside down from a low branch.

His confusion lasted only a few moments, for he noted the seared patches of grass, the hoof marks of hellsteeds. He buried Brie's face against his chest and pulled his cloak over her, shielding her from what he feared would be a gruesome sight.

Indeed, there was some blood, and a line of burned grass leading off to the south—the drow were in pursuit, he knew.

Chasing highwaymen, he realized as he came nearer the tree, or highwaybugbears, he decided, for the hanging figure, quite dead, wore a necklace of pierced handcrossbow bolts. Likely, it had fallen asleep and swung over, hanging, and there, one of Bregan D'aerthe's formidable soldiers had delivered a swift and bloody end, cutting the would-be thief from hip to shoulder.

Drizzt picked up his pace, the questions gone, and focused on the road ahead, suddenly anxious to get his beloved little girl to the shelter of the Monastery of the Yellow Rose.

They probably weren't in physical danger with this drow force flanking them, but there were more scars than those of the flesh. Brie didn't need those. Not now, not yet.

If Drizzt had his way, not ever.

GUENHWYVAR BURROWED INTO THE SNOW MOUND, DISAP-pearing from sight, snow flying out behind her. Jarlaxle tried to help, diving down into the panther's tunnel, pulling more snow out, trying to gauge the cat's progress.

Guen went down several yards, then leveled out and burrowed in, all but disappearing from sight, with just her twitching heavy tail flickering in the first tunnel. The drow heard Catti-brie's groan—she was alive!—then saw more of Guen's haunches, the panther backing out, then backing up the slope.

Jarlaxle went out of the mound and waited, calling Zak to the other side of the opening.

The panther's back end appeared, then more, and Jarlaxle and Zak dropped and grabbed at Catti-brie, helping to pull her free.

"Get Entreri, Guenhwyvar," Jarlaxle pleaded, and the panther disappeared into the hole.

Twisted, battered, her limbs locked in place by a coating of ice, Catti-brie was in rough shape here.

"We have to find some shelter," Zak said.

"Get her up on the nightmare," Jarlaxle instructed.

They almost had her secured in place across the hellsteed's shoulders when Guen appeared again, dragging Artemis Entreri.

Jarlaxle went to the man tentatively, fearing that he was dead. Surely he looked dead, blue in the face and unmoving. But as he neared, Jarlaxle noted the quiver of the man's lip. Jarlaxle fumbled about Entreri's pouch, producing a second hellsteed, and tossed it to Zak, who quickly summoned it.

"Go find us shelter, wonderful Guenhwyvar," Jarlaxle instructed. With a low growl, the panther turned and surveyed the land below them.

"A cave," Zak clarified.

"Even an overhang of stone," Jarlaxle said. "Anything, anywhere we can make a fire."

"With what kindling?" Zak asked, but Jarlaxle's responding look reminded the weapon master not to ask silly questions. For of course Jarlaxle had brought along a supply of fuel.

Guen was long out of sight by the time the two had secured Entreri. Up Zak went on the hellsteed behind Entreri, but to his surprise, Jarlaxle instead again went into the burrow Guenhwyvar had dug.

"What now?" Zak asked, but before an answer came back to him, Jarlaxle was crawling out. He stood and brushed off the snow, stuffing something into his belt pouch. He climbed up behind Catti-brie and led the way, walking the hellsteed down the hill in the direction in which the cat had run off.

"With the time we've been here, daylight has to be waning," Jarlaxle said, looking to the north, then more to the east. Curiously, the sun was a bit higher in the sky, he thought, and more fully out over the white plain to the north. He wasn't sure what to make of it, and wondered if perhaps he had used the orb incorrectly and was really looking south instead.

But still, why was the sun higher in the sky?

They resisted the urge to move across the mountainside, prefer- ring the route where the top layers of snow had already rumbled away. They were still on the mountain, but much lower, when they heard Guenhwyvar's growl, far off to the left. Zak spotted her on a high bluff of stone. The sun still seemed no lower, but fearing darkness and the deeper cold that would surely accompany it, Jarlaxle picked up the pace, following Guen, who kept coming up high on bluffs so they might see her. After putting several miles behind them, they finally caught up to the cat, standing on a high rock, a dark opening of what seemed like a deep cave below her.

The sun was much lower to the horizon now, seeming to almost touch the land, and farther to the right. The two drow went into the cave and helped Catti-brie to the floor, then lifted Entreri, who was not dead but still unresponsive, from the hellsteed, which was dismissed.

Jarlaxle went right back to the cave opening, Zak following, and looked again to the sun. Beside him, Zak did likewise, and when that fiery ball continued to move—not to set, but almost as if rolling along the horizon—they exchanged blank glances. Where in the multiverse had they gone, after all?

CHAPTER 10

All Out of Sorts

Catti-brie struggled to stand, putting her left hand on her injured hip for support. The movement sent her thoughts back across the centuries, to that other time when she had been gravely injured in this same hip. This wound was not nearly as bad as that, she was certain, and yet her healing spell had not brought her the comfort and strength she had expected.

It still ached, and barely supported her.

"What is it?" Zak asked, showing her that her discomfort was obvious.

Catti-brie shook her head. "The cold, perhaps. I don't know. I used a powerful spell, but the healing didn't quite revive me."

"The wound is worse than you believed?" Jarlaxle asked from deeper in the cave, where he sat beside Artemis Entreri, who was still unconscious. When she turned to regard the mercenary, he pulled his hand from his magical belt pouch, looked at the chunk of ice he was holding, and threw it aside with a huff.

"The pack seems to have opened when I dug and crawled into the snowpack," he explained, and thrust his hand back in, this time pulling forth a log, covered in snow. "I am quite sure I have enough of that avalanche in my bag to construct a mountain giant made of snow alone," he lamented.

He brushed the log, then tossed it to the floor before him.

"It is this place, perhaps," Jarlaxle told her while he continued retrieving the firewood from his pouch. "I have heard that magic might work differently this far north, as it is different in the Underdark. Perhaps there are limitations."

"I don't know," Catti-brie said again. "There is something . . ." She shook her head and looked out of the cave at the vast white plain down the rocky hill before her.

"Amiss?" Jarlaxle asked.

"Different," Catti-brie corrected, and she was still shaking her head, as if she couldn't quite put her finger on it. "Like the path of the sun out there."

"I've felt it, too," Zak admitted.

They left it at that, for none of them seemed to be able to express the sensations any more clearly. Catti-brie followed Zak to the pile of wood—kindling perfectly sized and split.

Zak took out his blade of light and ignited the sword as they went, but didn't immediately plunge it into the wood pile when he stood beside it. For Catti-brie put a hand on his shoulder and directed him to move away, then kneeled quite gingerly beside the pile and began properly arranging the firewood to best take and burn. With great effort, and an assist from Zak, she stood back up and stepped aside.

Zak thrust in the fiery blade. The wood, wet from the snow and ice, crackled and popped, and barely caught.

"Back up," the weapon master bade Catti-brie, and stepped away beside her, transforming his bright blade into a bullwhip.

Up it rolled over his shoulder, and Zak brought it snapping down across the firewood, cutting a line of fire down the side of the pile.

Catti-brie immediately reached through that planar tear with her ring, feeling the heat and power of the fiery plane, and sensing the preternatural sentience beyond the cut.

She coaxed forth a bit of that sentience as the tiny balls of fire dripped from the planar tear onto the logs, and she grinned as she dominated those living flames, instructing them to attack the wet kindling.

When the fire had more fully caught, Catti-brie called one of the living balls of flame off the pile and sent its light deeper into the cave, leaving puddles that quickly hardened on the floor, which was rock and ice. She limped along behind it for a bit, moving it deeper still—the cave seemed endless, a winding, slightly descending tunnel going deeper into the mountains—until the tiny elemental finally expired.

"Ice everywhere, even in here. How is it so cold?" Zaknafein asked. "It's summer."

"Icewind Dale can get quite cold in the summer," said Catti-brie. "But not like this."

"But the Sea of Moving Ice is always mostly frozen, and more so the farther north you go," Jarlaxle added. "My guess is that we're farther north than that, even."

"And it is still light outside," Zak remarked, motioning to the cave exit. "We've been here for many hours and it's not even twilight."

A sudden epiphany sent Catti-brie moving toward the daylight. She paused and cast yet another healing spell upon her bruised hip, sighing in relief as the warmth flowed through her. Jarlaxle nodded, and she returned the nod, then started on her way again, the two drow close behind.

Staring at the shining whiteness outside, the perplexed woman tried to get her bearings. The ground fell away before her still, moving toward that same white plain she remembered from the mountain, but the sun seemed to be moving west to east if she was indeed looking north. How was that possible?

"I am certain that is north, but it cannot be," Jarlaxle said, obviously sharing her confusion.

"No, it is," Catti-brie told him.

"But the sun . . ."

"I think we're looking right over the top of the world," Catti-brie explained.

"But—"

A cough from Artemis Entreri cut short Jarlaxle's reply, and the three rushed to get near to the man. Entreri rubbed his face and with great effort managed to prop himself up on one elbow.

"Bad choice, that drop," he said, his voice weak.

"The choice saved your life," Jarlaxle replied. "The whole of the mountainside rolled down and would have buried you and carried you all the way to the bottom, where we would likely never have found you." He looked at Catti-brie. "Even there beneath the ridge I was afraid we would not find you. Quick thinking, good lady, in bringing Guenhwyvar to your rescue."

"But where were you?" Catti-brie asked. "Why weren't you buried with us?"

"Because he's Jarlaxle," Entreri said.

"Because we're drow," Zaknafein corrected.

"How are you feeling?" Catti-brie asked, slowly kneeling again as Entreri managed to sit up.

"Like a horse kicked my head and the Hosttower fell on my back." He stopped short and looked all about. "Where's my hat?"

"Probably under the snow," Zak said.

"We have to go get it."

Zak scoffed. "That mountain is miles from here. And uphill."

Before Entreri could argue, Jarlaxle produced the chapeau and handed it to him. "I thought you might want it." He looked to Catti-brie, smiled, and produced another item that had been left behind in the snowpack: the figurine of Guenhwyvar. "Exhaust this day's healing power," he told her. "On yourself and on Artemis. Let us rest while the fire burns."

"In here?" she asked. "The cave goes very far back. In a land like this, I doubt many caves are uninhabited."

"Neither you nor Artemis is fit to travel, I fear. Don't worry. Zaknafein and I will take turns on watch," Jarlaxle said. "You two need the rest more than we. And I'll make a fine meal for when you wake. Zaknafein is a maestro with the blade, to be sure, but merely a novice with the ladle."

"I've seen him fight," Entreri said. "He could probably beat you with a ladle." He sucked in his breath, then let out a relieved sigh as Catti-brie sent a wave of healing magic through him.

She used most of her spells, and the effort exhausted her more than it should have, reminding her that she, too, had suffered some grave injuries. So she pulled out her bedroll, set it very near the blazing fire, and crawled in.

She was soon fast asleep.

ZAKNAFEIN CREPT ALONG THE WINDING, NOW DESCEND-ing tunnel. When he had left his companions, with Catti-brie and Entreri fast asleep, he had promised Jarlaxle that he wouldn't go far, but he wasn't about to consider their cave camp secured until they learned if this was someone, or more importantly, *something*, else's home.

He looked back the way he had come, much farther than he had intended. He couldn't ignore the smell, though. There was something more in here than the stone and ice of the floor and walls. He scanned back around, wishing there were more glowworms than the few that offered only a bit of light. Directly across from him, he noted the green eyes of his scouting partner, Guenhwyvar. He could still see the way despite the meager glow with his drow lowlight vision, but a little bit of illumination would help a lot.

Before them was a flight of descending stairs, crudely hewn but certainly crafted by tools, although, by the look of them, that might have been many centuries before. Since each step was almost half Zak's height, he hoped that to be the case.

Beyond the long descent, the wide passage leveled, then forked, although it seemed that after only a short way, both corridors emptied into the same room, which was lit by a soft red glow.

Zak motioned for Guen to go left, while he moved right.

He slipped into the chamber down low and along the left-hand wall, guessing correctly that the room opened wider to his left than to the right. He peered in and paused, trying to digest the curious sight before him.

The room was noticeably warmer, and Zak figured the heat to be coming from a large globe suspended from the ceiling, which was also providing the red glow. He gave it only a glance, though, too mesmerized by the rest of the chamber. The walls were natural and uneven, but had huge shelves cut into them at various heights, and on each shelf were bundles that looked like bedrolls, perhaps, or large piles of clothing.

Directly across from Zak stood a solitary figure, humanoid but truly giant and hulking, four times his height, he guessed. Stripped to the waist, the behemoth seemed a mass of muscle—it looked to Zak as if King Bruenor or one of his powerful shield dwarfs had been enlarged many times over.

A gigantic double-bladed axe leaned against the wall beside the giant, its pointed tip resting on the behemoth's shed heavy jerkin, beside a helm adorned with the antlers of a moose, and massive pauldrons fashioned of what looked like monstrous bear skulls.

Zak moved in a bit more to see the rest of the room, and to see if Guenhwyvar had exited the tunnel. He spotted her in the doorway, crouched and waiting, and motioned for her to hold.

The giant seemed to be fiddling with something, and finally turned enough for Zak to make it out.

At first he thought it a huge ball of snow or ice, but when he noted the loving care the brutish giant was showing it, Zak realized that it was an egg.

An egg as large as the ball of flame Catti-brie had produced on the mountainside. And there were more, many more, along the other shelves in the chamber.

The giant rolled the egg over in its hands, then lifted it up toward the glowing ball and peered at it intently.

That's when Zak noted the giant's face: shaggy, and with a beard that reached almost to its waist. He couldn't really tell the behemoth's skin color, as it was bathed in the red glow, but deep in his memories, all the way back to his studies at the drow Academy, whispers of *frost giant* entered his thoughts.

He was pondering that when the giant yelled, "Hey!" and put the egg back on the shelf and hoisted the massive axe.

Zak thought to run, even started to turn, but changed his mind and went into the chamber, standing upright and at ease, left hand open and raised. *"Bror,"* he said, a word he thought might mean "friend" in the ancient language of giants.

Didn't work.

The giant roared and leaped for him. Zak's right hand came up, holding a handcrossbow. He fired off a shot before leaping into a roll to his left, coming around to his feet expertly, Khazid'hea in one hand, the magical hilt in his other. Despite his clever evasion, he couldn't help but grimace at the thunderous sound as the massive axe slammed the corner where he had been, taking stone from the wall.

He noted the small quarrel hanging from the giant's chest as it turned to face him—the behemoth hadn't even grunted at the impact—and doubted that any of the poison had gotten through this one's thick hide.

The second missile to strike the behemoth was more effective, however, as a large black form flew over Zaknafein's shoulder, lifting high into the air, claws raking ferociously. Lines of blood erupted on the giant's chest, and Guen's claws pulled clumps of hair from the great beard as well.

Zak called upon his magical hilt, bringing forth the bullwhip, and charged.

His opponent roared in anger and in pain and brought its right hand slamming onto the panther's back, then pulled Guenhwyvar free—taking a fair amount of its own skin with her—and hurled her across the room with frightening ease.

The whip cracked at the giant's shins, cutting lines of fire and lines of blood, and the brute howled all the louder, now obviously in pain, and clearly not much liking the fire. It stumbled for Zak, who rolled between its legs, cutting a backhand across the tree-sized left calf with the fine edge of Cutter.

He saw Guen then, her haunches unsteady in the shadows, but stubbornly coming forth from the wall.

More importantly, though, he saw the giant, turning, roaring, coming on in measured, deliberate steps, cutting down the distance between them, boxing him in.

Zak backed slowly, trying to measure the room, trying to figure out his best escapes.

The giant charged suddenly, its huge axe sweeping large circles before it, its strides wide and balance steady, ready to spring out left or right as its puny opponent broke.

Zak noted all that instantly, and doubted he'd get far enough to the side in time to avoid being hit.

So, he turned and he ran—not to the side, but straight for the wall, floor shaking from the pursuit.

He reversed his grip on Cutter as he neared the wall, then leaped and stabbed the sword with all his strength and momentum right into the stone. The brilliant Khazid'hea plunged in deep—deep enough to provide a secure foothold as Zak pulled himself up, planting his foot upon the swaying hilt, then sprang from there, upward and turning. And as he came around, so too came the roll of his whip.

Even though he was high off the ground, the giant still loomed above him. But Zak's anticipated angle proved correct, and the whip snapped across his enemy's eyes.

Zak dropped, hoping to land and roll out of harm's way, but the giant just plowed forward into the wall, its leg smashing Zak into the stone, stealing his breath and, he was sure, cracking some ribs.

His whip became a blade of light, and he struck frantically, enough to loosen the dazed and blinded giant's press and allow him to half run, half fall out to the side.

"Oh, run away, dear Guenhwyvar," he said when he saw the wounded panther going in at the giant once more. He stumbled, leaning on the wall for support as he tried to catch his breath, and slipped, tumbling into a small alcove—or starting to, until a huge clawed hand smashed into his shoulder, throwing him out from the wall. As he flew away, he brought his sword across desperately, and in the flash of light he caught a brief glimpse of his new assailant.

It was mammoth, but not nearly as much so as the frost giant to the side, and surely not a giantkind or any other humanoid Zak had ever seen. Leaning forward as much on all fours as upright, neckless, it had a massive wide head that was all mouth, with more of a snout than a nose, and tiny, wideset eyes. Zak could barely comprehend it.

He looked into the stuff of nightmares.

And he wished that this was, indeed, just a nightmare.

Guenhwyvar flew above him, hurled again by the wounded giant, and slammed into the wall, where she dropped to the floor in a heap with one last squeal of pain. Zak took only a single step toward her before realizing the futility.

He turned for the hallway and he ran for all his life.

He heard the blinded giant flailing and screaming, then heard a second voice calling for the brute to calm, and in a language Zak understood.

Drow.

CATTI-BRIE SAT BOLT UPRIGHT, GASPING, "GUENHWYVAR."

She let her eyes adjust to the dim light, the fire burning low beside her. She spotted Jarlaxle a bit farther into the cave, crouching, ready, and peering into the deeper gloom. She looked to Entreri's bedroll, but he was not there, and she scanned all about for him, and for Zak. She did spot Entreri, moving toward Jarlaxle, but then, on the mercenary leader's signal, rushing across the cave and disappearing into the shadows as surely as if he had turned invisible.

She pulled out the onyx figurine, holding it close and immediately recognizing that Guenhwyvar was gone, back to her Astral home. And it had been a painful departure, Catti-brie sensed, and feared.

Catti-brie spent a moment considering her magic, sorting her spells, then scrambled to her feet and flicked her belt buckle, bringing Taulmaril into her hand as she rushed to join Jarlaxle.

"What is it?" she whispered. "Where is Zaknafein?"

He held up his hand to urge silence and whispered, "Coming, I think."

There was some sound deep down the tunnel. Catti-brie slipped to the side a few steps, near a protective jag in the wall. She nocked an arrow and went down to one knee, watching.

Zak came into view, running. Or, rather, stumbling. His right hand, in which he held his sun blade, was up against his left shoulder, while every step made his left arm bounce limply at his side. He started for Jarlaxle, but turned to Catti-brie as soon as he spotted her, and crumpled to the wall beside her.

She was with him immediately, her bow on the floor, her hands guiding her eyes as she tried to inspect his wounds. A deep and vicious gash had been torn right through his fine leather armor and the superb mithral shirt underneath, an ugly wound made by a powerful claw— Catti-brie had to wonder if he had somehow tangled with Guenhwyvar!

The woman dismissed the thought for now and closed her eyes, calling upon the divine powers of the goddess to bring forth a spell of healing. Then she inspected again and was dismayed, for the wound seemed no less foul.

She had to decide how much of her magical energy she would expend with potential enemies approaching, but it was clear to her that having Zaknafein back up and in the fight would be the greatest benefit of all. So she cast again, the most powerful healing she could offer.

The wound mended, though not as much as she would have liked or expected.

She shook her head in frustration. Was there something strange here, magically amiss? Was this a Spellplague returning of sorts? She prayed that it wouldn't be that, looked down to the tattoos on her forearms, and shook her head. She calmed by reminding herself that the magic had felt somewhat disjointed since they had arrived up here, like everything else. Was it now diminishing?

She put her arms around Zaknafein as he began to slump to the floor, guiding him down softly to a seated position. Then she rushed back to her bedroll and grabbed some bandages and salves, retuning immediately to her work on the weapon master.

His breathing seemed raspy. His entire side was soaked with his blood.

"Well met!" she heard, and it took her a moment to realize that it had been spoken in the Drow language. Not Common, not Undercommon, but decidedly Drow. She jumped up and turned back to Jarlaxle to see another figure approaching him: a woman, a drow.

She looked at Zak and went back to her bow.

THE EYE UNDER JARLAXLE'S MAGICAL EYEPATCH FLICKERED, and he knew at once both the truth of this visitor and the fact that she was trying to magically read his thoughts.

"Here," the drow said to him, holding forth Khazid'hea. "I am sorry for the confusion. The giant didn't know that you were not enemies. I hope your friend isn't too badly injured. And the great feline—I don't know where it ran off to."

It took Jarlaxle a moment to sort through the statements, for while this woman was speaking Drow, little of what she had said would have been understood in Menzoberranzan. She was using an older version of the language, archaic in wording and in dialect. And very different in sentiment.

Ched Nasad. Jarlaxle filled his mind with images of the City of Shimmering Webs and let go of the protective magic of his eyepatch for just a moment, letting the newcomer hear those thoughts. He immediately brought the mental shield back up, however, for the eyepatch's other property, truesight, had already shown him more than he needed to know.

"Ched Nasad," he said aloud. "Your accent makes me think you're from that city, or that your family came from there, at least." He gave a polite bow, removing his hat for just a moment, which was all he needed.

"Indeed, and quite perceptive," came the response. "And you're from?"

"An area not far from you," Jarlaxle said, and he used the more modern Drow language, hoping to give pause to one of those before him and a call to action to the other. "Near and behind you, if you're looking south."

Jarlaxle was looking south. He knew that Artemis Entreri, lost in the shadows of the cave, would understand.

The drow woman looked at him curiously. "And where is that?"

"You ask a lot of questions," Jarlaxle replied sharply, and he began to monopolize the conversation, excitedly so. He spoke of the City of Shimmering Webs, retelling his journey with Zaknafein, or at least, using that long-ago journey as a basis for his ridiculous and nonsensical blather. He saw the woman narrow her eyes, focusing intently.

Yes, she was indeed trying to get into his thoughts.

Yes, he was holding her attention.

Finally, she held up her hands and bade him to stop, and he did stop.

Talking, at least.

For he began pumping his arms, his bracers putting daggers into his hands that flew off with every downstroke, a line of missiles streaming at the creature, which was not a drow at all.

The monster threw aside the illusion, growing in size, towering over Jarlaxle, and suddenly resembling more a bipedal frog than a drow, with mottled skin, clawed hands, and a huge head and mouth. It batted aside many of the daggers, accepted the hits of many more. A ball of flame came into its hand and it threw the fire at Jarlaxle, forcing the drow to hold and defend, then to fall aside with a yip of pain.

Up came those huge clawed hands and the creature started for the drow, but an arrow sparking with lightning slammed it in the chest and drove it back a step. Another arrow came in, and a third, and the monster threw its hand out toward Catti-brie, and projected a magical, glowing replica of that hand right before her, which grabbed at Taulmaril and held it tight. A second attack on the woman came almost immediately, a ray of fear that enveloped her and told her to run away.

She fought it, and struggled against the grasping magical hand, growing strong enough in defiance to push aside the dweomer of fear and consider her spells.

Jarlaxle caught his balance and brought forth two more daggers, snapping his hands repeatedly to elongate them into swords before turning back to meet the foe.

He saw then another flame coming his way, a smaller one, a pea of fire.

When the massive fireball erupted a moment later, the creature croaked in victory, then snarled at Catti-brie. "We will be back for you," it promised in that same ancient dialect, only now croaking and trilling like a frog around the edges of the words.

Then, with a flash, it disappeared, and Catti-brie saw Artemis Entreri standing right behind where it had been, two hands on the hilt of his powerful sword as he thrust it forward to where the monster had been standing.

To where the monster was still standing, invisibly, she realized as the beast came back into view, now with the gleaming red blade of Charon's Claw sticking out of its chest.

Entreri retracted the sword with a great tug that brought it back up and over his shoulder, and wasted no time in striking again, a round-house swing that cut down across the monster's back with such power that it sent the beast flipping sidelong and to the ground, where it hissed and sputtered, and expired.

Catti-brie fell over from her tugging as the magical hand blinked out of existence. She looked to Jarlaxle, fearing that the fireball had destroyed him, for the heat of the blast had reddened her face, she was sure, even though she was well out of the killing radius.

"Jarlaxle!" she called, and Entreri followed suit, running forward, pausing only for a heartbeat to plunge his dagger deep into the monster's frog eye.

CHAPTER 11

The Overlight

L ook at it, Brie, always," Drizzt said, his daughter sitting on his crooked forearm up against his chest and shoulder, her eyes, like his, lifted skyward.

"Tahs," she said, pointing up. "Tahs."

Drizzt smiled at the simple joy of hearing the toddler pronouncing her new words, often mangling the first sound or forgetting it altogether.

"Stars, my little love," he said. "A million, million stars. Always remember to find time to look at them. They will show you the truth."

He paused and grinned. "Do you agree, Kimmuriel?"

The drow psionicist came out from behind a large bush and a pair of close-growing trees.

"I was not hiding," he said. "I simply did not wish to disturb you and your child in that moment."

"I don't mind the company," Drizzt assured him.

"Tahs," Brie said to the newcomer.

Kimmuriel looked at her sidelong, then to Drizzt.

"Stars," he explained.

"Ah, yes, the tiny sparkles of light."

"Not so tiny," Drizzt replied. "Just far away."

"How do you know?"

"Look up. How do you not know?"

Kimmuriel's smile gave him away.

"Have you ever wondered about going there?" Drizzt asked. "I have been to the Astral Plane with Guenhwyvar. I had thought that I might walk among those lights."

"But it wasn't that," Kimmuriel stated more than asked.

"No, it was quite strange, but it wasn't that. And that disappointed me. But only for a moment, until I considered the vastness of it all and the sheer beauty and power of such a creation."

The two stood in silence for a long while, broken only by Brie's reminder of "Tahs," and the call of a wolf, to which the little girl replied, "Woofie."

"Do you always remember to find time to look at them, Drizzt, as you counseled your child?"

"I try. I spent many a night upon Kelvin's Cairn in Icewind Dale looking up at the night sky, even sometimes feeling as if I were floating up among the stars, and thinking, 'Wouldn't that be grand?'"

Kimmuriel almost smiled and almost nodded, he noted.

"But yes," Drizzt went on. "I do not enjoy the dark nights when the clouds steal my pleasure of the starlit sky."

"Or the sunrise or the sunset, from what Jarlaxle has told me."

Drizzt nodded, his eyes remaining heavenward.

"Why?"

"Perspective," the ranger replied. "A reminder of the vastness of the multiverse around me, and that I am only one small man, after all. No, I don't find that diminishing," he answered Kimmuriel's predictable next question. "I find it properly humbling, and hopeful, for I would love to see them all, to walk everything that is in between and all that there is, and so I know that that journey will be everlasting."

"But you are a mortal man."

"That's not my hope."

"But if it is?"

Drizzt shrugged. "I don't believe that."

"But neither do you believe in the gods."

"I never said that. I only said that it does not matter." He looked down to stare the psionicist in the eye. "Because it does not. I believe there is more than this existence."

"And that is?"

"Understanding."

"Of?"

"Everything," Drizzt replied. He looked to Brie, who had put her head down on his shoulder, her eyes already closing. "But no," he said, "I am not impatient for that journey, because I have many roads left here that I wish to walk."

When he turned back to Kimmuriel, he jolted a bit, for the drow was looking up once again. It wasn't the direction of Kimmuriel's gaze that had caught him off guard, but the look of pure serenity upon the psionicist's face.

"It is beautiful," Kimmuriel said softly.

Heartbeats later, the psionicist finally turned away from the sky. "I had wished to speak with you, but it can wait. I will leave you to your night with your chil— with your daughter," he said, and bowed, and quietly left.

Drizzt rocked slowly, feeling Brie melting into his shoulder and watching the surprising Kimmuriel walk back the way he had come. His gaze lingered long after the psionicist had vanished into the night.

It was a mystery to Drizzt, like the sky above him, how such a simple but unexpected conversation could bring him such peace.

He knew that he would remember this night for a long time.

He knew that Kimmuriel would as well.

A MAGICAL HOLE APPEARED ON THE FLOOR WHERE JARL-axle had been standing. "It's quite deep," he said. "I could use a hand, or a rope to help me out of here, if you please. Or a ladder . . . oh, wait."

Catti-brie and Entreri paused, hearing some scuffling from within that hole, and then, sure enough, the top of a wooden ladder appeared above one edge and Jarlaxle came walking up easily, patting at his sleeves, which were still smoking.

"Potent blast," he said. "Are you all well?"

"All but Zaknafein," Catti-brie replied. "My healing has helped, but his wounds are deep and stubborn."

"What was that thing?" Entreri asked.

"Good question. And I'm afraid I know." Jarlaxle walked over to the dead frog-like humanoid and bent low, inspecting. "Slaad," he said, standing to face the others. "A green slaad, specifically."

Entreri and Catti-brie exchanged confused glances.

"From another plane of existence, I believe, although who can tell, since the gods seem to jumble the multiverse at a whim?" said Jarlaxle. "But yes, this corpse is that of a slaad, and they are quite intelligent, quite formidable, and rarely alone."

"Then we should be moving," Entreri said.

Jarlaxle paused and at first seemed doubtful, but then nodded. "Where is the panther?"

Catti-brie's expression went grim. "If it is as I suspect, she'll not be with us for several days to come."

"Do these slaad travel in packs? Or are there entire colonies of them?" Entreri asked.

"Slaadi, when more than one, I believe. I know little about them," Jarlaxle said, and that rare admission from the seasoned mercenary set both Entreri and Catti-brie back on their heels. "Only that there are several versions of them, all quite deadly, some with potent magic, all with brute force." He looked to the green slaad as he spoke, they all did, and the size of its maw and claws and the sheer muscle of the huge creature made his point all the more acutely.

"Let's get packed and get out of here," Catti-brie offered.

"He doesn't look fit to travel," Jarlaxle said, looking to Zak.

"Then summon your hellsteeds."

"The magic is limited," Entreri replied. "Much more than with Drizzt's unicorn. How long did it take to get us here? Hours, you said."

"Several," Jarlaxle confirmed. "The mounts did not move well upon the hillside, creating ice with every fiery step. We had to fly them more than once to get off that mountain, and use their levitational powers repeatedly, and that drains the magic even more."

"Let us just hike out of here, then, and now," Entreri offered. "If we need the nightmares to flee pursuit, then we'll call them."

"You feel well enough to travel, my friend? We thought you dead when we pulled you from the snow pile."

"She helped." He pointed his chin toward Catti-brie.

"But I'm not sure how much I can help again," Catti-brie admitted. "This place remains strange to me, and to my spells. Almost as if they are fainter, or perhaps as if I am farther from my goddess." She turned her gaze toward Zak. "There is an energy in this land. Or lack of energy, perhaps. Dimmer, like the sunlight. Regardless, we have to go. Let us gather our things. Don't dismiss your ladder, Jarlaxle. We'll use it as a litter."

"I don't need one," Zak said, surprising them. Grunting and growling with every movement, his left arm still hanging at his side, the weapon master stubbornly tried to get up.

"Giant," he said when he was up, leaning heavily on the wall. "Maybe a frost giant—I am not well acquainted with the type."

"Where? With that thing?" Catti-brie asked.

"I don't know what that is or where it came from," Zak answered.

"From the looks of your wound, I would think it knows of you. The claw rake is clear to be seen."

"I fought a giant," Zak said. He paused and remembered what had sent him spinning out from the wall. "Maybe," he admitted. "Wait, there was another. Yes." He nodded toward the dead slaad.

"A giant. A green slaad. Hmm," Jarlaxle murmured. He pulled the ladder from the hole, then lifted an edge of the hole itself and turned it back into a small, circular piece of black cloth, which he tucked into his hat, tapping the brim to Catti-brie, who was now over by the dead slaad.

"How did you do that?" Catti-brie asked him. "How did you get that hole out fast enough to escape the fireball?"

"I didn't really escape it," Jarlaxle said, looking at his still-smoking shoulder.

"Enough so," Catti-brie retorted. She kneeled and bent low, examining the terrible claws of the beast and its frog-like maw.

"You don't really think I'd bow to a slaad, do you?" Jarlaxle answered.

"But how did you know it was a slaad?"

"I know everything. I'm Jarlaxle."

Catti-brie huffed and quietly cast a spell of detection, one that would show her any poison or disease on or about the slaad corpse.

"You know little about the slaadi, so you said," Entreri put in, throwing Jarlaxle's own words against him.

"Eggs," Zak said before Jarlaxle could retort.

"Eggs?" Jarlaxle and Entreri asked together.

Catti-brie shook her head, finding no poison or disease at all. She looked at the claws again and figured that this monstrous creature didn't need it!

"They have eggs," Zak explained. "Dozens of eggs. Huge eggs."

"Lovely," Entreri remarked. "We're in a nest."

"A nest of what? Slaadi?" asked Entreri.

"Huge eggs," Zak answered. "Like the eggs of a dragon."

"We should definitely leave," Catti-brie declared. "Now."

No one argued.

They packed and departed the cave. Zak walked for a long while, then accepted the litter of the magical ladder, which Jarlaxle pulled out and unfolded from a seemingly simple block of wood that fit in the palm of his hand—only this time, it was only half the twelve-foot length Jarlaxle had utilized to get out of his portable hole.

"How much time do we have before sunset?" Entreri asked when he took up the front of the litter, following Jarlaxle and with Catti-brie bringing up the rear. The day had grown a bit darker, the sun now behind the mountain at the backs of the companions.

Jarlaxle looked to what he thought was the east, then turned to the south, then to Catti-brie.

"If we were in Luskan, we would be long into the night already," she answered. "Or even into tomorrow."

"That is my thinking as well," Jarlaxle replied. He directed Entreri's gaze to the brightest point behind the mountains, a position that seemed to be south-southeast. "If night doesn't fall soon, I'm not sure there will be one, as I believe the sun will be climbing from the horizon again when it moves out from behind the mountain wall."

"No night?" Entreri asked skeptically.

"The overlight," Zak chimed in. "The anti-Underdark."

"I just don't know," Jarlaxle admitted. "But if that's the case, we should consider it our good fortune. Even with our magical protection, you can feel how cold it is when the sun is up. What might a deep night bring?"

"We're still going to need to rest," Entreri reminded him. "And to find shelter."

Again, no argument was offered there, and the troop trudged on, all three walking and taking turns dragging the litter. Every time they changed positions, Zak promised that he would be walking beside them soon, but on each such occasion, the weapon master sounded weaker, not stronger.

The third time, when Entreri went back to pulling the litter, Jarlaxle took Catti-brie aside.

"I know," she said before he began to explain his concern. "I have expended most of my healing spells this day on him, but they seem to have had only minimal effect."

"Perhaps the wound is infected, or maybe the claw carried poison or a disease."

Catti-brie shook her head. "I checked. The slaad showed no signs of any such thing. And if that were the case with Zaknafein, then it is like nothing I have ever seen or heard tell of before," the priestess of Mielikki explained. "More likely, those claws went in deep and the wound was, or would have been had I not used the healing spells, mortal. I think our friend only barely escaped death, Jarlaxle."

"You saw the slaad," Jarlaxle said, and he curled up his hand as if mimicking its great claws.

Catti-brie nodded and had no answers other than to assure her friend, "I will prepare powerful healing spells tomorrow."

"If we cannot fully heal him, then perhaps you should use your recall magic and take him back to Luskan."

"Longsaddle," she corrected, for that was where her spell had been pre-aimed. "I am bound there. It is my home, and Drizzt's and Brie's . . . and Guen's. My spell is anchored in the Ivy Mansion. And if I go, I take all of us."

"I'm here for a reason."

"And you'll need me to use the sword to point you toward that reason; so you told me when you asked me to come along."

Jarlaxle's expression seemed a bit off to her, but for only a moment. She thought about that slight revelation, and dismissed it as merely a manifestation of Jarlaxle's concern for Zaknafein. At least, that's what she tried to tell herself.

"When do you wish me to hold Khazid'hea?" she asked. "Are we even going in the right direction?"

"Right now, we're just trying to find a place to shelter. And we're following the only course Doum'wielle could have taken after landing through the portal."

Initially, Catti-brie thought, but didn't say. "Doum'wielle went through that gate four years ago," she reminded.

"And she survived, I am sure, and so she went the right way."

That made little sense to Catti-brie, but she let it go.

They found another cave soon after, this one shallow and without another exit, something they carefully checked once, twice, and again.

They made a strong fire and ate a good meal, both the firewood and the food brought forth from Jarlaxle's magical pouch of holding, which seemed to be working, at least. Fed, Catti-brie took one last look at Zaknafein, who seemed a bit better, and gave to him the remainder of her healing magic. Then she went to her bedroll and crawled in for a much-needed rest. She couldn't fall asleep for a long while, though, for her conversation with Jarlaxle regarding Doum'wielle continued to nag at her, creating a stubborn suspicion that Jarlaxle hadn't come up here simply for the wayward half-elf, half-drow woman and whatever her return might offer him with regard to the war brewing in Menzoberranzan, and certainly not for some ridiculous scheme to cleanse Khazid'hea so that it would be a more suitable weapon for Zaknafein, who could never be dominated by it in any case.

No, there was something more, she thought, though of course with Jarlaxle, that could mean nothing more than his simple lust for adventure. He had taken Artemis Entreri halfway around Faerun, after all, simply for the joy of it. So maybe that was the true purpose, the true reason Jarlaxle had decided to bring them to the top of the world.

She found herself hoping that was it.

She found herself doubting that hope.

The sheer futility of trying to unravel the mystery of Jarlaxle allowed her to move far enough past that concern to finally drift off, for who could ever hope to unwind the schemes of the enigmatic rogue?

When she awoke, and she knew it to be a long while later, she first noted Zaknafein sitting beside the small fire, slowly eating from a bowl of porridge. She crawled over to sit beside him, trying to gauge his health. He smiled, but it was strained and Catti-brie knew that he was no better than he had been before she had slept.

"You snore like a dwarf," Entreri remarked to her from the side. "Bruenor would be proud."

"How long was I asleep?"

"Long time. I fell asleep well after you and when I woke up, you were still snoring."

She looked to the cave opening.

"Jarlaxle went out to scout the area," Entreri answered her unspoken question, then went on to the second. "And no, it never grew darker, and seems to be brightening already. We've landed in a land without night. The sun runs in a circle around us, like the spying eye of some giant flame god."

Catti-brie wasn't so sure of any of that, particularly the part about there being no night up here, but she had no answers and so offered no rebuttals. "That's probably how Jarlaxle figured out that our visitor was no real drow, for what real drow would live in a place without any night?"

In response, Entreri tapped his face just below his eye, indicating the eyepatch. "Polymorphs and illusions will never fool that one."

She turned back to Zak. "Let me prepare some spells and I'll see if I can do better for you this day."

"You should eat first," Zak replied, his voice weak. He looked at his bowl and held it out toward her. "Here, if you wish. It tastes foul to me."

Catti-brie wasn't really hungry, but she was curious. She took the bowl and ate a spoonful of the porridge. It wasn't foul at all, and was, in fact, quite tasty.

She nodded at Zak and rose, then moved back to her bedroll and the small reliquary she kept in her backpack, which contained a piece of a unicorn's horn. She was certain now that the internal wound was much worse than the external injury had reflected, and so she meant to prepare her strongest healing spells.

Jarlaxle returned soon after, announcing that he had found a pass that would carry them farther to the north, one sheltered enough so that the snow was not deep about it. "We should make fine progress," he promised, then went over to Zak and began a private conversation. A short while later, he looked past Zak to Catti-brie, and the woman nodded. She climbed to her feet and went to join the two, a small pouch in her hand.

She kneeled down beside Zak. "This should help you feel much better," she said. "If not, I have one stronger, though if I use that today, I'll never find the energy to recall us home if need be."

She closed her eyes and began to chant, calling to Mielikki, feeling the power growing within her, her hands warming, hot.

Not as hot as she had expected, however. She felt the tingle, she felt the energy, she felt the warmth, but they were all like the polar sun: a paler light by far.

Still, she placed her fingers on Zak's torn shoulder, then threw forth the energy, willing it deep inside the man.

Zaknafein gave a great exhale and slumped in on himself.

Catti-brie finished with her eyes closed, nose-to-nose with Zak, who was similarly looking inward. They opened their eyes together, the slightest nod of gratitude coming from the weapon master to the priestess. Catti-brie rose up, holding out her hands for Zak to grab as she helped him to his feet. By the time he was upright, it was apparent that he had taken her assistance only out of courtesy, for he didn't need it.

"Finally," he said to Jarlaxle and Entreri. He lifted his arm up over his head and rolled it about, nodding. "The pain is little more than a nuisance now."

Catti-brie accepted his hug and reciprocated, and breathed a sigh of relief at her other two friends, who nodded appreciatively. She didn't tell them the truth of the depth of her relief, though, and tried to dismiss her feeling that her spell was not quite up to the power it should have known.

"Good choice in bringing that one along," Artemis Entreri softly said to Jarlaxle.

"Her magic is wonderful," Jarlaxle agreed.

"Her company is better," Entreri said.

Catti-brie heard it all. She closed her eyes and pressed her head against Zak's shoulder, and despite her trepidations, told herself that this would indeed be a great adventure and that she had chosen correctly in agreeing to it.

"Come, let us be on the move," Jarlaxle said. "I have found a trail that I believe will lead us nearer our goal."

"How do you know where that goal might be?" Catti-brie asked. Because, pointedly, Jarlaxle had not given her Khazid'hea to hold, to see if she could sense the direction of Doum'wielle, as he had told her he would when he had convinced her to come along on this expedition. She had initially dismissed it as being lost in the necessity, first of getting off the mountainside and then in getting away from their assailant and its possible allies. Still, they had moved at least twenty miles from where they had first landed, north-northeast, so they believed, and Jarlaxle didn't seem concerned at all that they might be going the wrong way.

Jarlaxle simply answered, "Come," and he walked out of the shallow cave.

Some time later, they came to the trailhead of which Jarlaxle had spoken, a rocky affair winding back into the mountains. Catti-brie looked all about, trying to get a fix on where they had first arrived in this frozen land, but it was impossible. The sun's movement offered no real help, and the high-rising mountain peaks gave her little perspective. That windblown great white plain was still in sight, but to the right and back the other way. If that was north, then the trail seemed to be going more southwest.

She didn't argue, though. This was Jarlaxle's expedition, after all. But neither did the change do anything to alleviate her suspicions that there was more involved in this journey than the hunt for Doum'wielle. More than once as they started on their way, the woman glanced to Zaknafein's sword belt and the feline-shaped pommel of Cutter, the sword that was supposed to guide them, to guide Catti-brie.

The sword she had not touched since their arrival.

When they grew tired, they camped, day after day—or that one long day, as it seemed. The sun became even less help regarding direction when they left behind that one reference point, the white plain. For along the mountain trails, the path bent continually and without consistency of direction. More than once, Catti-brie saw Jarlaxle fiddling with that dull white orb, but whenever he caught her watching him, he just shook his head and shrugged.

They rested in caves or under overhangs of heavy stone. They ate the rations from Jarlaxle's supplies, supplemented by some magic by Catti-brie that produced bland loaves of bread and water. Catti-brie also kept tending Zak with spells of healing, just to make sure that he was fully recovered.

The journey proved uneventful, the only sounds the wind and an occasional rumble of something distant, likely another avalanche. Remarkably, they saw no signs of life. No animals, not even birds in the sky. It was a bit warmer than it had been near the ice pack with that constant freezing wind, and no longer did they feel the bite of cold beyond their magical protections, at least. But neither did they find the respite of a night sky, with the maddening sun circling them throughout their travels like a vulture waiting for them to lie down and die. They knew not how many days had passed, but some twenty or so rests later, so subtly that it went unnoticed by all for a long while, they came to an area on a high ridge, moving around the side of a mountain, where the ground below them was not white with snow, and even bore a few plants, scraggly and small, dotting the mountainside.

They moved through a narrow gorge, then came out to the mountainside at an angle that afforded them a wide view. Peaks stretched long and far before them, and endlessly off to the left, but to the right, the ground sloped down to a large box canyon, and there, some water, and small trees, far, far below, and huge birds coasting high on warm updrafts.

Beyond the valley, the mountains continued, but not so far, it seemed.

It was the lake that held Catti-brie's gaze. Silver and sparkling, it stretched out to the left below, narrowing to a river that ran deeper into the mountains. The source was not hard to see, for on the right end of that lake, the canyon was sealed by a mountain of ice—no, more than a mountain, a gigantic ice serpent, a frozen river hundreds of feet high and snaking away between the mountain peaks to the right, filling the valleys beyond sight.

"Are we in Damara?" Artemis Entreri asked.

"That's not the Great Glacier," Jarlaxle assured him. "Though I believe that it is *a* glacier."

The mercenary leader stepped off the trail, tentatively moving down the steep slope toward the lake far below. "Come," he bade them. "And take care in your every step." As he spoke, he dislodged a couple of small stones, which began rolling and bouncing down like a pair of racers. One stopped in a depression, while the other hit a half-buried rock and bounced up into the air, then disappeared over some distant ledge.

"Your every step," Jarlaxle repeated.

They moved down the slope several hundred feet, then came to a sheer cliff. Undaunted, Zak and Jarlaxle used some ropes and drow levitation to float down from shelf to shelf, hammering pitons to create a ladder for Catti-brie and Entreri.

The going was painfully slow, straight down the mountain instead of along any winding trails they might have sought.

Catti-brie kept a couple of arcane spells in the front of her thoughts, primarily one to make a falling person float like a feather, in case of catastrophe. She could only trust that it would work in this strange place.

More and more shrubs appeared around them. They heard the cawing of the great birds riding the updrafts, and the air was becoming comfortably warm. They touched down on a plateau full of blueberry bushes, hundreds of feet below the high trail. The air buzzed with gnats and flies and bees, so many small bees. Squirrels and other small animals darted about the underbrush, while one white squirrel climbed up on a scraggly little tree and stared at the intruders with obvious curiosity.

They couldn't see the lake from here at the back end of the plateau, but the top layers of the glacier that sealed it in to the right were visible above their level, showing them that they were well more than halfway to the valley floor.

A quick spell by Catti-brie assured them that the berries were safe to eat—that they were indeed blueberries and quite delicious—so they picked and picked and stuffed handfuls into their mouths as they made their way to the other side of the wide plateau.

There, they looked down to the tops of small trees, and on the lake, and, to their surprise (and Jarlaxle's delight) upon structures, houses of stone and thatch.

"All right, I have had enough of the climbing," Jarlaxle said. "Come, Entreri, bring forth your mount!"

"Why didn't we just do that at the top of the damned cliff?" a frustrated Zaknafein asked.

"Adventure," replied a smiling Jarlaxle, and he dropped his obsidian figurine, summoning the nightmare. He went up on its back, offering his hand to Zak. "Besides, would you have us plucked from the sky by one of those oversized vultures?"

"You really think it wise to swoop down on villagers on these beasts?" Catti-brie asked.

"I'm tired of crawling across the cliffs like a spider," Jarlaxle answered, "and I always do so prefer a grand entrance." And over he and Zak went, the hellsteed floating, gliding down toward the lake.

With a shake of her head and a sigh, Catti-brie accepted Entreri's hand and took a seat behind him on his mount. He trotted to the edge and simply kept going, out into the air and flying down for the silvery lake, the nightmare moving its hooves as if it were running across solid ground.

"The villagers will probably shoot us out of the sky," Entreri said, but Catti-brie wasn't really listening, her attention fixed on a bird sitting on a ledge far to the right—a blue-black bird with a black beak, like a raven, except that it seemed nearly as large as the nightmare and its riders combined.

"Are those rocs?" she asked Entreri.

"Babies, if so," he replied, and Catti-brie was sure that he felt her shudder.

She grew quite relieved as they descended and the bird hardly seemed to care, and when she turned her attention to the small settlement below, a different level of curiosity came over her.

The village seemed empty of life. It was on the lake's far bank, the stone houses stretching all the way to the towering glacier—no, right *into* the glacier, she realized.

Jarlaxle's hellsteeds touched down, he and Zak hopping off. Entreri's mount fell more than flew the last few feet, landing hard, snorting and turning. Catti-brie leaped from its back, Entreri quickly following.

"Dismiss it!" Jarlaxle warned, though his command was hardly necessary, for Entreri was already doing so.

The hellsteed became an obsidian figurine once more, Jarlaxle's fast following suit.

"Did it try to shake you with the landing?" Zak asked. "To throw you?"

Entreri shook his head, and Catti-brie agreed. "The glide down from above exhausted it," she said.

"Our sense of time passing is all confused," Entreri agreed. "The item wasn't ready for that much exertion and use."

Jarlaxle didn't appear to agree, but he just shrugged, and the friends went to searching the town. Jarlaxle called out a couple of times, Entreri and Zak moved into the shadows, and Catti-brie followed Jarlaxle, her hand on her belt buckle, ready to bring Taulmaril to her grasp.

The more she looked around, the less she thought she'd need the bow. Little things told her that no one was about, and no one had been for a long while. She noted several of the rails of a wooden corral were down, lying on the ground. A bucket sitting beside a well wasn't empty, but the little water left was green with algae. The doors on some houses were open, others closed, the splotchy clumps of grasses overgrown, the gardens untended—for many seasons, it seemed. There was a dock on the lake, but the boat beside it was submerged in shallow water.

"What happened here?" she asked Jarlaxle.

He shook his head, leading through the deserted settlement, moving toward the glacier. A large house at the end of the lane seemed half inside the glacier, half out. As its door was open, the two curious explorers entered. They found wooden plates, rotted bedding, metal utensils and tools—all of the things one would expect in a frontier town.

What did surprise her and Jarlaxle was the opposite door of the house, for it, too, was open, and led into a hollow within the glacier.

Catti-brie cast a spell of light on the tip of an arrow, and in that glow reflecting off the ice all around them, the two realized that the town was much larger than they had thought, with a line of structures that had apparently been claimed by the ice.

"What is this place?" Jarlaxle asked her. "What people live north of Icewind Dale?"

"There was one tribe rumored to be just north of the Sea of Moving Ice—a family of folk in the Ten Towns settlement of Lonelywood claimed heritage from there—but I never met anyone directly from the place; nor had anyone else that I know of, and most believed that it might be more myth than truth."

"Barbarian tribes? Like Wulfgar's?"

"No, no, very different. Smaller men and women." She put her hand at her chin height. "With round and flat faces. At least, the northern folk who had settled in Lonelywood had that appearance. I can tell you that I've seen houses like this before."

"I've seen houses, too," he said skeptically.

"Yes, but the design of these houses is specific. See where the hearth is? It's to let the heat from a single fire warm all corners, and to let the smoke easily escape."

"So maybe those people in Lonelywood came from here?"

"Maybe." But she was still dubious.

A loud creak and shudder reminded them that they were under tons of ice, and so they made their way back through the first house and out from under the glacier.

Entreri and Zaknafein were waiting for them, standing near an open door to a house near the lake. The weapon master waved for Jarlaxle to come to him, then pointed inside the doorway when they arrived.

Catti-brie led the way in, the glowing arrow up before her. Barely across the threshold, she understood why Zak had guided them here, for they had found their first villagers.

The remains of some villagers, at least.

The skeletons were small and humanoid, likely short humans, as Caiti-brie had noted earlier. Three distinct and nearly complete skeletons littered the floor, all lying on their backs and all with the fronts of their rib cages shattered.

Catti-brie kneeled down beside the largest, studying the breaks in the rib bones.

"These bones were broken from the inside out," she said.

"Or from the back through the front?" Zak asked.

The woman pulled her sleeve over her hand and rolled the skeletal torso to the side, shaking her head before she even looked more closely. "I see no wounds from the back, no wounds at all on the back ribs or the spine."

"Then maybe some beast stabbed him and tore out his heart, breaking the bones on the way out," Jarlaxle offered. "One of those giant birds, maybe."

Catti-brie didn't argue the point, but neither did she believe it. The killing wound seemed clear here, and seemed to have come from within the dead person. She moved to the second body, then the third, and found the same curious pattern.

She turned to Jarlaxle, her doubts clear on her face, she knew, when the mercenary assured her, "It was a long time ago."

Catti-brie couldn't argue that point.

They found a couple of other similarly situated and broken skeletons about the village, and a graveyard in the foothills across from the lake—which seemed unremarkable enough, except that two of the graves had been dug up.

Or dug out of. That was the first thought that came to Catti-brie, but she let it go when they inspected more closely, even digging at the remaining dirt, and discovered that bones remained in those graves, broken and twisted.

The four settled into one of the houses farthest from the lake. Catti-brie repaired the door hinges with minor spells of mending, while Entreri and Zak set traps about the outside, and clever barriers and deadfalls for anyone, or anything, thinking to pay them a visit. Jarlaxle, meanwhile, started a fire and cooked a fine dinner.

They sat around a table inside soon after, sharing that meal.

"Savor it," Jarlaxle warned. "The strangeness of this place's effect on our magic, as with the hellsteeds, is beginning to concern me, and so I'll save my stores until we find ourselves truly in need of them. After this dinner, we'll be reduced to the conjured food Catti-brie can create for us."

"There are fish in the lake," Entreri remarked.

"Let's be away from here as soon as we may," Catti-brie said.

"The villagers are long dead," Zak said—to reassure her, she understood, and the reminder brought some small comfort to all of them. "Very old. No one's been here for many years."

"It's still unsettling," Entreri answered before Catti-brie could. He turned to Jarlaxle. "Do you even know where we are? Or where we're going?"

"I have an idea."

"I thought Catti-brie could lead us by communicating with the sword," Entreri pressed. "Has she even held it?"

"Good question," Catti-brie said, turning a wary eye on the cagey mercenary.

Jarlaxle just leaned back against the wall.

"You didn't give it to me yet because you're afraid that Doum'wielle is long gone from this place," Catti-brie bluntly accused. "Perhaps you really do want to find her, but you brought us up here for another reason."

"Do tell," said Zaknafein.

"To stay out of the fight in Menzoberranzan, is my guess," Entreri said, and that didn't seem to sit well with Zak, from the way the weapon master arched his bushy white eyebrows.

"I wish to find Doum'wielle," Jarlaxle replied. "Our path to this point seemed self-evident. What I fear is that Khazid'hea will not show us what we believe it might. Nor am I keen on handing it to Drizzt's beautiful wife, given her sad history with the blade. It's all just a guess, after all, and perhaps I have simply harbored second thoughts."

"You brought us up here on a guess?" Entreri demanded. "And had us walking blind through this forsaken land for tendays, perhaps a month?"

"An adventure, and one with a purpose!" Jarlaxle countered. "We all needed some time on the road. That much you cannot deny."

"What road? A road implies an actual path. We've been stumbling about a mountain and deserted plain of snow!"

"A figure of speech."

"You wish to hear a few other figures of speech?"

"Don't," Catti-brie said to the assassin. "We're here now. What's done is done."

"We're definitely here—wherever 'here' is. He might have picked a more enjoyable place," Entreri grumbled.

"I didn't think it would be this cold, and this . . . empty," Jarlaxle admitted.

"At least we found some living things here that didn't try to kill us," Zak reminded them.

"And hopefully there won't be some walking dead things here that do," Entreri countered.

"This very night," Catti-brie stated in a tone that brooked no debate. "After this meal, I will hold the sword and we will see what it tells us." She wasn't asking. She left it at that, but she was done with Jarlaxle's evasions, and she wasn't buying his feigned fears for her safety with Cutter. Yes, the sword had once dominated her when she was very young, but now? Now, Catti-brie faced down primordials and battled a Lolthian avatar as she championed Mielikki. She had easily handled Entreri's sword, whose malignancy was many times more powerful than the telepathic suggestions of Cutter.

And Jarlaxle knew all that.

"After this meal," she said again, looking to Zak this time, and the drow who wore the sword nodded, clearly in full agreement.

She looked the other way to note that Jarlaxle, however, didn't seem so pleased.

SHE FELT THE REJECTION, ANGRY AND INSISTENT.

But the voice was faint.

"You know me," she whispered to Cutter as she tightened her fingers about the black grip.

Zaknafein! the sword screamed in her thoughts. Catti-brie was amused, but not surprised. Khazid'hea wanted one thing alone: to be wielded by the greatest fighter it could find. The sword would rather lose an epic battle with a great champion than win one in the hands of an untrained peasant.

Memories flashed for Catti-brie, of a time when she had shamelessly thrown herself at Drizzt, long before they had even begun any romantic relationship.

Khazid'hea had done that to her.

The recollections continued for only a moment before the woman realized that these were not memories of hers, but rather of the sword. The blade nicknamed Cutter was trying to remind her that it had once dominated her and could do so again.

"Hmm," she said aloud, and she heard the others shift about her curiously, but kept her eyes closed, her thoughts inward.

You cannot dominate me, she imparted to the blade. *I am beyond you.*

Zaknafein! the sword pleaded. She ignored it.

There is another who once wielded you.

An image of Artemis Entreri came into her thoughts, and Catti-brie got the distinct impression that the sword would not be upset with that choice, either.

Who else? she telepathically prompted. *Who have you known? Who has bent to your will?*

The sword offered her Jarlaxle.

She prompted again and was answered with a view of an old man sitting cross-legged on the roof deck of a great structure nestled on a plateau in a range of high mountains. It took her a moment to decipher this unexpected vision, until she remembered that Jarlaxle had gone to the Monastery of the Yellow Rose—and so had likely allowed Grandmaster Kane to handle the sword.

Who else?

An image of a young elf—or half drow, given the gray undertones of her skin—came to Catti-brie. She felt a connection distantly. On instinct, the woman held the sword out before her and loosened her grip enough for the blade to shift its angle from side to side.

Maybe it was the shape of her hand, maybe that she wasn't holding her palm level, but the sword did sway over to the left, pointing more toward the beginning of the glacier than at the lake, where Catti-brie was facing.

Show me Doum'wielle, she commanded. *Show me the other one who bent to your will.*

Zaknafein, Cutter responded defiantly, a demand and certainly no answer to her request. She felt an urge to hand the sword back to the weapon master.

But that was what Khazid'hea wanted, and she was no longer in its thrall. Catti-brie opened her eyes, waved her three companions to the side, then stepped over and smashed the flat of the blade hard against a large stone. She struck again and again, doing no damage to the magnificent weapon, but letting it know in no uncertain terms that she, not it, was dominating here.

And it was so easy for her! A stark reminder of how far she had come in her life. The young Catti-brie had fallen prey to Cutter. Now, she could not imagine that the sword could compel her to do anything, even if she were mortally ill or wounded and lying on her deathbed.

When she had finished the display of dominance, she offered a smile and a wink to her companions and went right back at the sword, demanding that it show her the way to Doum'wielle.

Again the sword shifted in her loose grip, again pointing toward the glacier—no, she realized, not toward the glacial wall, but far beyond. Beyond the glacier, or far to the back of it, at least.

Jarlaxle had told her that she could connect to Doum'wielle through the sword, but she felt none of that to this point, or very little, at least. Yet there was certainly a bit of Doum'wielle's consciousness within the magical mind of Khazid'hea. Catti-brie saw another half elf, half drow, his expression shocked. She watched in horror as the memory unfolded for her, the deadly blade choosing not this unknown young man, but the one who then held it, who was then sliding the blade into his chest.

She remembered the story of Doum'wielle and knew the victim to be Teirflin, her brother. She prodded and prodded, but found no memories from his perspective at all, though he, too, had wielded the sword.

No, because he was dead.

Catti-brie went back to her thoughts of Doum'wielle and asked the sword again to show her the way, demanding more insistently. This time, a most confusing and alarming sensation came over her.

Soldiers . . . serving . . . cold . . . we are not we . . . we are it in glory . . . soldiers . . . serving . . . cold.

She didn't know what to make of it. She felt like something more than herself—or Doum'wielle did, but also like she was no longer herself at all, as if she had been psychically consumed.

Catti-brie tried to press further, but then felt a deep chill within. She opened her eyes and thought she was looking through the blur of ice—no, looking out from within ice!

What was she really being told? With a vague direction and no indication of distance, the sword's answer seemed thin, very thin.

One last time, Khazid'hea tried to make her give the sword back to Zaknafein. She growled at it, opened her eyes, and tossed the blade to the ground.

"What do you know?" Jarlaxle demanded. "She is alive?"

"I think maybe she is, against all odds. But I cannot be sure."

"Where?" Jarlaxle and Zaknafein asked together.

"Somewhere out there," the woman replied, waving her arm toward the glacier, a direction she figured to be northeast, perhaps. She looked directly at Jarlaxle and admitted, "I don't know how far, though. She might be halfway around the world."

"You don't believe that."

Catti-brie considered that last feeling, the coldness in her bones, in her heart and soul. She walked to the door of the house and peered out at the glacial wall.

"But you think her alive?"

Catti-brie just shrugged. "I don't know. We don't need her to cleanse the sword, if that is truly one of your reasons for bringing us here," she replied. "I see its pride clearly and I am confident that I can break it."

"Then do it," said Zak.

"No," Jarlaxle snapped immediately, more insistently than was typical from the cool-tempered rogue.

Catti-brie, Zak, and Entreri all stared at him.

"No," Jarlaxle said more calmly. "Menzoberranzan is on the edge of war and Doum'wielle alone might help us prevent it. Perhaps she is long gone from this place, but we must try to find her, and that sword, with its memories and sentience and pride and all, is our only chance of doing that."

"You think too much of her worth in Menzoberranzan," Zak bluntly replied. "She is only half drow, and though she's of House Barrison Del'Armgo, do you really believe they'll put much credence in anything she advises?"

"She'll be our spy," Jarlaxle retorted.

"Which will probably get her killed anyway," Entreri put in.

Jarlaxle huffed and seemed quite out of sorts. "Then why did you all agree to come along, in any case?" he asked. "We knew it wouldn't be easy to find her, and were fairly certain that this land wouldn't be hospitable. No, we should use this and find the poor girl. If we can locate her and help her to heal from the terrible things she has done because of this sword, then would not that alone be a good thing? Surely you," he added, looking to Entreri directly, "understand and sympathize with such oppression from a magical weapon."

"I understand just as easily as Artemis. And yet you don't seem to want Catti-brie to cleanse the blade," Zak remarked.

"If she does, Doum'wielle is forever lost to us."

"Why does Jarlaxle care?" Zak pressed.

"Why does Zaknafein not?"

"I did not say that I do not care, nor have I pressed for our return to the more hospitable lands."

"Good, then pick up your sword and let us go onward. This empty village unnerves me."

"You didn't answer his question," Catti-brie said.

"I met her mother," Jarlaxle replied. "I looked into her sad eyes." He pointed to Khazid'hea, still lying where the woman had dropped it. "That sword broke her family, brought betrayal from her daughter and her husband and a terrible death to her son."

"So, let me relieve it of the malignant magic as I believe I can."

"She cares not for the sword, though. I want to bring her back her daughter, freed of the influence and terrible memories wrought by Khazid'hea," Jarlaxle said, and Catti-brie found that she believed him.

But he was still evading them. Every time they came close to the truth of their mission, Jarlaxle danced sideways. The girl, the need for adventure, the hopes for Menzoberranzan—they were all parts of the reason, she was sure, and they were worthy enough goals in her mind. There was more, though. Of that she was certain.

And she wasn't going to keep dancing much longer.

CHAPTER 12

Ruminations of the Gods

D rizzt sat on the railing of the large deck about the main back door of the Monastery of the Yellow Rose, his cloak flapping behind him in the brisk wind whistling down through the narrow passes of the Galena Mountains. The season was quickly changing, the leaves turning and falling away, and the air had that crisp feeling of forthcoming snow, with gray clouds rushing overhead.

Drizzt loved this time of the year everywhere he had lived, with the exceptions of Menzoberranzan, which had no seasons, and Icewind Dale, where autumn was just winter with a bit more light, after all. The smell in the air, the dance of falling leaves—all of it—just brought to him a sense of peace and calm.

Maybe that was because many of the conflicts he had known had ended in the fall, pressed to completion by the promise of a war-stifling winter.

He smiled widely as he watched Brie rushing about the leaf-speckled grass, hopping into a pile of leaves that Savahn kept putting back together for her. The sheer joy of the child's play was so obvious and infectious.

Or maybe it wasn't just play, Drizzt speculated, at least not for the monk. Savahn was Mistress of Winter, the third-ranking monk at the monastery, with only Grandmaster Kane and Master Perrywinkle Shin, an old man well past his fighting prime, ahead of her. Earlier that tenday, Kane had mentioned to Drizzt that he expected Savahn to become the first female Grandmaster of Flowers of the Order of Saint Sollars in many years.

Her only rival in her ascent had been Brother Afafrenfere, and alas, he was gone.

Drizzt's smile mellowed when he thought of the man. Afafrenfere had transcended his physical form and used every bit of his spiritual strength to pull Drizzt back from eternity, at the cost of any chance he, Afafrenfere, had of returning. Because of their soulful joining in that spiritual state, Drizzt understood the man's reasoning, but still, he couldn't escape the pangs of guilt. Afafrenfere believed that Drizzt had more reason to return than he. With a child on the way, a family strong and growing, Drizzt wasn't done in his journey through this life, Afafrenfere's every call had claimed.

But Brother Afafrenfere was ready and willing to transcend the physical world. He believed that his partner in life, his lover and best friend—the monk brother named Parbid who had given him true meaning and direction—was waiting for him in a shared existence on that higher plane.

Drizzt hoped that was true, both for Afafrenfere and for himself, and for all those others he loved. He wanted there to be more.

For some reason only a two-year-old could know, Brie gave a tremendous roar then and proclaimed herself a tarrasque. She lifted her hands like monstrous claws and stomp-walked toward Savahn, who feigned terror and began to run away, the little girl in close pursuit.

Drizzt's smile returned.

But was this just play? he wondered again. He had the feeling that Savahn was evaluating his daughter, as if trying to get an idea of when the child might become an appropriate candidate for the ways of the monastery. Drizzt had already told Kane that he would like such training for Brie, but also that she would not be a sworn member of Saint Sollars—at least not until she was old enough to truly make up her own mind regarding such an important life decision.

That hadn't bothered Kane at all. Drizzt had never converted to the faith—he still wasn't sure if what the monks had here was a "faith" in the traditional sense at all, and from the teachings at the monastery, the "saint" in question seemed more an example of true devotion to personal discipline and purpose than to any godly handmaiden. And, perhaps more than anything, that was what appealed to Drizzt about the monastery.

Yes, he would very much like the idea of Brie spending a lot of time here with the goodly monks.

"She moves as I would expect of the daughter of Drizzt Do'Urden," came Kimmuriel's voice behind him.

"She's not yet two," Drizzt replied with a laugh. He turned his head to look over his shoulder as the psionicist approached. "When did Kimmuriel become the purveyor of empty praise?"

"Is that your way of asking what it is I want from you?"

Drizzt laughed again. "It could be." He grew more serious immediately, though. "I am grateful that you came out on the road to protect my daughter in our journey here."

"It was my half of the bargain I hoped to make with you."

"And for the company, on those few occasions we spent together," Drizzt added. "I cannot say that those nights we spoke weren't . . . interesting. Certainly you've surprised me of late."

"I'm glad."

"You had your desired meeting with Grandmaster Kane?"

"I did."

"And he did not disappoint, I'm sure."

"He is beyond what I would expect of any human," Kimmuriel admitted. "His wisdom was much appreciated."

"For what? What is it you seek?"

"Answers."

"To that most elusive question of all," Drizzt said with a nod. "I doubt Grandmaster Kane did much to help in that regard."

"He let me into his mind," Kimmuriel said. "And so, intimate with his memories, I now better understand the feeling of transcendence."

Drizzt hardly heard the second sentence, for he was still stuck on the shock of the first part. "He let you into his thoughts? He invited you into his mind?"

"Yes," the psionicist said matter-of-factly.

"But . . ." Drizzt couldn't even find the words to respond to that.

"Because he was confident that he could expel me with ease," Kimmuriel explained.

"Was he wrong?"

"No," Kimmuriel admitted, still matter-of-factly, and if he was surprised or even humbled by the experience, he wasn't showing it. "I told you, he was much more than I would ever expect of any human."

"So, he let you in there and he gave to you his memories of transcending the physical form."

"And now I understand better. But of course, there remain limitations on that understanding, because such an act may or may not be a permanent state of being."

"There's only one way to find out the truth," Drizzt admitted.

"I am in no hurry to leave this life."

Drizzt didn't question that, for he felt much the same way. His transcendence fleeing the retriever had given him great comfort and hope in what might come next, but he knew that he could not know the permanence of that experience. He could not dismiss the notion that it had been no more than a trick his mind had played on him to ease the transition as his spirit diminished to nothingness.

"We are leaving in the morning," Kimmuriel told him.

"In a hurry to be away from this place, then?"

Kimmuriel smiled. "Would you choose to ride with us? The winter winds will come on fast and we'll be fortunate to beat the snows to Luskan."

Drizzt considered it for just a moment, then shook his head. "I have no business back there at this time. I'll stay with Brie—this is a good place for her. Catti-brie will come for me when she returns, I am sure, and I would like her to spend some time here as well. The discussions are stimulating, even enlightening. It is always good to speak of that we cannot fully know, to gain the hints from others who similarly ponder."

"As I found my discussions with you," Kimmuriel said.

"Why?"

Kimmuriel looked at him curiously—a rare expression from the drow who could so easily slip secretly into the thoughts of another person. But he hadn't on this journey, Drizzt knew. Not to Drizzt—at least since Drizzt had asked him not to. Not even once.

"Why everything?" Drizzt clarified. "You are suddenly so concerned with the gods and the afterlife. I've never known of such questioning from you."

"I never thought of them before. Not truly and deeply. The gods seemed inconsequential to me in a spiritual sense, and more a matter of pragmatic survival, particularly in Menzoberranzan. As to the rest, with possible centuries of life left before me, contemplation of the meaning of death seemed . . . remote. And probably pointless, after all."

"But now?"

"As I said, I never bothered to deeply think of it *before*."

"Before what?"

"Before I aided Yvonnel and Matron Mother Quenthel in their search of Matron Mother Yvonnel's living memories," Kimmuriel admitted, which was what Drizzt expected and hoped to hear.

"What did you learn?"

"That in the end there is no place to hide."

"Perhaps there is nothing there in the end from which you'd wish to hide."

Kimmuriel nodded and smiled, but kept the conversation moving forward. "No divine justice?" he asked. "Is an afterlife a matter of the choices we make, then? Do they decide? Those are the questions facing my kin, our kin, on a grander scale now, Drizzt Do'Urden. Those are the choices stark before them in the city of our birth. They are going to war against each other, do not doubt."

"I don't doubt it. What I doubt is whether the answers you seek will do anything about that."

"I think they will. And even if not, I seek these answers for my own sake. Consider it, Drizzt Do'Urden; why do you seem to so easily spurn religion itself?"

"'Spurn' is a strong word."

"Even when you found Mielikki, you did so only conditionally," Kimmuriel reminded him. "You have admitted as much repeatedly. You placed yourself, your conscience, above her."

Drizzt started to argue the point, but paused and considered his fights with Catti-brie over the true nature of orcs and goblins.

"Is that not spurning religion?" Kimmuriel asked as if reading his thoughts. Drizzt realized, though, that Kimmuriel didn't need any mental intrusions to know what he was thinking at this time.

"I cannot deny it," he said.

"What is religion, Drizzt Do'Urden?"

"That seems a wide question."

"What is it based upon?" Kimmuriel asked.

"Morals. A code . . ."

Kimmuriel scoffed. "To hear morals ascribed to Lolth is unexpected."

"Lolth is a false religion."

"And Mielikki? Who tells you to wantonly kill goblinkin, whom you believe might not be inherently evil?"

"That . . ." Drizzt stopped before he started, caught in the psionicist's trap.

"What is religion based upon?" Kimmuriel asked again, sharply.

"Fear," said Drizzt.

"See? We agree. It is based upon the fear of death and what might or might not come afterward. Take that away, and churches would be no more than mediators of commonwealth, if that. The gods of Toril promise power or riches or sublime comfort, even unbridled sexual gratification, in exchange for worship. They command us with threat or with pleasure, but only because we fear that we have so much to lose elsewise."

"That's why you came out here," Drizzt said. "To be truly free."

"Yes," said Kimmuriel. "I have lived for centuries, hiding away in the hive mind or in a library, trying to make sense of that which, ultimately, I cannot, for these destinations can only be answered when the road is finally traveled. But now I believe that I have come to the limit of my potential understanding of this unknowable matter until that final journey."

"And so you have escaped the fear."

"I have. Gone now is the coercive power of the gods, the terror of their warnings, the allure of their promises. Now I can see the world as it truly is before me, and make my decisions as best serves my own sensibility."

"Like with the coming events in Menzoberranzan. Kimmuriel knows which side he will fight with, then?"

"I do, if I choose to fight at all. I am just trying to decide if it is worth the effort."

That notion initially struck Drizzt oddly. If Kimmuriel knew which side was right and which wrong, did it really matter if the notion of some eternal reward lay in the balance?

Really, though, Drizzt now understood that he believed the same. Yes, he tried to do good in the world and for the sake of the world, for the sake of community and those he loved. But if he didn't believe in something beyond this life, would he be so quick to sacrifice his remaining moments of consciousness, of existence itself, for just those external rewards?

Yes, he would, he knew, and had thus lived his life, even surrounded by the doubts and the fears.

"It is worth the effort," he asserted to the psionicist standing before him, an intellectual who lived too much in the realm of the mind and not enough in the realm of the heart.

"I know you believe that."

Drizzt held up his hands, not about to deny it.

"And I hope you are right. And that's why I ask the questions I do. Who knows, my friend, perhaps we will soon stand side by side on the streets of Menzoberranzan, doing mortal battle against those who decide to remain in the thrall of the Spider Queen."

"In that event, can I count on Kimmuriel to stand with me no matter the odds?"

"You ask a lot," Kimmuriel replied, but then he flashed a rare smile and went back inside the monastery.

Yes, Drizzt mused, he was glad that Kimmuriel and the others had come out to join him on this journey.

THAT NIGHT, AFTER BRIE HAD GONE TO SLEEP, DRIZZT wandered out onto the back porch of the monastery and into the darkened yard so that he could bask in the starlight. His talk with Kimmuriel had given him hope, both for the psionicist and for his people and their coming great struggle. There were many drow of similar heart to his own, he knew without doubt. The vast majority of them, likely. They had been smothered by a demon goddess, but now the veil of darkness had been pulled back.

Would he go to Menzoberranzan for the fight that was surely to come? A big part of him wanted no involvement with any of this. Not now. He wanted to focus on his family. On their future, together. For so long, he had battled for the good of the wider world and now, perhaps, he was due his rest.

But this current situation was the crystallization of that which he had most wanted in all the struggles of his life. This could be his greatest contribution to his kin and his homeland. It could secure that future he hoped for.

Or it could be his death. And all for a cause that had little chance. Lolth would not let Menzoberranzan go without a terrific and terrible fight.

He lay on the leafy ground and let the millions of spots of light in the sky lift him up among them, as he had done so many times before.

Some time later, he headed back into the monastery. He stopped by Brie's room to check on her, then made his way to the small meditation chapel reserved for the masters, where he expected he'd find Grandmaster Kane. It was a simple place, with four benches set along the rim of a shallow pit, the whole of it open to the sky. At the bottom was a garden, mostly grass, but with a few flowers bringing color about its edges. The middle of it was an X formed of white stones of various shapes and sizes.

Kane was staring at that X, sitting up on a bench, his legs tightly crossed beneath him.

"They are leaving in the morning," Drizzt told him, and he nodded. "Kimmuriel is quite grateful to you."

"He seeks answers."

"He feels that he has learned a lot."

"He seeks answers to questions that cannot be answered in this life."

"He understands that," Drizzt assured the Grandmaster.

"I know. What he seeks most of all is a place where his understanding of the physical truths about him coincides with the hopes for the next part of the journey within him. If I gave him some valuable insights into his own heart, or some comfort against his fears, then I have done a good thing."

"Again, you have my thanks for agreeing to speak with him."

"I owe you the thanks, Drizzt," Kane replied. "You have granted me the opportunity to do a good deed in the world, and that is no small thing." Kane went back to staring at the stones set below.

"Will you leave with them?" the monk asked a few heartbeats later.

"I hope to stay longer."

"You can stay forever, of course. This is your home if you ever wish it to be."

Drizzt gave a quick bow of respect, although Kane wasn't looking at him.

"Have Jarlaxle's associates heard from him? From Catti-brie?"

"No," Drizzt answered. "Which surprises me, I admit."

"And worries you."

"It does."

"You know not how far they went? The northernmost north?"

Drizzt held up his hands.

"If so," Kane continued, "then they might find that magic is not quite the same up there."

"You've been there?"

"I've been to the northern reaches of the Great Glacier. Even beyond them. I was with Olwen Forest-friend on that occasion, a ranger of great reputation and power, and a disciple of Mielikki. His magical spells didn't work as powerfully up there, I recall, and even Treefeller, Olwen's axe, felt unwieldy to him. Perhaps it was just the cold wind chattering his teeth and numbing his fingers."

"But you don't believe that," Drizzt surmised.

"It was different up there, as it is in the Underdark. If they are in the farthest north, then they might be discovering that old things do not work as they believed, and might well discover many new things in their place."

He went back to staring at the X of stones then, and Drizzt did, too, falling within himself. He didn't find Kane's words comforting. Magic was the crux of Catti-brie's power, after all.

Kane did not seem to notice when he chuckled a moment later, as he reminded himself that what he was going through now was something he had put his beloved Catti-brie through on more than one occasion over the last couple of years. How she had stayed within her wits when he had gone to the deep Underdark, he did not know!

Trust her, he reminded himself. *Trust* in *her*. Catti-brie was among the most resourceful and powerful individuals he had ever known. And she was with Jarlaxle, who befriended dragons and toyed with kings.

And with them, too, were Zaknafein and Entreri, and Drizzt didn't doubt their loyalty to him, to Catti-brie, to the Companions of the Hall. Or their skill as warriors.

She is okay, he told himself, repeating it like a mantra as he fell deeper within himself through the peaceful image of the white stones, lit by the stars and a half-moon hanging in the sky above, shining a bit brighter than the dark garden that held them.

CHAPTER 13

Eleint the Fading

I t would make a fine traveling companion," Catti-brie argued when her suggestion had been met with head shakes and grumbles. She had awakened to find that she was a bit colder than she had been the night before. She conjured their breakfast magically, creating enough food to keep the bellies of ten large dwarves from growling the whole of the day.

But it should have been half again that amount.

"A companion that would turn on us the moment you let down your guard," Jarlaxle countered.

"I won't, and it won't be a powerful beast, in any case. Just a minor elemental to cut a path before us, to melt the ice that might take our feet out from under us." And to help keep the chill out of the air, she thought, but did not add.

Jarlaxle turned his gaze to Zak and Entreri, the weapon master responding with a shrug, Entreri hardly seeming to care either way, except to say, "Even with your damned ring, this cold wind is rooting in my bones."

Jarlaxle held up his hands in surrender. "All right, then," he agreed, and he motioned for Zak to move to the open ground between them and the small lake at the base of the towering glacier.

With a shrug, the weapon master complied, drawing the empty sword hilt from his belt. He fidgeted with it in his hand, closed his eyes, and called upon its power, flicking his wrist and bringing forth not the blade of light, but the whip of flame.

He rolled its length in the air before him, studying it for a few moments, then looked to his companions. "A large tear?" he asked, and not for the first time.

"The best you can manage," Catti-brie replied.

Over his head rolled the whip, and Zak snapped it hard before him, drawing a bright line in the air, dripping fire. He looked to Catti-brie, though, showing her a frown.

Catti-brie understood his consternation, for she, too, had recognized that the whip wasn't quite as formidable as it had previously seemed. Like her healing spell the previous night or the conjured meal, the whip's fires seemed somehow lesser, diminished.

"Let that one vanish," Zak prompted. "Tell me when you're ready, and I'll cut it deeper."

"Do it," Catti-brie replied, walking up beside him.

He rolled the whip out before him, cracking it in the air once, twice, thrice in rapid succession, each time calling forth the deeper powers of the enchantment to cut tears into the Plane of Fire.

Catti-brie lifted her open hand before her face, looking through her fingers at the small tears, three thin, short lines of what looked like floating lava. She reached into her ring, calling to the fiery plane, trying to bring forth an elemental.

She reached one, felt its strange sentience, connected to it, and forced it to move to the tear.

A wall of denial, of anger—a stream of invective she could not understand—struck her, along with a sudden blast of cold, cold wind.

"What?" she asked to no one, fully by reflex, and she lowered her hand and looked at the wavering lines of magma, the small drips of flame falling to the ground before them, landing and coalescing as they tried to form into a singular living being of flame.

Tried, and struggled, to little avail, much of the magma hardening almost immediately to dead black rock.

The ground began to shake beneath the companions, a sudden rolling rumble, followed by a sharp sound from the glacial wall to their left and high above.

Catti-brie felt the unbridled anger through her ring, but it wasn't coming from the failing fire elemental—in fact, she felt that being's fear and loathing, though neither was aimed at her.

No, this was bigger, stronger, a level of indecipherable power and outrage she had known only once before in her life.

"Run," she told her friends, and she backed up a few steps. She shook her head. It could not be . . .

"Run!" she said again, turning and sprinting off directly away from the towering glacial wall.

"You cannot control it?" she heard Jarlaxle calling as he rushed to keep up with her, and she realized that he was speaking of the fire elemental.

Another rumble knocked her off balance and nearly sent her tumbling.

Then came a deafening and long cracking sound, and she didn't dare look back or slow her stride.

"By the gods," she heard Entreri gasp, and now she did glance back.

The ground shook; the glacier calved, fissures appearing down the sides of a large jag in its facing, then the whole of it sliding down, striking the ground with tremendous force and falling forward, crashing over the town, shattering the buildings nearest the ice wall, burying the magma lines, extinguishing whatever being of fire had come through Zak's tear in the Material Plane.

Catti-brie was on the ground, and she was not alone. Only Jarlaxle remained upright, the clever rogue with an answer for everything enacting a levitation spell and getting just above the rolling, shaking, quaking stones. A great rush of bits of ice, water, and wind washed over the four.

Then it was quiet, settled, and the air cleared, revealing a gigantic chunk of ice half in, half out of the small lake, one that would have buried them all where they stood had Catti-brie not heard the threat and reacted.

"What do you know?" Jarlaxle asked her, helping her to her feet.

Her eyes never left the towering wall of ice.

"The glacier," she mumbled. "It is alive."

"Alive?"

"Maegera," she said. "Like Maegera."

"I take it that it didn't like my whip," Zak said dryly.

"Or my call to the realm of fire," Catti-brie replied.

They collected themselves and headed off with all speed, moving up out of the valley on the wall opposite the one they had descended to get here. Once they got far enough away, they paused and rested, looking back at the now-distant town and glacier.

"We should be far from that ice," Entreri remarked.

"But if Doum'wielle is alive, she is in there," Catti-brie admitted, and she felt the surprised stares of the others upon her.

A long while passed.

"The glacier? Well, how do you propose we get in there?" Entreri asked sourly, at the same time that Jarlaxle asked, "Are you sure?"

Catti-brie pondered that for a few moments, then shook her head. "It is a guess," she admitted. "But that's what I felt. And if she is in the glacier, or perhaps beyond the glacier, she is still far away, I believe."

"Then what do we do?" Entreri asked, his voice growing sharper with frustration with each unanswered question.

Jarlaxle moved to the mountain wall at the side of the trail, cast his levitation, and climbed up the wall.

"The glacier goes a long way," he called down from his high perch. "Beyond this last line of mountains and out onto the ice pack. Let us get down there and move alongside it. We'll use Khazid'hea often, and so perhaps we'll know when we pass Doum'wielle."

"*If* we pass Doum'wielle," Entreri corrected, too quietly for Jarlaxle to hear.

Catti-brie looked at the man and wanted to scold him for his pessimism, but in this instance, she thought that sentiment rather appropriate.

They picked their way along the mountainsides, roughly paralleling the glacier, and the sun still circled them, spying on them, hour after hour, and through the next day, though it seemed to be lower in the sky now than when they had first arrived in the far north, tendays before. During those hours when it went behind the mountains, the air was now dark enough for them to see stars above. Dull, but visible.

That brought a sobering notion to Catti-brie as she considered her years in Icewind Dale. The days there were long in the summer, but very short in the winter.

She didn't know the precise date, but certainly they were well into the ninth month, Eleint, now, with the autumnal equinox approaching.

Eleint the Fading, it was called.

The sun's continual stalk of them had been maddening indeed, but the woman wondered if she and her companions would soon miss it sorely.

She shuddered against the thought—or maybe the shudder was against the cold north wind cutting into her bones up here on the open mountain heights. Cold enough to bite through the magical protection she wore, which should have shielded her better than any clothing, any number of fur layers, she could possibly wear.

She shuddered again, and this time knew that shiver's source to be her fears of what would happen once that sun went below the horizon, once the northern night fell.

They had some cover from the howling wind as they descended along the last rocky trail heading down toward the icy plain. To their left, the mountains continued beyond sight; to their right a cliff, and when the trail bent slightly, they could see, too, beyond the mountain wall, the towering side of the massive glacier, which now seemed to Catti-brie like a sleeping giant white serpent stretched out long upon the ice and using the mountains to rest its head.

They crossed from the stone to the ice pack and continued on. At one point, Jarlaxle used the directional orb, but the mercenary, after several tries, just tossed it back into his pouch. He, it, could not determine which way was north, for some reason. Still, they pressed on, moving along the ice pack, the towering glacial wall barely a few hundred yards to their right. Wind-whipped bits of ice nipped at them with every step.

At one point, Jarlaxle brought forth his nightmare, bidding Entreri to do the same, and the four went up and galloped along.

But only for a short while, before one of the hellsteeds, Jarlaxle's this time, began to buck and snort and turn in protest, its magic quickly waning.

Jarlaxle dismissed the steed, Entreri following suit.

"We have to get farther away from that thing," a shivering Entreri said as he replaced the figurine in his belt pouch. He nodded his chin at the towering wall of ice.

"You think it's the glacier causing this?" Jarlaxle was also rubbing his hands briskly together. "You think it is attacking us?"

"No," Catti-brie answered before Entreri could. When the others all looked at her, she continued, "I don't sense its presence, and I doubt that it could know where we are, even."

"It threw a wall of ice at us," Entreri reminded her.

"Not at us," Catti-brie corrected. "At the tear into the Plane of Fire. It didn't much like the intrusion. I felt its surprise and anger keenly. I do not feel that malice now when I focus on my ring."

"So, it's an ice primordial?" Entreri asked. "Or a god of coldness?"

"I don't know," Catti-brie admitted. "I think it is a powerful elemental being of some sort, or that there is one within the glacier. I've never heard of an ice primordial, but I had never heard of a fire primordial until we went into Gauntlgrym. What I felt back in the town was a primal reaction to the fire."

"We had a fire going before that, with no complaints from the glacier," Jarlaxle pointed out.

"But not a tear into the Plane of Fire," Zak reasoned, and he pulled the hilt from his belt. "Ready your ring and let us see what we may," he said to Catti-brie, then he called upon the blade of light.

Zak's expression showed his surprise when the sword ignited, for it seemed meager indeed, almost like a thinner short sword or a long, narrow dagger than the weapon he had brought forth previously. He rolled it about in his hand and changed it from sword to whip, and again, the weapon seemed a pale reflection of its previous power.

Determinedly, Zak cracked the whip repeatedly, trying to cut a tear.

But no more than a few wispy fingers of flame extended from it. There was no planar rift left behind in the air.

The weapon master looked to Catti-brie, who shook her head. "I felt no connection to the fire plane, and no recourse from the glacier."

"It broke your weapon?" Entreri asked.

"No, maybe it's more than that." Catti-brie was sure of it, though she couldn't yet articulate her feelings.

"Whatever it is, it's getting too cold out here even for our magic," Jarlaxle said. He removed his hat and pulled out the small circular piece of black cloth. "Let's get some shelter from this wind, warm our toes, and figure out how to proceed." He tossed the cloth down to the ice pack, thinking to make a hole for them to crawl into, but the cloth just landed and lay there. Not elongating, not creating a portal.

It seemed no more than a piece of unremarkable velvet.

The wind picked it up and started to blow it away, and only Entreri's quick reaction to snatch it from the air prevented the loss of one of Jarlaxle's most coveted toys.

"What was that?" Entreri asked, but Jarlaxle stood there, hands on hips, staring dumbfounded at the wall.

"First the directional orb, then the nightmares, then the sun blade, now your portable hole," Entreri remarked.

"No," Catti-brie corrected. "First my spells." She looked at Zak and pointed to his shoulder. "The last healing spell I cast upon you."

"It worked," he reminded her.

"It did, but it felt . . . strange. The magic here is somewhat altered—perhaps it is the sun and the cold, the pale light. I don't know. But now I feel it is more than altered, and is, perhaps leaving." She looked Jarlaxle in the eye. "We should go home."

His jaw tightened. He shook his head and, very uncharacteristically, seemed ready to cry out in rage.

"And it's getting colder," said Zak.

"No," said Catti-brie. "It's not getting colder around us. Our magical protection is weakening."

Jarlaxle reached into his pouch and brought forth a piece of kindling. "We are not yet defeated," he told them. "Let us find some shelter and start a fire."

But Catti-brie shook her head. She took a deep breath and put the thumb and forefinger of her right hand over the ring on her left, the ring of elemental protection Jarlaxle had given her.

"If I remove it, will I once again have to acclimate to it?" she asked the rogue.

"What are you doing?" Entreri asked.

"I want to measure how much protection these items are actually offering us," she explained. "Can I put it right back on and realize the magic of it?"

"Yes," Jarlaxle said, "you are attuned to its power."

Catti-brie took a deep breath, then slipped the ring off. Her eyes widened and she gasped, then slid it right back on.

"Shelter and fire won't be nearly enough to sustain us if this magic fails completely. We have to be out of here right now," she said. "The ring is functioning, but not as before."

"We have come so far to abandon it all," Jarlaxle argued.

"We haven't gone anywhere," Entreri noted.

"You come with me or I leave you behind," Catti-brie warned, her tone offering no room for debate. She held out her hands and stared down the other three, Entreri and Zak looking to Jarlaxle for leadership here.

Catti-brie didn't flinch, didn't blink, and didn't lower her hands. "We have failed," she said. "And this is no death I want."

Zak broke ranks first, grabbing her hand and holding his other out to Jarlaxle, who hesitated. But when Entreri took her other hand, the frustrated drow had no choice but to concede. He took the offered hands, completing the ring, and Catti-brie cast her most powerful spell, one she had prepared extensively and fastidiously before they began their journey. This was the true escape, a dweomer to put them back in Longsaddle.

A word of recall.

Nothing happened.

Catti-brie stared blankly ahead. She knew the magic was weakening, but for this spell to have failed completely . . .

"Gods," Entreri breathed.

"We need to find shelter," Jarlaxle said. "Now."

They moved as quickly as they could manage, angling toward the glacial wall to see if perhaps there were any caves or crevices to be found.

After some time, Entreri spotted one. He directed them straight toward the massive glacier and a huge rift along its side.

"Doesn't seem like the best idea," Zak remarked.

"Do we have a choice?" Entreri countered.

"Go," Catti-brie told them, trying to lift fast-sagging spirits. "We'll be all right. Perhaps it was the cold that caused me to stutter or somehow else defeated my spell. Out of the wind will be better."

Off they went, moving faster across the ice pack now that they had a destination in sight, the glacier looming higher, higher. They slowed as they neared, with the giant river of ice towering hundreds of feet above them, the rift some thirty feet across and running from the base all the way to the top, open to the sky.

They went in tentatively, and felt some relief immediately as the wind diminished around them. But not enough for them to make a fire, and not enough for them to survive for much longer. They had no choice but to go in deeper, a hundred strides, two hundred.

"It's getting warmer," a surprised Zaknafein observed.

"The walls of ice are acting as a blanket for us," Entreri offered.

"No," came Catti-brie's correction from behind, and when the other three turned, they found the woman holding her protective ring in her hand, having removed it yet again. "This is more than that."

"How cold are you?" a surprised Zaknafein asked.

"Chilly, not cold," Entreri answered for her, for he, too, had removed his ring. He looked to Jarlaxle. "What is this place?"

"I know not. Is the beast warm on the inside?"

They went on and found a second surprise when the floor of the rift became a shallow puddle, then turned from ice to soil, hard at first like the tundra, but even that changing as they continued.

They heard the water running before they came upon it, a small stream flowing before them at a T-shaped intersection in the rift. The tunnel widened considerably in both directions, with enough solid and dry ground for them to walk along either side of the small stream, which was about as wide as a drow was tall. Steam wafted off the flowing water.

Entreri was the first to bend, gingerly tapping and then dipping his hand into the water. "Warm," he told them, pulling his hand back out. "Hot, even."

Catti-brie, Jarlaxle, and Entreri stopped there for a bit to take in the unexpected channel, while Zaknafein ran off to the left, deeper into the glacier, to scout.

"We should eat," Jarlaxle said, and reached into his belt pouch. His hand went in only a very short way, hitting the bottom. Jarlaxle's eyes widened in shock.

"What?" Entreri asked.

"The pouch, the food. I cannot access it."

Catti-brie began to cast a spell, a quick one, and when she finished with nothing to show for it, she shook her head grimly at the others. "I cannot summon any food. I hear no magic, no words of Mielikki, no songs of Mystra's Weave."

"Here!" they heard Zak's voice, and turned to see him at the beginning of a bend in the corridor, waving them to him.

Around that corner, the open-air passage became a high-ceilinged tunnel, but only for a short distance before it opened again to the sky, and to a wider chamber, the stream flowing along its right-hand side, and the rest of it, perhaps a quarter acre of land, covered in grass and flowers, and bushes full of berries.

And bees, buzzing happily and noticing the newcomers not at all.

"By the gods," Catti-brie whispered.

"What is this place?" Artemis Entreri asked again, but no one could find the breath, let alone the words, to answer him.

WHEN SHE AWAKENED AFTER A LONG AND COMFORTABLE sleep, Catti-brie had to spend a few moments to remind herself yet again that this was real. The flowers were real, the insects were real, and the blueberries and raspberries and strawberries were real.

And the warmth was real, here, in this place, hemmed in by mountainous walls of ice! And with a howling wind just beyond that would freeze her solid in short moments.

As her thoughts and senses came fully into the present, the first thing she noticed, looking straight up to the open sky high above, was how much dimmer the light seemed. She nodded, understanding. The long winter nights were coming. Would there even be a daytime?

"Shh," Jarlaxle said, sitting nearby, and she turned her head to glance at him. He motioned for her to sit up and look across the way.

She went up on her elbows, then, taken by the sight, and sat up slowly, making no sudden movements. A family of white foxes was over at the widest part of the flowing water. One adult sat watching, the other drinking, while three kits rolled in the grass and dirt along the bank.

"They've seen us and seem not to care," Jarlaxle whispered.

"They probably have no experience with people," Catti-brie whispered back. The canids were no more than twenty strides away. She thought to prepare some spells of animal friendship or communication, that she might use these intelligent little predators to get a sense of the area, but she didn't need those spells to understand that the foxes seemed perfectly at ease in here, and that they were familiar with this chamber.

Besides, she was pretty sure the magic wouldn't work, despite the obviously enchanted nature of this place.

Two of the kits continued to tumble about, but the third noticed them then, and began to approach curiously, though not cautiously. It halved the distance quickly, and the watching adult seemed to take note, but merely yawned.

Catti-brie felt the eyes of her companions upon her but could only offer a shrug in response. The kit kept coming, and began yipping. The adult foxes seemed not to care. The other two kits began rambling toward the unexpected visitors.

The first kit went right up to Catti-brie's feet and sniffed, then jumped upon one foot and began wrestling and gnawing.

"Domesticated?" Jarlaxle asked.

"By whom?" Entreri asked.

"By them," answered Catti-brie, who was at the end of the line, nearest the tunnel from which they had entered this chamber, and so looking past her friends and deeper into the rift. She sucked in her breath, her eyes unblinking.

The others slowly turned about.

Five figures stood at the far entrance of the chamber, strangely dressed in shiny black skintight suits that seemed to be a single piece of clothing, feet to collar, and with a cloak lined in thick white fur, very much like that of the fox family who had come into the chamber.

Each of the newcomers carried a handcrossbow at the ready, and that clue led Catti-brie to look more closely, to confirm what her eyes had shown right away but her mind had pushed aside due to the sheer strangeness, the alien nature, of their outfits.

They were drow.

CHAPTER 14

Where the Hot Springs Flow

W e have no magic, few weapons," Catti-brie whispered to her friends, lifting her hands in surrender. She stared in disbelief, for these were indeed drow, without doubt, in hair color and the varying hues of skin color, all with that dusky gray base. A patrol from Menzoberranzan would have appeared no different, except for the outfits they wore and the swords and short spears they carried. The material of these blades was not familiar to Catti-brie, for they were white, or bluish white, and one even shone fully blue. She couldn't really tell from this distance, but they looked more like ice than metal, somewhat translucent—or perhaps, she thought, it was some type of glassteel. She started slowly toward the newcomers, her hands raised and empty.

The other three companions, all sitting, made no move, just stared at the unexpected drow.

The fox family, though, went running at the sight, but not away. Yipping and barking, they rushed for the drow, the adults bounding up before them and skidding to a stop, sitting excitedly, one lifting a paw and patting at the air.

The figure farthest from the companions turned back to the tunnel and began signaling with his hands.

Zaknafein, who was closest to the newcomers, began moving his fingers to mimic the strange drow.

"He is calling to and for others," Jarlaxle whispered to Catti-brie.

"We should run," Entreri whispered.

"Back out into the cold?" Catti-brie said openly. "We'll die."

The sound of her voice had five handcrossbows coming up at them as one. One of the nearer drow asked, "How did you get here?"

It took Catti-brie a moment to understand the words. She recognized the language immediately as Drow, but it sounded to her quite different from the language spoken in Menzoberranzan in both dialect and syntax, and with one word she did not recognize at all. Frighteningly, the syntax reminded her of that used by the slaad creature masquerading as a drow in the cave they had taken as their first shelter in the northland.

"They know the silent hand language," Jarlaxle whispered so that his nearby companions could hear. "Could a giant frog even do that?"

"Yet they sound like the other one," Catti-brie replied in similarly quiet tones.

"If that monster thought it was fooling actual drow of this land, wouldn't it?"

"Tell them nothing of the fight in the cave," Entreri whispered. "Nothing."

"How did you get here?" the drow man asked again, more insistently.

"Well met," Jarlaxle answered in the drow tongue, using his most charming and gracious voice, as if they were old friends. "We came in to get out of the cold, nothing more."

"Keep talking," the nearest of the newcomers prompted.

"We would have died out there. We were surprised to find it warm in here, but without it . . ." Jarlaxle let it hang there with a shrug.

"That is not what we have asked from you. How did you come to this region in the first place?"

"We've been hiking for tendays, looking for a long-lost associate."

"It's been cold for tendays," the doubting interrogator replied. Catti-brie noted that his features were perhaps a bit less angular than those of most of the drow she had known. His white hair showed highlights of soft lavender and hung shoulder length, pulled back from his face. His eyes shone red. "You are hardly dressed for the wind and snow."

"Their magic failed," put in another of the group, a woman with long, thick white hair tied up on one side and set with a shining blue pin. The others nodded.

"You were protected, and now you are not," the first said to Jarlaxle.

"Nor could we get to our supplies," Jarlaxle confirmed, putting a hand into his belt pouch. "This, too, is enchanted." He looked around. "I am sorry, but yes, we took some of the bounty we found here in this place. We did not know that this land was claimed."

"It is of no concern."

"We would leave, but we'll die, surely."

The drow questioner looked to his companions and shared nods, and they lowered their handcrossbows. Others came around the corner then, and still more rappelled down the sides of the glacier walls to land at the ready in the exit tunnel.

"Who are you?" he asked Jarlaxle, then pointed to the mercenary and clarified, "You alone."

The rogue stood slowly, showing his hands all the while, then dipped a polite bow. "I am known as Jarlaxle."

"I am Emilian," the drow replied.

"Well met."

He gave a slight nod, nothing more. Unsurprisingly, the five seemed more focused on Catti-brie and Entreri than on their two fellow drow, a trio whispering among themselves.

"What is she?" Emilian asked, indicating Catti-brie.

"A woman."

"Clearly, but *darthirii? Kitrye?* And he? *Kitrye,* yes?"

"Humans, both," Catti-brie answered, for she understood Emilian's references, asking if she and Artemis Entreri were elven or half-elven.

"Humans?" Emilian remarked, clearly confused. "Never have I

seen humans who look like this. His skin is too brown, and she too tall."

"Southerners, then," said the drow woman standing beside Emilian.

"Yes, the south, from here, at least," Jarlaxle answered, and he shot Catti-brie a look begging her to let him do the talking here. "She is from beyond the Sea of Moving Ice, he from much farther, from the lands of hot sands and high sun."

"You are a long way from home," said the drow woman.

"A long-lost associate, you said," Emilian prompted.

"Yes. Well, an associate," Jarlaxle corrected. "A woman, half drow, half elf."

"Her name?"

"She was called Doum—"

"Doum'wielle," Emilian finished for him. "Little Doe."

Catti-brie gasped. "My god, the sword was right. She is alive."

"How do you speak our language?" Emilian asked.

"I speak common Drow," she said. "It is only slightly different from your . . ."

"What you call common Drow is polluted with the sounds of the lower planes," the woman drow told her. "Our distant kin have long lived near to other races in the deep Underdark, and thus, their language has changed."

"If you know Little Doe, then you know that we are not enemies," Jarlaxle said.

"Doum'wielle was an enemy when first we met," Emilian replied sharply. "You'll find no Queen of Spiders here."

"Good," Zak and Entreri both said together, and both blew heavy sighs of relief.

"I'm not going back into the dungeon of a drow priestess," Entreri quietly added. "I'll die here first."

"This is Catti-brie," Jarlaxle explained, and he wagged his hand to silence Entreri. "Perhaps you have heard of her, or of her husband, Drizzt Do'Urden."

Emilian looked around, but all of them just shook their heads. "He is aevendrow?" Emilian asked.

"Aevendrow?" Catti-brie echoed.

"Evening," Jarlaxle told her. "Starlight drow, aevendrow."

Catti-brie and the others spent a long moment letting that digest, Catti-brie staring at Jarlaxle and measuring him. A lot of the previous puzzles were beginning to make sense to her here, but this wasn't the place to throw her accusations.

"I am a priestess, but not of Lolth," Catti-brie said. "Hardly of Lolth. My goddess is Mielikki." She took a chance here with the admission, but if these people were living in such obvious harmony with such a brutal environment, there was a chance that they at least knew of the goddess of nature. "The Forest Queen."

Their expressions and nods told her that she might have hit on a positive thing here.

"I'd call to her for you," she continued, "but she doesn't seem to hear me right now."

"I am Ilina," the woman said. "Your magic has diminished because of Twilight Autunn. The day is ending, the night begins. In this transition, the air will fill with magic of its own making. There is no room for the whispers of your gods or the enchantments of the ancient Weave of Mystra. Even the dragons will not take wing for the next tenday. After that, your magic will slowly return to you."

"Dragons? Lovely," Entreri muttered.

"In that case, if we may indulge your patience, we will remain—right here, if you please—until then, when we take our leave," Jarlaxle said. "And if possible, perhaps we might bring Doum'wielle with us."

"No," said Emilian. "You will not remain here. As to your leaving, that remains a question for others to answer."

"And Doum'wielle?" Catti-brie asked.

"Shed your weapons," Emilian answered without answering. "All of them, and come along."

The companions looked to each other doubtfully, but they really had no choice. Without magic, without Taulmaril and Guenhwyvar and the sun blade and their hellsteeds—without all of Jarlaxle's toys—they had little chance of fighting their way out of there, and where might they go, in any case?

In silent accord, they stood up and placed their weapons on the ground. Surrounded by a dozen of the drow, weapons drawn, they started off soon after, deeper into the glacial rift.

Catti-brie took some hope when they departed, for Ilina and another of the group stayed behind and were feeding and playing with the family of foxes.

The joy of the play was unlike anything she remembered from her short time in Menzoberranzan.

PART 3

CALLIDAE

What a powerful force is this fascination with, this fear of, death. How could it not be so for a reasoning, mortal creature? Mortal in this form, at least.

We are groomed from childhood, or perhaps it is even innate in any logical being, to prepare for the future, to take actions that will lead us to the place we believe we wish to be. The gods of Faerun have made their positions of power based upon this! For the ultimate future for us all, we know, is not in this short life, but in whatever might come next, if anything (and if nothing, that is perhaps the cruelest possibility).

Yet, how can we properly prepare other than to give ourselves to a matter of faith? We seek evidence—I have found great hints in my journey of transcendence—and yet that which we can see as such remains hints and little more. This is the ultimate mystery of life, the greatest of all.

My journey with Kimmuriel has surprised me in a most wonderful way. To see him, the most emotionless person I have ever known, drawn into such discussions of purpose and place, of the point of life and the hopes of what might come next, was more than unexpected. It was shocking, nothing less.

There is no question of Kimmuriel's brilliance. He often resides in the vast library of the illithid hive mind, his consciousness flitting effortlessly among the memories and conclusions of that vast repertoire of experience and history. He has mastered a magic very different from that of priestesses like Catti-brie, a spellpower irrelative to the notion of divinity. He has mastered a magic very different from that of Gromph, for Kimmuriel's is also a spellpower independent of the Weave, the elemental powers, the harnessing of natural energies. His magic is purely intellectual, purely a matter of controlling his own thoughts and emotions and using that intellectual force as a weapon or a thief's tool.

Yet here he was beside me, acceding to my demands without questions, revealing his own vulnerabilities in the form of his hopes and fears as he tries to unravel this greatest of mysteries.

And more than that, I watched him bringing that journey back beyond his personal mind space and to the world around him, including responsibility to community above his responsibility to self—that he is even considering joining in the coming fight for Menzoberranzan for altruistic and moral motivations is something I could never have anticipated. Not from Kimmuriel, whose journey surprises me more than that of Jarlaxle. Jarlaxle's heart was always hinted at in his actions, whatever other excuse he might make for his consistent generosity and caring. Kimmuriel's revelations here surprise me more than the journey I have seen in Artemis Entreri, whose path had to lead him through personal darkness, his own inability to look into a mirror and not be horrified by the reflection. For Entreri was as much victim as villain.

It surprises me even more than the journey of Dab'nay, or that which I am hoping is real within the Matron Mother of Menzoberranzan and the other "true" devotees of the horrid Demon Queen of Spiders. While I suspect, and not without evidence, that much of these doubts regarding the Lolthian clergy is also unintentionally in the service of Lolth, a demonic goddess who values strife and chaos above all else, I am convinced that those who have now seen the awful truth of Lolth will never go back, indeed, will die before reverting.

Watching the spiritual journeys of all these others, including my own wife, is a powerful reminder to me to ever hold tolerance for those who come to different conclusions than I, and to humble myself in my conclusions.

For much of my life, I have envied those who have found their answer, their savior, their planned and expected afterlife. I do not say that in any condescending manner, or with any thought at all that because I am not at the same place as those people, I am somehow better or more informed or more correct than they. For what I have understood from the beginning is that this place of faith, this understanding of the multiverse and the continuation of self beyond the mortal coil, is not something one can reach by power of will, or reason. It happens or it does not. It is an epiphany or it is not. I'm not talking about those who follow a religion simply out of tradition, but of those who truly believe.

Thus, when I say that I envied those who have had their epiphany, I mean it, for I long awaited my own. Now I have found it. At the very least, I have come to understand that there was for me, albeit temporarily, something more, something grander, something freeing—freeing from the fascination and fear of the ultimate conclusion.

Long ago, I proclaimed my freedom because I knew that I would one day die. That certainty reminded me to grab at every sunrise and sunset, to appreciate the things so many take for granted.

Now I am freer still, because I have had my epiphany.

And now I feel even more certain in my agnosticism because I find myself joined by Kimmuriel, a drow of great intellect and great scholarship.

—Drizzt Do'Urden

CHAPTER 15

The Aevendrow

T his cavern is called Cascatte," Ilina explained to Catti-brie and the others as they came up over a rise and into a large chamber that was mostly covered by an ice shelf, but with much of the area open to the sky to allow in enough of the meager daylight to convey Cascatte's size and majesty.

The cavern was multitiered, full of blue-white ice formations, the most spectacular of which were the frozen waterfalls, some wide and with thin fans of ice, others narrow and matted to stone walls. It seemed to Catti-brie like a mountain cavern in the spring melt, water bursting from the stones but then flash-frozen, locked in time as if the scene were an artist's rendering.

It was colder in here than in the previous area, where the hot spring was more central and dominant, but not brutally so. It warmed comfortably as their hosts led them to the wider floor, where one area was not icy and cold at all, but had that stream running, banks lined with growth—flowers, mostly. Wisps of fog lifted off the warm water, creating a blurriness that sharply contrasted with the crispness of the view from the higher vantage point. Peering past the icy formations, glistening pillars of frozen water, stalagmites of dark rock and blue ice, and fans of waterfalls, Catti-brie noted other lights—home fires, and even a structure or two.

"Just a few families live here," Ilina explained, and even as she finished speaking some dogs began to bark. Echoes came at them from every direction. Or perhaps it was more dogs answering. Catti-brie could not be sure. The entire chamber seemed to be alive with the calls, the music.

The group moved around a procession of stalagmites near the chamber's left-hand wall. It opened abruptly to the right and the four companions from the southlands were treated to yet another strange sight and shocking surprise. Under the roof of a waterfall fan sat a small cottage of wood and stone. It had a front yard, fenced in with spaced wooden pickets, that was stone near the house, but then more soil and then, nearest them, a long and narrow garden.

"We should have brought Pikel," Jarlaxle mumbled, and Catti-brie nearly giggled, thinking that yes, the druid dwarf would have loved this sight, particularly the way the garden had been set to perfectly catch reflections of the daylight off of various sheets of sparkling ice.

She was about to say that to Jarlaxle when she looked up and even better understood why the rogue had thought of the unusual dwarf. For standing before her on the small porch of the house was a family of dwarves more unusual still—if they even were dwarves! At first she thought them all children, for they were diminutive, shorter than Regis, even, and only one of them had a beard, albeit a small one, to go along with a twisting mustache.

"Dwarves?" she asked, gasped, more than stated.

"Inugaakalikurit," Ilina explained.

"The what?" Zaknafein asked.

"Or the kurit, if you will, if that longer name ties your tongue."

"So dwarves."

Paler than a field of fresh snow, with pinched faces and curly white hair, the folk had the muscles and thick limbs of Delzoun dwarves, to be sure, but with their short frames, they seemed as wide as they were tall. And despite all of that strangeness, the prominent features on each of the five standing before them were their huge eyes, so blue— bright blue, almost glowing from within.

"Yes."

"Then why not call them that?"

"That is what they call themselves," said Ilina.

"What do you call them?" Zak asked.

"I call that one Kanaq," the drow woman said with a laugh. "Because that's his name."

"A'aha'ile, Ilina," said the dwarf with the beard and twirling mustache. "Found some more strays, have nyu, what no, eh?"

Catti-brie looked to Jarlaxle, who just shrugged his shoulders, as perplexed and stunned as she.

"They found us."

"New aevendrow?" Kanaq seemed truly surprised, as did the other dwarves on the porch.

"So it would seem, *amico*," Emilian answered.

"What no, eh," Kanaq said, shaking his head, long and curly white hair bouncing about his broad shoulders.

"*Amico?*" Zak whispered under his breath.

"*Abbil*," Jarlaxle answered, the Drow word for "friend."

More of the diminutive folk, the inugaakalikurit dwarfs, appeared then, a group of about a dozen, and with them a pack of large, broad-chested, golden-furred dogs, who barked and leaped, charging the group of intruders. Catti-brie went into a defensive crouch, thinking they were about to be attacked, but the dogs had no such intent. Their barks became yips of playfulness, and with their tails wagging they assaulted the drow hosts not with bites and scratches but by leaping up at them and licking.

Catti-brie watched Ilina reach into a pouch and pull her hand out carrying a pile of small treats, which she tossed into the air, sending the dogs into a scramble to catch, then snuff about happily on the ground for any they had missed.

"We need the chamber," Emilian said to Kanaq. The dwarf nodded and sent one of the littler ones—one of his children, it appeared—running into the small house, to return a moment later holding a giant key ring that held only a single large key.

"That doesn't sound good," Entreri whispered to Jarlaxle, but Catti-brie heard.

"Just trust," Jarlaxle whispered back.

"As if we have a choice," Zaknafein sourly added.

Another handful of dog treats went flying, the dogs bounding away after the falling kibble, and the aevendrow and inugaakalikurit exchanged some parting words as the dwarf child bounded up and handed the key ring to Emilian.

The companions were led across the chamber to where several tunnel openings presented themselves in the high stone-and-ice wall. Also in the wall was a small carved structure made mostly of stone with a heavy wooden door. Emilian unlocked and opened it, revealing a darkened chamber within.

"You first," Ilina said to Catti-brie, and she took the woman by the arm and led her through the door. Emilian left the door open, letting in enough light for Catti-brie to see a small side room and beside it a large wardrobe of soft white clothing and thicker white robes with furred cuffs and collars. On a rack below sat pairs of simple, soft shoes.

"Take one set of clothes and find some shoes," Ilina instructed. "Then remove all of your clothing—all of it. And all of your jewelry."

"Not this, I beg," Catti-brie replied, tapping the unicorn scrimshaw she wore on a chain about her neck. "And this," she added, revealing a circlet that was mostly hidden by her thick hair, a green-gray band of leather set with two gems that looked very much like the feline eyes that gave the magical item its name. "The first is the symbol of my goddess and the second grants me vision in the darkness."

Even as she finished, the door closed, leaving them in near-complete blackness, reminding Catti-brie that her cat's eye circlet really wasn't functioning anyway.

She heard a scrape and Ilina lifted a lit candle.

"All of it," she repeated. "I am sorry, fellow priestess, but we know enough of the world beyond our homeland to understand that even the simplest and seemingly most innocuous of things can bring disaster if the magic within them is powerful enough. A small emblem can become a weapon, a circlet an alchemist's grenade. I cannot inspect them for magic in the time of Twilight Autunn. Remove them, everything."

"Will they be returned?"

Ilina didn't answer.

Catti-brie sighed and nodded. She stripped down to nothing, then found a suitable pair of pants and shirt from the wardrobe, pulling them on. The clothes were comfortable, at least, amazingly so, with the soft interior fur caressing her road-weary skin. She folded her own clothes and put all of her items together, her jewelry in a small pouch, then stepped aside. Ilina handed her a robe, then gathered up the discarded items and put them in a bag, tying it tightly before leading her out of the room and back outside the chamber.

A couple of the aevendrow had gathered near a large cart that had been brought out of a nearby tunnel by a group of dwarves and orcs.

Orcs! Catti-brie watched curiously as one orc helped Emilian lift a large white slab.

"The ice from the bottom of the glacier," Ilina explained to her.

Catti-brie looked to the priestess's sword, with its beautifully decorated white blade.

"It has been pressed by the weight of the glacier walls for centuries, millennia," Ilina explained. "It is very hard, as hard as metal."

"But brittle, and able to melt."

"No. We know how to treat it to prevent such problems. I assure you, you do not want to feel the bite of an aevendrow weapon."

That last sentence rocked Catti-brie back on her heels. She wasn't sure that Ilina had meant it as a threat, but she also wasn't sure that Ilina hadn't, and so it came as a pointed reminder of her predicament here, in her prisoner's garb, perhaps, and without weapons or magic to protect her.

Her gaze reflexively went back to the orcs, mostly the one with the white slab of ice, talking and laughing with Emilian.

One by one, the outsiders were brought into the chamber and relieved of all their items, including their clothing. Soon the party was on its way once more, the four companions dressed identically in white clothes and robes and soft skin shoes.

They felt comfortable, true.

But most of all, they felt vulnerable.

And felt, too, marked for easy identification, as if they were prisoners.

From the time they had left Cascatte, they walked through channels open to the sky, which was darker than they had seen it since arriving in the north, though more of a predawn light than a true nighttime sky. Only occasionally did they have any ice over their heads, and only for very short distances. Beside them, the stream continued to flow, with plants on either side, occasional insects buzzing or crawling about, and once, the walls falling away enough to present a wide meadow chamber inundated with white rabbits, dozens of them. Like the foxes, they showed no fear of the drow or the newcomers, and just went about their way, eating the thick clover that filled the chamber.

Catti-brie bent low near one large rabbit. She plucked a clover and held it out with an extended hand. She was testing the animal, which did indeed hop up and take the offering, but she was also testing their drow hosts here, watching Ilina mostly out of the corner of her eye.

The drow priestess smiled, and neither she nor the others hurried Catti-brie along.

By the time they came to a fork in the channel—the stream coming from straight ahead, another tunnel, enclosed, moving off to the right—Catti-brie had come to feel a bit better about this place and their hosts. So when the aevendrow indicated the smaller tunnel, she followed without question and led the way among her companions.

Except for Jarlaxle, who passed her just inside the tunnel, moving swiftly, eagerly.

Oh yes, she thought, she would later have a word with that one.

The tunnel wound and climbed. The floor was of ice, but not slippery, as it clearly had been roughed over. They went up carved stairs, then into a long straight corridor, the other end of which seemed to open into a wide chamber. It wasn't until they came to the end of the tunnel that Catti-brie and her friends began to understand just how wide.

It wasn't until they came to the end of the tunnel that Catti-brie and her friends had to remember how to breathe.

"Behold Callidae, the borough of Scellobel," Emilian announced, leading them out onto a wide ledge.

It was a long while before Catti-brie and the others were able to close their slack jaws. Below and before them lay a valley within the glacier. Callidae, the city of these northern people who called themselves aevendrow, spread wide and sprawling, with gardens and houses and trees, even. A wide stone ridge climbed almost to the top of the glacial ice, its side lined with houses of stone and wood, and carved avenues climbing like a giant snake, back and forth.

"It's bigger than Menzoberranzan," she heard Zak whisper to Jarlaxle, and so it was, undeniably.

Catti-brie studied her drow companions. She saw the awe on Zak's face, his jaw still hanging open. He shook his head several times, as if not knowing how he should act.

As expected, she found that this moment was different for Jarlaxle, less surprise, less awe, but more emotion. She saw the tears welling in his eyes, a sight she had never imagined, and one that filled her with sudden hope.

And why not, she realized, looking again at the grand vista before her, the drow city of Callidae spreading wide.

Several large buildings stood out from the normal structures, but none dominated. One, at least, and perhaps two or three others seemed to be chapels. Another large rectangular structure looked like something one might find along Waterdeep's docks. A warehouse, perhaps. But Callidae, or at least this section which they had called Scellobel, was not defined by the buildings, far from it. Wide fields lined by walls of piled stones covered much of the ground, including one right below the ledge, full of neat rows of leafy plants, among which many people moved, carrying large baskets.

A shift in the breeze brought the aroma from that field up to the ledge.

"A vineyard," Entreri said, his surprise clear in his voice.

"How many?" Jarlaxle asked Emilian.

"How many?" Emilian echoed in response.

"People," Jarlaxle clarified. "How many live here in Callidae?"

"This is Scellobel, one of four boroughs that make up Callidae," the drow explained. "And the largest because of the number of people here who are not aevendrow. Perhaps fifteen thousand of the aevendrow live within your sight from this ledge, but almost half that number of others as well, like the kurit you met in Cascatte, the Ulutiuns—humans, somewhat like your two companions—and the arktos oroks."

"Oroks?" Zaknafein said with some alarm.

"Orcs," Catti-brie said. "Like the ones in Cascatte."

Emilian nodded.

"Slaves?" Catti-brie dared to ask, and the shock on the faces of those aevendrow who heard her was all the answer she needed.

"There are no slaves in Callidae," Ilina answered sharply. "Never before, not now, never."

"We are truly glad to hear that," Jarlaxle intervened.

"Orcs and dwarves and . . . what did you call them?" Catti-brie asked.

"Ulutiuns," Emilian replied, his voice strained, as it seemed clear that Catti-brie's previous question had truly unnerved him. "Humans, like you, but a bit different."

"But no elves?" Catti-brie asked.

"Oh yes, but not in Scellobel," said Emilian. "There are just a few who happened upon us many years ago. They call themselves eladrin."

"High elves."

"Yes. They have found great joy here and have made their own families."

"Families of eladrin?" Catti-brie pressed, suddenly very interested.

"One, I think," Emilian answered.

"Yes, one couple," Ilina added. "They have two children. Two of the other three who stayed with us have sired or birthed children, too, but they are only half-eladrin, of course."

Catti-brie bit her lower lip.

"Fifteen thousand aevendrow here, or in the four boroughs combined?" Jarlaxle asked.

"Here in Scellobel. Almost twice that number in the other three boroughs. Come, welcome to my home."

"Forty thousand drow," Jarlaxle whispered to Zak.

"Twice Menzoberranzan," the weapon master answered.

To the left of them was a long stairway carved in the stone, but Emilian didn't go that way. He went right, to the lip of the wide ledge, where he sat down, looked back and smiled, and disappeared over the edge. When the companions went up to that spot, they found an icy slide with high walls running down the side of the glacier.

Emilian was already far below, lying back and speeding along. He went left suddenly, onto a high bank, then turned back fast to the right, disappearing feet first into the glacier.

Catti-brie gasped, and she was not the only one.

"It is fun," she heard Ilina say behind her. "Exciting. You will see."

The last time she'd gone down an ice slide, an avalanche had been chasing her. Not exactly what she considered fun.

Yet when Catti-brie glanced back at her, Ilina nodded for the woman to go with a gentle smile.

She had no magic, she had no weapons, she didn't even have her proper clothing, and she found herself in a strange land at the mercy of her hosts or captors or whatever these aevendrow were.

Completely at their mercy.

So Catti-brie shrugged, sat down, and shoved off.

"Lie back!" she heard Ilina call behind her as she slid faster. She did so and her speed increased immediately. She tried to keep steady, feet out before her, but every slight turn sent her up on one bank or the other.

She screamed when she went out to the left suddenly, and the fright became childlike glee when she abruptly went into the tunnel, speeding along in what soon became near-complete darkness! More sudden turns, breath-stealing drops, even what she thought might be a complete loop kept her screaming, half in terror, half in joy, before the tunnel finally straightened out in a long run, only slightly descending.

She came out of the glacier wall just to the right of the vineyard she had seen from up above, shooting fast, deeper into the town. The slide ascended then, gradually slowing her so that when she came to the end of the ride, she was on a raised platform nearly a hundred long strides out from the wall.

Emilian stood above her, holding down a hand for her to take. "Better than two hundred stairs?" he asked.

Catti-brie brushed down her robes, which had climbed halfway up her belly, taking her shirt with them. She sat up and took the offered hand.

"Can I do it again?" she asked, grinning from ear to ear.

Emilian laughed. "I have done it a thousand times and it still steals my breath," he told her. "I often *forget* things when we leave on patrol and have to come back to Scellobel, but don't tell Ilina that I do it on purpose."

Zaknafein came in next, then the other companions in quick succession, with Ilina coming last. The other three Callidaeans remained on the high ledge and waved their goodbyes.

"Ilina will take you to a place where you may eat and rest," Emilian explained. "I will arrive later to take you to the inquisitors."

"Inquisitors?" Jarlaxle echoed.

"They will hear your story," Emilian explained. "They will pass judgment."

"It would be easier if it were not the Twilight Autunn," Ilina added. "Then they could use magic, of course, to arrive at their answers. But fear not. Just tell them the truth of your journey and your arrival and your intent."

"You are not among enemies unless you make it so," Emilian explained. He singled out Jarlaxle and Zaknafein. "You two, in particular, will draw great curiosity. You are not of the aevendrow, yet you are obviously drow. This is most remarkable."

"The aevendrow," Jarlaxle echoed, simply because he liked the sound of it.

"*Aevensussin yndadrow*," Emilian explained. "The starlight drow, the *aevendrow*."

"Come," Ilina bade them despite the numerous questions hovering on their lips, and she led them across the city, past a sea of curious eyes, aevendrow, kurit, and arktos orok alike, and one group of a dozen or so that seemed to be humans, or perhaps halflings, or some combination thereof. They were short, the tallest still several inches shorter than Catti-brie, with dark hair and eyes, bronzed skin, flat round faces, and curious smiles showing broad white teeth.

"Ulutiuns?" Catti-brie whispered to Ilina.

"Yes, the Geelah family. Their people came from a nearby village in the mountains."

That perked up Catti-brie's ears. Family, yes, she realized when she looked back at the group as they passed, and realized that she was staring at three, perhaps even four, generations.

"Evil befell their home and the glacier encroached upon it," Ilina explained as they continued their walk. "Many were killed, but the Geelahs and some others escaped. The two oldest there, Jissi and Anji, were just children when they came to us for shelter. They became our most accomplished handlers."

"Handlers?"

"Of the teff, the sled dogs you saw back in Cascatte."

"Sled dogs?"

"Mukteff," Ilina told her. "The golden coats. The heteff are white, the okteff black coated, and of course there are combinations of all, as one can expect from dogs."

"As one can expect from eladrin and aevendrow?" Jarlaxle slyly asked, and Ilina laughed.

Catti-brie just shook her head. It was all too much. Too much information, too much . . . difference. She felt as if she were in a delusion, in some strange land she could never have imagined and surrounded by people familiar and yet not. Like friends one might meet only in a dream.

But thus far, at least, it was just a dream and not a nightmare.

Her eyes went to Ilina's sword, and her thoughts went to Ilina's warning.

"I TRUST YOU ARE COMFORTABLE," THE INQUISITOR SAID to Catti-brie.

She sat in a straight-backed wooden chair, a plain table before her set with a glass of cold water. A trio of aevendrow, who had identified themselves only as inquisitors, sat in the shadows on the other side of the room, on a raised dais and in taller chairs, so as to tower above her in an obvious attempt at intimidation. The only light in that area came from a candelabrum on the floor, uplighting the inquisitors, which made them even more imposing.

They hadn't threatened her with their words, but their posture and positioning were hardly neutral.

"You understand that we must ensure most of all the safety of our home," the woman on the left end explained.

"We are no threat to you."

"You came here, you found us," said the man in the middle. "That alone is a threat."

"An accident, a fortunate one for us, and no threat," said Catti-brie.

"So you say," declared the first.

"Ask your questions," Catti-brie invited them.

"You are a priestess, we are told," the woman went on, "and so you know that there are ways in which we could magically determine the veracity of your claims, and perhaps even search that which is in your heart unsaid. But you also know that we are in the time of Twilight Autunn, the fading, and in this time, magic is unpredictable and greatly weakened, if accessible at all.

"Thus, our task is doubly difficult, for without those dweomers, we are reduced to evaluating the impression that you and your companions make upon us, and we must trust in that, and only that, for another several days."

"So we will be imprisoned for that time," Catti-brie reasoned.

"Hopefully not," said the woman. "We do not wish to keep you in a dungeon."

"But will if needed," the stern man in the middle said.

"We would like you to enjoy Scellobel, perhaps all of Callidae," the woman pressed past him, and Catti-brie knew the technique, where one tried to be soft and friendly, the other playing the threat. "It is ironic, but in this time of the great reduction of our magic, Callidae itself approaches its most magical day, Quista Canzay. Magic swims in the dark sky, waves of beauty and song. I hope that you will partake in the celebration, but to do so, you need to tell us how and why you came here, to this land that is rarely visited by those who live in the southlands."

Catti-brie complied. She told them of the sword and the hunt for Doum'wielle—even why she had been asked to come along, as another who had once, long ago, fallen under the domination of Khazid'hea. She offered a warning with her tale to her captors regarding handling that malevolent blade, for if its magic returned and it caught a wielder unaware, that person would likely be overtaken and perhaps driven to dangerous deeds.

A chuckle from the man in the center stopped her there.

"Many years ago?" he asked skeptically. "We are to believe that? We know humans. You expect us to believe that many years ago you wielded such a weapon though you were but a child? Are you nobility, then, in this land you left behind?"

"No," Catti-brie replied with a nervous chuckle. "No . . . although, yes, I am now considered such by some, since my father is a dwarven king." She laughed helplessly. How could she begin to explain her life and all the twists and turns and adventures? How could she explain her death, if the time in Iruladoon even was death, or her return as a chosen of Mielikki sent to do battle with the woman who had inadvertently become the chosen of Lolth?

How could she begin to explain it all?

"I am much older than I appear, but thank you for the compliment," she answered. Before the man could reply, she went on with her story, of the magical portal that had put the four of them in this place they did not know, of their journey across the northland before they happened upon this glacial rift—pointedly, she did not tell them of the cave and the fight with the giant and the frog-like monster, as the four companions had agreed back in the original glacial chamber. But she did tell them of the abandoned town and the reaction of the glacier itself when they had torn a small rift to the Plane of Fire with Zak's whip and Catti-brie had tried to reach into that plane with her ring.

That brought some nods, for all of those possessions, although mostly inert at this time, it seemed, were in the hands of the aevendrow. Still, sages among these drow should have been able to identify, or at least guess, the general powers of the distinctive items.

"Doum'wielle Armgo is dead," the drow in the middle told her.

"No, she isn't," Catti-brie replied. "Or at least, if she is, it happened only recently, within the past day or two."

Even in the shadows, she could see the man shaking his head.

"Forget her," he said. "She fell victim to the uninhabited, and so Doum'wielle as you knew her is forever dead."

"The unin—" Catti-brie started to ask, but the woman cut her off.

"Now that you know the futility of your search, perhaps you would like to leave. But you cannot, not now. You would die in the cold wind without your magic, of course."

Catti-brie shrugged. What was to be said?

They led her out of the room then, bringing her through the door on the right-hand wall, opposite from the door through which she had entered, and where her friends waited, each in their own small cell in a large room of many such tiny chambers—a place that reminded her of the meditation hallways of the Monastery of the Yellow Rose.

Ilina and Emilian were waiting for her beyond that door.

"A REMARKABLE STORY," THE LEAD INQUISITOR TOLD HIS two companions when the door closed once more. "One of many, I suspect, that we might hear from this human."

Both he and the woman who had questioned Catti-brie looked to the end of the table at the third of the group, a strong woman sitting with perfect posture, a reflection of the discipline she carried through her every day. Her white clothing was pressed and sharp, her blue hair cut neatly. She held a small coffer, mostly glass, a reliquary showing the skull of a white fox inside.

"Mielikki," the other woman said. "She is another name for your own god, yes, Galathae?"

"A sister goddess, at least," the drow paladin answered.

"What did you sense?" asked the drow man. "And can you trust it in this time of Twilight Autunn?"

"I sensed no evil in her," Galathae replied. "Not in intent or in memory. I believe I would trust the safety of Callidae on that feeling, even in this time, and particularly since the lightness and warmth of this one resonated so strongly. Let us bring the others through to see if they are of similar weal."

JARLAXLE WAS THE LAST OF THE GROUP TO SIT BEFORE the inquisitors, and he wasn't the least bit intimidated. He worried that perhaps he was letting his elation at simply seeing Callidae and learning of this place and these people put him off his guard, but it was really of minor concern to him.

If the aevendrow had wanted him and his friends dead, they'd already be dead.

He told the same story to the panel of three that Catti-brie, Entreri, and Zaknafein had related. He, too, resisted telling them about the fight in the cave, although he wasn't sure that they should bother to keep that secret, and expected that it wouldn't hold for much longer anyway. Why had the green slaad impersonated a drow? Was it because it had seen Zak in the deeper chamber battling a frost giant, or because it knew of these drow?

Both, likely, but that hinted to Jarlaxle that the slaad and the frost giants, that clan at least, were not in league with the folk of Callidae.

"You are the leader of this expedition?" asked the man centering the three on the dais.

"I organized it, yes."

"But you don't even know where you are?" asked the woman to his right. "You ask us to believe this?"

"Have the others told you of Archmage Gromph?" Jarlaxle answered with a question of his own.

"The one who created the portal," the woman confirmed.

"A great wizard, one of the most powerful in the south, and perhaps the most powerful of all in the Underdark when he lived there, serving as the archmage of Menzoberranzan, the city of your relatives."

"The City of Spiders, so said your fellow drow companion."

"Yes. I will tell you more of it."

"You presume our interest," said the man in the center. "And our ignorance."

"Our concern is Callidae, and Callidae alone," the woman who had been speaking added. "You do not give us confidence in our ability to trust you by speaking to us of great wizards and Underdark cities. We know well that some of our kin traveled there in the great separation of the peoples."

"They are very unlike you," Jarlaxle remarked.

"Are you?"

The drow shrugged. "We did not come here just to find Doum'wielle and to try to break the demonic influence within a sword," he admitted, and that raised the eyebrows of the two, though the woman on the other end of the stage remained wholly impassive, outwardly at least. "My friends likely believed so, but I had other intent.

"Do you know of Silverymoon?" he asked.

"Yes," came a surprising answer.

"I was there recently, following a rumor of an elf, another eladrin, who once found a most unusual civilization in the frozen northland, beyond the reach of the known kingdoms of Faerun."

They didn't react.

"A drow civilization," Jarlaxle added. "Or aevendrow, perhaps."

Still no reaction.

"Or maybe it was just a dream. That is what those around this very ancient eladrin believed, or that his old mind had become incapable of distinguishing fantasy from truth. Fear not, for he is not taken seriously."

"Yet you are here," the woman answered.

"Because above all, I wanted his dream to be true. Because I needed it to be true . . . and also, because the hunt for Doum'wielle is true and good and holds great importance for a coming conflict among my people. Thus I had another reason to come here, and to convince my companions to follow."

"That reason is gone now, as is Doum'wielle."

"So you said. Would you have us be on our way?"

"You have no magical protection. You would die."

"Lend us your clothes."

"No. You cannot leave before the fall of night and the end of Twilight Autunn," said the man.

"When magic returns. When our magic will protect us."

"Of course."

"And when your magic will protect you." Jarlaxle understood. He thought of the old elf in Silverymoon, who hadn't told his tale of drow in the north for many years, and now whispered it as gibberish more than reality, like the waking dreams of one caught more in memory and fantasy than in the world as it was around him.

Perhaps that old elf was confused, his mind diminished. Perhaps his tale held no truth at all and the presence of the aevendrow here was mere coincidence.

Or perhaps the magic that had erased his memories of Callidae for all these decades, centuries even, had worn away enough for that old elf to now dream of a place he once knew.

"We have no desire to meet the people of the south," the woman inquisitor explained to him. "Nor anyone of the Underdark, surely."

"Yet your people came out to find us. You could have let us die."

"It was by chance—and of course we could not leave you to die. Like the Ulutiuns who lost their town to the glacier, or the inugaakalikurit wanderers who were found out on the ice, or the ones you call orcs, who roamed the region. We have made their lives better as they have made our lives better. They have become a part of Callidae, a part we treasure. They fight in calci, tend our fields with us, create artwork, share their songs and dances. That could be your future, too, if your tales are true and your heart is good. Perhaps a future you might consider."

For all the complexities and thrills of his life in the south, such a notion was not one Jarlaxle found he could easily dismiss. But neither did he miss the first mentioned contribution.

"Calci?" he asked. "Is this an enemy?" He thought of the slaad and the frost giants, hoping to find an opening here to further solidify any alliance he might forge.

"Cazzcalci," the man answered. "The battle of Twilight Autunn. Take heart, my friend, for you have come to us in a time of feast and play."

"And battle?"

The two inquisitors who had been questioning him looked at each other and grinned.

Then they looked to the third, who nodded.

"Go to your friends, Jarlaxle," the man told him. "You are free to wander the borough, indeed, the whole of the city. Emilian and Ilina will guide you if you choose, or you can make your own way. You will find food and drink plentiful."

"And dance and song," the woman added. "Add to that if you can, or tell great tales of old, and you will find many smiles of gratitude."

When they quieted, Jarlaxle rose and bowed, starting for the other door.

"One more thing," the woman called after him. "On my advice, do not miss the persimmons."

"Persimmons?"

"A small orange—"

"I know what it is," Jarlaxle interrupted, too surprised to maintain his polite decorum. "Fruit . . . tangy."

"Ah, but you have not tasted it paired with aged kurit muskox cheese and chased down with Hollico, the Scellobelee ice wine!" She pursed her lips, pressed her fingers against them, and smacked her lips, extending her hand wide as she threw it forward, toward a very confused Jarlaxle.

He didn't know the details, of course, or what a muskox might be, or Hollico for that matter, but that wasn't the real source of his confusion. No, it was the pride, the welcoming pride, this inquisitor whose name he did not know had just relayed to him.

"Fine advice, Jarlaxle," the man agreed. "That delicacy alone may make you think your journey to this difficult land worth the trouble."

Shaking his head, trying not to chuckle, Jarlaxle went through the door and soon rejoined his friends.

CHAPTER 16

Making Wine

I have been tasked with showing you your way around Callidae," Ilina told the four companions when they left the inquisitors. "It is not a difficult place to navigate, and I can give you some advice on sights that might prove of interest to you."

"And we're completely free to go where we will?" a skeptical Artemis Entreri asked.

"Well, you cannot barge into private homes, of course. I expect your customs are similar. And you cannot leave, not even to Cascatte."

When eyebrows arched at that, Ilina quickly added, "The elements would kill you. It is cold out there, and will grow much colder quite soon. You wouldn't survive it."

"Even if we had the clothing you and your companions were wearing when we first met?" Entreri quipped, staring at the drow priestess hard.

"But you do not," Ilina sharply replied.

"And even if we did, could we carry enough food, and would we even be able to find our way?" Jarlaxle said, and Catti-brie nodded her approval at his attempt to ratchet the tension down.

"The storms will begin soon," Ilina added. "The wind can blow you from your feet, and fill the air with tiny crystals of ice so thickly that you cannot see five strides ahead. However you might decide to leave this region, you would have to cross mountains that will soon be impassable, and will remain so until the Conception Verdant."

"The what?" Entreri echoed.

"Mid-Ches, the vernal equinox," said Catti-brie, who understood it now, and realized that the coming night would be very different from the nights they knew back home. "Six months. We live a year of days back home, but up here, they have only one true daytime and one true nighttime."

"But why not Cascatte?" Jarlaxle asked Ilina. "It was not too frigid in that place of beauty."

"The dwarves and orcs of Cascatte haven't the resources on hand to accommodate visitors. They have their work and are somewhat independent of Callidae, by mutual agreement. In that spirit, we do not like to intrude upon them unless there is no avoiding it, as with our patrols. If you truly desire to return there, you would have to do so with a full Callidaean guard. It can be arranged, but there is enough here to hold your attention, I expect."

"Show us around Callidae," Jarlaxle relented.

"And watch over us, of course," Zaknafein added.

Ilina laughed at that. "I will show you to a place where you can then show yourselves about the boroughs of Callidae. There is no one watching over you in any intrusive manner. The inquisitors have determined that you are not prisoners here, but guests."

"Who cannot leave," Entreri replied, refusing to surrender the point.

"You will be able to leave, but first we must have our magic," Ilina answered.

So they can erase our vivid memories of this place, Jarlaxle realized, but did not say aloud.

"A tenday, then," Catti-brie said.

"Callidae is easy to navigate," Ilina said, leading them away from the inquisitor house and toward the nadir of the rocky prow that cut this borough nearly in two. At the base of that prow, with land rolling out before them and climbing both left and right, they found an intersection of five wide avenues. At the center of the resulting plaza stood a tall pole, and as they neared, the companions noticed four directional signs upon it, and a large plaque on a shining metal ball atop it.

"Callidae Scellobel," Ilina said, pointing to that plaque up top. "You are in the heart of Scellobel, the most populous of the four remaining boroughs of Callidae. This is the guidepost of Callidae. You can only reach the world beyond through here, unless you were to climb or fly to the top of the glacial walls. You see the water stream you followed into the glacier? That is the River Callidae, the only way out without climbing."

Catti-brie surveyed the distant glacial wall in a straight line from the narrowest point of the prow.

"Due south," Ilina explained, and then expounded, "If you are ever lost in the side avenues of Scellobel, always look to the prow. From its highest point to this place where we stand is due south. Shift your gaze just a bit to the right, and you can see the stairs and the slide where you entered from the tunnels back to Cascatte."

"It's not on the signpost," Zak remarked.

"Cascatte isn't a borough. There are just a few families of dwarves and a dozen or so arktos oroks, which you call orcs, living there. These are the boroughs." She pointed to the signpost and lowered her hand past each sign as she explained. "Scellobel, here, then to Mona Chess, the seat of the Siglig, which is a larger canyon than this, and almost as populous, but with many more aevendrow and fewer of the other cultures."

"Siglig," Jarlaxle whispered as if trying to decipher the word.

"Council," Catti-brie replied.

"Yes, the Siglig is the building of our council, which we call the Temporal Convocation," Ilina confirmed. "Emilian served on it just last year, and Kanaq, whom you met in Cascatte, spent many years there until a dozen sunsets ago."

That these drow had allowed a dwarf to serve on their council was a point that did not pass by the four companions without notice.

"I thought you said the dwarves had their own rules out there," Jarlaxle noted.

"Kanaq moved his family out of the boroughs when some new kurit came to us," Ilina explained. "They are still full citizens of Callidae, and he of Scellobel, but they are often on their own to deal with . . . well, whatever monster wanders in from the ice pack. Because of their heightened patrols and their most important work, we think it prudent to only minimally bother them.

"Mona Chess is the oldest of the boroughs," she continued, "and the one most natural in size, but also most resplendent in structures. All of the other boroughs were expanded by great effort and labor as our population expanded. This next avenue follows a parallel road, which runs through the northwest corner of Mona Chess to Ardin."

"Garden," Catti-brie translated.

"Very good," Ilina congratulated her. "Yes, the garden, and also the place of the muskox herd. You can visit there now, but I would not advise it anytime around the Conception Verdant, for the muskoxen tend to smell quite terrible when they are chasing mates!"

"What is a muskox?" Entreri asked.

"A huge animal," Ilina said. "Huge and hairy, with great horns and cloven hooves. They are peaceful enough and feast on grasses all the day long, and the kurit make of their milk the most delicious of cheeses."

"To put with persimmons," Jarlaxle said.

"You make light of it," Ilina said with a chuckle of her own, "but once you taste it, you will offer me your gratitude, I promise."

"I look forward to it, lady," Jarlaxle said with a grin.

"Most of the carts you will see along the streets here in Scellobel are full of food from Ardin. Every day, the farmhands load their wagons with the produce from the gardens and walk the miles to the other boroughs, then return with carts laden with goods from each."

"And muskox steak?" Entreri asked, and Ilina cast him a puzzled look.

"Meat," he explained.

"Oh, no no no no," the woman said. "We do not slaughter the

muskoxen, or the eider or puffins you see around you who give us fresh eggs." She pointed to a nearby house, where a group of black-and-white duck-like birds with distinctive circular orange plates above their bills milled about.

"I know puffins," Catti-brie said. "There are colonies on the Sea of Moving Ice."

"Do they taste like duck?" Entreri quipped. "They look like ducks."

"They are tasty," Ilina said, "but we do not slaughter them."

"Then how do you know what they taste like?"

"We are past that," the aevendrow explained. "Our priests create food. We do not slaughter any animals."

"Yes, of course," said Catti-brie.

"Bland bread," Entreri put in.

"We have spent centuries perfecting the spells of conjuration," Ilina said. "Our creations are wondrous, particularly the food."

"Take some lessons before we leave, I beg," Entreri told Catti-brie.

"B'shett," Ilina said, pointing to the bottommost signpost, indicating a boulevard that ran to the northwest, along the western hillside of the prow. "A small and narrow forest of tall larch that provides the wood you see in the fences, the doors, the handles of our spears, and even some houses. The passage from Scellobel to B'shett is not long, but I would not bother with the journey at this time of the year if you have other things you wish to see or do. The birdsong is wonderful—sometimes you can hear the melodies echoing all the way into northern Scellobel—but B'shett is the darkest of the boroughs, with little sky above, and the coldest by far, as the narrow channel catches the wind and tightens it. If you do decide to spend some time there, I will take you to the inquisitors to see if they will grant permission for you to visit the tailors and get some clothes like mine." She tapped the dark gray sleeve of her snug-fitting shirt. "It replicates the skin of the seals, as the fur on the robes you now wear replicates that of the white foxes. It is incredibly warm, and the cold rain or melting snow can't get through. It would be better, of course, if you were to visit after the Twilight Autunn, because the tailor could make you clothes to fit perfectly. But they have extras on their racks that will do, I am sure."

"Replicate?" Jarlaxle and Catti-brie asked together.

"We don't hunt the seals or the foxes," Ilina said. "There is no need. What is magic for, if not comfort and food?"

Jarlaxle could barely hide his grin, and Catti-brie knew that he was seeing a marvelous economic opportunity here.

"This fifth sign, the one you skipped and whose name is crossed out?" Zaknafein asked. "Cattisola?"

A dark cloud passed over Ilina's face. "It is gone. Many decades gone. It was wooded, less so than B'shett, and with many tunnels leading deeper into the glacier and even some moving outside through cracks in the ice. It was a place of great conflict—my mother and father fought there for many years. One of my uncles was killed there. But that is a century and more past, and it is quiet now, forevermore, we expect."

"In the hands of enemies?" Jarlaxle asked with concern.

"Devoured by the advance of the glacier," Ilina said.

"But enough of that," she added, clapping her hands together. "Explore as you will, but hear my word that you are in the best of the boroughs. We make the wine."

Her eyes lit up with infectious enthusiasm.

"Here in Scellobel, you hear the calming, chanting songs of the kurit, the drums of the arktos orok, the flutes of the Ulutiuns. Here we have the widest sky, and you will appreciate that when twilight turns to night and the air fills with waves of magic, I promise. And we Scellobelans are the best of fighters. We won cazzcalci last year and will win again! You will see.

"But I have kept you long enough," she said. "I can go with you if you insist, but I think it better that you wander as you will. Throw away the weariness of your journey. Enjoy the smells and the sounds, and the food—just ask. There is no cost, though you might be asked to trade a tale. We don't get many visitors, as you must understand. Indulge in the ice wine, but take care. It is so tasty that you do not realize how much you imbibe until it is too late and your head feels as if it had been stepped on by a fat muskox."

She bowed and turned to go.

"What more will you ask of us?" Jarlaxle said, turning her back.

"Oh, much, I expect," Ilina answered. "Stories, I mean. We would like to know of your lands, especially from your human friends. You understand our curiosity? If I walked into your homeland, would your Temporal Convocation not wish the same from me?"

"Oh, indeed they would," Jarlaxle said, and he felt his eye twitch at the mere thought of Menzoberranzan's Ruling Council.

Ilina smiled and left them.

"At the end of a serpent scourge," Zaknafein added when she was gone, now talking in the Common tongue of the surface world, far removed from the Drow language they had thus far heard spoken here. "I hope there are no snakes up here."

"I'll settle for no spiders," Entreri said.

"We've been invited to explore, so let us do so," Jarlaxle told them, and Catti-brie saw right through any pretense of seriousness and did not miss his bubbling excitement.

"They said Doum'wielle is dead, and was lost far from here," Catti-brie reminded him.

"We haven't got Khazid'hea," Jarlaxle replied. "Nor you your magic."

"We can make quiet inquiries," Zak offered.

Jarlaxle nodded. "Very quiet, but our quest is on hold if everything we have learned is true. If Doum'wielle is here, why would they have tried to conceal it?"

"Maybe she's in a prison," said Entreri.

Jarlaxle shrugged, and seemed to Catti-brie to so easily discount that possibility. "And what would you have us do about that? No weapons. No magic."

"We can get weapons if we need them," Entreri assured him.

"Don't be a fool," said Jarlaxle. "They may call themselves the aevendrow, but they are drow, and so they are formidable. We are four, only four, and they are what? Fifteen thousand here in this borough alone, to say nothing of the thousands of other peoples? If you had been dropped into Menzoberranzan, would you be quick to make such a suggestion?"

"Were I dropped into Menzoberranzan, I'd already be fighting my way out, or dead," the stubborn Entreri answered.

"But this is not Menzoberranzan," said Jarlaxle.

"So you believe."

"Indeed," he answered.

"Because you *want* to believe," Entreri replied, and Catti-brie was glad he had said it so she didn't have to.

Because when the remark led to another dismissive shrug and a nod from Jarlaxle, she found her suspicions regarding the too-clever rogue, regarding this entire expedition, more fully confirmed.

"Come," Jarlaxle told them. "The best way to learn of a new place is simply to walk the ways and meet the commonfolk. We have already seen so much, yet have barely hinted at the surprises of this place, I am confident."

Too confident, Catti-brie thought.

"You know that they are watching us," Zak said as they started on their way.

"I'd lose respect for them if they were not, and so would you," Jarlaxle answered.

Very soon after they left the signpost, Artemis Entreri's hope were dashed, for down the far end of the very first avenue they traveled, the companions found a fenced-in field of abandoned old carts, scraggly trees and bushes, and spiders. Huge white spiders, as large as a fist, spinning beautiful webs and long filaments that reached from tree to tree to upturned cart.

At the end of the fence was a small cottage, and beyond that a waist-high stone wall and some kind of a waterwheel, creaking and sloshing.

Entreri turned a sly look on Jarlaxle. "Well?"

"It means nothing," he replied, but not very convincingly.

"It means they have spiders," said Entreri.

"Luskan has spiders," Jarlaxle countered. "Gauntlgrym has spiders. Waterdeep has spiders. Calimport has spiders. Everywhere has spiders!"

"Like that?" Entreri retorted. "If we saw a field like that in Luskan, we'd hire the Hosttower to reduce the whole of it to ash in short order."

"Assume nothing," Jarlaxle told him.

"I'm not. But you seem to be."

The companions moved down the fence line toward the water-wheel on the other side of the cottage for a closer look, and began waving hands before their faces at the smell. They stayed, though, caught by a most curious sight.

A large yard, perhaps a quarter of an acre, was hemmed in by walls, even one built against the glacial ice, which had been carved into a deep and wide alcove. Both in the alcove and here near the opposite wall were pools of water, and the turning wheel seemed now in the process of transferring the fluid from the nearest pool back under the icy alcove.

The water nearest them lowered with every turn of the wheel, and they could soon see the pool teeming with writhing eel- or snakelike creatures.

Catti-brie crinkled her nose and brought her hand up over her face.

"Not everything here is beautiful, it seems," Jarlaxle admitted, and he contorted his mouth to get the taste of the stench out.

"What in the Nine Hells?" asked Zak when one of those creatures came forth—slithering out of the water, seeming more snail than snake. Or maybe it was an eel, or maybe a long and narrow fish. He couldn't tell, but whatever it was, it began crawling across the stony yard, and also secreting a thick mucus.

Then came the others, dozens of them, crawling, even somewhat swimming through the viscous liquid that spread about them, covering the ground in a gooey sheen and filling the air with a most disgusting odor.

"Hags!" came a call from the door of the cottage, and the friends turned to see an aevendrow standing there, hands on hips. "Ah, newcomers! Well, don't stand there when the hags are crawling. You will taste that smell in your food for a tenday!"

They started back along the wall, and the drow waved them into his cottage—his boutique, they soon discovered.

"Hags, you called them," Catti-brie said as she entered beside the drow.

"Phlegm fish," he explained. "Hags, yes, or hagfish."

"Why do you let them so near your house?"

"Oh, I don't live here. I, we . . ." He waved his hand around at several others, drow and kurit dwarf, working looms or needles, a pair of dwarves wearing full masks over at a long trough at the far end of the room, stirring long paddles. "We create here."

"Tailors," Entreri realized. "That explains the spiders." The look on the drow's face clued the others in to the fact that Entreri had spoken in the Common tongue of the surface, not in Drow. Entreri caught it, too, and quickly repeated his words so their host could understand.

"Ah, yes, wretched eight-legged little beasts," the aevendrow said. "They eat the bugs, and there are plenty, but sometimes, alas, a baby puffin wanders too near. We are constantly reinforcing the fence to keep wandering chicks out and the spiders in."

"They are caged?" Jarlaxle asked, and he cast a hopeful glance at his companions.

"Caging a spider in Menzoberranzan would get you killed," Zak told Entreri and Catti-brie in surface Common.

"They are native to the land and Qadeej," the aevendrow answered. "Whenever a Scellobelan finds one, if they don't reflexively stomp it, they call to us and we collect the beast. You see, the white spiders create the very strongest and smoothest threads."

"A spider can crawl over a fence," Entreri reminded him.

"Ah, but they won't cross the hag phlegm," the tailor replied.

"So that's why the hags?" Catti-brie asked. "But still, that smell!"

"The smell doesn't last when the mucus is treated and dried," the aevendrow told her. "But no, the hags are not just for the spiders—we could cage them in other ways. That mucus helps us make the finest armor in the world, and it will keep you warm, too. You won't even know you're wearing a glove of it when you put it over your hand. Let me show you."

"MAGNIFICENT," JARLAXLE SAID AS THEY WALKED AWAY from the small cottage a short while later. He flexed the fingers of his left hand, stretching and bending as he admired the silk-and-mucus gloves he had been given by the tailor. They were mostly white, but shot with lines of bright orange in the delicate design of a calendula, the stitching so fine and intricate that it made the glove appear almost as if it were lace instead of solid cloth.

"You're welcome," said Zaknafein, whose rousing tale of Jarlaxle's hair loss had paid for the gloves.

"They are beautiful," Catti-brie admitted.

"They are more than that," Jarlaxle explained. He pulled off the glove and handed it to her. "It feels as if I am wearing nothing at all, as if my skin is simply smoother and softer. And yet, there is something of weight stitched into it—there is some mucus in there, I am sure."

Catti-brie slipped it on, considered it for a moment, then nodded her agreement.

"Armor, he said," Jarlaxle said. "And perhaps a weapon, like the metal knuckles the thugs in Luskan often quietly put on before a brawl."

Entreri snorted and shook his head, looking positively disgusted.

"What is it?" Jarlaxle asked.

"Nothing."

"There is no 'nothing' here," Catti-brie scolded him. "We are guests or we are prisoners in this strange land. No feeling, intuition, or fear should be kept silent."

"Look around us," Entreri said, and he directed the attention of the others to a wide stair leading up to a grand building one block over, where several aevendrow were engaged in what seemed to be a dancing contest while a crowd at the base of the steps clapped out a rhythm. "They show a gaiety, a zest, a soft edge. Like that glove. Are they, too, lined with weighted mucus?"

"It's their time of celebration," Catti-brie reminded. "They survive up here in as difficult a terrain as any we've known. Perhaps they just set aside some days to enjoy life? Is that such a bad thing? They take pleasure in beauty, clearly," she added, pointing out a group of younger drow moving along the road, dressed in revealing and seductive clothing in bright colors.

"You think it all a ruse?" Jarlaxle asked Entreri.

He seemed to be contemplating the question, so Catti-brie said, "Even the people who fear and loathe the drow of Menzoberranzan could not deny the beauty of a high priestess's robes, or even the garb of a houseless rogue, for that matter. It seems that we've stumbled upon an enclave of drow who collectively favor Jarlaxle's flamboyant style."

"They are pale shadows of Jarlaxle," Jarlaxle assured her with a grin.

"Maybe that's why Artemis Entreri is uncomfortable," Zak remarked.

"They're not coaxing us into vulnerability," Catti-brie stated flatly. "This is not a show before us. What would justify such an elaborate ruse to four weary travelers who are without weapons or power?"

"Or it's all an illusion," Entreri said. "Such things are not unknown."

"Magic isn't functioning," said Catti-brie.

"*Our* magic isn't working," Entreri corrected.

Jarlaxle looked to Zak. "And I thought you the most cynical," he said, shaking his head.

"Have you forgotten the story of Wulfgar's torment in the Abyss?" asked Entreri. "The worst of the torture was showing him that which he most desired, then tearing it from him. It's not cynicism on my part, just proper caution."

"Or perhaps we've all just gone mad from a circling sun," Jarlaxle scoffed. "It is what we see. It is only our fear that makes it more."

"You seem very certain of that," Catti-brie accused.

Before Jarlaxle could answer, Entreri reminded them, "They have spiders."

"And keep them in a manner highly illegal in Menzoberranzan," said Zak.

"We survive with preparation," Entreri continued. "I know how to relieve a guard of her spear or sword, as do you."

He looked to all three of his companions, his expression intense, and repeated, "And they have spiders."

Jarlaxle, then Catti-brie, let go of their argument, for neither could deny the prudence of Entreri's reminder. They were, in truth, captives in a very unusual place. For all the pretty dressing and the apparent delight of those folk about them, the four companions, so far from home, had to keep that in mind.

It proved a difficult task, though, as they made their way through the streets and plazas of Scellobel, for the most prominent sound that came to them was that of laughter. Not mocking, cruel laughter, but a sense of pure joy. Every aevendrow or kurit or orok they passed gave them curious looks, of course, particularly aimed at Entreri and Catti-brie, who, they had been informed, didn't look anything like the Ulutiun humans of Callidae, but all offered a nod and many even added a passing greeting, with "A fine day to dance" being the most common.

"Have you noticed the details on their buildings?" Zaknafein asked at one point as they neared a plaza where a large group of drow had gathered. "On every surface?"

"Yes," Jarlaxle answered. He glanced at Catti-brie and Entreri, then guided them to a nearby archway leading to a house with a small garden.

Catti-brie understood Zak's observation quite clearly as she moved to the base of that arcing trellis, for like most of the structures about them, it was fashioned of pressed ice, blue-white here, and covered in delicate carvings. At first, those designs just looked like a mishmash of lines, but as they drew her eyes in deeper, she made out shapes: a battle on one panel, aevendrow against giant; a dance of kurit on another; an aevendrow riding a great bearlike creature on a third.

"This is hopeful," she said, pointing out the giant fight.

"None told the inquisitors?" Jarlaxle asked.

"Maybe we should have," said Zak. "It could prove important."

"We'll trust them when they trust us," Entreri said, again a voice of prudence and caution.

"They've let us walk freely through their city," Catti-brie argued.

"If you think we're not being shadowed, you should pay more attention," Entreri countered.

"Again, that is to be expected," Jarlaxle said, ending the debate.

They moved toward the plaza, politely veering to travel around the edge of the place when they realized that a gathered group—all standing, dressed in matching blue-white robes trimmed in a deeper blue—were posing for an artist feverishly painting behind a huge easel.

"Wait! Wait!" one aevendrow called as the foursome passed behind the painter (who was doing a remarkable fast and fine portrayal, and seemed near completion).

"Who are you?" asked another, a tall woman with purple-and-white hair and a generally soft purplish tone to her skin, particularly bright about her cheeks.

"Visitors to Scellobel?" asked a third, a tall, thin, muscular orc.

"Spies from Ardin, no doubt!" another said, to great laughter.

"No, we've never been to Ardin, or any other borough," Jarlaxle answered. "We are new to Callidae and have just come from the inquisition."

That brought many excited discussions among the two dozen or so gathered for the occasion.

"Bring them in!" cried the one who had called them Ardin spies. "It will mark this year forever, a triumph for Biancorso!"

"Especially her," said the first who had called out to the companions. He was short and wiry, thinner than most of the drow Catti-brie had seen up here, with very angular features. His bright white hair was cut short on the sides and the back, but long in front, parted to the side and covering his right eye. "The beautiful one!" He rushed out from the group, moving toward the foursome.

"Why, thank you," said Jarlaxle with a slight bow.

"They said 'her,'" Entreri said.

"Catti-brie," Zak agreed.

"Come and join us, all, it will not take long," the aevendrow said, waving them to him in a very animated manner as he quickly approached. "All of you, but you most surely, beautiful lady." He hopped up and flipped his hair back from his face, then took Catti-brie's hand and brought it to his lips. "Magnificent! What are you?"

"What?" Zak repeated.

"She's a woman," said Entreri.

"A *married* woman," said Zak.

"Of course she's a woman," said the aevendrow.

"Human, from the south," Catti-brie explained.

"A married woman," Entreri reiterated.

"To you?"

"Not to me."

"Do you not think her beautiful?"

A flummoxed Entreri didn't answer.

"Of course you do," said the aevendrow. He looked closely at Catti-brie. "The color of your eyes! I have never seen such blue as that. Are you part kurit?"

Catti-brie started to reply, but thought of Bruenor and found herself just giggling at the unexpected complexity of the question.

The aevendrow turned to the artist. "Giville, make sure you get the eyes."

The artist stepped over, looked at Catti-brie, then nodded. "Humans from the south?" he said, glancing from Catti-brie to Entreri and back again. "Welcome."

"Come," said the female aevendrow from the group. "Please, join us. It will not take long."

"We don't wish to intrude," said Jarlaxle.

The man with them held up his hands, smiled and scoffed at the ridiculous notion. "We do this every Twilight Autunn on the eve of our war, so that the painting can be displayed behind the victory cup."

"Victory!" cried the orc from the group, and all the others joined in.

"We are Biancorso, the Scellobel Whitebears," the drow explained. "I am Vessi, or Alvinessy, but they call me Vessi. You may call me Vessi. We would like very much for you to join us for this. We do not get many visitors to Callidae, and having you in our portrait will mark it as particularly significant when we vanquish our enemies in cazzcalci."

The four companions looked around at each other curiously.

"Come, come," Vessi insisted, and he pulled Catti-brie forward by the hand, to the cheers of those behind him.

Giville the painter came over and posed them, front and center, then rushed back to his work. As promised, it didn't take very long at all, but still, Catti-brie had to keep being reminded to look forward, for she couldn't help but study those around her.

Particularly the tall woman with the purple-and-white hair, very striking, with features that seemed both angular and soft. The aevendrow bore a wide, joyful smile, and shining eyes similar to those of a drow man Catti-brie knew so very well—purple eyes to match the streaks in her hair! The woman gave a wink and blew a kiss, catching Catti-brie off guard, until she realized that the aevendrow was matching stares with Zaknafein at the time.

"You have just arrived, then?" Vessi said when the painting was done and the group began to scatter. All of the others made a point to come by the companions and pat them on the shoulder or the back before they left, though, and to promise victory for Biancorso in honor of the gracious visitors.

The woman with the purple eyes moved up beside Vessi, dropping her forearm familiarly upon his shoulder.

"We have just arrived, yes," Jarlaxle answered Vessi, though his stare never left the woman.

"All of you?" the woman asked, surprised. "Even you two?" she added, pointing out Jarlaxle and Zak. "You are not of Callidae?"

"No," Zak and Jarlaxle answered together, and that seemed to shake the two aevendrow profoundly.

"From Chult, then?" asked Vessi.

Zak shrugged and shook his head in obvious confusion, but Catti-brie caught a glimmer in Jarlaxle's eye. He knew of the southern forests of Chult, as did she. Had this aevendrow just informed them that there was another surface drow city in that southern jungle land?

"It is a long story," Jarlaxle replied. "But we've yet to introduce ourselves. I am Jarlaxle, and my friends are Catti-brie, Artemis Entreri, and Zaknafein Do'Urden, the great weapon master."

"A warrior?" Vessi asked, his face brightening as he looked to Zak. "This is my friend Azzudonna, and she, too, is a great warrior, as you will see in cazzcalci."

"Twice you have mentioned that," said Catti-brie. "Cazzcalci?"

"The battle of Quista Canzay," Vessi answered. "We fight it every year, borough against borough."

"The representatives of the borough," Azzudonna clarified, clueing Catti-brie in to the somewhat trepidatious expression that she—and likely her friends—wore at that moment. "Biancorso, the Whitebears, champion Scellobel."

"A joust," Zak offered.

"I do not know that word," Azzudonna said.

"A . . . game, a tournament," Zak tried to clarify.

"Yes, yes, a tournament," said Azzudonna.

"Should I look forward to it?"

"Once you have seen cazzcalci, you will think your life empty if you cannot see it again," the woman promised.

The tone between the two had changed, Catti-brie noted, and when she looked to her other friends, Jarlaxle's knowing grin and Entreri's resignation showed her that they hadn't missed the flirting, either.

"Where are you going?" Azzudonna boisterously asked them all, breaking the spell.

"We're just looking around, trying to learn the ways of Scellobel," Jarlaxle answered. "Priestess Ilina told us to see what we could see."

The woman smiled—rather slyly, Catti-brie thought—and whispered something in Vessi's ear. He, too, beamed.

"Do you like wine?"

"Quite!" Jarlaxle answered.

"Making it is more fun than drinking it," Azzudonna told them.

"Ah, but making it after you have had too much of it to drink is the most fun of all," said Vessi, and the two laughed.

"Come," Azzudonna bade them. "They have filled the barrel. Perhaps your warrior will find an opportunity to prove himself."

"Filled the barrel?" Jarlaxle quietly asked when they started off, the four friends trailing their two drow escorts.

"An old pirate joke," Catti-brie said.

Entreri snickered.

"I hope that's not what they mean," she added.

"If it is, better Zaknafein than me," Entreri agreed.

"What are you talking about?" Zaknafein demanded.

"You don't want to know," Catti-brie assured him, and Entreri laughed again.

Catti-brie, too, chuckled, and her reaction gave her pause. She was at ease. Up here, helpless in a city she did not understand, she found that beneath her forced caution, she was at ease, as were her friends, and even Entreri, it seemed, was giving in to the celebratory atmosphere so obvious around them.

What might Drizzt and Brie make of this place, Callidae? The thought intrigued her, but also reminded that her two greatest loves were not here beside her.

Vessi and Azzudonna led them into a vineyard, the smell of grapes both white and red thick in the air. A crowd of folk, mostly drow but with all others as well, had gathered near two buildings set beside the glacier wall. One was a house, similar to the others scattered throughout Scellobel, but the other, much larger, seemed more like a barn. Beside this barn on a slightly raised platform was what looked like the bottom quarter of a gigantic barrel, covering an area the size of a small room.

As they neared, Catti-brie noted that large buckets were being passed shoulder-to-shoulder from the barn to the platform, to be dumped into the barrel.

Grapes, Catti-brie realized. They were filling the barrel with grapes.

"This is a dance, then," she said aloud.

"Ah." Vessi sighed. "White. Less fun, and harder to judge."

"Red a bit later," said a nearby drow, and Vessi smiled at the news.

Jarlaxle, Zak, and Entreri all looked to Catti-brie for answers.

"The halflings of Bleeding Vines dance on the grapes in casks much like that to make their wine," she explained.

"How would that prove the worth of a warrior?" Jarlaxle asked.

"It is no dance," Vessi told them. He pointed to a group of around a dozen aevendrow standing off to the side and talking among themselves. "Those are the scouts for Biancorso and the B'shett Boscaille, for the Ardin Tivatrice and the Mona Chess Guardreale."

It took Catti-brie a moment to translate, but she had a feeling that Vessi was naming the teams of cazzcalci: the Whitebears, the Lumberjacks, the Farmers, and the Royal Guards.

"We of Biancorso discovered Azzudonna in a barrel," Vessi added with a laugh.

"But you wouldn't fight me in one," the grinning woman replied. "Not then and not now."

"Perhaps I did not wish to ruin your chances of joining Biancorso," he returned, batting his eyes, "because I thought you so beautiful and wanted you near to me."

She swatted at him, but he ducked aside.

"They will be leaving, of course, for they can only watch the fighting when the warriors are of their own boroughs," Azzudonna explained. "You must fight in cazzcalci for the borough of your home, with your heart and your pride. You live for cazzcalci. You carry the scars of cazzcalci. Some have died for cazzcalci, and it is a fate that we all accept."

The bucket brigade ended then, with a kurit climbing up on a platform behind the barrel and signaling that there were enough grapes. To great cheering, two drow women climbed to the platform, moving to either side of the huge barrel. They wore bits of clothing that left little to the imagination, just short white shifts of light material, and white ribbons wound about their upper legs and arms. They raised their hands, accepting the cheers, their names and nicknames being roared all about by their adoring fans.

The dwarf on the platform lifted a small gong and banged on it. One of the aevendrow combatants placed her hands on the rim of the barrel and inverted into a handstand, revealing quite a bit, before flipping over gracefully to land on her feet on the grapes.

The other hopped up into a sitting position on the edge of the barrel, where she sat facing the crowd for just a moment before straightening her arms and lifting up just a bit, then bending her legs out to either side to hook her feet over the edge. Remarkably, she released her grip and lifted her hands up beside her head.

The crowd hushed in anticipation.

"That can't feel good," Entreri muttered, for she was balanced there on a narrow ledge by only the fronts of her ankles.

Down went the woman's hands, then up again, when she threw her arms and threw herself, springing off her ankles into the air, into a backflip that landed her on her feet within the barrel.

The crowd roared with approval, many chanting, "Biancorso!" as if they expected the team to recruit the woman before the fight had even begun.

"Just an acrobat's trick," Azzudonna quietly remarked.

"You know her?" Jarlaxle asked.

"I know her opponent," Azzudonna replied. "Qvisi. This one will need more than gymnastics to beat Qvisi."

"You cannot bite," the kurit told the competitors. "You cannot claw. You cannot kick the head if the other has fallen."

He looked to the crowd and lifted his hands. "Tell me!"

"Zio!" came the roaring reply, and the fight was on.

The fighters ran together into a crashing clench, like the clash of rutting elk, followed by a desperate, full-bodied tug-of-war. They growled and ground, each pushing forward with all her strength while the dwarf counted. He held his fists up to either side and whenever a fighter gained a step, he raised a finger.

"Arktos oroks always win this part of the fight when they enter the barrel," Vessi told the friends.

"Except when one fights a clever kurit," Azzudonna added. "Then it is quite amusing."

Catti-brie was hardly listening, staring transfixed at the sheer intensity of the fighters. They ground their chins into each other's collars, occasionally snapping their heads to butt. Their arms worked to either side, each trying to tie the other up. And all the while, they bulled and bucked, anything to push the other backward.

She glanced at the dwarf. Four to two, and the one Azzudonna had named as Qvisi was winning.

The acrobat jumped backward just as the dwarf raised his fifth finger for Azzudonna's friend, and Qvisi pitched forward, nearly slipping down, and the acrobat hit her with a vicious right hook to her cheek. She turned to the side, went down to at least one knee—Catti-brie couldn't really see their legs from this angle—and came up immediately, turning as the acrobat jumped onto her back, trying to drive her down.

But Qvisi, so strong, stood straight instead, even snapped her head back against the face of the acrobat.

"She should let go," Azzudonna remarked.

Qvisi began to spin about and the crowd began clapping a cadence for her. She nearly slipped several times, but somehow held her balance, finally turning for the center of the barrel, putting her head down and rushing forward. She reached up and slapped her hands at the acrobat's head, but the lithe woman managed to fend off one, at least.

Qvisi pitched forward in a somersault, such a tight turn that her opponent couldn't get away from her fast enough and so served as a cushion for the landing.

"Beautiful," Vessi whispered, his remark buried under the roar of the onlookers.

The two came up almost immediately, near each other, facing each other, their fists flying, their light shifts plastered wet against them—and the acrobat's showing the blood dripping from her nose.

"Sanguine white," Vessi said. "This will be a fine batch."

"You *want* their blood in the wine?" Entreri asked him.

"Of course," he answered. "Brings it strength."

Catti-brie realized that her jaw was hanging open. She wanted to look away from the sheer viciousness of the exchange continuing in the barrel, but she couldn't. They were fighting with fists the way Drizzt and Entreri had fought with swords: rapid strikes, slaps, and blocks, but the precision was less apparent since they were slipping about on squishing grapes. As many swings wholly missed as hit, but the attempts to block were also less effective.

"How do they know who is winning?" Jarlaxle asked.

"You'll see," Azzudonna promised. "Oh, Qvisi!" she added when her friend seemed to have an opening as the acrobat staggered, but Qvisi, too, slipped, and her right cross that might have ended the fight just clipped the other on the cheek and ear.

Qvisi recovered quickly, though, falling back in a turning slide before coming ahead with a sweeping left hook that looked like it would rip the acrobat's head from her shoulders.

But she ducked, just dropped from sight, under the blow as if she had expected it.

To her credit, Qvisi caught herself short with the swing, and squared up almost immediately.

But up came the acrobat, like a fish leaping out of a pond, her arms down against her sides, her chin tucked, her head leading.

She caught Qvisi under the chin, snapping the warrior's head back, throwing her over backward, blood flying, and maybe a bit of tongue or a tooth as well, the acrobat falling down upon her.

As quickly as she had attacked, up sprang the acrobat, hands raised, leaping and dancing about.

"How does the wine taste with teeth in it?" Entreri asked their hosts.

"Eh, we will strain that out," Vessi answered.

The four companions stood and stared in shock, but the crowd was roaring in delight.

Azzudonna sighed heavily.

"Qvisi won't be invited as the next replacement to Biancorso that way," Vessi chided his purple-eyed friend. "She is strong and fast, wonderfully balanced, but not so smart, I fear."

He turned to his guests. "What do you think?"

"Violent," Catti-brie said before the others could form their replies.

"We live in a violent land. We are prepared, or we die."

"That's not the impression we got from our walk across Scellobel," said Catti-brie. "We see beauty and hear song and music. And dance. Everyone is dancing and smiling. Is it all a lie, then?"

She heard Jarlaxle suck in his breath, an unsubtle reminder that they were fairly helpless here at this time.

"Perhaps we view beauty all the more vividly because we know that our life here is ever on the edge of doom," Azzudonna said. "You believe you have felt the cold bite of the wind, but you truly have not. For the day is ending and the night is colder by far."

"Breaking someone's face open teaches one to fight off the winter's cold?" Entreri asked.

"Did the sight trouble you?" Azzudonna countered, and Entreri couldn't help but laugh. If only she knew . . .

Catti-brie, too, snickered a bit at that. Artemis Entreri's reputation had not preceded him, which was almost certainly a good thing!

"This is a land of dragons," Vessi said. "And great bears and yeti. And warrior giants of murderous intent."

Catti-brie wasn't the only one to perk up a bit at the remark about giants.

"And darker beasts still," Azzudonna added. "We fight to be prepared. We dance and sing and create beauty and make love to be alive."

She looked to Zaknafein. "What did you think of the fight?"

The weapon master shrugged, obviously trying hard not to appear impressed.

"The next barrel will be red," the woman continued. "Are you ready to feel alive?"

Another shrug from Zak, and he looked to his friends.

"I can't heal you at this time," Catti-brie reminded him.

"Their faith in you is truly heartwarming," Azzudonna teased.

Zak flashed her a wicked smile, one Catti-brie had seen her husband wear many times, usually right before he leaped into a wild battle.

"Red wine, then," Zak agreed.

THE WEAPON MASTER FELT A BIT FOOLISH AS AZZUDONNA wrapped white ribbons about his upper legs. He was wearing only a shift, after all, a short dress.

"If there is no clear victory, the amount of stain on you—grape, not blood—will be measured," she was explaining, though Zak was hardly listening—something a bit too obvious, he realized only when she stood and slapped him hard on the butt.

He turned a glare at her.

"Your challenger is Ahdin Duine," Azzudonna said into that stare. "Do not take her lightly. If Biancorso loses a center guard in the first fight of Cazzcalci, Ahdin Duine is likely to be named as replacement."

"I don't even know what any of that means."

"Center guards are the true brawlers of cazzcalci. The strongest. They open the way or defend the way for the dashers," Azzudonna explained. "Vessi is a dasher."

"And you?"

"I am a warrior, as are you, so they said. I support both guard and dasher. Strong and fast, I patrol all the way from my base to the Biancorso line in the enemy territory, two-thirds of the total battlefield."

"And the dashers go all the way into the enemy territory?"

"Dashers can go anywhere on the battlefield. Warriors are limited to two-thirds, guards to the middle third of the battlefield alone"

Zak nodded, beginning to catch on. There weren't many sports in Menzoberranzan, since there were few rules for fighting there, but the drow did have a couple of games, notably sava, where pieces on a board were given the ranks of Menzoberranzan's castes—slave to priestess—each with specific movements and powers. On the streets of Luskan, he had seen contests where teams kicked cloth balls about, trying to score in opposition goals. In Gauntlgrym, the dwarfs played "capture the keg," where, as far as Zak had ever figured it out, the point was to drink enough of your opponent's beer to forget the pain of the bruises you got getting to it.

"If Ahdin Duine gets in close to you, she will overpower you," Azzudonna warned him. "She is as strong as any orok, quicker than most. But she has a weakness."

"Do tell."

"Of course I will not."

Zak laughed.

The gong sounded and Azzudonna leaned forward and kissed him on the cheeks, left and right. "Now we will see."

She ran out of the small room. Zak took a deep breath and slowly followed, digesting the little information he had been given. He figured that the dashers were more like the acrobat he had seen in the earlier match, nimble and fast, whereas the warriors, if he was judging Azzudonna correctly, were a combination—Zak figured that he would likely be a warrior under that cazzcalci definition. What that meant, though, was still uncertain.

What *was* certain was that his opponent was probably stronger than he, but possibly not as quick.

He nodded and strode out to the platform, then up to the side of the barrel, filled now with dark grapes. He didn't have his hands raised, as did his opponent, a tall and broad-shouldered drow woman with dark gray skin and hair to match. Her face was set into a scowl, her eyes simmering red.

She looked at Zak, snorted derisively, then, to his surprise, walked away from the barrel. She turned, laughed, and ran full speed and hopped sidelong into the barrel wall, using the impact at midthigh to launch herself into a flying somersault, landing on her feet and skidding across on the grapes—all the way across, where she grabbed the edge right before Zak and roared in his face.

The crowd loved it, and cheered her all the way back as she sauntered to her side.

Zak tried hard not to laugh. He walked slowly up to the barrel, then went over carefully, deliberately, one leg moving in as he turned, then the other.

Hisses and laughter followed him.

He didn't care. He wasn't giving anything away. He noted something curious and unexpected as he touched down with his bare feet, though. The grapes were frozen.

"You cannot bite," the dwarf barker recited. "You cannot claw. You cannot kick the head if the other has fallen."

To the crowd, he lifted his hands and bade them, "Tell me!"

"Zio!"

Zak charged to meet Ahdin Duine's furious rush. He figured he'd get the worst of "zio," so he focused on minimizing the damage, getting his shoulder properly aligned at the last moment to fit across the widest area possible as the two collided.

Still, his breath was blasted away, and he felt Ahdin Duine's powerful hands grab him tightly, the woman already driving forward like an angry rothé.

Zak tried to dig in and fight back, but he was skidding.

To the side, the dwarf barker's fingers went up for his opponent, one, two, three, four . . .

Zak caught a foothold and braced, breaking her momentum finally.

Before he could celebrate, even as he started reversing the flow, she pulled back suddenly, slammed her forehead into his face, then slipped down just enough to grab him lower, hoisting him.

Five fingers raised for Ahdin Duine as Zak made his second mistake, trying to disengage as he had seen earlier, as he thought customary following zio.

Not so, he realized as he went up into the air, then flying over backward with Ahdin Duine atop him. The grapes padded his fall only minimally, as they were indeed frozen, and it was clear that his opponent was going for a quick kill as she slid to straddle him and began raining blows at his head.

"OOF," CATTI-BRIE SAID, SIGHING HEAVILY AND DROPPING her face into her hands.

Vessi laughed. "You still think us simple dancers?"

They couldn't see Zak, as he was below the rim, but they did see his hands coming up, trying to cut short the punches.

Jarlaxle paid particular attention, noting that Zak's defenses were improving against every punch.

"You think this fight ended?" he said.

"He lost zio five to none and he is already fully stained red, no doubt," Vessi replied as Azzudonna came over, her eyes fixed on the fight.

"Perhaps a wager, then," said Jarlaxle.

"All she has to do is stay awake and her victory is assured," Azzudonna put in.

"So wager," the mercenary repeated, but he winced as he did, seeing one of Ahdin Duine's heavy punches avoid Zak's block, resulting in a solid smacking sound. "Gold?"

Vessi and Azzudonna looked at him as if they didn't understand.

"Money?" he clarified.

"Money?" Azzudonna echoed.

"We have no need of such things, if I understand you," said Vessi.

Out of the corner of his eye, Jarlaxle saw a clever block and a second, and Zak got his hands looped about the woman's extended arms.

"Then what?" he asked quickly, thinking they might change their minds soon enough. He thought, perhaps, that he shouldn't be so confident here, but this was Zaknafein Do'Urden, after all, and when had Zak ever let Jarlaxle down?

HE TASTED HIS OWN BLOOD, HIS LEFT EYE WAS FAST swelling—and he knew that he had caught her punching right arm only because of the feel. He fought hard to hold on, and moved furiously to entangle her left arm. Ahdin Duine was beyond thinking here and was just pummeling.

And it was very near to working!

He wasn't done yet, though. Zak caught her left and didn't hesitate, pulling her forward with all his strength, sliding himself beneath her more than actually moving her. But no matter, for he got enough of his length out behind her. He bent at the waist, legs whipping up high, knocking her forward a bit, but to little real effect.

Little was better than nothing. He bent his legs and slammed them down, timing it perfectly to thrust his hips and arch his back, while reversing his pull and tugging Ahdin Duine straight down instead.

She lost her balance. Zak got out farther behind her, turning onto his belly, then up to all fours, still with his shoulders and head beneath her. As Ahdin Duine tried to stand, he came up under her and shoved off with all his strength, sending her head over heels into the grapes.

He too went down, but no matter, for he rolled away, putting distance between them, then came back up at the ready.

Ahdin Duine was smiling, laughing at him, even, and stalking in. Trying to cut the ring, he knew, thinking to keep him in close. But he thought of her attitude when she had been atop him. It had been a painful lesson, but Zak had learned it and survived. And now he knew her weakness.

"THERE ARE BETS ALL ABOUT," JARLAXLE SAID. "WHAT ARE they betting with, if not money?"

"Servitude," Azzudonna said. "There are chores to be done. Or a proper back rub."

"Or a foot rub," Vessi added. "Or even a kiss."

That might be fun, Jarlaxle thought, but he had another idea. "If Zak wins, then you two will show us all around Callidae, to all the boroughs."

Azzudonna and Vessi glanced at each other.

The crowd roared and the three turned just in time to see Ahdin Duine's flip, then the two coming up across the barrel from each other.

"After cazzcalci," Vessi agreed. "We of Biancorso are not permitted to go to the other boroughs until the wars are decided."

"And if Ahdin Duine wins?" Azzudonna asked.

"Then you will dance," Vessi told Jarlaxle. "In front of all Scellobel, you will wantonly dance."

"He'd do that anyway," Entreri remarked from the side.

"And you will dance with him," Vessi replied.

"Doubtful," Entreri started to say, but Jarlaxle cut him short with "Agreed!"

And they turned back to the fight, except Entreri, who paused a moment to glare at the troublesome rogue.

HE HAD HIS OWN WEAKNESS NOW, TOO, ZAK UNDERSTOOD, for he could barely see out of his left eye, and even that minimal vision seemed to be diminishing by the heartbeat. He turned his right shoulder forward toward the approach of the grinning Ahdin Duine and got his hands up defensively before him.

He had to fight her from a distance. Her advantage was that she was stronger than he.

She waded in confidently, hands rolling over in a furious barrage as she tried to force him back. He went low instead, turning left at the waist, then back to the right as he came up, his left arm rising fast and powerfully to connect with Ahdin Duine's left, driving it and her off to the side just a bit.

Then up he rose, turning with a fierce uppercut from his right hand, his body weight fully behind it. It came from his ankles, from his hips, from his fast-turning shoulders, all of his power, as his right fist connected just under the left side of Ahdin Duine's rib cage.

He heard the blast of her breath as he immediately rewound, then drove up again in the same spot, this time lifting her right from the floor.

She was staggering when Zak came around on her left, ducking low, but then springing upright and into the air. Now he pressed his middle knuckle out from his fist, a sharper point, and as he came down, the woman covered her ribs, so he drove that hand into her shoulder. He jumped back as he landed, measuring the damage as Ahdin Duine straightened and turned.

She was still smiling, but betrayed herself with an occasional wince, and even more so by the fact that she was holding her left arm a bit lower now. Zak inwardly smiled, thanking his old Melee-Magthere instructor, who had taught him that a properly angled knuckle could be as numbing as a sword pommel.

To those watching, the next exchange seemed no more than a wild blur of slapping, punching, and grabbing hands, but in the ring, both combatants methodically moved for their next play. Ahdin Duine was trying to finish him with a heavy punch, or to simply grab hold of him and get him in close, while Zak's movements and strikes were simply meant to prevent either of those events.

He was biding his time, hoping he could keep up, and very well aware that one mistake would cost him the fight.

Her right hook flashed above him as he ducked. She grabbed his right arm with her left, but Zak turned and tucked that arm in tight, breaking the hold and completing the circle quickly enough to stick a right cross into her stung shoulder yet again.

Enraged, Ahdin Duine came at him, her weakness, her overconfidence bringing her left foot too far forward, signaling her move.

Across came a vicious and sweeping right hook, but Zak was dropping into a deep squat even as it began, and even adjusting the angle of the swing, Ahdin Duine couldn't do more than graze the top of Zak's head with a glancing blow. No such problem for Zak, though, as he shot up straight with a snapping left jab, palm out instead of fist, connecting right under Ahdin Duine's nose.

She staggered back, stunned for just a moment, just long enough for Zak to step right and jab her shoulder once more. Then, as she was too late in executing a block, he stepped right again and jabbed, and a third time.

All to the same spot, the front of the shoulder ball joint.

Her arm sank more and she knew her vulnerability and swung about to get her left shoulder out of reach, but Zak wasn't going for it, instead reversing his slide, going back to the left. He launched a heavy left uppercut, the mirror image of the first body punch he had landed, taking her breath and sending her back.

He meant to follow with a running leap, but a sudden and overwhelming bolt of pain exploded within him at his own left shoulder, radiating down into his chest and arm. He saw Ahdin Duine recover and turn for him and tried vainly to get his left arm up in defense.

He couldn't. He couldn't stop her, but he didn't have to.

For Ahdin Duine halted her rush even before it really began and lifted her hands up before her, fully defensively.

"Phage!" she screamed, stumbling backward. "Phage!"

Zak's one working eye began to flicker. The pain did not relent. He heard her scream but knew not what it might mean. He glanced at his agonized shoulder and saw red lines pulsating out from under his smock, garish and angry.

He was on one knee and sinking, but didn't know how or why.

CHEERS TURNED TO SILENCE TURNED TO HORROR, VOICES screaming "Phage!" all about the three companions.

Vessi spun on them. "Deceivers!" he yelled at Jarlaxle, and he backpedaled along with everyone else about them.

"What is happening?" Catti-brie asked.

Her answer came as a host of armed aevendrow rushed at them through the mob of retreating onlookers, a line of spears leveled. Although their presence raised even more questions—and she was certain she wasn't going to like those answers.

CHAPTER 17

The Lie of Omission

They were spying on us as we expected, that much is clear," Jarlaxle told his two companions, pacing back and forth as Catti-brie and Entreri sat helpless in a darkened room back in the building of the inquisitors. Their robes had been taken from them, their arms bound behind their backs—not tied, but glued with some goo not unlike the one Jarlaxle often produced from his favorite wand. Their arms were stuck, their entire forearms locked in place, and all of them had mittens packed with the same gluey substance over their hands, preventing any coordination of fingers for spellcasting or anything else—never mind the fact that their magic didn't work right now. "You saw how fast they were on us, and in such force, when the cry went out from the fight."

"The cry, yes," Catti-brie answered. "Phage?"

"I don't know the word," Jarlaxle admitted.

"Then what?" Catti-brie asked. "What happened? Did Zak say something? Did our hosts become incensed because he was gaining strength in the match and even seemed to be winning?"

"It cannot be that," Jarlaxle started. "It makes no—" He stopped abruptly when the door banged open, a blue-white glow filling the room.

"Up," an aevendrow sentry demanded of the two humans. He held a "torch," a glass globe atop a small post filled with water and a trio of luminescent fish.

"What did we do wrong?" Catti-brie dared ask as she shimmied her back up the wall to stand.

"We should have just killed you in the first chamber," said a second aevendrow, entering.

Ilina.

"But why?"

"Shut up," Ilina told her. "From this moment forward, you will speak only when told to speak, and anything else will be answered with punishment."

"I . . ." Catti-brie fell silent and looked away.

They were marched out to the same anteroom where they had remained while each had earlier had their turn with the inquisitors. They expected the same, but this time, Ilina just kept marching them, bringing all three before the panel, who stared down at them from the shadows at the far end of the room.

On the other side of the room stood Emilian. He came forward to join Ilina, and it was they who started the questioning this time.

"You lied to us," Emilian said. "We welcomed you into our home, yet you lied to us. You brought phage to us. You put us all in peril."

The three looked to each other, none of them sure how to respond, or if they even could, given the warning Ilina had offered in the other room.

"Who will speak for you this time?" Ilina asked. "Just one."

"I will," Jarlaxle answered without even looking to his friends.

"Then speak."

"We did not lie."

"Another lie. You brought phage," Ilina countered.

"I don't even know what phage is!"

Emilian scoffed.

"The scar," Catti-brie realized and blurted before she could stop herself, and she stiffened as she heard the guard moving up quickly behind her, expecting to be punished.

Ilina held up her hand to stop the guard.

"Let them all speak," said the woman at the right end of the table, the straight-backed one who hadn't spoken at all when Catti-brie had first come before them.

"Scar?" she asked Catti-brie.

"Zaknafein's scar, on his shoulder," Catti-brie replied. "You saw the wound."

"Scar?" Emilian said, and scoffed again. "It is phage, chaos phage! Scar, you fool? He is plagued! He will become slaad! A red slaad, or perhaps even a green."

Catti-brie felt her knees go weak beneath her. She held her balance only barely, and noted the same from Jarlaxle.

"Green?" Artemis Entreri whispered. "The frog we killed was green."

"You lied to us," Ilina said, aiming the accusation at Jarlaxle.

"No," he corrected somberly. "We left out one encounter, one battle, one day of our travel."

The woman's lip curled in a snarl.

"We did not mean to deceive, we were simply afraid of you," Jarlaxle explained. "We battled a slaad, yes, and killed it, and it was green, as my friend just told you. But it came to us in the form of a drow, and spoke much like you spoke, that more ancient drow language than the one spoken in my homeland, one still fused with the softness of the language of the surface elves."

"Surface elves?" Emilian whispered, his expression skeptical.

"The elven peoples who are not drow," Catti-brie quickly put in, guessing his confusion easily enough. "Like the eladrin."

Emilian nodded and it was obvious that he had never heard them referred to in that manner.

"You fought a slaad?" Ilina prompted.

"We killed a slaad—a green one," Jarlaxle repeated. "Who came to us as a drow, masked by illusion."

"Your actions here reveal your lie," Emilian said. "Why would you have come with us, then? Why didn't you four start the fight when first we met, thinking that we, too, were not as we appeared?"

"You have the answer in your possession," Jarlaxle admitted. "My eyepatch. In the same way that I saw through the slaad's deception, so I saw that you were drow, as you appeared. The item has a great enchantment upon it, one of truesight."

"That's not true," Catti-brie said immediately, stopping and surprising Jarlaxle.

"Take them," said the male inquisitor as he and the other two stood. The woman on the right lifted a beveled shield of pressed white ice and a large blue sword.

"Just shut up, I beg," Catti-brie told Jarlaxle, and Ilina shoved her and told her to be silent. "For once in your life."

Escorted by the three inquisitors, the two guards, Emilian, and Ilina, the companions were led out of the house and down the streets to the northwestern corner of Scellobel and a large door fashioned of opaque pressed blue ice that appeared starkly different from the surrounding natural ice of the glacial wall.

Through that door, they entered a dark tunnel, the guard with the fishbowl torch rushing up front to lead the way with the armed inquisitor.

Barely inside, the friends felt the coldness of the place, a deep chill that increased with every step away from the city. They were shivering before they got to the first stairway, and that was only one of several they had to climb, so that by the time they had reached the apex of the tunnel, with only a short corridor leading to daylight, their fingers and toes were numb or throbbing with pins and needles, their breath thick before them with every exhale.

It got much worse when they came out of the tunnel, onto a ledge high on the side of the glacial wall, the ice cap spreading wide before them, and far, far below, the incessant hum of the cold wind sounding like a giant hornet, burrowing to the bone.

"I could be merciful and just throw you from this ledge," the sword-wielding inquisitor told them. "Or you may sit and wait for the wind to take the rest of the heat from your bodies. You will just fall asleep then, never to awaken."

"Then it was all a lie," Jarlaxle said through chattering teeth.

"*You* lied," the inquisitor replied. She lifted her sword and put its tip under Jarlaxle's chin, forcing him to look her in the eye. "We welcomed you and you repaid us with lies."

"No."

"The magic of the eyepatch, if it is even what you claim, would not have worked at the time when you were found in the outer chamber," the aevendrow told him.

"That's why I denied it," Catti-brie dared to put in.

The inquisitor lowered her blade and walked up to Catti-brie. "A priestess of Mielikki, you said."

Catti-brie nodded, though she feared that she was shaking so hard that the movement hardly registered.

"Perhaps we should judge you separately."

"No!" she replied. "We are together, in trust and in love. You cannot do that."

"Your friend lied to us."

"We didn't resist, we didn't fight, because we couldn't," Catti-brie growled through the freezing pain. "We didn't want to, anyway, but we were caught without hope, and so we could only hope that you were not what we feared."

"You used the silent hand code of the drow," Jarlaxle added. "A frog couldn't do that."

The inquisitor turned sharply on him. "If that is true, then why wouldn't you tell us of this fight, as you were instructed?"

"Because how were we to know that you weren't allied with them?" Catti-brie answered, determined to take the lead here. "The slaad we met, who wounded Zaknafein, was not alone in the lower tunnels of that cave. It was with a giant. A frost giant, Zak believed."

"A green slaad?" Ilina asked.

"Yes, as we told you."

"No green slaad did this to your friend. Their birth is one result of the chaos phage, but they are not the traffickers of the disease."

"We assumed the source of the injury to be the slaad we killed," Jarlaxle explained when Catti-brie hesitated. "Zaknafein wasn't with us when he fought in the lower tunnels. He went off to scout. Nor was he in the fight when the slaad came to us bearing the sword he had left behind, for he was sorely wounded then and being tended off to the side of the cave by the priestess Catti-brie. We didn't go back down to the lower tunnels after that fight, we left with all speed, especially since Zaknafein was so grievously wounded. Our friend only told us about the giant much later, and about the strange room he had stumbled upon."

The inquisitor looked past Catti-brie to her peers, then back at Jarlaxle.

"Eggs," he said. "Huge eggs being tended by the frost giant. White dragons, perhaps? Either way, we left, and did not pause or slow a moment to look back."

The inquisitor stared at him and back at Catti-brie for a long while—a time that seemed longer because the wind was surely taking the life out of the three standing in light clothing and nothing more. But Catti-brie had hope, for she recognized that Jarlaxle's information had shaken them profoundly, and more importantly, that the story had resonated.

"I sense no ill intent," the inquisitor announced. "I believe they are speaking truthfully."

"You believed that before," said the male inquisitor.

"And they were," the woman answered. "I cannot judge that which they do not say. Give them their robes," she told the guards, and as the friends were wrapped in the incredibly warm garments, the inquisitors led the way back into the tunnel, then back to Scellobel, to the hall, where again the three companions were presented before them, sans robes.

"My deepest apologies," Jarlaxle began when he was told to speak.

"Our apologies," Catti-brie corrected. "We agreed among us before you ever brought us to Callidae that we would keep the encounter in that faraway cave private until we could learn more of our captors, of you. Had you been aligned with the giants and the strange creature we had battled, a beast unknown to us, then—"

Ilina held up her hands to stop her.

"Where is Zaknafein?" Entreri demanded. "Did you heal his wound?"

Emilian snorted. "Heal? We are simply trying to keep him alive right now, and to fend off the encroachment of the chaos phage. If he is lucky, he will only lose his arm and shoulder. If he is already too far diseased, he will become one of them and will have to be destroyed."

"You can't kill him!" Catti-brie said.

"It is not a choice we would make easily, but it is also a choice we will not hesitate to make if the need arises. In another time, we could easily cure and heal him," Ilina explained. "But not now, not in the Twilight Autunn. Zaknafein will need better luck than he found in being struck by the claw of a blue slaad in this season without magic if he is to survive."

"Tell us your story again," the man in the middle of the inquisitor trio demanded. "From the time you came here to this land to the time you left that cave after your battle. And any other details you have kept from us. All of it." He looked over to the guards by the door. "Go and get us food and drink. We are going to be here for a long time, I expect."

The woman to his right added, "We had thought to let you enjoy the festival and to learn about you over the days from your actions and interactions, and only then demand of you the full story of where you come from and how you came here. You don't have that benefit now."

"I'm older than I look, I fear," Jarlaxle said with a chuckle—a rather pitiful attempt to lighten the mood, Catti-brie thought. "That will take a long time."

"We would all rather be outside in the revelry," the woman agreed. "Your deception has cost us that. Every detail, Jarlaxle, from the time you came to this land, to the fight in the cave, to your departure from the cave. And every other detail of your time here that you omitted. And either of you may correct him as you see appropriate. I warn you all, you will not be forgiven a second time for any lapses."

"Bring me to Zaknafein," Catti-brie pleaded. "I may be able to help."

"We are no strangers to the chaos phage," the same inquisitor woman answered. "It is a matter of existence for us, for we do battle with the slaad"—she looked at Jarlaxle and sharply added—"and the giants, both day and night."

"Please, he is my husband's father, the grandfather of my daughter."

"There is nothing you can do that we cannot. If you wish to see him again, then speak fully and truthfully here and now. He must be kept alive and the disease must be held back until the fall of night and the return of our healing powers."

"There's nothing you can do for him?" Jarlaxle asked.

"We have herbs. We are doing all that we can."

Catti-brie started to speak again, but the woman silenced her. "Worry about yourselves," she said. "You are here to tell us a story, a complete story. And if you fail now, know that we will not expend our healing efforts on your friend. The surest way to prevent the transformation of chaos phage is quite the opposite direction than that. The next time we must take you to that ledge is the last time."

The inquisitor looked to Ilina and nodded toward the door. "Go and check on Zaknafein," she said, and Ilina left the room.

Jarlaxle told again the story of how they had come to the north, of Gromph's magical gate, of the avalanche on the mountainside that nearly killed them, and of their desperate rush to find shelter. Now he told them the full tale of the cave, of Zaknafein's scouting descent while Catti-brie tended Entreri and then rested with him, of the fight with the slaad that had returned disguised as drow and carrying Zak's lost sword, and of their flight from the cave, to be far, far away.

When he told of the abandoned town, Catti-brie added a detail, fully describing her feelings when Zaknafein had torn the rift in the planes.

"I sensed that this glacier that serves as home to your colony is itself alive," she admitted, and held her breath.

"Our legends say it is one of the Vaati," Emilian replied to her after a moment.

That only brought confused looks from the companions.

"The Wind Dukes of Aaqa," explained one of the inquisitors.

"I do not know this lore," Catti-brie said.

"Nor I," Jarlaxle agreed.

"It is a tale for another day, if . . ." said the man on the dais. He held up his hand, as if changing his mind. "Our legends name this icefall as the remains of Qadeej, one of the Wind Dukes of Aaqa, who lay down here in the madness of Ygorl and called upon the cold north winds to protect him in the armor of ice."

"Ygorl?" Catti-brie asked. "The Lord of Entropy?"

"A slaad lord," Jarlaxle said.

"Enough," said the straight-backed woman on the dais. "Tell us the rest, all of it. Tell us of your homeland, of what you left behind. We had hoped this might wait, but no more. If you wish to have a chance at walking the ways of Callidae once more, then you will tell us this tale of why you came to us in full."

Jarlaxle bowed. "Again I ask you to accept my apology—*our* apology—for omitting the fight in the cave. I hope that you can understand."

"The apology is irrelevant," the straight-backed woman answered. "Right now, we care only whether or not you present to us a danger."

"We do not."

"That's what we'll find out," she said firmly before continuing. "Now, the town you found was Ulutiun, and most were killed by slaad. The few who escaped are among us now, or mostly, their descendants are among us."

Catti-brie thought back to the remains they had found, to the ones whose rib cages seemed to have broken outward, as if something was trying to escape from within . . .

Her legs nearly failed her as she thought of Zak, and she gave a little wail.

"What is it?" Emilian demanded.

"The skeletons we found there, ribs broken out from within. Is that this chaos phage?"

"No," Emilian answered. He looked to the inquisitors, who motioned for him to continue.

"Your fight with the green slaad was how long ago?" he asked.

"Tendays, perhaps a month," Jarlaxle answered.

"Those are two very different measures of time."

"I'm sorry—we lost track of time in the white."

More nods. "And you were four when you came to the north? You lost no friends along the way?"

"Just us."

"You will all be inspected again, more fully, for wounds," Emilian explained. "It will be quite thorough."

Before they could protest, the woman inquisitor on the left side of the bench asked, "You are certain that it was only that one green slaad that you slayed, and perhaps the blue slaad who struck your friend in the lower chambers?"

"We thought them the same," Jarlaxle replied. "The green one we killed was the only one we saw, and Zaknafein mentioned no other."

"You will all be inspected," Emilian said again. "Head to toe. If any wounds or scars of recent wounds are found, the inspection will grow more intrusive, I am afraid."

"Zak was the only one injured in that fight," Catti-brie said.

"Yes, and it is a great tribute to your goddess that he is still alive," Emilian replied. "Chaos phage usually kills the host, transforming the victim into a slaad, red or sometimes green, within a few days, at most, but that is not the only way the slaadi expand their numbers. One type produces eggs."

"Zak saw the eggs in that cave," Jarlaxle said, but Emilian shook his head.

"The eggs are small, and cut into hosts at the end of a red slaad claw, and there they gestate and hatch, and grow inside the victim until the tadpole devours the innards and bursts forth from the chest. It can take a matter of months."

Catti-brie remembered the out-broken ribs, and she shuddered at the horror of it. "So Zaknafein had an egg inserted into him?" she asked. "I'll admit I'm more than a little confused."

Emilian laughed. "Not as confused as the slaadi," he said. "And no, Zaknafein has no egg within him. For the slaadi, those who are not evolved to the greater ranks of their kind, there are three types: red, blue, and green. And they hate each other viciously. But they need each other. The red slaadi inject the eggs, which burst forth when they are ready."

"Like the bones we found in the Ulutiun town," Catti-brie said.

"I'm so glad we followed you here," Entreri sarcastically remarked to Jarlaxle.

"Yes," Emilian said. "Those tadpoles become slaadi, most blue, but some, if the host was powerful in the ways of magic, green. The blue slaadi inject the chaos phage, as with your friend Zak, who would, who still may, become a red slaad or a green."

"He is not wizard or priest," Jarlaxle said.

"Red, then," Emilian told them.

"And the green? We battled a green," Catti-brie explained. "What do they make of their victims?"

"Dinner," Emilian replied.

"Cooked with fireballs," grumbled Jarlaxle.

"They were spellcasters before; they are spellcasters still," Emilian explained. He clapped his hands together as if to put an end to that troubling conversation. "So you see that our most prudent course would be to simply kill you all and burn your corpses," he finished. "But that is not our wish. So tell us the full story of your journey to Callidae and make yourselves worthy of our mercy."

MANY HOURS LATER, AND AFTER POSSIBLY THE MOST careful and intrusive inspection any of them had ever known, the three friends emerged from the inquisitor house beside Emilian, their gooey shackles removed.

"Go where you will," Emilian told them. "I will accompany you."

"To watch over us," Entreri remarked.

"Of course you are being watched—you were watched the first time you traversed Scellobel. Would you expect less of us? But no, I am not accompanying you to watch over you, but to watch out for you. Word of the revelations at the wine battle, of the chaos phage, has spread wide, no doubt. You will find many questions confronting you as you move about Scellobel."

"We are glad to have you, and thank you," Catti-brie said.

"We wish to see Zaknafein, of course," Jarlaxle said.

"Not now," Emilian said, shaking his head, but then brightened a bit as he motioned for them to look out to the street, where Ilina was coming quickly to meet them, along with Vessi and the woman Zak had been battling, Ahdin Duine.

"He fares a bit better," Ilina told them before they could even greet her. "The herbal wraps are in place. Zaknafein is strong."

"Azzudonna is with him," Vessi added.

"Our apologies," Jarlaxle said with a bow. "We did not know that he was afflicted."

"I thought his wounds cured before we arrived here," Catti-brie explained. "I pray to Mielikki that you are not in danger," she told Ahdin Duine.

The drow warrior woman shook her head.

"The danger would have come if the chaos phage had taken him fully," Emilian replied, "for then we would have had a slaad among us. Chaos phage spreads only from the claw of a blue slaad."

"If it were more contagious than that, we'd all likely be hopping instead of walking," Ilina added with a chuckle. She looked to Emilian and held her hand out toward the three strangers to Callidae. "The inquisitors are satisfied?"

"They are. Our visitors should be glad that Holy Galathae sits on the dais at this time. Galathae is most sensitive to the words and movements of one being questioned," Emilian explained to the three. "She can discern not only whether one speaks truthfully, but the intent behind the words."

"She is a paladin," Catti-brie realized.

"Oh, by the gods," Artemis Entreri muttered, but in Common, not Drow, and he heaved a great sigh.

Jarlaxle laughed a bit too much, Catti-brie thought. "My friend here has suffered some difficult—perhaps the better word would be 'annoying'—encounters with paladins in the past. A paladin king, in particular. Pay him no heed, for he is ever cynical."

"I find that I like him all the more," Vessi said, and Emilian and Ilina laughed.

"Vessi was once paired with Galathae," Ilina explained, and Vessi's sigh was as heartfelt as Entreri's had been.

"Paired with?" Jarlaxle asked. "Married, you mean."

"No, no," said Vessi. "We did not get near to that!" This time, he joined Emilian and Ilina in their laughter.

"I find Galathae most wonderful," Ahdin Duine said, clearly surprising the other Callidaeans.

"You marry her, then," said Vessi.

"One never knows" was all that Ahdin Duine would say.

"When can we see our friend?" Catti-brie interrupted the ensuing cheers.

"Azzudonna will bring him to us, to you, when the healers are done with him and he is able," said Vessi. "Until then, let them keep to their work, and Zaknafein to his rest. I warn you, he is doing better now, but until powerful spells can be put upon him, the phage will remain, and will grow."

"He has had the disease within him for a long time," Ilina told Catti-brie. "It might require the greatest spell of all."

Catti-brie returned a blank stare, not sure what she might be speaking of, and very sure that she was not enjoying the implications.

"This talk is for another day," Ilina announced. "The healers work with your friend and they are very hopeful that he will be kept alive and as drow until the magic returns to us. And then, of course, fully restored. Let us go about and enjoy the festival of Twilight Autunn. The smells and the song and the dance call to my heart."

Vessi pointed at Entreri. "I sense a kindred spirit here," he said. "Come . . ." He paused, prompting Entreri with his wagging hand.

"Artemis," he answered.

"Come, Artemis," Vessi continued, "I will show you places of great enjoyment for those of our common . . . shall we say, temperament?

Places paladins do not enjoy. This is the last day I am allowed to travel to the tunnel taverns between the boroughs, and I wish to go into my seclusion with Biancorso holding my head in my hand!"

"I think you would have more fun with him," Entreri replied, pointing to Jarlaxle, but Jarlaxle wouldn't hear of it, and pushed the man forward.

"Go," he told Entreri. "Learn something."

"Would you show me the herbs?" Catti-brie asked Ilina as Entreri and Vessi started off.

"Ardin is a long way," the priestess answered. "But yes. It will give us the chance to speak at length. I wish to hear more about your goddess."

"Well, that makes you the fortunate ones," Jarlaxle said when the two women departed, leaving him with Emilian and Ahdin Duine.

"I hope your friend will recover," Ahdin Duine said.

Jarlaxle paused, collecting himself. "Thank you. He is indeed my friend, my oldest friend. I will tell you of our adventures together, or of those we have the time for."

"He had me defeated," Ahdin Duine admitted.

"He did," Emilian agreed. "Though you fought brilliantly, Vessi told me. He and Azzudonna will speak highly of you to Biancorso."

That brought a smile to the young aevendrow woman.

"Zaknafein was the greatest warrior in Menzoberranzan in those many years we lived there," Jarlaxle told them. "He is to this day the greatest drow warrior I have known, and I have known many. Well, the greatest with one exception—his own son, the husband of Catti-brie."

"I would like to hear those tales of adventure," Emilian said.

"And I," Ahdin Duine agreed. "I have been told that the vintners have brought forth the bottles filled in Twilight Autunn the year I was born in honor of my battle with your friend."

"We mustn't miss that," Emilian said.

"Not for the world," Jarlaxle agreed, and let himself be led away.

CHAPTER 18

Softness

C old, yes?" Azzudonna said when she crawled into the access tunnel to Zaknafein's bedside.

Propped up in a sitting position, the weapon master didn't need to nod to confirm the obvious, for his smile showed chattering teeth. His shoulder and arm were wrapped in a giant ice-pack bandage, and his bed itself was no more than a bit of padding cut into the glacial ice wall.

"They will take you out soon," Azzudonna told him. "It's believed the cold may slow the progress of the phage, particularly when it is in an arm or a leg, and it allows the herbs to better battle it."

Zak nodded. "The w-woman I f-fought," he chattered. "Did I infect her?"

"Oh no, put your heart at ease. You cannot transfer the phage. Only the claw of a blue slaad can do that."

Zak nodded again and took a relaxed breath.

"You fought well," the woman said. She moved a bit closer and turned sidelong, mirroring Zak's position. She lay on her side and propped her head up on an arm bent at the elbow, her thick mane of purple-and-white hair cascading down to the ice floor of the crawl space.

"She surprised me with her strength," Zak managed to get out, and he finished with a shudder and a puff of frosty breath. "It almost ended before I knew it had begun."

"We saw that. Ahdin Duine is no minor opponent. It is likely that she secured a rank among those we would elevate to Biancorso if we lose center guards. And yes, we all saw, she almost had the match won. All she had to do was survive the fight and she would have taken the victory, since your grape stains were—"

"Are," he corrected, bringing his working arm to his red-and-purple-stained shift.

"Yet, if you had not fallen to the phage, she would not have held out," Azzudonna said.

Zak shrugged, and shivered.

"I do not say that in false flattery," she assured him. "As soon as you recovered your footing, you found her weakness and exploited it."

"She was too forward with her attacks," Zak said. "She lowered her off-hand guard in trying to hit a bit harder." He smiled ruefully. "I'll admit, she hit hard."

"If you remain in Callidae, you will fight in cazzcalci next year, I do not doubt. I hope that you will choose Scellobel as the borough of your home." She paused and gave him a playful smile. "Because I would not wish to have to beat you senseless."

Zak managed another wide smile, but winced in pain as he shifted. "Will I ever fight again?" he asked, as much to himself as to his guest.

He looked to Azzudonna as he finished, though, his eyes redirecting the question to her.

She wasn't smiling.

She was trying to smile. But she wasn't smiling.

THE COMPANIONS WERE HOUSED IN A LARGE LOW STRUCture near the crossroads of Scellobel. This was the only inn within the entire borough, typically used for visitors from the other three who didn't feel like hiking back after a visit. And occasionally, very occasionally, it was used for outsiders who had wandered into the glacial rift, or who would have been doomed had not the aevendrow gone out to rescue them from the unforgiving elements. The placard outside named the inn as IBILSITATO, a word Jarlaxle did not understand until he broke it down and rearranged a syllable.

"It's just a welcome to visitors," he explained to Entreri and Catti-brie.

"No wonder, then, that you had trouble with it," Catti-brie quipped. "It's not something you would readily read in Menzoberranzan."

"Not true. The dungeons of House Baenre have a similar greeting above the entry door," Entreri said.

But they were not in the dark city of the drow, and this was no dungeon. The place was more a common room, a tavern of sorts, than an inn, with just a few bedrooms set in the back. It didn't take long for the companions to realize that one of their newfound friends had eased the way for them here, for they were met with warm greetings by the kurit busing and waiting the tables and the two aevendrow moving in and out of the kitchen with trays of food, the round-faced Ulutiun chef close behind and reminding her team repeatedly, "Dance and serve. Food is the lust of life, remember!"

They were given a table near the middle of the room and felt the eyes of Callidaeans upon them as the establishment filled up around them. There were no harsh words aimed their way, though, and more than one of those gathering came up to them and offered well-wishes for their afflicted friend, with assurances that the healers of Scellobel were very familiar with battling the chaos phage.

Catti-brie noticed that Jarlaxle was saying less and less to those who came over, and seemed to be looking inward more than outward, a quite unusual posture for the clever, detail-devouring rogue. She couldn't miss the look in his eyes (and how unusual it was to see both of his eyes!), however, as he took in the sights and sounds of mirth about him.

She understood that, and felt it, too.

"Do you see the future here, Jarlaxle?" she asked after a while.

"The future for me?"

"For your people," the woman clarified. "Is this place a vision of your hopes for Menzoberranzan? For Luskan, perhaps?"

"I don't yet know what to make of it," he admitted. "I don't doubt the sincerity of our hosts, nor do I even fear that there is a more vicious underbelly to this place. Not much of one, at least, and that is more than I can say of almost any city I have ever visited."

"It's not Menzoberranzan," Entreri agreed.

"But there are flashes of Callidae in Menzoberranzan," Jarlaxle pointed out. "In the Stenchstreets, mostly, where the influence of the matrons is minor."

"And where bodies are often found in alleyways," Entreri reminded him.

"Ah, my friend, but that is the spillover from the political and familial rivalries, most often."

"Menzoberranzan is a noxious place," Catti-brie said. "I don't feel that here, and I don't believe that we are being deceived. Their smiles are real, and grounded in joy."

"They play hard, and drink harder," said Entreri, who was nursing a tremendous headache. "They dance, they love, and they sing with abandon."

"And they drink," Jarlaxle repeated with a knowing grin.

Entreri groaned and held his head.

"You enjoyed your time with Vessi?" Catti-brie said with a laugh.

"Too much so. But yes. He took me to a place he called De'lirr. I did not know that drow could sweat so much."

The other two looked at him curiously.

"It was half a dance, half a fight to see who could stay on the floor the longest. Few left alone."

"Including Entreri?"

The man just shrugged and even seemed to blush a bit, which caught Catti-brie off guard.

"They are alive," Entreri went on. "Maybe more alive than any people I have known. They play harder than many fight."

After a moment of quiet, Catti-brie surprised her companions when she looked to Jarlaxle and asked, "Are you ready to admit it yet?"

"Dear lady, whatever are you talking about?"

"That this, Callidae, is why we're really up here in the far north," Catti-brie replied. "It wasn't about Doum'wielle, and certainly not about Khazid'hea. You brought us here because you knew of this place."

"I did not," Jarlaxle said, somberly and evenly, fully without flare. "I did not know of it, but . . ."

"But?"

"But yes, I suspected its existence."

Catti-brie sat back and sighed. Artemis Entreri locked his stare upon the rogue.

"On the same trip I took to visit the Moonwood, I met a very old elf in Silverymoon who was known to spout wild stories of drow in the north, at the top of the world."

"What a wonderful coincidence," Catti-brie sarcastically remarked.

"It was no coincidence," Jarlaxle admitted. "I had heard of Free-windle before, and had already commissioned a lord of the region to look more deeply into the rumors, and also to arrange the visit with Sinnafein. You see, it has always been about Doum'wielle as well, and yes, though it is a minor thing, about Khazid'hea. Finding Doum'wielle, if she is who I believe her to be, will prove no small thing in the coming trials of Menzoberranzan. I knew she was in the north and had somehow, so it seemed, survived. I thought she might be here, if *here* even really existed."

Entreri snorted.

"What?" Jarlaxle bade him.

"I do not much like being used," he said, "though I wonder why it even surprises me where you are concerned."

"You were not used, and not deceived."

"This sounds like your words to the inquisitors," Catti-brie said. "You remember, the ones that almost got us thrown from a cliff."

"I knew only whispers of such a place as Callidae from an elf nearing the end of his life and seemingly more lost in fantasy than present in that which was truly around him," Jarlaxle said. "I didn't even know its name, and had no idea that it might be within a glacier, or that it would be anything like this."

"Except for the drow," said Catti-brie.

"Yes, and that they were not Lolthians, that their society was neither cruel nor unjust. Quite the opposite, for if what Freewindle told me in his rambling tales of these drow is true, we have come upon a society that is egalitarian and moral, a place where you survive because you can rely on others and where they survive because they know they can rely on you. Do you now understand what such a promise means to me, who had to survive Menzoberranzan? To Zaknafein, who gave his very life simply so that his matron wouldn't murder her own son, and for no better reason than him denying the vile demands of the Spider Queen?"

"So Zak knew," Entreri said.

"No," Jarlaxle sharply replied. "I told no one but Dab'nay, who was with me in the east, and swore her to secrecy as well. Do you realize how great the disappointment would have been for Zak if Freewindle's tales were indeed rambling fantasies? I could not do that to him, or even to Kimmuriel or Gromph."

"Gromph?" Catti-brie echoed incredulously.

"Gromph," Jarlaxle declared. "Or any of the others. Any of Bregan D'aerthe, and most of those in Menzoberranzan, as well. I didn't tell you for the same reason Dab'nay wouldn't: because we understand the stakes here for those of us who escaped Menzoberranzan and the Spider Queen. This, Callidae, the aevendrow, all of it, is something we dared not even hope.

"So, no, I reject your anger and your claim that I deceived you, because this is, too, about Doum'wielle, for her sake, for the sake of her poor mother, and for the hope that we can do something to prevent, or mitigate, or at least make sure the correct side wins in, the coming storm in Menzoberranzan. That may not matter to you, but it matters to me, deeply."

"It doesn't matter to me," Entreri said, but he looked down as he did, not making eye contact, and Catti-brie thought he had just wanted to say something, anything, to strike back for being deceived.

"It matters to me," Catti-brie said to Jarlaxle. "It matters to my husband, to my family." As she finished, she considered Drizzt's mood of late, and silently added to herself, *I think.*

"That said, I add this warning: we don't really know what Callidae is," she added.

"We've seen them fight," Entreri interjected, looking up again, his expression deadly serious. "You don't learn that in knitting circles or from painting pretty pictures. And in my night with Vessi, I saw them fight even more, weapon duels with blunted blades. If a score of aevendrow fought a score of Menzoberranzan drow, the only bet I would take is that both would lose."

"It's a harsh land," Catti-brie reminded him.

"Perhaps," Entreri replied. "But it is my experience that those who fight so well fight often."

"They are as they seem," Jarlaxle insisted. "They play hard, they love free, they live for life itself. I saw this on the Stenchstreets of Menzoberranzan. For all my life, I thought that merely a response to the strict edicts of the matrons and Lolth, but now I see that the ways of the Stenchstreets were because the drow there, for all the pressures and threats upon them, were free."

Entreri scoffed, but said nothing as a woman came over to the table then, carrying two drinks in each hand. Her hair was more blue than white, and her skin showed bluish shades amid the dusky gray of drow heritage. Her eyes, too, were blue, light blue, though, not the same deep hue as Catti-brie's. Still, blue was an eye color none of the three had ever seen on a drow. She was dressed in a beautifully laced and revealing gown, trimmed with golden fur that seemed soft enough to fall into and never return. She placed down three of the mugs, which looked like glass but were, in fact, made of ice, and were filled with a heady beer.

"To new friends," she toasted, lifting her own mug for a large swallow. "Billibi," she said after she had wiped her foamy lips, and she indicated one of the aevendrow, who was pushing a large cart. "He will come by with a fine assortment. Take what you will, but if you are very hungry, take the *tagliog*. It is the steak of the tail, full of fat." She smacked her lips together and winked, then started away, but paused and turned back. "I spoke with Ilina," she said seriously. "You haven't done as she asked."

The three looked at the woman curiously.

"Persimmons," the blue-eyed drow explained. "With kurit muskox cheese and Scellobelee ice wine, of course. I have some coming for you shortly. You will thank me."

Another wink and she danced away.

"I've found the answer of the gods," Jarlaxle said, "for surely I've died and gone to paradise."

"This is a place where danger is all about," Catti-brie said. "They survive by counting on each other. Maybe that's the key to their love of life. I think you are right, Jarlaxle."

"*Gioi*," the rogue said. "The love of life and the appreciation that it is temporary." He hoisted his ice mug and Catti-brie tapped it with her own.

"I'm surprised there is such a word in your language," said Entreri. "But as to what you claim as the reason," he added to Catti-brie, "haven't you also described Menzoberranzan? What *gioi* do you find there, surrounded by danger?"

"The Stenchstreets," Jarlaxle said again.

"The murders," Entreri countered again.

"The Stenchstreets without the shadows of Lolth, then," said Catti-brie, and to that, she and Jarlaxle lifted their icy mugs again.

This time, after a grunt and a grumble—because he was, after all, Artemis Entreri—Entreri joined in.

The tail steak was every bit as delicious as promised, and the trio were devouring large cuts when the blue-eyed woman returned.

"You are a priestess, I am told," she said to Catti-brie.

The woman nodded, her mouth full.

"When magic returns, I will teach you how to create this," the drow promised.

"What is your name?" Jarlaxle asked.

"Ah, I know yours and forgot to tell you my own! I am called Ayeeda, but my real name is Aida'Umptu."

"I'd love to learn to make it," Catti-brie said. "I'm amazed that this can be accomplished without killing an animal."

"It's a necessity, since there are so few animals around. Besides, we love our animals. Consider this: I share my house with two mukteff. I would no sooner skin them than I would skin . . . well, you! And I must admit, I do find the color of your skin quite beautiful."

"Should I worry?" Catti-brie asked with a laugh.

"No, but maybe he should," Ayeeda answered, and she poked Entreri's shoulder, then laughed and spun away.

"So it is true, as we were told. They have learned to shape their magic to replicate beautiful things," Catti-brie said when she was gone. "You really are in your paradise, Jarlaxle."

The look Jarlaxle returned in that moment truly gave the woman pause, for she had never seen such an expression on the face of the irascible rogue. He looked like he was about to cry.

Ayeeda returned soon after with the promised persimmons. She pulled up a chair and joined the friends, and showed them how to properly eat the Scellobelee delicacy, with the perfect and necessary ratio of cheese to the fruit, with the wine chaser close at hand.

"As I promised!" came a voice when the four took their first bite and sip of wine, and they turned to find Ilina, Emilian, Ahdin Duine, and several others coming over to join them.

"There is only one greater joy to be found in all of Callidae," Ayeeda said, and she cast a glance at Entreri. "And even that is a contested opinion!"

"Yes, cazzcalci," Ahdin Duine immediately countered. "Cazzcalci. There is nothing to exceed cazzcalci."

"To Ahdin Duine, then," said Emilian, lifting a mug. "If she does not find an opportunity to get on the rink this festival, then may she find a full battle next sunset!"

"Ahdin Duine!" the others cheered.

"Where is Vessi?" Entreri asked, looking about to see if he was among the group.

"He is in seclusion, of course. Biancorso will not be seen until their first battle under the shimmering night."

"The shimmering night?"

Filled mugs were brought to all and the next toast roared throughout the common room. "Biancorso! Quista Canzay!"

"Your head will hurt even more tomorrow," Catti-brie warned Entreri as he put his mug back to the table and suppressed what clearly would have been a tremendous belch.

"Worth it," he replied.

Catti-brie sat back and joined in the toast. She still couldn't dismiss the fear that this was all a deception, but as the revelry wore on, she came to realize that her fear remained only because she truly didn't want it to be a ruse. Even aside from whatever danger such a deception might mean for her and her friends, she didn't want this to be anything other than what it seemed.

For Jarlaxle.

For Zaknafein.

And more than that, for Drizzt.

And most of all, for Brie.

"I MUST SAY GOODBYE FOR NOW," AZZUDONNA TOLD ZAK.

Zak spent a moment catching his breath, which was becoming increasingly difficult. He felt as if he had a feather in the back of his throat, one that constantly tickled him. "Where?" he managed to ask.

"I must go into seclusion with Biancorso before cazzcalci," the warrior explained. "Sunset is only three days away. We must prepare. We must consider nothing but cazzcalci."

Zak nodded and turned his head back to a neutral position, staring straight up at the ice. He thought of his son, and now believed he would never see Drizzt again. He thought of Catti-brie—yes, he would have them bring her to his bedside. He owed her an apology for those early days when he had first come back to life, when he hadn't quite been able to get beyond the prejudices that had been ingrained in him since the day of his birth. Even if, especially if, it was with his last breath, he wanted to tell her that one more time. He hoped for a better world for his granddaughter, and now, seeing this place, he dared to believe it could be so.

But still, he could not die happy. He could not leave again now and accept it.

"I will fight," he declared, though he really didn't even know what he was fighting. He had no feeling in his shoulder or his arm, but that was mostly the ice, he figured. What was scaring him, though, was the creep of tingling numbness and the crackling lines that now covered half his chest and had crossed over to his other hip and down his right leg.

"I wish you would fight beside me in cazzcalci," Azzudonna said. "Next year, yes!"

Zak heard the false optimism in her declaration, her exaggerated exuberance for his sake. She understood what he was facing here. He turned his head to regard her again and, despite his discomfort, was struck by the image. A fire burned in the room behind her, its light dancing into the deep alcove. She was on all fours, the tunnel being too low to stand in, and was shifted just a bit to the side, her head bent that way, her smile wide.

Too wide for the fears that were in her heart, Zak knew, but he couldn't help but appreciate her effort here.

Her long hair bundled on her shoulder and rained down from there, like a sparkling waterfall, the flickers of firelight flashing between the strands with her every movement.

There was something about her in this moment, in this light, a softness that struck Zak profoundly, and it took him a moment to understand why.

He had never seen a drow woman this . . . gentle. This emotionally open. This giving. The closest had been Dab'nay, and his scattering thoughts began to summon those tender memories with the priestess. He began to lose himself in that past.

Azzudonna lifted her hand from the floor, holding something, and Zak was brought back to the present.

His shirt?

"This was yours, yes?" she asked.

He managed a slight nod.

"May I tear it?"

The question confused him.

"A strip of it," she explained. "I wish to wear it about my wrist in the battle. I will be Zaknafein's champion, if he will allow."

Zak nodded.

She gave a tug, creating only a minor tear.

"Mithral," Zak whispered as the woman inspected the garment and noted the light metal inside the fabric layers. She smiled and separated enough to rip a piece off the tail of the shirt. She looped it about her right wrist, rolled it under into a knot, and looped it again, then tightened it, tugging with her left hand while holding the other end in her teeth.

She stared at him with those lavender eyes so much like his son's, smiling all the while. "There," she proclaimed when she was done, holding her hand out to him, the back near to his face.

"Do you give me your blessing?" she asked when he didn't respond.

He started to say he would when Azzudonna moved her hand a bit, showing him what she meant. Zak leaned forward and kissed the back of her hand. Then she took his hand and similarly kissed it.

"Biancorso will win," the woman said. "I will throw with the strength of Zaknafein."

"Throw?" he tried to ask, but barely a sound came out.

"Rest, my new friend," she answered. "Rest and fight against the affliction. Sunset is soon and the wane of magic will turn to wax. Hold strong and we will win your fight soon after Biancorso wins its battles. I promise."

She came forward more then, and pressed her lips against Zak's cheek.

"I promise," she said again, and she crawled back out of the alcove.

Zak closed his eyes and tried to focus his will. But it was harder now. He was glad for her promise.

Even if he didn't believe it.

CHAPTER 19

Cazzcalci

H e looks terrible," a devastated Catti-brie said to Galathae when she and the paladin left the building housing Zak's vault. It could not be denied. Catti-brie had been coming to him every few hours since the aevendrow had allowed it, and Zak's accelerating disease was plain to see. Now the entire left side of his chest was swollen and red, almost glowing red, and his mouth had stretched, reaching nearly from ear to ear, making him almost unrecognizable. He was failing, clearly, and he was changing.

Galathae offered her a hand on the shoulder for support, but said nothing in reply.

"I thought your people had experience with this," Catti-brie said.

"Vast experience. Too much experience."

"And knew how to counteract it, to heal the phage."

"There is a reason we have increased our watch about the city in this time of the year," Galathae replied. "There is a reason why none but those patrols are outside of Callidae at this time. We have little experience with the chaos phage in the time of Twilight Autunn because we do not engage the slaadi in this time, nor do they—so dependent upon magic themselves—press their attacks against us. Twilight Autunn is a time of peace because there is no magic, no illusions, no healing, no escape.

"Zaknafein has to survive through the first few days of this sunset," she went on. "He must find it within himself to resist the final bites of the transformation until our magic returns. Perhaps the herbs and the ice will help to slow the progress, but it is his will that will carry him through."

"And if not?"

"He will become a red slaad."

"And your magic? You said the greatest of spells . . ."

"We have nothing to save him, then," Galathae grimly replied. "Once, so say the histories, we had a wizard who reversed the transformation, who wished the victim back to her previous life as aevendrow. But it cost the wizard greatly and he was not able to cast that most powerful of magic spells ever again, to the day of his death."

That thought jarred Catti-brie's thoughts. A wish spell? Who did she know who might cast such a legendary dweomer? No Harpells, certainly. She thought of the Hosttower of the Arcane. If anyone there could perform such a great feat of magic it would be . . . Gromph Baenre.

Could he? More importantly, *would* he?

"If the transformation is completed, Zaknafein will be quickly and mercifully slain," Galathae said, jolting the woman from her thoughts.

"No," she argued. "We will take him back to the south. We have powerful wizards—"

"No," Galathae interrupted. "You would have no way to get him back there in time for any wizard to perform such a reversal."

"And you would not allow it," Catti-brie said.

Galathae didn't confirm that, but Catti-brie could see that the paladin was truly torn here. The slaadi were obviously mortal enemies of the aevendrow, and the thought of letting another of the beasts free was not one the paladin could easily digest. Red slaad were prolific procreators, so Galathae had told her.

"Sunset is tomorrow," Galathae said. "Take heart. Zaknafein is strong—most would have succumbed long before now. Our magic will return soon, as will yours."

Catti-brie nodded and took a deep and steadying breath, steeling herself against the grim possibility before her. Because she saw the decline and doubted Zak would live another day.

"The battle is tomorrow," she said, hardly thinking.

"Cazzcalci, yes. It is glorious."

"Have you ever fought in it?"

"Almost. But my journey and my piety took me to another place, one that I value greatly," Galathae explained.

Catti-brie nodded. "Glorious and vicious, yes?" she asked. "Few rules and the violence of a weaponless war, so I've heard."

"What you have heard is true, though I doubt you can fully appreciate it until you have witnessed it. All of Callidae turns out for the four battles, each cheering for their borough, each cheering for the tradition of this place we call home, and the determination that keeps us here alive."

"Why would you do that in this time?" Catti-brie asked. "If people are wounded, you have no magical healing, no potions even."

"If?" the paladin echoed with a chuckle. "Many will be wounded, some terribly."

"Then why now?"

"Exactly because of that!" Galathae said. "They risk great injury, even death, though that would be a rare thing, for their belief in Callidae, for their loyalty to their neighbors, their willingness to serve with all. Because it is in this time that their wounds have meaning, their scars last, their risks are real. Don't you see? To fight when there is a priest standing ready shows little real courage."

Catti-brie nodded. It made sense, brutal though it seemed.

"We live in a dangerous place," Galathae told her. "We have enemies—giants, slaadi, vicious beasts, dragons, white worms, the land itself. There were five boroughs when I was younger, but now there are four, for the glacier took one. The heat of the River Callidae disappeared in the west and Cattisola was overwhelmed by Qadeej, eaten house by house, her citizens scattered to the remaining boroughs.

Qadeej's advance continues, and it is fostered, we are certain, by the slaadi."

"How is that possible?"

Galathae shrugged and shook her head. "They prod Qadeej, perhaps. They irritate him so he growls and his breath freezes and tilts the balance."

Catti-brie remembered her encounter with the glacier when she had called into the Plane of Fire, and she knew that there was within this vast river of ice some sentient, elemental power. Perhaps not malignant, but nor was it moral in any way a mere human would understand.

And because of these memories, Catti-brie understood the gravity of Galathae's words. Of the desire, the need, for balance. This society, ancient and stable as it was, survived on the very edge of destruction solely because of where it existed. And if that went away, so did the society and home of the aevendrow.

Catti-brie had to put those notions aside, though, as Zaknafein regained her attention and forced a heavy sigh from her.

"Zaknafein is strong," Galathae said to comfort her one last time. "The sunset is tomorrow."

THE THREE COMPANIONS WERE AWAKENED THE NEXT morning by roaring chants. They climbed from bed, wiped their eyes, grabbed their clothes, and went out into the abandoned common room. When she got outside, Catti-brie came to believe that she and her two companions were the last people to wake in Scellobel, and the last to come out onto the street.

Drow, kurit, Ulutiuns, and oroks came down every side street onto the main lane, cheering "Biancorso, victory! Biancorso, victory! Champion, champion, champion!"

The throng south of them parted, moving to the sides of the street, and down the lane came the cazzcalci fighters dressed in the same shift outfits with leg and arm ribbon wrappings that had been worn in the wine barrel fights, only blue-white in color. Their skin glistened, and

Catti-brie suspected that they were smeared with the mucus of the hagfish.

The fighters walked past silently, some with fists raised, and the crowd filled in behind them, following them, cheering every step.

"I want to go see Zak," Jarlaxle remarked, speaking loudly so that his two friends, who were right beside him, might hear.

"But I don't want to miss this . . . whatever it is," Catti-brie replied.

Entreri pointed to the south, and the others noted Emilian and Ilina coming their way.

"Cazzcalci!" the two said, rushing up to them.

"This is the most important day of the year. Quista Canzay!"

Great Holiday, Catti-brie translated in her thoughts.

She didn't have time to think any more than that as their two escorts pulled them out into the lane and they were swept along with the crowd. The cheering became singing, somber and prideful:

Pey'pey Biancorso thalack nadoon
A'braze jivvin questa'tel
Quista Canzay o R'pusk Autunn
Pey'pey Biancorso ultrin akh'nadoon
Qu'ellarianfere z'ress a'Scellobel!

Catti-brie wished that she had her spells available, particularly one to comprehend the language better as the songs wound on. She understood enough of the main refrain to translate it on the third singing, though:

Hear, hear, Whitebear, who march to war
Burn to victory before all eyes
This holiest day of Twilight Autunn
Hear, hear, Whitebear, supreme army
For our home, our strength, O Scellobel!

She couldn't keep up with the rest, but the words really didn't matter. The power of their rhythm, the joy and strength and determination of the singers, ten thousand, perhaps fifteen thousand, voices lifting as one, was all she needed to know, and all she needed to be swept away in the moment. Even Jarlaxle seemed to have forgotten Zaknafein for now.

The parade wound through the streets of Scellobel, ending at a stair of stones that reached to the top of the glacier, and beside them a wooden counterweight lift.

The members of Biancorso trotted along the stairway, the cheers growing as they came into view of all the gathering crowd. Only after they crested the top and disappeared from sight did the borough folk begin following, all those who could climb the stairs doing so, the very young or very old or infirm being hoisted on the lift.

Emilian and Ilina led the companions up the stairs.

"We were hoping to see Zak before the battles begin," Catti-brie said to the drow priestess, snapped momentarily from the pageantry.

"I was with him earlier," Ilina said. "He fights valiantly."

"But he's losing," Catti-brie said, clearly interpreting her tone. "He won't fend off the phage long enough for the return of the magic to heal him."

Ilina didn't respond.

She didn't have to.

Catti-brie looked to her two companions and realized that neither Jarlaxle nor Entreri had heard the exchange. She decided not to tell them, not then, and so as they ascended the stairs and came out atop the huge glacier, Catti-brie bore a great weight upon her shoulders, one that she was determined to suppress in this most important of holidays among the aevendrow.

Daylight was meager, the sun below the line of mountains to her right, across the glacier, and the wind blew cold. She tucked the heavy robe tighter about her and pulled her fur hood lower.

Emilian rushed to her side. "Here," he offered, holding a pair of gloves much like those Jarlaxle had gained from the clothier, only much less fancy in design. "These will help. It will be warmer in the Grande Coliseum, with all the people huddled about, but if you're still too cold with your thin southern blood, do speak up. We have other ways to help!"

Catti-brie nodded her thanks, and indeed, the gloves proved quite helpful and warm, surprisingly so since they were so thin. Even with that grim news regarding Zak pressing on her, it was hard for her not to be astounded when they followed the line across the ice sheet to the place Emilian had named the Grande Coliseum. It was carved into the ice, a depression whose nadir was a level field of ice perhaps fifty or sixty yards across and nearly twice that from end to end. Even more remarkable were the rows of elevated benches, vast seating stepped up from a few feet above the frozen field to many, many rows above.

The scale of the place was beyond anything the companions had ever seen, something that became more evident as the viewing benches began filling, thousands and thousands of people from the four boroughs collecting in their allotted grandstands.

Scellobel was on one of the longer sides, with Mona Chess across from them. The people of B'shett were seated to the right of Scellobel's stands, with the folk of Ardin far across from them at the other end of the playing field. Catti-brie noted that a wall separated the B'shett grandstand from another, smaller one. No people were going there, clueing her in that this had been the seating for the folk of the borough that had been reclaimed by the expanding glacier.

As a few people came out through tunnels onto the playing surface itself, the dimensions became clearer, including a wall of almost twice a drow's height encasing the rink. Tenders pulled sharp rakes, scratching the sheet of ice, while at the far ends, others were measuring and smoothing the edges of long, narrow windows centered on shorter walls, one on each end perhaps twenty feet wide and five high. Catti-brie couldn't make out much behind those openings, but at the base of the wall below each was a hole.

"What comes out of that?" she asked Ilina, who sat beside her. "Or goes in?"

"The gah," she replied. "The ball. If you put the gah in the window, the rectangle, of the enemy side and it remains, you gain a point.

If it goes in deep enough to reach the slide that brings it down so that it comes out the hole at the bottom, it is two points. If you put it in the hole at the bottom, it is two points, and if you do that with enough force to bring it up to the window, it is three points."

"You throw it in?"

"It doesn't matter how you get it in there. Kick it, throw it, place it, throw in an enemy who is holding it. It doesn't matter."

"That doesn't seem very difficult," Entreri remarked.

Ilina's smile widened. "The closer you get to your enemy's window, the fewer allies you will have defending you."

"The enemies try to block you?"

"They try to hurt you," Ilina corrected. "To block an enemy would stop her from gaining points for her army. To hurt her gets her off the rink, and she cannot be replaced. The armies start with twenty-five soldiers each. Few cazzcalci battles end with fifty still fighting."

After some chuckles, Jarlaxle asked, "What are the other rules?"

"You cannot bite, you cannot kick the head of a fallen player, and you cannot gouge the eyes with a finger. A knuckle, yes, but not an extended finger. Oh, and you cannot grasp and twist the genitals of a man." Ilina laughed. "I think the war was more fun before that rule was added, but I have heard that the damage was not always repairable."

That had the three companions exchanging dumbfounded looks, head shakes, and nervous laughter. What truly amazed them, however, was the continuing line of spectators coming to cheer on their respective boroughs, and the sheer scope of this gathering.

"How many?" Jarlaxle breathlessly asked when the place finally settled, most in their seats.

"Forty-seven thousand, perhaps fifty," Emilian answered. "Almost all of Callidae."

To the three companions, it was overwhelming, and more so when the four armies marched out from separate tunnels to stand for review before their fellow borough-dwellers, Biancorso shining in their blue-white uniforms, across from Guardreale of Mona Chess in their regal purple, with the Boscaille of B'shett in the woodland greens to one side, and the colorful yellow, red, and green patterns on the uniforms of the Ardin Tivatrice, the garden borough. Most of the soldiers were drow, but several orcs and at least a dozen dwarves were also in the fight. No Ulutiuns, though, and Catti-brie made a mental note to later on ask Ilina why the humans weren't involved.

The cheering echoed across the glacier, to the mountains and back, it seemed, and once again Catti-brie couldn't help but be caught up in the excitement of the moment.

"I wish Zak could see this," she heard Jarlaxle say to Entreri, and she felt herself deflate. Should she tell them?

She decided against it. She would tell them later, after the battles, when they returned to Callidae and might go and see their dying friend. Telling them now would do nothing but ruin this magnificent display before them, as it was being ruined for her.

As one, the crowd quieted, and the four armies turned toward the center of the rink and stood at attention, hands behind their backs. A tall woman in a huge flowing purple robe walked out to the very middle, climbed on a small wooden dais that had been dragged out before her, and raised her arms to the crowd.

"She is Mona Valrissa Zhamboule," Emilian quickly explained to the visitors. "The current Mona of the Temporal Convocation."

"The queen," Jarlaxle replied.

"No, not that," Emilian quickly and vehemently corrected. "Such an idea . . . it doesn't exist here. She is the governor, the maire, of the Temporal Convocation of representatives, serving until the next referendum. It is rumored that Galathae may aspire to the office. Perhaps if you choose to settle in Callidae, you will be asked for support from her. For all her annoyances, she would be a wonderful choice."

From the looks upon their faces, the concept he presented was obviously foreign to Jarlaxle and Entreri, but Catti-brie had some experience with elections from her time in Icewind Dale, where several of the Ten Towns chose their leaders in such a manner. Certainly this was a matter the newcomers wanted to explore further, but this was not the time, as was clear when Mona Valrissa Zhamboule lifted her voice in song.

The acoustics of this Grande Coliseum were truly amazing, for they heard her intonations clearly, and then it didn't matter, as fifty thousand joined in. It was more a chant than a song, Catti-brie soon realized, and more a matter of music than actual words, extended syllables and sounds. It was more feel than information, a beautiful chorus and harmony tugging at the spirit, not the mind, at the heart and soul.

And yet for all its beauty, Catti-brie thought it a dirge, a funeral song for the long day, a greeting to the fast-approaching night. It comforted her a bit, but soon she burst out in tears, fighting sobs, as she thought of Zaknafein, as this dirge became to her a tribute to his life well lived. A final tribute. She looked around, hoping not to draw attention to herself, but found that she was hardly alone here, that almost all the cheeks around her, even Jarlaxle's, were wet with tears.

When it was done, there came one great roar, then a hushed and anticipatory silence.

The mona turned about dramatically and slowly on her dais, raising the tension, then lifted her arms suddenly above her head, right arm straight, left arm curving to meet it fingertip to fingertip.

The tens of thousands went wild. Down on the rink, the soldiers of the four armies all pumped their fists and patted each other on the shoulder or the back.

Catti-brie, Jarlaxle, and Entreri turned to their guides for some answer.

"She signaled that the nightfall will be without clouds," Emilian explained.

"The half-moon waning," said an excited Ilina. "We will need no torches for the champion battle!"

"Biancorso and Tivatrice!" Mona Valrissa Zhamboule declared.

The two armies named walked out in formation to the center to confer with the mona, while the armies of B'shett and Mona Chess went back into their tunnels.

"Azzudonna," Entreri noted, pointing down at the woman.

"Vessi beside her," Jarlaxle said.

While the teams conferred, more attendants rushed into view, some bearing one-wheeled contraptions, others with buckets and brushes. In short order, lines were drawn across the rink, dividing it into sections, and the rim of the window to Catti-brie's right was painted blue, the one to the left painted in a red and yellow swirl. About a third of the way toward the center from each window were lines of the same color as the respective window, and near the center of the rink, two parallel black lines were painted about ten yards apart.

The armies aligned, leaving the mona alone in the center, twelve each on the black line nearest the window painted in the other army's color, eight more on the colored line, the remaining five behind them. The companions spotted Azzudonna on the red-yellow line shouting instructions to her fellows, which included an orc, then found Vessi moving about with four others behind her, conferring near the window.

"The center guards are restricted within the middle third of the rink, between the lines showing the team colors," Emilian explained. "Those in the second rank, the warriors, can go all the way back to our goal, but cannot cross the line of their own color."

"Like Azzudonna," Catti-brie said.

"Yes, she cannot cross the Biancorso attack line." He pointed to the blue line drawn down to the right.

"Those in the back, the dashers like Vessi, can go wherever they wish," Ilina added.

"About!" the mona ordered, and all fifty soldiers turned their backs to her. She nodded to a man sitting on the wall across from the Scellobel grandstand. He reached behind it and produced a sphere about as large as a head, a ball that appeared leathery. He hopped down and rushed forward, then rolled it the rest of the way to the mona, who deftly scooped it up in her arms.

Mona Valrissa Zhamboule then knelt upon the wooden dais and lifted what seemed to be a small disk off the center, leaving a hole upon which she placed the ball.

She stood and bowed to each stand of fans, then turned to the ball again, kneeled and whispered something none could hear, and kissed the ball.

She left the rink, climbing onto the wall beside the man who had sent her the sphere.

"Ahhhhhhhhh," the entire gathering began to chant, lifting their voices, stomping their feet, as Mona Valrissa Zhamboule slowly raised her hand to the sky. She dropped it as they dropped their chant, and there came a great thump, then a whoosh of air from below, a geyser of pressure that sent the ball flying high into the air.

The armies spun about to face each other, all eyes lifting to locate the high-flying orb, which began its descent from a hundred feet or more above the rink. The winds caught it in its fall, moving it toward the second rank of Tivatrice soldiers.

"Aggress! Aggress!" Emilian, Ilina, and most of the Scellobel fans chanted, and the army did indeed. At the center of the rink, the two guard forces came together in a sudden and furious melee, punching, kicking, grappling. Azzudonna led the second rank of Biancorso warriors through that melee, running hard on the somewhat slippery surface toward the blue line.

A Tivatrice warrior caught the falling ball at about the same moment that Azzudonna caught him with a flying body block, hurling him to the ice. She, too, went down, sliding hard and crossing the blue line, and so she had to come up fast, raise her hands in temporary surrender, and retreat with all speed back behind that line.

The ball, meanwhile, went bouncing and sliding to the dashers of Tivatrice. They passed it all the way to the right side of the rink, then ran back to the left as Biancorso's defense set up to stop them.

They never got near to the center, where one dasher threw it desperately to a guard before being buried in a tackle, and that guard, with nowhere to run, the opposite black line looming before him, just kicked the sphere as far as he could toward the Biancorso goal.

Back and forth it went, the crowd cheering and gasping, roaring at wild brawls that erupted mostly in between the black lines at center rink. There was blood, lots of blood, and grunts of pain. The frenzy and fury of the melee wracked Catti-brie and the others, even Jarlaxle, who had grown up in Menzoberranzan.

The discordant reality of the sheer violence of these people who sang such mellifluous songs, whose intricate and beautiful art was shown on every wall, every bridge, every pole in Scellobel (and probably the other boroughs), who wore such colorful and creative outfits and danced with joy, and spoke of love and friendship, staggered the woman.

This was the fight in the wine barrel multiplied many times over.

Vessi captured the first points, slipping past a Tivatrice defending warrior with a clever sliding maneuver that had him dropping to his knees below the warrior's attempted grab, then coming up beyond him and sprinting far ahead to catch a powerful flying kick of the ball from the orc Azzudonna had conferred with at the beginning of the battle.

With no one else near him, Vessi easily outran the Tivatrice warrior and got alone to the window goal, where he dropped the ball down right before the hole and kicked it hard. He pulled it out from the window, gaining three points for Biancorso.

The match never got closer than that. As Catti-brie at last managed to look past the violence, she began to understand the flow of the battle, the quiet tactics playing out away from the ball. The violence and the fury ebbed as time wore on, with several, mostly Tivatrice, carried off the rink, and simple exhaustion turning many of the center-rink brawls into melting grapples.

Biancorso was clearly superior here, faster and stronger and more practiced in the scheme executions, and when the battle ended, they were declared winners with thirteen points to Tivatrice's two.

"As expected," Ilina told the three. "The gardeners have not won a battle in three years, since the four orc brothers all decided that it was time for them to leave cazzcalci behind. This is a young person's war, after all, and orcs do not live so long. An aevendrow soldier might fight for forty years, but for an orc twenty would be a long, long time of such service. Now, come, I will show you to the banquet. You should eat before the next match."

Beyond the grandstands on every side, long tables heaped with food and drink had been set out. There were even outhouses, far back from the food, fashioned of ice and with deep holes bored into the glacial mountain.

"Cazzcalci is the joy of Twilight Autunn, and the sunset of Quista Canzay is our most solemn moment of reflection, a reminder of the good we have in the midst of harshness," Ilina explained as they made their way. "For two millennia, the aevendrow have lived here beside the blessing of the hot River Callidae. We remember the strife of the times before that, the wandering, the hopelessness, the grief. This day, this war of cazzcalci reminds us that our peace is earned by vigilance and by sacrifice, and that we must all be ever ready to do whatever is asked of us to preserve that which we have built. There is no aevendrow, kurit, orok, or Ulutiun of Callidae who would not die to save the city, or even to save another borough. When Qadeej breathed upon Cattisola, more people of the other four boroughs died trying to save the Cattisolans than Cattisolans themselves! For that, we are all proud, and we are all one."

"Until you beat each other senseless in cazzcalci," Entreri remarked.

"The pain is temporary, the glory eternal," Ilina answered. "When the brothers Nurgu, the four orcs I spoke of, visit Scellobel or any of the boroughs, they are hailed as heroes, and will be spoken of as such until long after they are dead."

"Zaknafein would be a hero here," Jarlaxle said. "And if Drizzt ever finds his way to the rink of cazzcalci, with all that he has learned from Grandmaster Kane, he will dominate the ice, I don't doubt."

Ilina didn't know all those details, of course, but she stiffened at the remarks. "Do not underestimate us," she warned. "The armies you see in battle before you train for this fight throughout the year, every day, and think of these battles every waking moment and in their very dreams."

Jarlaxle bowed to her. "I meant no offense, good lady," he said.

"None taken. Let us all pray that Zaknafein recovers from the phage and so can try to earn his way to fight for Biancorso next cazz-calci."

Ilina said it clearly and powerfully, but she glanced at Catti-brie as she did, and the priestess of Mielikki noted her slight grimace.

Again, Catti-brie had to remind herself not to tell Entreri and Jarlaxle. Not now. Let them enjoy the day.

"The next battle will be one of finesse against true power, Guard-reale against Boscaille," Ilina told them as they made their way back to the grandstands after a fine meal. "Many think Guardreale will win, and that is my hope. They may be too fast for the timber folk."

"So they are better, but you wish them to be victorious?" Jarlaxle asked.

"Biancorso's warriors are fast enough to defeat Guardreale, I think. You witnessed Azzudonna in the first moments of the fight! Boscaille is stronger, across all three lines. They are lumberjacks and swing heavy axes all the day long, and so, too, swing heavy fists in cazzcalci. Biancorso is better suited to beat Guardreale, I think. That is how we won last year, and the teams have changed little."

When they got back to their seats, they found that the blood had been cleaned and the lines and window trimmings repainted, now in the colors purple and forest green.

The second match began exactly as the first had, with a burst of pressure from some mechanism below the rink throwing the sphere high into the air. The battle played out along the lines Ilina had predicted, except that Boscaille prevailed, the decision coming down to a last charge where a Guardreale kurit dasher leaped for the window, thinking to go right in with the ball. But at the very last moment, a Boscaille warrior hit him broadside, deflecting him enough off target that, while he still managed to get the ball into the window, he didn't follow, cracking his chest and skull against the side rim and bouncing hard to the ice.

That same warrior kept enough presence of mind and situation to reach into the window and pull forth the gah, stopping it from going in deep enough to catch the slide, preventing a tie.

Catti-brie found herself breathless as fifteen thousand Mona Chess onlookers groaned as one, and six thousand B'shett fans roared in victory.

Ilina informed the friends that it was late afternoon when an exhausted and dispirited Guardreale lost to Tivatrice in the consolation battle. She and Emilian took the companions back to the banquet for dinner, and when they returned, they found a most unexpected surprise awaiting them.

Their hosts had brought Zaknafein out to witness the final battle, bearing him on a litter, which they had set beside the long bench seat reserved for the visitors to Callidae. The joy the three felt at the sight didn't hold, however, for Zak couldn't even respond to them with anything more than an eye blink and a half-hearted raise of his still-drow right arm. The left side of his torso and his right leg seemed almost twice their normal size, and much of his skin shone with a burning red hue.

"We knew he would not find the strength to sit through all the battles in this long day," Ilina whispered to the three a few moments later. "But we wanted him to see this last battle, to share this with you, at least, under the magic of Twilight Autunn. And it is magic. You will see."

But Catti-brie had a hard time accepting such claims with her friend so clearly dying.

CHAPTER 20

Sunset for Zaknafein

Catti-brie couldn't take her eyes off of Zaknafein. His breathing was labored, likely from the weight of the swelling on his chest. Ilina had quietly assured her that he wouldn't die this night. The chaos phage was accelerating now, as it had taken more than half of his physical body, and the aevendrow had seen this before and so could now, they believed, accurately track the demise. Ilina hadn't admitted it openly, but Catti-brie thought that he would certainly expire the next day.

The magic wouldn't be back by then. Catti-brie couldn't help him. That was the worst part of all, the helplessness.

Jarlaxle sat between her and Zak's litter, holding his oldest friend's hand, often tenderly stroking the back of Zak's hand. This was tearing him apart, Catti-brie could see. All of the companions had watched friends die in battle, suddenly, brutally, but in an unsubtle way. This withering was worse.

She was so focused on Zak that it took her a moment to realize that the Grande Coliseum had gone perfectly silent around her. She turned to Ilina to ask about it, but the priestess put a finger over pursed lips to silence her, then pointed to the sky.

Catti-brie looked up.

It was a long while before she looked back down.

The last couple of days had been low daylight, the circling sun barely below the horizon locking the land in perpetual twilight. Now, for the first time since Catti-brie and her companions had arrived here—and for the first time in half a year, if her guess was correct—the sky above deepened in darkness, a true fall of night. The stars seemed as soft lights gaining in intensity, igniting a million tiny fires in the black void about them. The "distant celestial smoke," as they called it in Icewind Dale, came clearly into view—as clearly as anything she had seen atop Kelvin's Cairn, like a double streak of parallel clouds running across a section of the sky.

The waning half-moon hung low, a backward D, its pale-hearted light turning the Grande Coliseum a bluer white, much like the uniforms of Biancorso.

She took a deep breath, relieved to see the night sky again, and yes, thinking it magical as Ilina had told her.

"It is beautiful," she whispered to the woman beside her.

"Wait," she replied. "It has only just begun."

Catti-brie wasn't sure what she might be talking about, but before she could ask for clarification, the whole of the Callidae gathering began to chant again, somberly, a different tune whose few words made Catti-brie think they were calling to the sky itself, asking for something.

She blinked then, a few times, thinking it a trick of her eyes when she saw a ribbon of green light appear. She even rubbed her eyes.

But no, it remained, and grew, and was limned in purple and blue here and there.

It became a floating curtain, drifting fabric folds of shimmering green undulating in waves, as if the bottom half of a rainbow had torn free on hurricane winds to hang here at the top of Toril. On rare occasions, she had seen this as a green glow, she believed, from

Icewind Dale, but never had she imagined anything of this magnitude and magic.

For it was more than the sight of the waving colored sheets of light. Catti-brie could *feel* the tingles of magic in the air. In her gut and in her mind, she knew that there was magic all about her, energizing her. She broke her gaze from the beauty and turned it upon Zak.

She thought his breathing seemed steadier, maybe, just a bit.

"The healers expected that the Alle'Balleri would be good for him," Ilina confirmed. "It helps with injuries, though only marginally. Still, it might bring him some relief here, at least, that he can better enjoy these final hours of his life."

The last few words shook Catti-brie, but still the name Ilina had used, Alle'Balleri or "Merry Dancers," struck her as perfect for the windy ribbons above her.

The singing transformed then into "Ahhhhhhhhhh!" climbing explosively, and then the thump sent the ball high into the air, beginning the Battle Finale between Biancorso and Boscaille.

It was hard to tear her eyes from the sky, but the action on the rink demanded it of her. The players were surely tired, and battered—their uniforms were all stained with blood. But from the moment the ball descended, the intensity of the battle made the previous three Catti-brie had witnessed seem gentle. She thought she was watching a fight to the death.

Bodies flew and crashed together. A scrambling swarm of guards and warriors turned the middle of the rink into respective battlements, shield walls without the shields, burying anyone passing through one line or the other, whether that person was carrying the ball or not.

The crowd cheered and gasped with every shift, every punch, every throw that got anywhere near one of the window goals. Catti-brie couldn't tell which team the Mona Chess or Ardin fans cheered—it didn't seem to matter. The volume itself was all-encompassing and never diminished.

Above the rink, the Merry Dancers swayed and intensified, as if drinking the rising noise and drawing energy from it.

It seemed to be reciprocal, for the minutes wore on and the game did not slow. As one, the crowd cheered a Boscaille guard who remained and fought, even though his forearm was clearly broken—Catti-brie could see the weird bend in the limb even from this distance!

But he didn't stop, even throwing himself in a cross-body block to take down two Biancorso soldiers, including Vessi, who was trying to break free around the end of the line to get behind the Boscaille defenders.

Ilina and Emilian cheered the valiant guard from the other army, then went right back to urging Biancorso to punish and vanquish the "lumberjack blockheads."

Catti-brie thought she knew all of the swear words in the language of the drow, but she learned many more that first polar night.

Back and forth it went, a purely defensive battle. At one point, all fifty soldiers were entangled in a vast melee, the ball lost somewhere beneath them, and not a one even looking for it. When finally the scrum relaxed, a Biancorso dasher scooping the ball and sprinting out toward the goal, it looked almost as if a third line, a bloody red one, had been drawn in between the two black central lines.

The cheering reached volumes not heard earlier in the day, the players ran harder, fought harder than they had earlier in the day, and Catti-brie began to understand when she, too, started to scream. It was the sky above urging them on. The Merry Dancers were lending power to the soldiers and the fans alike, lifting them with energy as sure as any empowering spell.

She couldn't believe it. She looked to Zak, to see him panting with excitement, to see that yes, his pain had seemingly diminished and he, too, was caught up in the moment.

She knew that he wished he could be down there, fighting, competing. She closed her eyes with that thought, knowing she would miss him, fearing that she would have to tell Drizzt that he had lost his father yet again, sad that Brie would never know this wonderful man.

She shook it away. "Enjoy the night," she determinedly whispered under her breath.

"What happens if no one scores?" she asked Ilina, and that seemed more and more likely, for they were certainly nearing the end time of the battle.

"Then there is no champion."

"They won't play on?"

Emilian and Ilina both laughed at that. "Even on this magical night, there is only so much to give," Ilina said. "Glory shared, glory diminished." She shrugged.

Catti-brie focused again on the battle. Certainly it seemed to be going toward that scoreless end, as no soldier from either team was getting anywhere near the opposite goal. The game went into a lull then, with both sides shifting and moving formations as if trying to plot one last chance to steal victory.

Biancorso possessed the ball, though, and that gave them the advantage. Suddenly the whole team swerved to the left, moving near the far wall. A pair of Biancorso dashers broke away just as suddenly, running hard across the rink, along the wall below Catti-brie.

But Boscaille caught on to the ruse, and defenders angled to intercept the breaking dashers.

But that was the feint-within-a-feint, Catti-brie suddenly realized as Vessi ran up full speed into the scrum across the way, and the Biancorso allies parted the defenders enough for him to slide through. He popped up and seemed to be running free as a Biancorso warrior heaved the ball through the air toward him.

But no, a Boscaille dasher, half kneeling, was only faking injury along that far wall, and she came out low, where the hurling Biancorso warrior couldn't even see her, and undercut the angle, rushing right behind the reaching Vessi to pluck the ball from the air, and in full stride toward the near wall, running free before Vessi could react, before any of the Biancorso soldiers even realized what had happened.

Except for one.

Azzudonna broke from the scrum when the ball went into the air, angling across the rink, and now was the only one with a chance to stop the speedy Boscaille dasher. The crowd gasped and cheered as the two neared, Azzudonna desperately trying to find an angle to intercept, the dasher sprinting harder—if she could get by this lone defender, no one could catch her all the way to the window goal.

The Merry Dancers swirled above, the crowd roared, the dasher put her head down, and Azzudonna, at the last moment, pumped her legs furiously, driving forward, then threw herself to the ice in a slide.

She clipped the legs of the dasher, sending her flying head over heels to crash awkwardly to the ice, then slide fast to slam into the wall below the companions. Azzudonna couldn't slow her desperate dive, either, and slammed into the wall as well, and the Scellobel fans groaned as one.

Catti-brie couldn't see her, but thought from the impact and the groans from those onlookers who could that she might be terribly injured—or even dead!

But no. She climbed to her feet and dove upon the fallen dasher, grabbing the ball, fighting for it, tugging the dasher along until the battered Boscaille woman finally fell free.

On ran Azzudonna across the center lines, blood pouring from her nose.

And yet she had nowhere to go, as the defenders who had chased after Vessi and the other dasher were moving to block, and all the others were now swarming across the ice.

With a scream that rose above the cheers, Azzudonna put her head down and charged forward for the blue line.

"She can't cross that line," Catti-brie reminded herself and her friends.

But Azzudonna wasn't slowing. No, she instead threw herself to her knees in a forward spin, around and around, and right before she reached the blue line, the last spin around, she planted a foot to throw her up to her feet, still turning, her right arm far back behind her turned shoulders, the ball cupped in her bent wrist.

Around she came powerfully, heaving the ball with all her strength.

It cleared the approaching Boscaille defender, cleared the other two and Vessi and his companion, and flew on, and the Grande Coliseum fell silent in a communal gasp of anticipation.

The ball arced down gracefully and hit the inside far rim of the window. It ricocheted back, then back again, disappearing from sight, and still the crowd gasped, for if it stayed in, the point would count, but if it fell out, then no victor seemed certain.

The ball came out, but not through the window. Somehow, whether from the spin, or a chip of ice on the jamb of the goal, or simple luck, or force of will from Azzudonna under the magical light, the gah made it deep into the goal and fell down the slide, exiting through the hole at the base of the wall.

"Two!" Emilian, Ilina, and nearly twenty thousand other Scellobel onlookers screamed.

A Boscaille defender scooped up the ball, but Vessi buried him where he stood, bearing him to the ice, tying him—and the ball—up to kill the time.

That very dimension seemed to stop on the rink, seconds lasting almost minutes, minutes practically years, all the while Boscaille soldiers grabbing at their hair and Biancorso soldiers leaping and cheering.

Not Azzudonna, though. The woman moved to the wall directly below where the companions were seated, and held up her arm, her wrist adorned with the strip of cloth torn from Zaknafein's shirt.

"*Perte miye Zaknafein!*" she yelled. "For you, my Zaknafein!"

And she kept yelling, "*Perte miye Zaknafein!*" with all her voice, with all her strength, with all her tears for this doomed man whom she had championed this night, this stranger in whose honor she had found the strength to make that throw.

"*Perte miye Zaknafein!*" she yelled.

"*Perte miye Zaknafein!*" the Biancorso soldiers joined in on the next refrain.

"*Perte miye Zaknafein!*" the Biancorso fans joined in on the next refrain.

And then something happened that somehow seemed more magical still, something that touched Catti-brie and Entreri and Jarlaxle more than anything they had yet witnessed in Scellobel. An arktos orok Boscaille warrior had pulled the ball from Vessi and was sprinting up the rink, but he skidded to a stop and dropped the ball to the ice, stepping upon it with a heavy foot.

"*Perte miye Zaknafein!*" the orc cried, and all of the Boscaille soldiers similarly stopped and shouted, in the next refrain.

And then, "*Perte miye Zaknafein,*" the fifty thousand Callidaeans chanted in unison and harmony. On and on it went, louder and louder with each refrain, and the Merry Dancer lights above seemed to sway and dart with every syllable. Fifty thousand voices lifted in the chant. Fifty thousand aevendrow, kurit, Ulutiuns, and arktos oroks jabbed their fingers to point at Zaknafein, this stranger they did not know, this poor fellow who had stumbled upon their land and seemed to be in the last hours of his life.

"*Perte miye Zaknafein!*"

Catti-brie sobbed, and then began laughing uncontrollably, she didn't know why. "What is happening?" she asked those around her, and noted that Entreri, too, was rocking between tears and laughter, and Jarlaxle's shoulders bobbed with sobs or perhaps with confused joy.

"What is happening?"

"*Perte miye Zaknafein!*"

"I don't know," Ilina yelled back at her. "I don't know!"

No one knew.

But they all felt it.

And they chanted and they pointed, and almost as if they were directing the Merry Dancers, or maybe it was just a trick of the angle and glow, a green-and-purple ribbon seemed to Catti-brie to reach down from the polar night and touch Zak, and he smiled.

His huge, stretched, frog-like mouth smiled.

The chant began to diminish, but then Zak suddenly pulled himself up from the litter, and growled and fought and stood, crooked and broken.

But he stood.

And all of Callidae cheered for him.

Catti-brie looked down to the rink, to Azzudonna and the Boscaille dasher she had flipped, leaning on each other for support, the both of them calling for Zaknafein.

Zaknafein straightened. No more did he labor for breath. Swollen and twisted, his skin angry red, he wouldn't surrender, and Catti-brie knew then.

She just knew.

He would fight the phage until the magic returned.

Zaknafein would live.

"What have we just seen?" Catti-brie managed to ask Jarlaxle.

"Everything I always dreamed of," he answered through sniffles and embarrassed little chuckles of joy.

PART 4

CHOICES

Never had I imagined that Kimmuriel Oblodra could become so obviously emotional over anything. He had watched his house torn down by Matron Mother Baenre, his entire family eliminated in but a few moments. He had watched his mother pulled back from her torment in the Abyss to serve as a connection to the illithid hive, only to be obliterated thereafter.

He spoke of it often, to me, to Jarlaxle, and never, not one time, did I see anything but a calculated and intellectual approach to the personal tragedies.

Even now, in our journey together to the east, when he recounted those events, they were offered only as lessons in the potential power that Lolth's chosen might bring to bear against usurpers and heretics. There was no hint of grief, no mention that he had ever cared for K'yorl and the others. But when he spoke of the coming storm, and more than that, of the history of Menzoberranzan as revealed by the memories given to Yvonnel and Matron Mother Quenthel, there I saw the desperate longing, a clear sparkle, a clear sense of both eagerness and trepidation—a combination of emotions that can be found only when the outcome matters quite a lot to the person speaking.

338 R. A. SALVATORE

As I ponder this seeming inconsistency in the cold-hearted psionicist, the knot of Kimmuriel's heart unravels. He had been trained to resignation. He had not flinched, or barely so, when his family had been destroyed, when his house and legacy and inheritance of stature and wealth had been so brutally and abruptly stolen from him—all because it was not an unexpected event in the cynicism that had been ingrained into Kimmuriel, into so many of us in Menzoberranzan, from birth.

A combination of helpless resignation and sheer numbness from the daily assaults and atrocities is a deadly mix to the emotions of any drow.

But these days, a sparkle in Kimmuriel's eye.

Now he comes to ride with me, to speak with me, to hope with me.

That is the key to his awakening: he dares to hope.

I cannot hide within myself now, though I truly wish I could. My excuses against that light of hope ring hollow in my own ears, but I cannot deny the resistance to this hope within my own heart.

What will be my role, I wonder?

The action of the matron mother and Yvonnel on the field was stark and shocking, I admit, and no doubt many witnessing it felt that same surge of hope.

Initially.

When I think back to my days in Menzoberranzan, what I remember most of all is the zealotry of the Lolthian priestesses, of my own mother, Matron Malice. I expect that, had this great event and great heresy occurred back in those times, I would have seen the sparkle in the eyes of Zaknafein, surely, and likely in those of my sister Vierna, perhaps even in the eyes of Maya.

Those embers of hope would have been quickly extinguished by Malice, I am sure, and even if not, even if Malice had heard the hopes and promises of her children and consort, the idea that she would have turned from Lolth would derive only from her belief that whichever side she chose would most favorably affect her. Malice loved the fight. In this time, she would side with Matron Mother Quenthel only if she thought Quenthel would win, and that she, Malice, would then be given ample reward.

But even that would have happened only if Malice had come to believe that Lolth was pleased with the chaos and the carnage, that the Spider Queen, in the end, would reward the victors and forget the vanquished.

Perhaps that is the unavoidable outcome of this impending fight. How many of Matron Mother Quenthel's allies will be so only for self-serving purposes? And how many only because they are confused, or afraid? Will mighty House Baenre, leading the revolt against Lolth, even be able to hold tight its own members? Will the driders-turned-drow even prove loyal soldiers to Quenthel, or will we quickly discover that they, too, were no more than a force planted by the Spider Queen, to test her children, to wreak chaos and root out those insufficiently devout?

I cannot escape these thoughts, no matter how clearly I recognize within myself that same cynicism that allowed Kimmuriel Oblodra to shrug at the loss of his family! And this is not who I have striven to be since my first days out of that cursed city. Always, I choose against fear.

But I cannot deny that my heart has not yet come to accept this glimmer of hope.

I have too much to lose.

I have Catti-brie and we have Brie, and the joy of that is more than I could ever have imagined. They would live on, and well I think, were I gone. Brie could not ask for a better mother than Catti-brie, and Catti-brie could not ask for better friends than the companions about us, her father and Wulfgar and Regis most important among them. She would not be alone were I to die in Menzoberranzan, a point made all too clear to me when I returned from my journey to everythingness to find my wife and new daughter surrounded by so much love.

I neither doubt nor discount the grief Catti-brie would experience were that to happen. Simply thinking that she might now be lost in the north has my gut churning with twisting fears and imagined horrors and the most profound sense of possible emptiness I have ever known. On those occasions when the fears overwhelm me and I come to believe that perhaps she is truly lost to me, I am broken. Even while in the light of Brie's smile, I am empty.

I remember that feeling so keenly. I remember that morning in Mithral Hall when I awakened to find Catti-brie lifeless beside me. I remember my horror, my helplessness, in watching her spirit fly away, just out of reach, *until it was gone through the solid reality of stone. It is not a feeling I ever want to experience again.*

And it is not a feeling I want to inflict upon Catti-brie.

Nor do I wish for Brie to grow up wondering about her father who is not there. Will she see drow men walking toward her and think them her da? Will she feel as if I chose to be away from her, that I left her because I cared about something more than I cared about her? Or will she understand that I left because I cared so much about her that I needed to try to make the world better for her?

And that is the rub. At what point might this greater struggle become someone else's to pick up and fight? At what point—is there a point?—will it be someone else's turn, when I am free to bask in the quieter and more personal responsibilities of my life?

Or am I doomed to be so consumed by future hopes that I would miss out on all the present joys?

The conflict is clear and jarring between my personal responsibilities and the wider mission, the purposeful road I have walked since I rejected Menzoberranzan, since I vowed that I would fight for that which, in my heart, is just and good. I know that the coming war in Menzoberranzan, as terrible as it will be, is to be waged to break free of the demon Lolth, that it will be fought in the hopes of the ultimate win for my people. For the shattering of crushing dogma that has hurt so many and will hurt so many more.

For freedom.

Yet for all that, what is my place?

If Catti-brie does not return from the north, am I to leave Brie with the monks? With Bruenor? In either instance, am I abandoning my greater responsibility to her, to make sure she will grow in the arms of a parent?

It is the first time in my life that I have had to ask myself this question.

It is the first time that I have had so much to lose.

It is the first time I've really had to ask: What is my place?

—Drizzt Do'Urden

CHAPTER 21

Did You Not Feel It?

I
bilsitato was so full it seemed as if the walls might bow out and collapse. The ice wine and beer flowed, the conversations collapsed repeatedly as another Biancorso soldier was announced, the murmuring din exploding into a singular roar of approval.

And none louder than when Azzudonna was hoisted up onto a table, to stand victorious above the gathering.

Artemis Entreri chuckled when he saw her, but said nothing.

Catti-brie and Jarlaxle didn't have to ask why, for they, too, offered little sounds, half in sympathy, half in amazement.

"She's got herself a nose like Bruenor," Entreri said a moment later.

"My da's is longer, but only just as wide," Catti-brie replied.

Indeed, Azzudonna's nose had taken the worst of her slide into the wall. It was obviously broken, with a little wad of cloth stuck up each nostril—ones they were likely changing often as they soaked through with blood. The rest of the woman's face was puffy as well, one eye blackened and nearly closed from the swelling, and her neck, her blue-white shift, her hair, even, were sticky with drying blood.

Mostly her blood.

She didn't seem to care up there on the table. She held her arms out wide, then dipped low and turned her right shoulder back, arm extended, to mimic her victorious throw.

The roaring resumed, full-throated.

"Guardreale!" came a cry from outside, from the main avenue of Scellobel, and many more voices echoed the arrival of the army from Mona Chess.

The gathering squeezed for the door, pushing out onto the lane, the three companions following. There seemed little reason to be inside, they thought when they came out, and realized, too, that the inn of Ibilsitato had merely been a staging area to collect the soldiers of Biancorso.

Now they were out again under the Merry Dancers of the magical sky, and all the borough was out about them. True to the calls, coming down the lane from Mona Chess marched the soldiers of Guardreale, and what seemed like the whole of that borough flowing behind them.

So the party expanded, and then again and again as the other two boroughs joined in.

It became a long celebration of Callidae and of cazzcalci, of the victors and of the vanquished, of the viewers and the Merry Dancers, of the food and wine and beer, of life itself.

Even Artemis Entreri could not help but get caught up in the dance of Quista Canzay—Catti-brie took note of the man singing at one point, and when he realized she was watching him, he answered her grin with one of his own, rushed out from the line of singers, grabbed her by the hand, and dragged her back to join in the song.

She didn't resist. She did note, however, that across from her—on the other side of Entreri, and with his large arm draped across Entreri's shoulders—was, amazingly, an orc, and one wearing the uniform of a Boscaille soldier.

Artemis Entreri was allowing an orc to drape his arm across his shoulders. A moment of near-panic came over Catti-brie, a reminder of the surreality all about them, a warning to hold her guard.

But no, she remembered this particular orc, and it all became more confusing still. Or perhaps, she told herself, it was less confusing. Perhaps it was just as it seemed.

When the song was over, the line began to disperse into the throngs all about, and the orc slapped Entreri hard on the shoulder and started away.

Entreri caught him by the arm.

"Wait, one thing," Entreri begged. The orc looked at him curiously.

"At the end, after Azzudonna's score, weren't you the one who got the gah and started the other way with it?"

"I am," said the orc. "I am warrior Lurnik of Boscaille."

"Why, then?" Entreri asked. "Time was not out."

"Yes, why did you stop?" Catti-brie added.

The orc looked at them both with obvious puzzlement. "*Perte miye Zaknafein!*" he then roared, lifting a fist. The crowd around him responded in kind, the words reverberating down the street.

"But you don't know Zaknafein," Entreri pressed.

"Warrior Azzudonna championed him," the orc said, tapping his wrist where Azzudonna had been wearing the torn strip of Zak's shirt. "She is honorable and fierce. Would you have me dishonor her?"

"Of course not," Catti-brie answered. "Forgive us. We are new here and do not know your customs."

"Besides," the orc added with a grin, "did you not feel it? I have fought in cazzcalci five times. Three sunsets ago, Guardreale became champions. But even on that great night, I felt nothing to match the song for Azzudonna's Zaknafein. Did you not feel it?"

"It was among the most incredible things I have ever felt," Entreri confirmed as Catti-brie nodded her agreement.

"The magic," she said quietly.

"Yes. It will be remembered long after I am gone," Lurnik said, and he saluted, repeated, "*Perte miye Zaknafein,*" and melted into the throng.

Catti-brie sighed, digesting it all, and watched him go, then turned to Entreri.

"He's not wrong," the man said. "I've never felt anything quite like the sheer power of that chant in that magical sunset."

"I want to feel it again," Catti-brie agreed.

Entreri lifted his eyes and one hand upward. "It's still there."

"It'll be six months before the sunrise, you understand."

He looked at her skeptically, but she nodded, certain.

"Then I guess I shouldn't feast for the entire night," Entreri said, and he, too, walked off into the throng.

"Or at least, not drink the night through!" she called after him.

The woman looked around for Jarlaxle, but it was impossible. So many faces, so much dancing and singing and feasting and drinking and cheering. The city was alive now, as much as anything she had ever known, and it proved truly infectious.

She wandered about, not even bothering to ask where Jarlaxle might be. It didn't matter. She was safe here, they all were. She wished that Zak could be out here, enjoying this, but Galathae had told her in no uncertain terms that it wouldn't be wise. He was still sick and had to fight through the phage for a few more days. That moment at cazzcalci had brought him great strength and comfort and relief, and had indeed pushed back the onslaught of the phage.

But that moment was gone. They all knew it, and everyone in Scellobel understood that the one moment of Azzudonna's victory, of the full-throated voice of Callidae demanding relief from the Merry Dancers, could not be replicated.

A short while later, back in the inn along with Vessi and many other Biancorso soldiers, Catti-brie heard inquiries about Azzudonna, who had apparently slipped out.

"She has gone to rest," one woman insisted, to which a dwarf complained, "She will have the whole of night to rest! She must sing and tell us again of her throw!"

Catti-brie knew that Azzudonna wasn't resting. She took her leave of Ibilsitato and made her way along the avenues of Scellobel, casually drifting toward the cold infirmary where the aevendrow had put Zak. She wasn't surprised when she entered to find Azzudonna sitting across a small candlelit table from her father-in-law, plates and glasses set before them.

"Persimmons?" she said with a grin when she neared. Both turned to her with a start and Catti-brie nearly laughed aloud at how ridiculous they appeared, as if they had gone through a war and had dragged their battered bodies off to the side for a moment of respite.

"This cheese!" said Zak.

He looked better, more like himself, and the swelling had mostly subsided. And he sounded better. Stronger. His mouth was almost its normal size again.

"You call yourself his friend and you did not share this with him?" Azzudonna said to her, shaking her head with an expression of feigned dismay. "Come, sit," the drow woman bade her, pulling up a chair. "I brought more than enough."

Catti-brie took a seat and Azzudonna pushed a plate of persimmons and kurit cheese and a glass of ice wine before her.

"To life," Azzudonna said, lifting her glass, and Catti-brie and Zak did likewise, the three tapping together with a marvelous chime.

"I'm going to live long enough for you to cure me of this affliction, daughter," Zak said. "Are you up to the task?"

"Our hosts have many who are."

"That's not what I asked."

"I am," Catti-brie assured him. "When my spells return, you will feel the full warmth of them."

"Soon," Azzudonna promised.

"What of you?" Catti-brie asked. "That must hurt." She reached gently for the woman's broken nose.

"What? You don't think I'm pretty anymore?" the woman said, leaning away from her reach and striking a playful pose.

"I think you're quite beautiful," Catti-brie told her. "I think everything up here is quite beautiful."

Azzudonna smiled and tipped her glass.

"Should I leave you two alone?" Catti-brie asked a few moments later, after she had eaten the two persimmons and the cheese and finished her wine.

"Please stay," Azzudonna answered before Zak could. "We will have plenty of time to be alone later," she added with a wink at Zak. "When kissing you doesn't hurt so much, nor leave me in fear that your slaad mouth will swallow my head."

The laughter was cut short as the door to the small room opened, and they turned to see Galathae enter, carrying a small pack.

"I hope that is more food," Azzudonna said.

"It is."

"Then sit, join us," said Zak, motioning to a chair across the way. But the paladin shook her head.

"No, I actually came to find you," she answered, indicating Catti-brie. "I wish to speak with you."

"Now?" Azzudonna protested. "It is Quista Canzay! Biancorso are the victors!"

"It will not take long," Galathae replied, and motioned for Catti-brie to follow. Curious, the priestess did.

The paladin led her to a second chamber cut into the glacial wall, one very similar to Zak's infirmary.

"This seems serious," Catti-brie said when Galathae shut the door behind them and pulled out a chair for Catti-brie.

The aevendrow woman nodded. "Nothing you didn't expect, I am sure."

"I honestly didn't expect anything serious now."

"Yes, but the magic will begin returning soon. For some, perhaps when we next awaken. My business with you must be concluded before that time."

Catti-brie held out her hands, inviting her to continue.

"You were brought to this land because of your magic, so you told us," Galathae said. "You are priestess and wizard, correct?"

"Priestess mostly, but yes."

"And you were asked to come because of your magic?" Galathae asked again.

"The others have their tricks and magical items," Catti-brie told her. "But you have it correct. I am here because I can, or could, heal them if we found battle."

"You came through a magical gate. You don't even really know where you are or how to get home."

"That is true."

"So you are here to take them home when your business is done. A word of recall or dweomer of teleportation, perhaps?"

"Recall," Catti-brie confirmed. "I am not powerful enough in the arcane acts to teleport in that manner."

"But you are the one assigned that task, and without you, the others would have to try to walk their way out of here?"

Catti-brie nodded.

"You are aware of the obligation of geas?" Galathae asked.

The question caught Catti-brie off guard. She had heard of geas, a magical spell placed to restrict or impose some conditions upon another person.

"A bit," she replied warily.

"We cannot have you leave until our magic is fully returned. When Twilight Autunn is at its end, we must go and finish what you and your friends started in that cave on the first day of your arrival. We cannot allow the slaadi and the giants such a hatchery."

"We'll lead you there of course," Catti-brie said with full confidence. "Return to us our weapons and gear and we'll gladly fight beside you."

Galathae nodded. "We will accept at least the first offer, but still, we cannot have you leave until . . . well, you will see. It is hard to explain."

"We still want to find Doum'wielle."

"You should forget her. She is lost to this world forevermore."

"We have to know if that is true. We came here because she offers great hope to the drow among us. It is a long and complicated tale."

"We will point you in the direction where your friend was lost, then," Galathae told her. "But most of all, we will point you away from Callidae."

Her somber tone as much as the words began to clue Catti-brie in here.

"I will ask you to accept a geas from me," Galathae explained. "One to prevent you from your magical recall home, or from sending messages to the southland, until the Temporal Convocation of Callidae have agreed that you may leave. The obligation of the geas will be removed if you then still wish to depart Callidae, I promise."

Catti-brie's thoughts swirled in a thousand different directions. She was sure that at that point, they would use new and different magic on her and her friends before they were sent on their way. She thought of Freewindle and his "dreams." She knew of spells that could make a person forget something, and others, more powerful, that could even modify a person's memory—the Harpells used those quite frequently at the Ivy Mansion when one of their more eccentric wizards was stubbornly researching and experimenting along what was surely a disastrous road. Never had she heard about any spells powerful enough to do what she was now fearing, though, in terms of the memories she and her friends had of Callidae. But then, never had she witnessed spells to create food as intricate and tasty as she had seen here. It made sense to her that the aevendrow would perfect such spells if they didn't want to imprison or execute people who stumbled upon Callidae.

Still, the thought depressed her completely—she didn't want to abandon this place forever! The very idea that she might not be able to bring Drizzt or Brie here broke her heart.

She hoped her suspicion would prove wrong, but in any case, she certainly understood the reasoning.

"So when you say that you cannot have us leave until your magic returns, it is not only because of the fight you will wage against those in the cave."

"That is part of it," Galathae said. "The slaadi are much more formidable when their claws inject their eggs or the chaos phage and our healers cannot easily counter it."

"We could draw you a map to the cave, but that would not suffice, would it?" Catti-brie asked, trying not to sound too accusatory here.

"Yes, that would suffice."

"But we still could not leave—not until your magic fully returns."

"No," Galathae admitted.

"We would not be the first who have come to Callidae and left, and you have magic to make sure that we are not the first to leave with the ability to come back."

The paladin didn't reply. She didn't have to.

"What would you have us do?" Galathae asked at length. "What would you do?"

Catti-brie rubbed her face. She saw their dilemma and truly sympathized, but that didn't make it hurt any less.

"When do you wish to enact this geas?" she asked.

"As soon as my powers return. I will need your word that if your own powers return before that time, you will not recall to your homeland, nor magically send any messages beyond Callidae."

Catti-brie considered it for just a brief moment. "I agree. I will not prepare spells of that manner at all until I have your blessing."

"I believe you, Catti-brie," Galathae said. "And as we know the relative power of the spells involved, it is likely that my geas will precede your ability to recall. Still, until it is done, we will not allow the four of you to be together at the same time. If you somehow manage to leave us, you will leave one of your friends behind."

Catti-brie sucked in her breath and tried to remind herself how much the aevendrow had at stake here.

"If someone finds a key to your safe, you change the lock," Galathae said.

"And the key to Callidae is?"

Galathae just stared.

"The memory of Callidae," Catti-brie finished for her.

She stood and went to the door. "And I am glad—we are all glad, that your friend has found his strength. *Perte miye Zaknafein* was real and true. The chaos phage will not take him."

She stepped out of the room, then turned back suddenly with a smile.

"But Azzudonna might."

Catti-brie remained alone in that room for a long while, mulling it all over. For the simple joy and elation here, this was becoming very complicated emotionally. She would be true to her word and would allow the geas to be placed upon her—she and her friends owed the aevendrow that and more, clearly.

But she desperately hoped that she was wrong in the rest of it. She didn't want her memories of Callidae turned into dreams, just out of reach, or erased altogether.

She hoped she was wrong, or, if not, that she, or maybe the ever-persuasive Jarlaxle, could effect a different course.

CHAPTER 22

When It Matters More

Catti-brie took a deep breath and rubbed her fingers together.

"Twilight Autunn has passed," Azzudonna assured her.

"And I am still alive," said Zak, who seemed perhaps a little worse off than he had been after the miracle of Quista Canzay, but still so much better and stronger than he had been before that startling event. "I told you that you would not be rid of me so easily."

"I shouldn't be nervous, but . . ." Catti-brie told him.

"Your spells will be followed by my own, and by Galathae's," said Ilina. "We two alone could cure Zaknafein of the chaos phage and restore his full health. We brought you here as a courtesy, and thought that you would prefer to begin Zaknafein's healing."

"I do, and I appreciate the opportunity," Catti-brie replied. She unfastened the pouch the paladin had given her, dumping a small bit of diamond dust into her hand. She closed her eyes and took another deep breath, then began to quietly chant to her goddess. She felt the magic growing within her, felt its beautiful release, and heard the profound sigh of comfort from Zak as the waves of restorative healing washed over him, attacking the chaos phage and bringing almost instantaneous relief.

As soon as the last wave left her, she began anew, using a spell dedicated to healing wounds more than diseases. She placed both of her hands on Zak's still-swollen shoulder and chanted, closing her eyes, feeling and freeing the warmth.

She fell back when she was done, taking a moment to steady her balance and slowly opening her eyes.

A smiling Zak stood before her, the swelling gone, his face back to normal. Catti-brie heard Ilina and Galathae whispering behind her, but she didn't turn around, instead accepting a great hug from the weapon master.

"You scared us so badly," she whispered into his ear.

"I know. I'm so sorry to put—"

She pulled back and pressed her fingers over his lips, silencing him. "I'm not letting you go anywhere. Brie needs you. Drizzt needs you. I need you."

Zak hugged her again, but then made a curious, questioning sound. Catti-brie looked at him, then followed his gaze back behind her to the two aevendrow women, both standing with their jaws hanging open, their matching expressions showing no small amount of shock.

"He is fully healed and fully cured," Galathae said when she found her voice. "This, I did not expect."

"Your power is great," Ilina added.

"It is given by Mielikki," Catti-brie replied. "I am but the conduit."

"A powerful conduit," Galathae said.

Catti-brie accepted the compliment with a humble shrug.

Galathae pulled her aside, motioning for Ilina to go to Zak and examine him more closely. To distract him, Catti-brie knew, when the paladin whispered to her. "Strong enough to resist my geas?" she asked.

"I know little about your spell—about that particular spell, I mean," Catti-brie answered. "But I have no desire to resist it. I accept it, and on my word, will not betray Callidae in any case. I do not like what you believe you must do, both with this spell and the one you soon intend, but I cannot argue the prudence."

The paladin nodded.

"We must go now," Galathae told Zak. "Your other friends will find you soon. They are on their way to you. Catti-brie will return to you a bit later on."

She led Catti-brie and Ilina out of the infirmary and across the city. They passed Entreri and Jarlaxle at one point, and Catti-brie winked at them and smiled, sending the two running in anticipation of finding a healthy Zak.

Catti-brie kept glancing back at them as they rushed along. She wanted to join them, wanted the travelers all together again.

"It won't take long," Galathae assured her, obviously catching on to her anxiousness.

Catti-brie didn't complain, but her jaw clenched.

"This is on your agreement, yes?" Galathae asked.

"Have I a choice?"

The paladin stared at her hard. "Do you want one?"

Catti-brie considered it, chewing her lip.

"It is very temporary, and it will merely prevent you from taking yourself and your friends back to your homeland for a short while," Galathae explained once more. "And a geas is about intent, not merely about this spell or that action. You have said to me several times now that you would not betray Callidae. If that is your truth, then the geas does nothing you claim you wouldn't already do."

"That is where I must trust you."

"Yes," Galathae answered.

Catti-brie didn't reply.

"We saved him," Galathae told her. "I mean, you cured and healed him now, but we would have, and had it not been for the people of Callidae in cazzcalci . . ."

"I know, I know," she replied, holding up her hand.

"Understand something, Catti-brie," Galathae told her, and locked stares with her. "I could have had you bound and gagged—the hagfish mucus is quite adequate for both—until this time when my magic returned, then forced the geas upon you without your acquiescence. That is not something that I, or any of us, wish to do to you or your friends, who have brought so much of interest to us."

Catti-brie couldn't dispute the truth of Galathae's words, so, wary as she remained, she nodded her agreement.

She owed them this.

CATTI-BRIE RUBBED HER TEMPLES AS SHE EXITED THE IN-quisitor house, Galathae beside her.

"You feel it in there, buzzing?" the aevendrow paladin asked.

"I do. It is very strange."

"It will diminish into the background of your thoughts shortly," Galathae assured her. "I am glad you agreed."

"I fear it foolish," Catti-brie admitted. "The spells you now block are ones that could extract me and my friends from the coming fight if it turns desperate."

"All we ask of you and your friends is that you show us the cave," said Emilian, walking over with Ilina, both clearly overhearing the remark. Both had sacks slung over their shoulders.

"It could remove you or your friends as well," Catti-brie said.

"If you wish to prepare another word of recall, you may," Galathae told her. "The geas will not stop you. But the place of recall must be here in Callidae. As I told you, the geas is about intent, not a particular action. You might think such a spell prudent, but—"

"But it will be unnecessary," Emilian said. "We are bringing a powerful force. We are not strangers to these fights and we do not intend to lose."

"Of course, you are under no obligation to join in the battle at all," Ilina added. "So perhaps you can guide us to the cave entrance and recall yourself and your friends to the city and await our return. We would think no ill of you in that event. This is our fight."

"Then it is ours as well," Catti-brie answered without hesitation, and indeed, she was shaking her head with their every word excusing her from the expected battle. "Do you think we have forgotten that you took us into your homes in our time of desperate need? Do you think we have forgotten cazzcalci and the Merry Dancers, and what you, all of you, did for our beloved friend Zaknafein? Your biggest challenge, Emilian, if you are leading the battle, will be to keep us from getting too far ahead in the fight. All we ask is that you arm us."

"Ah yes, that," Emilian said, nodding to Ilina, who pulled the sack from her shoulder and handed it to Catti-brie.

"Your items," she explained. "That is a most wonderful and clever belt buckle!"

Catti-brie fished about and found the belt, holding it up for them with a grin. "Thank you. I fashioned this at the Great Forge of Gauntlgrym. The bow is Taulmaril the Heartseeker, whose creation, I believe, traces to the eladrin. You will see it in action, I'm sure."

She bent over and again fished about in the sack. "But that is not the most favored of my possessions," she explained, standing back up and holding a beautiful onyx figurine. "I doubt you've had any success in trying to sort out the magic in this one."

Ilina and Emilian shrugged.

"Do not be startled," Catti-brie warned. "I promise you are safe."

The three looked at her curiously, as did a few other nearby Callidaeans.

Catti-brie second-guessed herself a couple of times on her impulsive decision, but eventually wound up back at the beginning. She closed her eyes and whispered, "Guenhwyvar."

"Not poison?" Ilina asked when the gray mist appeared and began swirling before the human woman.

Catti-brie shook her head. "No, no. Not poison."

"Oh, it is an artwork of smoke," Emilian said as the swirling fog began to take shape, but the last word of that remark came out as a gasp when the huge black panther arrived right before Catti-brie, who reached down immediately and stroked the cat's head and ears, assuring Guen that everything was peaceful and calm.

"By the Wind Gods," Galathae gasped.

"She is beautiful," Ilina said.

"Her name is Guenhwyvar," Catti-brie said. "I name you as my friend, and so she is your friend. She likes to be scratched just above the shoulder."

Ilina hesitantly moved toward the panther, but pulled back. When Emilian laughed, the priestess stepped forward again.

"And yes," Catti-brie told them, "Guenhwyvar will join in the fight. She, too, was wounded in Zaknafein's battle in the lower chamber, I know, because she was banished to her Astral home for recovery. Now she is healed, and quite angry with whatever it was that harmed her so. She'll get her revenge."

SEEING JARLAXLE IN HIS OUTRAGEOUS HAT AND EYEPATCH once more brought a sense of normalcy to Catti-brie, and she was surprised how much she appreciated that feeling. As enchanting as Callidae and the aevendrow had been, as strange and beautiful and wonderful all of this had proven, she had been away from home for a long time.

She wondered if Brie would look different when she returned. They'd been gone for more than forty days; Catti-brie had lost track of time in those early days, with no real day or night to guide her, but she knew the date of the autumnal equinox they had witnessed at cazzcalci.

In some ways, it felt as if she had just left her home, but in others, it seemed like she had been gone for months and months. She wanted to see Drizzt and Brie. She needed to kiss her husband. She needed to hold her child.

She took the remaining seat at their table. The common room wasn't crowded this day for the first time since cazzcalci, but the streets outside remained full of Callidaeans, most sleeping on the grasses near the warm water of the many tributaries that crossed Scellobel.

"I'm surprised they returned everything to me," Jarlaxle said.

"Everything," Catti-brie agreed. "Even Guenhwyvar. She is healed—I brought her to show my aevendrow friends, but dismissed her right after, as I expect we'll be wanting her company soon enough."

"Not everything," Entreri answered.

Catti-brie returned a curious glance only for a heartbeat before catching on that there was no gauntlet on Entreri's right hand, and no sword on his left hip. When she thought about it, she wasn't really surprised, for Charon's Claw was among the most powerful and malignant of magical weapons she had ever seen—much more so than Cutter, even.

"Likely they're still trying to figure out the malice of that red blade," Catti-brie told him. "I hope that none tried to hold it without the protective gauntlet."

"Were that the case, then I doubt our hosts would have been so cheerful in returning our other items."

"You still have your dirk?" Catti-brie asked Entreri.

He pulled forth the signature jeweled dagger, spun it by its tip on the table, then gathered it up and slid it back into its sheath.

Jarlaxle nodded at Catti-brie, then turned back to their other two companions and continued, "It is a ritual, I would guess, and not one that pleases me."

"You must understand their reasoning," Zak said. "They've been more generous with us than we might ever expect. What do you think might have been the reaction had a group of aevendrow stumbled upon Menzoberranzan?"

"Or Waterdeep, even," Entreri added.

"What are you talking about?" Catti-brie asked.

"Jarlaxle believes they intend to dull our memories of this place before they allow us to leave," said Zak.

"I would agree. Galathae has stated exactly that to me." She looked to Jarlaxle. "You think they did that to Freewindle."

"Maybe he was just old," Entreri put in.

"I am sure that they did it to him," Jarlaxle replied. "They took his memories and blurred them, or reshaped them into dreams, indistinct and without an anchor anyone might act upon."

"Act upon to find Callidae, you mean," Catti-brie said. "Do you blame them?"

"Of course not."

"But that doesn't mean we have to like it," said Zaknafein. "I'm not too keen on allowing such an intrusion into my thoughts and memories."

"He has often wanted to murder Kimmuriel, I fear," Jarlaxle said lightly, drawing a laugh from Catti-brie, but a glare from Zak.

"A common thought," Entreri remarked.

"Isn't it possible that this elf you met was driven mad by the spell these aevendrow cast upon him?" Zak asked.

"Many thought him mad," the undeterred Jarlaxle continued, shaking his head, "but only in regard to this place, if it even was this place."

"Of course it was Callidae," said Catti-brie.

"We do not know that. The world is full of coincidence. In truth, Freewindle was very old, ancient even, and he could not be sure of anything. Perhaps it had just been a dream—Freewindle was convinced it was, and then he was not, and then he was again. And certainly the old elf didn't tell me anything to match what we have witnessed here—and truly, I don't even know if this is the same place he dreamed of, or visited, if he even did come north."

Catti-brie fixed him with a glare. "Perhaps we could have had this conversation in the Hosttower in Luskan."

"I did not lie to you," Jarlaxle protested. "I merely did not reveal my hunch."

"Your what?"

"My hunch, I say, for it was only that."

"But you took us here on that *hunch*," she scolded.

"Not on false pretense! No, Khazid'hea's sensations are real. Perhaps we will cleanse the sword, perhaps it cannot be done, but that was never the point, after all. Doum'wielle is alive, the sword tells us. Finding her is still paramount to me. Do not underestimate her value in the cause of Menzoberranzan. If she can help us keep Barrison Del'Armgo allied with House Baenre, vile Matron Zhindia has little chance of finding friends, and so, no hopes of prevailing. And Doum'wielle is no Lolthian. It was the sword that drove her to evil deeds. We know that. Being freed of it, conquering it, will perhaps bring her to a place of desired redemption, and that place will be back in Menzoberranzan, in House Barrison Del'Armgo. Doum'wielle might help us avoid a war. Is that not a chance worthy of our efforts? Isn't that—"

"Yes, Jarlaxle, we know," Zaknafein interrupted him.

"And yet you should have told us all of it," Catti-brie said, angry. "From the moment you asked us to accompany you. The very notion that there was a place akin to Callidae up here is rather important, don't you think?"

Jarlaxle replied with a slight nod—what could he really say, after all?

"It doesn't matter now," Entreri put in. "We found it and know more about it than any old elf in Silverymoon might recall, yes?"

"Agreed, and so it is settled," said a sardonic Zak. "Callidae exists." He lifted his glass in a toast. "And glad am I that it does. *Perte miye Callidae!*" The others smiled at that, but didn't toast.

"I agree with Jarlaxle's assessment of our hosts," Catti-brie said, bringing the topic back to the original discussion. "They will not hold us here, for they are not jailers and have no designs to do us harm in any way that I— that we, have seen. Quite the opposite. But it makes sense that they will hold many of our memories of this place."

"As long as that's all they demand," Entreri said. "Though I have to admit, it is a painful price. I don't want to forget Callidae."

"The aevendrow will do as they must," Catti-brie decided. "They have a lot to lose. Everything to lose."

"You could take us home now," Jarlaxle said. "Right now. And we could return—with Drizzt, even! Should he not see this place before it all becomes but a dream to us?"

"I cannot."

"We will come right back," Jarlaxle assured her. "Doum'wielle is out there, and she is important to our cause. Even if Callidae were not here, it is worth our attempt."

Catti-brie shook her head. "We cannot."

"Why?" a surprised Entreri asked. "I am in no rush to be away from this place—I rather like it—but why can't we?"

"For one, we have our own obligation to them. We must take them to the cave where we fought the green slaad."

The others nodded.

"And we will, with even more help. We can come right back to the north and fulfill that obligation," Jarlaxle repeated.

"We can't." She was almost sighing at this point.

"I don't understand," Jarlaxle said.

"I'm unable to cast the spell," Catti-brie explained.

"But the Twilight Autunn is over—"

"No—it's not that. I'm not allowed to remove us from this place. On my word and my acceptance of Galathae's geas."

"Her what?" Entreri asked.

"A geas? You accepted a geas?" Jarlaxle asked.

"I had little choice. But yes, I did, and would have even if offered the choice."

Entreri held up his hands, at a loss.

"It is a magical prohibition," Catti-brie explained. "The spell would not execute to take us home even if I tried, for the geas, much like a curse, would prevent it. There is no way around it."

"I can't believe you let her do that," Entreri remarked.

"I wouldn't have cast it anyway," Catti-brie answered him. "I gave her my word that I would not cast it, and I'll not break my word."

"Still," Entreri said, staring at her, his expression catching her strangely. She could almost see him playing it all out in his thoughts, and watched as his initial resistant surprise seemed to be melting away.

"Then we have to let it play," he said after a moment.

"Then let's go kill some frogs," Zak said.

After a few exchanged glances, Jarlaxle nodded his agreement, but the old rogue also rubbed his face.

He was calculating his options, Catti-brie realized, as he always did. This land of Callidae was everything to him, as she knew it would be to Drizzt. She wondered then if perhaps Jarlaxle would not return with her and the others when this was all over, and would instead choose a life here among the aevendrow.

What would that mean for her memories of Jarlaxle if their theory about the aevendrow ritual proved accurate? She couldn't help but give a little laugh at the prospect of Jarlaxle the rogue becoming no more than a confused dream to her, Entreri, and Zaknafein. The thought of the ever-present Jarlaxle somehow being wiped from their minds seemed impossible.

There was no magic in the multiverse powerful enough to do that, Catti-brie expected. Not with Jarlaxle, whose sheer presence mocked such a possibility.

Jarlaxle started to say something, but went quiet abruptly and looked toward the inn door, past Catti-brie. She turned to see Galathae approaching, wearing a familiar gauntlet.

She removed it as she arrived, dropping it on the table in front of Entreri.

"Quite remarkable," she told him.

"I warned you, or your friends at least, out in the rift. I hope no one ignored that warning and held or even touched the sword without the gauntlet."

Galathae smiled and reached over her shoulder with her now-bare hand, lifting a familiar sword up and over.

"Quite remarkable," she said again. "You were wise, and kind, to offer such a warning." She widened her gaze to take in the others. "You do carry some powerful magic, and some with designs of its own. Evil designs, or wicked at least."

It didn't escape the notice of any of the four friends that this paladin drow so casually held Charon's Claw in her bare hands. Only a powerful and veteran warrior could hold Charon's Claw unshielded from its malignancy. The sword had no sway over her, it seemed, a keen reminder that many of these aevendrow were even more formidable than the southerners might have thought.

"I do not put it to evil use," Entreri answered her. "Once I was a prisoner to the power of that sword when it was wielded by a Shadovar tiefling. But now . . ." He shook his head.

Galathae studied him for a moment, then very deliberately laid Charon's Claw on the table before him. As she reached to unfasten the scabbard set across her back, Entreri put his bare hand on the backbone-like hilt of the wickedly beautiful sword and lifted its decorated red blade up before his eyes.

"The inquisitors argued over whether we should return the blade to you at this time," Galathae admitted, handing over the scabbard. "Or substitute a white ice sword and wait to give this back until your ultimate departure from Callidae."

"I understand your concern."

"I was the tie-breaking vote among the inquisitors, who were tasked with deciding the fate of your various magical items," the paladin told them all. "Pray you do not prove me wrong."

"The only ones who will regret your choice are the giants and the slaadi," Entreri promised.

"So you do plan to join us in the coming fight? I was told as much by Ilina and Emilian."

"We do," Catti-brie answered.

"Gladly," Zak added.

"That is why I came to you now, and I am pleased to hear of this." Galathae pointed to a nearby chair. "May I join you?"

"Of course," all four replied, or at least nodded.

"I will tell you all that we know of battling the slaadi and the giants, in tactics and in the most and least effective magic to use against them, both to attack and to defend. These are lessons long and painfully learned by the peoples of the north."

They all leaned in, particularly Catti-brie and Jarlaxle.

"Tell us, friend," Zak said, "how we can kill these awful enemies."

A LARGE PARTY OF AEVENDROW, OROKS, AND KURIT SHAD-owed the four southerners from Scellobel, through Cascatte, and down the tunnel, out of the glacial rift and back toward the mountains. Night remained deep about them, the sky cloudy and hinting of snow, and no Merry Dancers were shining above later on that day's march when they came into the dead Ulutiun town.

There, they found the calved ice block the glacier had thrown at them.

"Near the glacier, we will be careful with Zak's whip," Catti-brie told Ilina and the others. "And I will be careful not to reach through my ring." As she finished, she held up her hand and rolled the ring about on her finger.

"Until we are far away," the nearby Azzudonna replied. "Even if you think us to be safe from Qadeej's response, the force following us is large, and may have support groups trailing distantly and still within reach of Qadeej if you anger him."

"Of course. I saw groups of dwarves bearing heavy litters," she agreed.

"The cave will be cleansed," Azzudonna said, as if that explained the burden of the dwarves. She moved away then, called by some others.

"Dwarves and orcs accompany us, but I have seen no humans other than myself and Artemis Entreri," Catti-brie mentioned to Ilina as they continued on their way.

"This is no business for Ulutiuns. We are in the mountains and so they are not needed."

"I noted none in cazzcalci, either—fighting, I mean."

"Those Ulutiuns who have joined Callidae do not believe in battle," Ilina explained. "They are fine hunters—or were—but they are not warriors and do not wish to be. It is not their way. I doubt they would raise arms against the giants or even the slaadi if they invaded us in Callidae."

"They would not protect their homes?"

"Not in battle against reasoning beings," Ilina explained. "I don't think it general among their peoples, but for this tribe, such things as war are forbidden."

"Yet you value them as citizens," Catti-brie asked as much as stated.

"Of course." Ilina gave a little smile. "Many think their beliefs aspirational. Perhaps if the practical necessities weren't ever-present, we would all seek their peaceful ways. Besides, you will see, they are quite important even if they will not lift weapons. They are not needed here, but if they were, they would be here, certainly."

Catti-brie let it go at that, thankful for yet another little look inside the aevendrow, layer upon layer of confirmation that all of this experience was exactly as it seemed.

They moved through the town and along the mountain trails, the four outsiders retracing their course, even breaking for rests in or around the same caves that they had previously used. Several snowstorms slowed the journey, but with their magical protections (and the strange clothing of sealskin, white fox, and hag mucus worn by the others, which seemed as good as the boots or rings), their progress continued. Deep snows were rare up here—just a few, if any, big storms each year—but the small flurries came repeatedly, or maybe it was just crystallized blowing snow. Catti-brie could not be sure.

The moon was up and nearly full in a bright and cloudless sky tendays later, when the targeted cave came into view. The four friends were very near where they had first come through Gromph's gate, and Catti-brie noted that Jarlaxle, in particular, seemed to be continually glancing all about. He was setting markers, identifying peaks, she knew.

Even if the aevendrow cast their ritual and dulled their memories, Jarlaxle intended to get back to this place.

She couldn't blame him.

They set one last camp near the cave entrance, the large force, nearly two hundred strong, catching up and breaking into their assigned assault groups.

"After the kurit sneak to the entrance and check it structurally, we will be the first to enter the cave," Emilian told the four as they ate their dinner. "You four, myself, Ilina, Galathae, Vessi, and Azzudonna. Once you have shown us what we need to know to direct the fight, then you can move back to this place, where we'll stage an infirmary."

"We asked to remain at your side," Azzudonna said, noting herself and Vessi. "We will return to this camp with you."

"But we won't be returning to the camp," Zak said before Jarlaxle could reply. "I won't, at least. I was down in the lower tunnel and remember it well, so I'll be of help. And if the frogs and giants are still there, well, all the better."

"None of us will remain in the background," Catti-brie said with confidence. "We are seasoned warriors all, and know each other well.

Too, I ask that you don't remain with us, my friends. Stay with familiar comrades."

"We've perfected our own . . . style," Jarlaxle added. He looked right at Galathae, whom he had been told would be leading the expedition, and who was now coming over to join them. "If there are objectives you wish us to meet once the fighting starts, just point them out and take confidence that we'll get it done."

"Just you four?" Galathae asked skeptically.

"Five," Catti-brie corrected, lifting the onyx panther figurine from her pouch.

"Six," said Jarlaxle, tapping the feather on his huge hat.

"Maybe eight, if there is room for hellsteeds," Entreri put in.

Galathae looked to her fellow aevendrow, none of whom had any answers to the claims of the four.

"This is our fight," Galathae said. "You need not—"

"Then it is our fight," Catti-brie insisted.

"*Perte miye Callidae*," said Jarlaxle.

"*Perte miye Callidae*," he said again, this time with the voices of his three friends echoing every syllable.

"Indeed," said a nodding and smiling Galathae. "Sleep well and prepare yourselves."

ARTEMIS ENTRERI CREPT INTO THE CAVE, HUGGING THE right-hand wall, scanning constantly for any signs of movement, both from other shadows and from the large body of the frog-like green slaad lying on the floor right where they had fought it and left it.

All was quiet, not a twitch from a webbed foot nor a flicker of movement from the creature's four-fingered hands.

Patience, Entreri silently reminded himself. He squatted below a jag in the wall, tucked tight in the shadows, and he waited.

And he watched.

Sometime later, he crept out from the wall, staying low all the way to the corpse—and yes, he confirmed, it was that same corpse all these tendays later, showing the same wounds inflicted by the very sword Entreri now carried. It hadn't decayed much at all—because of the cold, he knew.

Back to the wall he went, then he crept all around the chamber and even down the descending tunnel.

All was quiet.

Entreri moved back outside. "The slaad is dead where we left it, just inside," he told them. "All else is quiet, well into the tunnel."

"Maybe they deserted the place," Zak offered.

"The corpse still being there means nothing," Galathae answered. "Slaadi care nothing for their dead or for each other."

"The room with the eggs was far below," Zak added. "A few hundred strides down that tunnel, then down a great stairway and along yet another corridor."

"Any turns or side passages?" Galathae asked.

"Not many and nothing to confuse. Large steps down to a straight run to a single fork right before the room, but both ways from the fork led into the chamber, although the tunnel to the left might have had another branch."

Galathae nodded to Emilian and he ran off.

"Then let's be done with this," the paladin told those remaining. To the four newcomers, she added, "You are certain you wish to engage in this fight?"

"Right up front," Jarlaxle answered.

Galathae motioned to the cave entrance.

Zaknafein and Entreri led the way, the aevendrow paladin and Azzudonna close behind. Catti-brie, Jarlaxle, and Ilina trailed, while Emilian organized a second strike group to move in as reinforcements, as well as a team of kurit with a litter to collect the long-dead green slaad.

Down the tunnel they went, silent as the shadows, silent as death. They came to the descending stairs and continued to the flat, straight tunnel below. Entreri and Zaknafein crept up to the fork, the red glow from the chamber beyond evident, and there Entreri held, sword and dagger now in hand, while Zak moved back the way they had come a short distance. When their companions came off the stairs and into the flat tunnel, Zak motioned back to Galathae, pointing left and right.

Which or both? Zaknafein's fingers flashed at her in the drow code.

Galathae glanced over her shoulder and flashed some hand signals that way, then turned back and silently told the point runners, *Left.*

Zak moved back to join Entreri and they started down side by side. They paused almost immediately, though, hearing movement ahead.

The room wasn't empty.

Zak turned back, his fingers working fast to relay the news.

How many? Entreri heard in his thoughts, and he recognized that it was Catti-brie who had sent the silent magical message.

He crept forward, paused, then moved again.

Several huge forms were shuffling about, including a trio of giants lifting and turning eggs. While it didn't seem so huge near the towering frost giants, he noted a slaad, hulking and thick and blue and nearly twice his own height, then a pair of slightly smaller and leaner red slaadi farther to the right.

He relayed it all back to Catti-brie with the connection of the message spell, then added that there was at least one more down the deeper hallway from this nesting room, for he heard its croaking call to its fellows.

He moved back to Zaknafein, who relayed to Catti-brie, *Put a fireball in there to start the fight.*

A few moments later, while Jarlaxle, Azzudonna, and Galathae moved up to join the pair, Catti-brie and Ilina remained back at the tunnel fork, waiting for Emilian's squad to arrive. Ilina sent them off down the right-hand tunnel, her fingers relaying the information, while Catti-brie began quietly casting her spell.

The five in the tunnel ducked and covered as one when the small ball of flame soared over them, flying into the room beyond. A wash of heat swept past, accompanied by screams of pain and great gurgling croaks of surprise.

Entreri and Zaknafein led the way, diving into rolls as soon as they reached the room's entrance, crossing paths in those dives to confuse the nearby enemies, and coming up shoulder-to-shoulder, leaping away as one for the nearest giant, which was frantically trying to balance a huge egg in one hand while it patted at the biting flames with the other.

The giant reached for its axe, which leaned against the wall to the side, but then brought its hand back across to block a stab from Zak.

A cut from Khazid'hea.

Three giant fingers and half of its palm went spinning to the floor. The behemoth reacted without thinking, hurling the egg at Zak.

Zak ducked, rolled forward and turned as he went, stabbing Khazid'hea downward on the turn and leaving the sword sticking up from the floor as he rose into a crouch facing Entreri, his hands cupped before him.

Hesitating not at all, Entreri rushed forward, stepped into those cupped hands, and leaped away, Zak propelling him up and over.

Both hands gripping the hilt of Charon's Claw, Entreri drove it home with all his strength, the fine blade slicing through the thick hide jerkin and stabbing deep into the giant's gut. Entreri could see and feel the behemoth's skin smoking and curling away from the wound, and knew that the giant's innards were faring no better. He was glad that the gash widened itself, for he slipped free and down, ducking fast as the giant slapped at him, then reached for him.

The crack of a fiery whip straightened the giant and sent it falling back a step, reflexively grabbing at its burned face with both hands, then howling again and tucking its half hand under its other arm, trying to stem the spurting blood.

"Behind you!" Entreri told the weapon master, for the egg had hit the floor, skipped to the wall, and bounced back, but now with a cracked shell. A blue creature that looked like a weird cross between a baby dragon and a giant centipede had pushed through the compromised shell and now swayed very near to Zak, toothy maw coiling, ready to strike.

JARLAXLE APPROACHED IN MEASURED STEPS AS HE WATCHED the opening charge of his two lieutenants. Even though it was all so perfectly predictable, he was still shaking his head in awe. The coordination, the improvisation, the precision of Zak and Entreri, although typical, could never be less than amazing to him, even though he himself could have joined these two experts and been complementary to their movements.

He managed a little smile when he heard the slight gasps of appreciation from the two drow beside him.

He planned to fight this battle with a pair of wands, mostly, but since this first giant was already getting ripped apart, he began with his conjured throwing daggers, one, two, and a third as Azzudonna and Galathae rushed past him into the room, veering left. He noted the egg flying past Zak and held his fourth shot when the weapon master came up in a turn with his hands cupped, realizing that Entreri would soon be leaping up high.

But then Jarlaxle let fly that fourth dagger when the serpent appeared from the cracked egg.

Azzudonna and Galathae were already around the corner, out of sight and out of range of the serpent, and there, Jarlaxle heard, another fight was already beginning.

AROUND WENT THE WEAPON MASTER TO ENTRERI'S CALL, only to find the hatchling too close for his whip, its head up high and swaying, then snapping forward, maw spreading wide, fangs pointing from either side.

Zak growled a curse and tried to get away, but only a thrown dagger saved him from a vicious bite, as it clipped the hatchling's head and deflected the strike wide.

A quick rush to the side brought Zak past Khazid'hea, which he pulled free as he spun back on the serpent.

He cracked his whip at it, and it hissed—but the fire didn't hurt it!

He did it again, cutting the tear, letting the opaque magma drip down before the beast, which struck again, its face plunging right through the hot residue.

If the heat bothered it at all, it didn't show it, but it didn't matter,

Zak saw, for the magma was upon its face, upon its eyes. It shuddered and swayed, trying to get free, but Zak came in fast.

Cutter slashed across viciously, and the creature and the breaking egg rolled to the side, the hatchling falling in half and both ends squirming wildly about on the floor.

Zak didn't see that, but confident in his strike, he had already dismissed the serpent as a threat, for there remained a huge frost giant, wounded and angry, not far behind him.

An arrow of lightning soared right over him as he spun, and he turned just in time to see the giant stagger from the impact. But still it roared and pressed on, gathering its axe, taking several more hits about the legs from Entreri's sword and dagger, taking another arrow, then a third.

Yet it kept coming.

The behemoth answered with a great sweeping swing at Entreri, but a flare of light flashed between the combatants, surprising the giant and giving the man enough time not only to get below the strike, but to come up behind it and drive his sword into the bending behemoth's side.

Zak came in, snapping his whip at the giant's face again and leaping into a tremendous downward slash with Cutter that finished off the giant's injured hand, stealing its grip, the huge axe spinning out to the side wildly.

Another arrow struck home.

A flying panther crashed in right behind the lightning missile, landing fully on the giant's head, bearing it to the ground.

In went Entreri and Zaknafein to finish the brute.

JARLAXLE NODDED HIS APPRECIATION TO ILINA WHEN SHE placed the warding flare between Entreri and the giant.

"Brilliant," he told her, and he realized he might as well have been speaking of Azzudonna and Galathae. If any doubts remained in Jarlaxle about the power of the aevendrow after cazzcalci and after the paladin so casually handled Entreri's sword, they were thrown aside in but a few moments of watching the two brilliantly working about a giant, Galathae with sword and shield, Azzudonna spinning a sword and short-spear combination with such deftness that Jarlaxle wondered why such a weapon combination was so rare in Menzoberranzan. The masters at Melee-Magthere would learn a bit from this one!

And those white blades, ice so tightly compressed as to be unbreakable, enchanted and treated with such skill, drew bright lines of blood all over the frost giant they faced.

For all that skill, Jarlaxle understood that the two could use his help, and he rushed in support as a second giant came up on them, along with the blue slaad.

A brilliant light appeared in the eyes of that second frost giant, blinding it, as Ilina joined in, and Catti-brie, too, turned her attention here, Heartseeker raining shots above the drow fighters and into the huge giants.

Now with wands in hand, Jarlaxle called upon the magic in a ring, magically blinking through a short dimensional gate that landed him at the back of the room to the side of the growing melee, and with the three massive monsters in a perfect line.

One wand, then the second sent a powerful lightning bolt shooting down that line, scorching all three.

Jarlaxle nearly laughed aloud when Azzudonna cleverly leaped forward behind that flashing blast, jabbing her spear at the blinded, outraged giant who stood in the middle. At the same time, she gracefully and fearlessly danced between the giant and the slaad. The giant reacted with a great sweep of its axe, but Azzudonna was far too quick to get caught by that.

The surprised slaad, however, did turn with her.

From his new angle, Jarlaxle could see the fight across the room, Emilian's group battling fiercely. He breathed easier when Entreri, Zak, and Guenhwyvar joined in with Azzudonna and Galathae, and Catti-brie kept her line of lightning arrows flying true.

Behind Catti-brie, Ilina bided her time, picking her magic. A silvery spectral hammer appeared in the air beside the slaad and immediately engaged, and when that slaad managed to clip Azzudonna with a claw, sending her into a defensive roll out the other way, her wound began to knit almost immediately.

Ilina's magic, Jarlaxle realized, and he was glad. The aevendrow knew what they were doing against these enemies, clearly. If they won out here, he was confident none of them would leave this fight infected with the chaos phage.

The mercenary reached for the feather in his cap, but just shook his head and moved on, picking targets.

The diatryma wouldn't be needed. Not yet, at least.

The pair of red slaadi fled the fight down the tunnel at the back of the room, and Jarlaxle went in pursuit. He turned the corner to see them fleeing, but also to see, with the magic of his eyepatch, a second pair of slaadi, almost identical to the green beast they had killed on their first journey to this place, cloaked in invisibility and standing on either side of the wide tunnel.

The mercenary skidded to a stop and reversed, putting his back to the wall and motioning to his friends. Zak and Entreri rolled away from their fight, which the aevendrow by then had in full control, and toward Jarlaxle. Catti-brie came, too, her bow working with every stride, pummeling the unblinded giant most of all.

As the two warriors quickly approached, Jarlaxle put both wands in one hand, motioned to the tunnel entrance, and showed his friends two fingers. He pulled something from his pouch with pinched fingers and reached about, throwing it into the tunnel.

Around went Jarlaxle, a wand in each hand, the air before him filled with glittering dust that outlined and clearly showed all four of the slaadi within.

The corridor flashed twice with shocking blasts of lightning, and Jarlaxle flipped the wands, holstered them, and brought daggers into his hands that elongated into swords as his three friends joined him.

The red slaadi tried to get forward in the fight to fend off the fury of Entreri and the two drow, while both green slaadi began casting.

But the friends knew what to expect, and had already been protected from fireballs as they had seen them used in the first fight, and Catti-brie, too, was casting as she arrived.

Swords rang out and then they didn't, and a whip cracked loudly and then silently.

The battle raged in complete and utter quiet. The green spellcasters, their dweomers lost in the muting silence, tried to flee, predictably, but Guenhwyvar leaped far and high and bore one down beneath her.

Catti-brie hit the second square in the back with an arrow as it half ran, half hopped away, obviously trying to get beyond the radius of her silence spell.

And then it was clear, and turning, and casting . . .

. . . only to catch a glob of green goo right in the face. The slaad tried to claw it away, sputtering.

As Jarlaxle was still in the globe of silence, his laugh could not reach its ears.

That slaad turned and fled.

A red slaad fell, its face cut in half by Charon's Claw. The other turned and tried to get away, but Zak was with it, step for step, then Jarlaxle, too, stabbing it over and over until it stumbled down, while Entreri helped Guen finish the green-skinned monster.

Catti-brie, still back in the room and outside her spell of silence, turned and leveled Taulmaril, picking her shots. She found few opportunities, though, for more drow and dwarves and orcs had joined in the fight, the few remaining giants and slaadi being taken down under the furious, coordinated assault. Catti-brie put away the bow then, and turned her attention to her wounded allies. And there were many, Galathae among them, though the paladin continued to battle, her shining blue sword almost fully red from the blood of her enemies.

THE BATTLE WOUND DOWN QUICKLY IN THE ROOM AND IN the tunnel, with Jarlaxle, Entreri, and Zak running off after the fleeing green slaad and Guen returning to Catti-brie's side.

The woman moved about, casting her spells of healing and restoration where needed, where there seemed any possibility of disease or of injected eggs. She kept looking to Ilina for confirmation, and the aevendrow priestess kept nodding.

"Take no chances with any wounded by a slaad," Ilina called to her, as Galathae had instructed her back when they had first set out. "Cure an infection, whether you think there is one or not."

Catti-brie nodded and went at her work with fervor, fueled by her memories of Zak's brutal trials. She hoped—she could only hope—that her spells would be enough.

One poor dwarf writhed about, having been stepped on by a giant, and the aevendrow priest working over him had no spells to deal with such a brutal injury. Catti-brie nudged him aside, closed her eyes, and called to Mielikki for her greatest healing gift. She held the dwarf steady as the magic flowed between them, as the waves of warmth flowed through him.

When she let him go, he was no longer writhing, no longer gurgling in agony. He looked at Catti-brie with sincere appreciation. She kissed him on the forehead and thanked him for his courage this day, promising him that he would fully heal.

When she stood up, she felt a hand on her shoulder, and turned to see a smiling Ilina. "Come," the drow told her. "Galathae is resting."

They started away, but Catti-brie stopped and motioned to the far wall, to a giant who was sorely wounded but still stubbornly struggling against heavy silk cords that were being wrapped about it, holding it down and helpless.

When it began to scream, one of the orcs walked up to it and slapped a handful of goop—hagfish mucus, Catti-brie believed—over its mouth, but pointedly kept it clear of the behemoth's nose.

Scanning the rest of the room, Catti-brie noted drow moving about, stabbing falling slaadi with their white swords and spears, and checking fallen giants to make sure they were truly dead. Others ran the shelves, collecting the surviving eggs, placing them in secure boxes set on some of the litters.

"A prisoner?" Catti-brie finally asked when she and Ilina moved near to Galathae, who was leaning against the wall.

"We need some clarity on what this portends," Galathae answered. She pointed to the original battle in the room, to the baby creature cut in half and lying dead on the floor.

"It looks like a remorhaz," Ilina said.

"The polar worms, yes," Catti-brie agreed.

"This is a dangerous turn," Galathae said, her gaze locked on the giant. "We'll get our answers from that giant."

"Then what?" Catti-brie asked. "I saw no giants among the folk of Callidae."

"Nor will you" was all Galathae would reply. "When our priests and wizards are done interrogating him and scouring his thoughts, he will be mercifully and quickly dispatched."

Catti-brie wasn't about to argue. She looked to the giant, fully bound now but still kicking at anyone moving too near, even throwing itself over at one point in an attempt to crush an aevendrow under its bulk.

Catti-brie turned to the now-quiet tunnel, diving farther down into the mountain. Some aevendrow were there, discussing options. She moved past them, seeing the three fallen slaadi.

She heard a shout from far below. The aevendrow came past her, weapons ready.

"Go to Zaknafein," Catti-brie instructed Guenhwyvar, and the panther leaped away, rushing past the surprised aevendrow and down into the darkness.

CHAPTER 23

Writhing Riddles

D own through the near-darkness Guenhwyvar ran, speeding along the corridors, quick-stepping down a long, enclosed rough-hewn circular stair of huge proportions,
coming out on a ledge overlooking a natural chamber
where a battle was well under way.

To the side she saw Zaknafein and Entreri rolling and running
circles about a giant, stabbing where they could find an opening, diving and dodging swings from a heavy club. A second giant was on the
floor, crawling, pulling itself along, destroyed legs behind it, leaving a
trail of blood on the uneven stone, its very life pouring out with each
labored movement.

Not far away, a green monster hurled flame at Jarlaxle, who responded with a lightning bolt, a duel of magic back and forth.

Guenhwyvar leaped high and far, silently flying across the room.

She felt the impact as she crashed down on the green slaad. She
felt it folding up beneath her, dug in her claws so that as it crumpled
and tumbled, she would not let it go.

She bit deep and hard into the side of the monster's head, back claws raking fiercely, front claws and teeth digging deeper, holding fast as the beast thrashed.

Raking, digging, long after the beast lay still.

FREED FROM HIS MAGICAL DUEL—ONE THAT HAD STUNG him painfully in many places, including his forearm, where the skin was licked and shriveled by a fireball—Jarlaxle gave a yelp of surprise, then a great deal of thanks for Guen's unexpected intervention. He turned his attention to the remaining enemy, to his friends staying one step ahead of disaster and slowly, painfully, wearing the giant down.

Jarlaxle lifted his uninjured arm, waiting for the giant to come around, then shot a bolt of lightning into its ugly face.

The brute howled and dropped its club, its hands going up to slap against its destroyed eyes.

Entreri and Zak went for the kill, leaping up and stabbing, leaping and stabbing, Charon's Claw in its belly, Zak working Cutter against a treelike leg while repeatedly snapping his powerful bullwhip up across the giant's hands and face. They had it disoriented and off balance.

They weren't about to let it ever find its balance again.

The behemoth came down hard to one knee, its left leg torn apart by the fine edge of Khazid'hea. Entreri went to work methodically, his razor-like red blade sliding up to the hilt with every thrust.

The giant crumpled and expired, not far from where the other one now lay still.

The area fell quiet. Looking about, Jarlaxle said, "What is this place?" It was a large chamber, mostly natural but with shaped sections like the ledge and the stairs. Several tunnels ran off it, most of them worked stone, hinting at a much larger complex.

"The green frog is dead," Zak replied. "We should get back with the others. There's too much here for us to risk getting separated."

"Agreed," said Jarlaxle. "But I'm still curious. What is this place?"

"A nursery," Entreri answered from a large door he had just opened near to the last kill, one that led into a chamber that opened back under the tunnel that had brought them here. Jarlaxle and Zak hustled to join him.

"Amazing," Jarlaxle murmured when he got there and peered in. The room before them was brighter than this one, with the same glowing globes as the room above, except this glow was purple instead of red, with one enormous light globe hanging over an open stone pit with angled walls so that the bottom was wider than the top.

So that the polar worms could not crawl out.

The three companions moved to the edge of the hole. Below them, scores and scores of young remorhazes squirmed and tangled. Some flapped tiny wings set just behind their heads to lift up toward the newcomers, toothy jaws opening to reveal their gullets, like baby birds when the mother returns to the nest. These were larger than the hatchling in the other room, some twice, some thrice, some four times that length. Several of the larger ones showed a heated glow along their spines, and the friends could feel the warmth from twenty feet above them.

"Why would . . ." Entreri started to ask, but the question trailed off and he just shook his head.

"Building an army, perhaps," Jarlaxle answered. "To send them all crawling for Callidae."

"How could they even control them?" Entreri replied. "And how big do these ugly things get?"

"Look at this," Zak said, walking over to them and holding out his hands, showing them several crystals. He motioned behind him, and the other two followed his gaze to the corner, to a pile of crystals.

Down in the pit, the worms began to click their mandibles frantically, and soon almost all of them had the front parts of their centipede-like bodies upright, small wings filling this room with a furious fluttering sound.

Jarlaxle motioned to Zak, who tossed one of the crystals down. The worm nearest its descent snapped at it, but missed, sending it clattering to the floor, where a cluster of polar worms attacked it, cracking it, powdering it with those powerful jaws.

"They eat crystals?" Entreri said skeptically.

"Look at the floor," Zak said, for indeed, now that they knew what they were looking for, the friends noted bits of crystal all about.

A low growl from Guenhwyvar and movement in the other room reminded them that this place wasn't secured, but they were relieved indeed when they turned about to find a sizable contingent of Callidaeans moving into the larger chamber.

Azzudonna and Emilian joined the companions at the edge of the pit.

"These beasts are among the most feared monsters to us in Callidae," Azzudonna explained. "They can burrow through the glacier walls at great speed and come upon us anywhere in the city. That our enemies are apparently breeding them is unwelcome news." She turned back to the other room, calling upon the soldiers. "Destroy them. All of them."

Aevendrow and orcs filtered in, all armed with long spears.

"I pray we've caught them early in this devious plot," Emilian said, moving to join the friends. "These are all young, very young, I think. I have seen some truly monstrous examples of their kind, several times larger than the largest in this pit, fierce and huge enough to swallow a drow whole. They do not feel the cold, they cannot be hurt with fire, and their jaws bite with more power than our armor can deflect."

"So we've seen," said Zak.

"Come," Emilian bade them. "Let us finish our tasks here and be quickly to Callidae to alert the Siglig."

"This bodes ill," Azzudonna agreed.

More than you think, Jarlaxle thought but did not say, for he was afraid that he was beginning to piece this all together now. He glanced over at the pile of crystals, then back to the pit, as the high-pitched screams of the doomed creatures began to fill the air.

The cacophony did not bring any more giants or slaadi into the room, and the scouting parties discovered that the other tunnels led mostly to empty rooms or back up to empty caves on the surface. Their job here completed, the expedition soon after departed for Callidae, the bound frost giant, unhatched eggs, and several dead young remorhazes in tow.

"THEY'RE GOING TO KILL THAT GIANT TONIGHT," CATTI-brie told the other three as she joined them for dinner one night, the expedition about halfway back to Callidae.

"If you expect me to speak against that, you'll be sorely disappointed," Jarlaxle replied.

"If they need any help . . ." Entreri offered.

"Their priests and wizards have used spells to scour his thoughts and have learned little," Catti-brie explained. "He is a dull-witted brute, more than you would expect, and it seems as if he has been tending this place for a long while. He doesn't even know what they do with the remorhazes when they leave the hatchery—and it would seem from what the aevendrow have learned that many have indeed left this place, unfortunately."

"It seems obvious enough what will be done with them," said Zak.

"Does it?" Jarlaxle asked, his serious tone catching them all off guard.

"You heard Azzudonna and Emilian," Zak reminded them.

Jarlaxle threw the question out to any of them. "Why do you think the hot springs flow? What brings all those small tributaries to create the lifeblood of the aevendrow city, the River Callidae?"

"Probably a volcano deep below," Entreri answered. "Maybe a god of fire, like—"

"Like Maegera," Catti-brie finished. "I had thought that. Is it possible that this glacier lies atop a captured primordial of fire?"

"I thought the glacier was an elemental of ice, or a wind god, Qadeej, or whatever they call it," Zak added.

Catti-brie shrugged. They could not know.

"Did you feel such a primordial back in the town near to the glacier?" Zak asked her. "When you reached through the ring, was there another Maegera there to answer?"

"I didn't sense anything like that. Just the glacier itself."

"Yet the aevendrow have been here for millennia, so they claim," Zak put in. "This area they have carved out has been stable all that time. Could opposing primordials be that evenly matched for that long?"

"Is it stable? Weren't there five boroughs until fairly recently?" Catti-brie countered.

"Yes, as with the abandoned Ulutiun village," said Jarlaxle. "Is the glacier gaining the edge?"

"What are you getting at, Jarlaxle?" Catti-brie asked.

"They ate crystal," he replied.

"Yes?" she said, not getting his point. "We have seen polar worms in Icewind Dale. They eat anything and everything, including humans and drow. I have heard it said that they eat crystals to gain the power to so wickedly heat their back scales. Others say they eat crystals and stones to sharpen those teeth, or mandibles, or whatever they might be."

The mercenary nodded and looked to Zaknafein. "They ate crystal."

A look of epiphany came over the weapon master. "The breathless rooms," he said, his voice barely above a whisper.

"There are places in the Underdark," Jarlaxle explained to his surface-dwelling friends, "vast chambers of great heat and energy, though few are anywhere near to Menzoberranzan. We call them the breathless rooms, because if you remain in one, the heat of it will burn your lungs so that you will never again be able to speak, or perhaps even to draw breath. Huge, vast chambers full of crystals. Beautiful, like flowering gardens of stone, but deadly. Crystals the size of the tallest trees of the Crags. Even the svirfneblin, who value such pretty baubles above all else, cannot mine them, because the heat is too much for them. Their priests would have to work harder than the miners simply to protect them from the burning energy of the massive crystals."

"I have heard of drow priestesses whose faith was doubted being locked into such a chamber, where only their fealty to Lolth could grant them enough spells of protection to survive the duration," Zak added.

"So, you believe that the slaadi and giants are breeding the worms to . . . what? Eat crystals?" Catti-brie asked.

"They feel no heat and feel no cold," Jarlaxle reminded. He noted the doubting expressions coming back at him.

"Breathless rooms wouldn't bother remorhazes," Zak said.

"It is only a possibility," Jarlaxle admitted.

A LARGE STORM CAME UP THE NEXT DAY, BUT THE FOL-lowing few days went along uneventfully, with no enemies but the wind and the ice coming up before the expedition. When the clouds finally broke, they were swept away on bitterly cold winds, but the four friends had their magic to protect them, and the clothing of the Callidaeans clearly kept them all warm enough.

The stars sparkled above; the moon made its return, and the Merry Dancers, too, green curtains setting all the frozen land aglow. On a high pass, the friends saw the river of ice, which they were now calling the Qadeej Glacier, in the distance, stretching out over the ice pack far away from the mountains.

"It really must be a primordial or a god," Catti-brie remarked. "How could such a glacier as that exist? Glaciers are rivers of ice that lock into mountain passes or spill down from higher peaks, but this . . . this looks like the legends claim, like a giant, frozen, now ice-covered creature that just lay down atop the ice and died." She shook her head. "It makes no sense."

"Have you not seen Anauroch, the Great Desert?" Jarlaxle asked her.

Catti-brie, who had been reborn after Iruladoon into a Bedine family, well knew Anauroch, a landscape equally out of place, and whose origins were legends no less exotic than the aevendrow explanation for this formation.

"Come," Azzudonna bade them. "We are almost to a place you must see."

She took them to Galathae and Emilian, who joined them in the hike for another hour, then turned the four friends away from the marching line and down a different trail, one going higher on the mountain the expedition was traversing.

"Do you see?" Emilian asked at one high plateau. He pointed out across the ice.

The friends peered and stared, studying the distant vista. They noted the glacial wall, but weren't quite sure what they were looking for.

The dancers in the sky shivered and swirled as if offering their light to the search, and Zaknafein spied it first. "There, on the glacier," he said. "Near the top, down there to the right."

Catti-brie started to ask what he meant, but then she saw it, too. At first, she thought it just the wind-beaten and -created sculptures of the ice wall, but as she looked more closely, she realized it to be more than that, more than natural.

It was a castle, gigantic and intricate, cut against the glacial wall hundreds of feet from the ground and still hundreds of feet high.

Now that they had seen it, they couldn't unsee it. It was many miles away, certainly, but so grandiose, so huge, that it mocked them even from afar.

"That is the castle of the frost giants," Emilian explained. "Or it was, until the slaadi came. Now it is shared, and I doubt the frost giant jarl, whoever leads them now, has much command above their guests."

"Have you ever been there?"

"I have," said Galathae. "On two occasions. It is not a place we raid regularly, for the cost is always too high. Your friend Doum'wielle fell there when we went in pursuit of a raiding party that had captured several kurit.

"We didn't rescue them," the paladin added somberly, "and I was one of only a score who managed to escape."

"We believe Doum'wielle to still be alive," Catti-brie told her. "I felt it through the sword. She could still be there."

"I don't know if she is or not. We don't go there unless we have no choice," Galathae said. "If she is alive, it would be in the ice dungeons below. But down there looms the frozen death, the cante and the n'divi, the uninhabited and the overtaken, and in great numbers.

Worse, even Qadeej will wage war on invaders in those depths. If Doum'wielle is alive there, she's still as good as dead."

"Cante and n'divi?" Catti-brie asked.

"The uninhabited and the . . . " Galathae began.

"I know what the words mean, but what are they?"

"Living water, or ice," explained the paladin. "The cante hunt for living beings to encompass and possess, though it is more than possession. Together, the cante and the victim become n'divi."

"Well, that sounds lovely," Catti-brie said, turning to Jarlaxle. She remembered the strange sensations she had known when seeking Doum'wielle with Khazid'hea.

"You said you'd go only if you have no choice. I don't think we have a choice," Jarlaxle said, ignoring her concern. "She is truly important to us, both in duty to her poor family and because she might hold the power to stop a war. As you went for yours . . ."

"I do not doubt your desire or intent," Galathae assured him. "You will speak with the Siglig when we return to Callidae. Make your case there, but do not expect that any of the aevendrow, the kurit, or the oroks will accompany you beyond the entrance."

"We only wanted to show you," Azzudonna explained. "This vantage alone along our trail reveals the ice castle under the light of the Merry Dancers. You kept asking about your friend . . ."

Catti-brie look at Jarlaxle, then both turned to Zaknafein.

He understood and drew out Khazid'hea, handing it over to Catti-brie. The woman closed her eyes and held forth the sword, her grip loose.

The sword swayed like the lights above, its tip going true to point at the distant castle.

"I feel her," Catti-brie whispered. "She is alive. I feel her."

"Perhaps what you feel is one not truly alive," Galathae said quietly.

"Either way, we must find out," Jarlaxle said with conviction.

CHAPTER 24

The Siglig

M ona Chess," Ilina announced to the companions as they came to the end of the long, straight corridor, open to the night sky but still lined with multicolored faerie fire.

Stepping out behind her, Catti-brie was greeted by a sight very different from that of Scellobel, and she could only think of the first time she had looked upon Menzoberranzan for any type of comparison.

Ilina had told them that Mona Chess was a bit larger than Scellobel, but at first glance, it appeared much larger. Perhaps it was because this borough wasn't split down the middle by a prow of stone. Perhaps it was the construction of the dwellings here, the whole of the borough punctuated by taller structures constructed of the magical blue and white ice, some reaching almost halfway up the towering glacial walls with their minarets and spires. All of the facades danced in waves of green and purple, reflections of the sky above, and still they were lined with faerie fire of all colors, accentuating the turrets and sweeping stairways, the columns and the decorated windows.

"So much like Menzoberranzan," she said quietly.

"Or Silverymoon," Jarlaxle added. "If you put the two together . . ."

"Mona Chess was originally the whole of Callidae," Ilina explained. "The other boroughs were set for defense and as staging grounds for patrols, much as we use Cascatte today. Come, across the way is the Siglig. We are expected."

Every side avenue they passed showed them more beauty. Every wall, every bridge had been sculpted with care, with myriad designs and perfect placement of highlighting magical light. The aevendrow greatly outnumbered the other peoples here in Mona Chess, which made sense since those not of drow heritage had come to the city later, and mostly, from what they had heard, few by few.

Soon after, the group turned down one wide lane, and Catti-brie didn't have to ask which structure housed the assembly. For across the way, at the far end of the boulevard and cut into the glacial wall, loomed the most wondrous edifice of all, stately and huge, with wide stairs leading up its front to a landing set with gigantic columns, thick as a frost giant and twice as tall. Magical lights circled the columns, but in a way Catti-brie had never seen before. Rather than simply a line of faerie fire, these seemed more like rolling globes of varying colors, running up and around, up and around. Red, chased by orange, chased by yellow, chased by green, chased by blue, chased by indigo, chased by violet. Indeed, it seemed as if she were watching multicolored sprites at play, trying to form a true rainbow but never quite getting there.

It took her a long while to break her gaze from the enchanting displays, and she shook her head in embarrassment at first, until she understood that Ilina was patiently waiting for her and her three companions, who were similarly gawking.

"The Siglig," Ilina told them. "The seat of government and the great library of the aevendrow."

They moved down the lane and up the steps, pausing frequently to note the reliefs carved into the triangular facing of the roof supported by the six columns. Such a contrast in those panels. Some showed battle, with giants mostly, while others spoke of love and dance, a contrast so evident in Callidae.

The sublime and the profane, the joy and the struggle.

Like cazzcalci, Catti-brie thought, remembering the Boscaille army halting in the final battle even though it cost them any chance to even the score or perhaps claim victory, in order to lend their voices to the champion of their opponents.

Like Azzudonna herself, and all the other soldiers of the four armies, wearing the broken noses, the missing teeth, and all the other scars of that battle still, though the magic had returned and they could have become again such beautiful drow. Only the serious wounds inflicted in the four battles of cazzcalci had been treated by the priests.

They were people of love and joy and beauty in a land that demanded of them ferocity and strength.

The great doors of the Siglig were open, with guards standing to either side, silent and still as the columns, resplendent in purple waistcoats above the black sealskin clothing common about Callidae. Their polearms were of polished wood, capped with blue ice three-way heads: pointed tip, axe presented forward, and hammer opposite.

The guards didn't even turn their eyes as the five passed. Ilina led them into a maze of hallways and smaller chambers, all comfortably lit, the walls set with tapestries and paintings that evoked the same aesthetic as the panels on the roof facing outside. Multiple alcoves lined the hallways, every one set with a sculpture or a bust of a particular aevendrow or simply a posing figure, some naked, some scantily clad, some in regal arms and armament. There were kurit dwarves, too, and orcs, and the Ulutiun humans, all gathered in still and silent celebration.

Each of the friends, even Entreri, kept pausing to consider one or another of the artworks.

It occurred to Catti-brie that half of Luskan's docks or all of Bleeding Vines could fit in this one building, but still, every bit of it, every inch of wall, every corner, every stairway or door they passed was carefully and lovingly designed, both functional and undeniably beautiful, provoking emotions and thoughtfulness.

At last they came to a large set of decorated double doors, flanked by a pair of guards attired and armed like those outside, and with two more aevendrow standing right before the doors, dressed fully in purple with silver trim, and each wearing a single white glove, on the left hand of the doorkeeper to the right and the right hand of the doorkeeper to the left.

They bowed as one and turned, each taking a doorknob in hand and drawing open the portal. They didn't blink, they didn't move beyond their prescribed ritual, they said nothing at all.

Until the companions passed them, when one whispered, "*Perte miye Zaknafein.*"

Caught by surprise, Catti-brie turned sharply, and the aevendrow flashed a wink and a smile, then became again his stoic self.

The chamber before them was the largest they had seen by far, and perfectly befitting the rest of this creation. Obviously this was the Siglig itself, the assembly for what they called the Temporal Convocation. The room was rectangular, except that the far wall opposite the doors was concave, curving about in a semicircle around a raised platform. Bench seats escalated up that curving facade, and there milled scores of aevendrow, and a fair number of the other three peoples of Callidae as well. It took Catti-brie just a moment to make sense of the sashes each wore, for they reflected the colors she had seen at cazzcalci for the armies of the four boroughs, and though the representatives were not separated into distinct groups, she soon discerned that the numbers of each color were an appropriate ratio to the number of the cazzcalci onlookers, thus the population of each respective borough.

On the center dais stood Mona Valrissa Zhamboule in her grand robes, flanked by two of the inquisitors who had spoken with the companions when they had first arrived in Scellobel, with the third of the trio, Galathae, standing before the dais on the main floor.

Galathae turned as the five entered, and pointed toward chairs of blue ice set on the floor several strides out before the dais.

Ilina led the companions to them and took a seat on one end, motioning for the others to sit.

As soon as they did, Mona Valrissa clapped her hands sharply three times, calling the Temporal Convocation to order, and the representatives all found seats along the multiple levels of the arena.

"Welcome to the Siglig," Mona Valrissa told them. "And our assembly, the Temporal Convocation. Holy Galathae, whom you know, will speak for this bench and this gallery, but let me first assure you that this is not an inquisition, nor a trial of any sort. All who happen upon Callidae must come here to speak before us. It is a necessary formality and an open discussion of your coming choices, nothing more.

"And be assured that we are well aware of your actions during your time here, and your assistance. This congress is grateful to you for directing our warriors to the hatchery of the slaadi, and impressed that you chose to lead the way into battle. Your exploits have not gone unnoticed." She paused and smiled warmly at them, and Catti-brie thought it sincere.

"Holy Galathae," Mona Valrissa prompted.

"I trust you are all rested from our great expedition," the paladin began. "Your single transgression in not telling us of your encounter with the giants and the slaadi is understood and excused, as you have more than corrected the issue.

"And so I must echo the words of Mona Valrissa: this is no inquisition. I do not expect that you are surprised by our caution here in Callidae, or ignorant of the purpose of this meeting. I will guide you through this assembly. Mona Valrissa might take the floor, as others might be recognized by her if there is a pressing matter they wish to inquire of you, but please rest assured that you are not among enemies here, nor judges. None in attendance may speak without the recognition of Mona Valrissa except for me and for you. Any questions, any additions, anything at all you feel should be said, please—"

"I understand," Artemis Entreri interrupted.

Catti-brie and the others turned abruptly to regard the man, whom they all expected would be the least likely of the group to jump in. But Catti-brie figured it out as Entreri went on, realizing that his somewhat rude interruption of Galathae was done more to measure the reaction of the gathering than because his thoughts could not wait. Also, the first remark in such a setting was always the hardest to voice, she knew. Entreri had just broken that emotional spell of silence for all of them in this intimidating place, whether intentionally or not. For that, Catti-brie was grateful to him.

"I understand the purpose, I mean," he went on. "This is akin to the geas my companion Catti-brie accepted from you, a continuation of that which you deem necessary for the security of Callidae. We may leave, but on your terms alone."

Galathae nodded. None in the audience gasped or seemed surprised, or annoyed at all by Entreri's interruption, Catti-brie noted. A good sign.

"The choice we must soon put to you is straightforward," Galathae explained, "and yet not. You are welcome to remain here, to choose a borough all together as one household, or individually, or in any combination you decide, in which to make your home or homes. In short time, perhaps as early as Conception Verdant, the vernal sunrise, you will be acclaimed as full Callidaeans, with all rights of voice here in the Siglig, with all opportunities to become as you will and as you can achieve, in trade, in art, in battle, or in governance."

She paused and offered the four a little smile. "I hope that will prove your course."

"And if we do not?" Entreri pressed, rather brusquely.

He's pushing too hard, Catti-brie thought, given the generosity of their hosts. And yet, she wanted to know the answer to that, too.

"Then you will leave," Mona Valrissa replied before Galathae could. "When you decide, and when you are able. The winter draws deeper. The cold and snows will not relent. Beyond this place is cold death, I warn." She looked directly at Catti-brie and added, "Unless, of course, you have a magical journey prepared.

"But this should be the discussion at the end of our session, not the beginning," Mona Valrissa decided. "We have other matters to attend before you make such a choice. There is no urgency here, in any case. You may wander the ways of Callidae freely through the coming hours and tendays, with but one condition that we must place upon you."

"A continuation of the magic-muting geas," Catti-brie stated. "I accept, and assure you that I alone among my party can perform the evacuation magic, or whisper across the distances."

Mona Valrissa and Galathae exchanged looks, then the mona nodded.

"Distant whispers?" Jarlaxle asked Catti-brie. "Messages to the south?"

She nodded, not quite understanding his eagerness here.

The mercenary reached for a chain around his neck and produced a small ornament hanging upon it. "A whistle," he explained to the assembly. "A whistle with which I can sometimes call to a faraway friend."

He pulled it over his head and handed it to Ilina, who seemed pleased. They all seemed pleased.

"I did not know," Catti-brie apologized, side-gazing at the ever-surprising rogue, and to Galathae, she added slyly, "You should inquire more deeply with this one, as he is ever the clever fellow."

"Not so clever," Mona Valrissa said, and she turned to the man at her left, the inquisitor from Scellobel, who reached for a chain on his own neck and produced a whistle remarkably similar—indeed physically identical—to the one Jarlaxle had just handed over.

"The one we gave back to you would have only called a mukteff," Mona Valrissa assured Jarlaxle, who laughed in reply, as did most of the assembly.

The rogue stood up from his chair and bowed low, sweeping his hat.

"He wouldn't make that particular gesture if he knew what it meant up here in Callidae," Ilina whispered to Catti-brie. "Not adding the hat sweep, at least."

Catti-brie eyed her curiously and the aevendrow priestess whispered in her ear, "I'll tell you later," in a very salacious tone.

Catti-brie figured in that moment that they'd never get Jarlaxle out of this place, and that, yes, he probably would have made the inviting bow in an even more exaggerated form if he knew the customs!

"And the rest of our gear?" Jarlaxle politely asked.

The mona offered the floor to the male inquisitor, who stood up.

"You'll find that everything else is as it was. This whistle is the only thing we withheld," he replied. "We do not understand the magic of it, other than that it is used to communicate across the miles. You understand, I hope, that we had to be certain, given our vulnerable situation here."

"I have witnessed cazzcalci, and now the fight at the caves," Jarl-axle replied. "'Vulnerable' is not a label I would affix to Callidae."

"We have learned to defend ourselves, yes, but we are few in number compared to those that might come against us," Galathae said, motioning for the inquisitor to sit back down, which he did. "We are not ignorant of the southland. We know of Silverymoon, of Cormyr, of Baldur's Gate and of great Waterdeep. We know, too, of the southern-most reaches, of Calimport. If all of Callidae moved to mighty Calimport, the people there would hardly realize the addition."

"Your argument is noted," Jarlaxle conceded, "but still, you could have simply withheld the whistle, could you not? Or spoken to me of it, perhaps offering a geas agreement as you fashioned with my friend here. You didn't have to go to such lengths to replicate it, unless of course, you did so as a test. Tell me, Galathae—Holy Galathae—did you have a mukteff on watch and at the ready to alert you if I chose to use the device?"

Catti-brie held her breath, but relaxed almost immediately as Galathae and many others of the assembly took no offense and indeed, laughed in reply.

"Well reasoned, Jarlaxle," the paladin congratulated him. "A small test, as it turns out, and one where you confirmed our confidence in these weighty matters when you simply admitted to having such a necklace, and one you have not used. Mostly, we held your whistle longer simply because we cannot construe the magic of it, and now that our own spellpowers have fully returned, we wish to unravel the mystery."

"It is a curious item, I freely admit" was all Jarlaxle said of their befuddlement. "I can contact only a single person with it, and then only if he happens to be listening at the time." He paused and chuckled a bit. "And if he chooses not to ignore me."

He hadn't mentioned psionics, Catti-brie noted, for that was the basis of Kimmuriel's whistle. She thought his omission of the mind magic curious, but began to wonder if there might be some other reason Jarlaxle would not want the aevendrow to know about the true nature of the item.

Given what she and her companions already suspected to be the terms of departure, she had a hunch of what that reason might be.

"It will be returned to you, likely," Galathae told him. "But yes, with conditions."

Jarlaxle swept another bow, and Catti-brie joined in the giggling. Ilina put her hand on Catti-brie's then, simply to lend support. A small but hardly unimportant gesture.

"You have told us several times that you seek Doum'wielle, our lost Little Doe," Galathae said. "You tell us that you are convinced she is alive, and so you must go seek her."

"The sword—" Jarlaxle began, but Galathae stopped him.

"You need not explain it again, and I have relayed to all of the Temporal Convocation that which you have told me of that sword and the connection you believe leads you to Doum'wielle. Their response, in unity, is the same that I said to you: perhaps she is alive, but even if so, she is not what she was. We have seen this before. Once encased by the cante, the victim becomes merely a physical extension of the monstrous magic, and the new joined being, uninhabited and victim, transforms into what we call the n'divi, the overtaken, an undead creature controlled by the slaadi. Doum'wielle was encased, and that was many months ago, soon after the last Conception Verdant."

"But you can't be certain," Jarlaxle said.

Galathae conceded that with a shrug.

"Doum'wielle was never a good friend to any of us," Jarlaxle admitted. "Though we, mostly Catti-brie, know of her, and know well her family, who live in a great forest we call the Moonwood."

"Doum'wielle told us of them," Galathae replied.

"Yes, and she likely told you that she could never return because of her crimes," said Jarlaxle.

"She did, to some degree. We knew that it was not a good series of events that brought her to us."

"It was terrible," Jarlaxle assured them. "But that is her story to tell, not mine. What I will say is that it was not Doum'wielle who did these things, but Doum'wielle under the domination of the sword Khazid'hea. The very same sword you returned to Zaknafein."

"A prideful and powerful blade," Galathae admitted.

"And now, because of circumstance, Doum'wielle, freed of the sword, might find some redemption, and do great good," said Jarlaxle. "Good for a drow city with almost as many people as this one, a city on the edge of civil war. The crux of that war is the Second House, Barrison Del'Armgo, the house of Doum'wielle Armgo, and of her father, who was a noble of the house but is dead now. She can sway them. She can turn them."

"By telling them of us, so you believe," Mona Valrissa Zhamboule sharply interrupted.

Jarlaxle seemed to have lost his voice.

"I . . . I . . ."

"That, she cannot do," Mona Valrissa flatly stated. "That, none of you will ever do. Understand that."

"You must understand," Jarlaxle countered. "What I speak of is everything to our people. *Our* people, yours and not just mine! In my homeland—"

"We know quite a lot about your home, Jarlaxle," Mona Valrissa replied.

"But it is more than that," Jarlaxle protested. "Do you know of Gauntlgrym, home again to the Delzoun dwarves?"

The aevendrow and others looked about, most shaking their heads.

"Of Luskan, the City of Sails?" Jarlaxle asked.

"Luskan, yes," said Mona Valrissa. "That sounds somewhat familiar."

"It is a city just south of the frozen lands on the Sword Coast," Jarlaxle told them. "A great port, which is now under my direction. And with that guidance, it is becoming a center of commerce. Wondrous trade of wondrous items from such varied sources as would never have considered such arrangements before. With your white and blue ice magic, with your alterations of simple conjurations, with the clothing you wear alone, I could create great avenues of trade for you."

"There is nothing we desire from the world beyond Callidae," Mona Valrissa answered. "What do you suppose you can offer? We have no need of your money or jewels or weapons or anything else.

That which you treasure is not what we cherish. We survive, we thrive, we live in the highest joy, because we have made of this place that which we desire, as one and as each of us."

"But there is so much," pressed Jarlaxle, ever the salesman. "From my home alone—"

"From Menzoberranzan, the City of the Spider Queen Lolth," Mona Valrissa cut him short. "We know, Jarlaxle, of Menzoberranzan, or at least, of how it came to be and how it was doomed to fall . . ." She struggled for a word. "*Virtuperd*," she decided. "Doomed to corruption. In the Grand Dispersion, so say the histories, when the drow peoples fled their elven cousins, they tried to leave the world that was ever shaken by the whims of kings and queens, of lords who claimed divinity, of churches that demanded fealty, of purest greed and callous projection, of damnable differences instead of celebratory diversity. In this time, several of the great clans traveled downward, what they believed the obvious path to security, into the Underdark. The stone ceilings and tunnel mazes provided ways for them to guard against great armies, of course, but alas, as with the cleaving of many of the dwarven peoples, sheltering in the Underdark meant settling near the barrier between our world and the lower planes, and so they were corrupted. *Virtuperd*."

"Yvonnel and Quenthel," Catti-brie whispered, and her friends heard her and turned to her. This was a bit of a confirmation, so it seemed, that the recounting of the memories of Yvonnel the Eternal was not far-fetched.

"Alas for the drow and for the duergar . . ." Mona Valrissa was saying when Catti-brie turned her attention back to the aevendrow, but the mona's voice trailed off.

"And now they have the chance to break free of that spell," Jarlaxle pleaded with her, with them all. "Doum'wielle might prove critical in that effort. To shake off the curse of Lolth!"

"It is not our fight," Galathae said. "It cannot be our fight. But we will not stop you in your quest to find Doum'wielle. We will take you there, to the lower caverns beneath the fortress of the slaadi, where she and many others were lost to us. There will be but one condition.

Prepare your word of recall, Catti-brie, but your destination will be Callidae and not the southland, and accept the geas that will hold you to that. When we are agreed upon that, you may go to find your lost friend."

"And then?" Catti-brie asked.

"We will speak of that at the end of the congress," Mona Valrissa reminded her.

Catti-brie tried to hide her grimace. Thoughts of Drizzt and Brie flooded through her; she knew that when she returned to Callidae from their rescue of Doum'wielle, she would demand that the aevendrow do whatever ritual or spell they needed to blur her memories of this place, and then, when they were satisfied, she would fly away to her home with whichever of her companions decided to join her.

It was a pleasant thought and it was not, for the idea of forgetting this place, of never returning here with Drizzt and Brie, stabbed at her heart.

Galathae nodded. "Now we ask something of you in exchange for our hospitality. We would have you tell us your stories, of your homelands, of how you came to be together. Of who you are, that our scribes may record your tales for our library, that our bards might put proper context on *perte miye Zaknafein*."

The unsubtle reminder made the request seem perfectly reasonable to all of them, of course.

"Are we wrong in expecting that your own tale might prove the longest and most . . . interesting?" she asked Jarlaxle.

"He'll make it seem so," Entreri muttered, to laughter.

"I am sure," Galathae replied.

"I do not wish to bore the assembly," Jarlaxle said with obviously feigned humility.

"We do not know much about you, Jarlaxle, but we strongly doubt that 'boring' is a word often associated with you."

"Would that it were," said Zaknafein.

"We'll starve in this room," Entreri moaned.

Catti-brie just watched Jarlaxle taking it all in, truly in his glory here.

"Very well," he said. "I will tell you great tales of many lands, of heroic adventures, and terrific battles, of dragons loved and demon lords destroyed. But I have a price."

"Truly?" asked a perplexed Galathae.

"I would think it already paid," Mona Valrissa stated evenly. "But speak your ransom."

Jarlaxle waited, the hall thick with curiosity, if not tension. To either side of the floor, aevendrow filed in and lined the walls, books in hand, ready to record. When they were all in place, pens at the ready, Jarlaxle let the suspense linger just a few moments longer before blurting out his price.

"Persimmons!" he shouted. "Persimmons with kurit muskox cheese, chased by Scellobelee ice wine. That is my price."

"He is so good at this," Catti-brie mumbled as the whole of the Siglig reverberated with cheers and laughter. In a moment of tension, Jarlaxle had struck the perfect chord, and while he had them tittering and settling, before any could slow him, he launched into a long tale, the story of Jarlaxle, the story he enjoyed telling most of all.

He began with his days as a houseless rogue in Menzoberranzan, explaining in detail the structures of the noble families and the lesser families striving to become more powerful—but being ever careful, for if they gained too much, they would be obliterated in short order by those who desired no rivals.

Catti-brie watched the faces of the representatives, mostly of the aevendrow, and she came to believe that, though they knew of Menzoberranzan and had found out bits of information here and there, never before had they, this particular group at least, heard such details of the wild ways of the City of Spiders.

Jarlaxle stressed how he had survived, forming Bregan D'aerthe— Catti-brie was truly surprised that he disclosed his organization so openly!

But then, what did he have to lose?

The rogue turned about to regard Zaknafein as he described the battle between houses wherein he had rescued Zak at the behest of yet another matron, and though he turned back to the assembly,

Catti-brie let her gaze remain on Zak as Jarlaxle detailed their time together, right up to the point when he alluded to Zak's sacrifice for the sake of his son.

Zak nodded through it all. It was clear to Catti-brie that he thought Jarlaxle to be offering an honest recounting, even if the rogue was surely leaving out a few details, like Zak's gory actions on the night Drizzt had been born.

As soon as he finished that bit, Jarlaxle pivoted to the events that had led him to a life more focused on the surface world.

At that point, Galathae stopped him. "The mona has called a recess for dinner," she announced to the chamber, and to the four visitors, she added, "You have a side room prepared where your food will be brought. This seems a good time for a break in the tale. Come."

When the mona formally dismissed the assembly, Galathae led them to one of the smallest rooms they had seen in the Siglig, although it was still quite large and comfortable. A long table was set with a dozen chairs, with plenty of room between them. Fine settings of white and blue ice were etched in various ways: beautiful designs of sled dogs and dancers, frozen waterfalls, and even a pair of grapplers in a grape-crushing battle.

"You heard them, yes? The Grand Dispersion, they called it," Jarlaxle said after the aevendrow servers filled the table with a wondrous bounty and departed. "I don't know the timeline of this event, but it would seem that these drow have a view of history similar to what we heard from Yvonnel and Quenthel."

"It makes sense," Catti-brie said. She took a large serving plate from Zak, then paused a moment to consider the fatty slabs of baked meat, topped with a red and green sauce she did not know that smelled delicious. "Why would the drow of Menzoberranzan have gone down that path of violence and deceit if so many are of different weal? How many did you know among you in all those years who truly loved Lolth and the daily horrors of a city caught in her grasp?"

"There were plenty of zealots, do not doubt," Zak warned. "They relished the power the infernal Lolth brought to them and their cruelty was to them nothing more than a joyful expression of that power."

"But most, I expect, just went along, secretly loathing it all," Jarlaxle put in. "What choice was there for so many? For Zak, for me, for priestess Dab'nay, who doesn't even understand why Lolth grants her spells?"

"But there was a choice," Catti-brie reminded him. "I am married to one who took a different path."

"Drizzt wasn't unique in leaving, and certainly not in wanting to leave," Jarlaxle replied. "What was unique, to us at least as far as we know, is that he made it and thrived."

"Unique until your recent efforts," Catti-brie said. She hoped Jarlaxle wouldn't bow at the compliment—after what Ilina had hinted, she never wanted to see him bow again.

"My son survived by sheer will, and then because he found such wonderful friends," Zak added with a warm smile to his daughter-in-law.

"This steak is delicious," Entreri told them through a mouthful of food. "I don't even want to know what it is, and I really don't want to know what is on top of it."

"Probably the hagfish mucus," Catti-brie teased, and all three told her to shut up at the same time.

Galathae entered the room then, declaring, "The ransom paid," and Azzudonna, Emilian, Ilina, and Vessi came in close behind, each with a bottle of ice wine in one hand, two or three smaller blue ice plates in the other, and after them Ayeeda, pushing a rolling cart overflowing with blocks of white cheese and persimmons.

"Simply amazing," Catti-brie heard Zak quietly say.

The conversation turned lighthearted when the aevendrow accepted the invitation to sit and join in the feast, and it really struck Catti-brie just how easy all of this was, as if it were a joyous dinner with old friends. Too much so, she feared. She and her companions had come upon this place so unexpectedly, relatively a short time ago, and yet already it seemed as if bonds were being formed.

Was it all just an elaborate ruse?

But to what end? From the first meeting, the adventuring companions had never been in a position of advantage over their hosts. The aevendrow could have killed them out in the tunnels before they even got to Cascatte, and quite easily.

But here they were, and there was no reason for such a display, for any of this, if the aevendrow were not as they appeared, if Callidae itself were some grand illusion, or worse, some grand deception.

When she looked at Azzudonna talking with Zak, the aevendrow woman so near to him, smiling and with a certain look so obvious in her lavender eyes, Catti-brie knew she was being foolish here with her doubts. She had seen such fears as her own manifested before, after all, when Drizzt had been afflicted by the Faerzress and had come to believe that everything he was being shown was a trick of the eyes.

"The secret is to dry the persimmon just so," she heard behind her, and she turned about to see Galathae holding another cheese-covered fruit chip toward her. The paladin motioned with her hand that she meant for Catti-brie to take it, so she did, gladly, and Galathae produced a second one and held it up between them.

"I look forward to hearing your story most of all," she toasted.

Catti-brie likewise lifted her treat, then took a small bite, savoring the explosion of flavors.

"Why mine? Jarlaxle has lived a most incredible and long life, as has Zaknafein, and none have grown in soul more than Artemis Entreri."

"Because we are the most alike, and not simply because we are both women. Jarlaxle has not mentioned his faith in his telling thus far, and I do not expect that to change. He only mentions the goddess Lolth at all to rightly cast aspersions on the fiend. And I expect little on the matter of the gods from Zaknafein or Artemis Entreri."

"I would agree with that," Catti-brie told her.

"But from you, I will hear the voice of Mielikki, a sister goddess to one I have pledged my life to serve, and through that perspective, I believe I will come to understand your friends and your land so much better."

"Though you'll never be able to visit that land."

"Who can say?" Galathae replied, piquing Catti-brie's interest.

"Perhaps a decade hence, I will wander the ways of your land and see again the face of Catti-brie."

"I would like that," Catti-brie replied. "But tell me, in that event, would I even remember you?"

Galathae went quiet suddenly, her expression a bit pained. "Maybe it will be just a feeling, a spark of knowledge to make you wonder if somehow we are old friends, though to you it will also seem as if we have only first met."

It couldn't be spoken more clearly than that.

"Maybe we've met before," Catti-brie answered. "Perhaps you did come to my home once, long ago, and we did to you that which you intend to do to us."

"Why would you?" the paladin asked in such a logical manner that Catti-brie paused and considered her analogy.

"What would the great cities of the south have to fear from an aevendrow enclave so far away?" Galathae continued, quite seriously.

"It was just a thought," Catti-brie deflected. She finished the delicious treat, then wiped her bottom lip with her index finger and scraped a piece of cheese onto her teeth, determined to enjoy every last bit.

"Maybe you've been here before," Galathae said. "Or perhaps there is more to reality than we can know."

"Perhaps Mielikki will show me the way back here," Catti-brie remarked. "What then?"

"Persimmons, of course," the paladin teased.

The door opened then and a sentry—the same one who had tossed the comforting remark at Zaknafein when the group first entered the assembly chamber—announced, "The Temporal Convocation is now reconvening."

Galathae leaned in toward Catti-brie. "I do wish to hear your story. Be at ease and be comfortable, Catti-brie. You are not among enemies."

"I know," she replied, and she wanted to believe that she did. And yet . . .

The other aevendrow rose and began collecting the plates. Galathae moved for the door, telling the companions to follow along.

Rising from her seat, Catti-brie glanced again at the smiling Azzudonna, her purple eyes locked on Zak.

"Does it still hurt?" Zak asked her, his hand coming up and almost, but not quite, touching her nose.

"You think me ugly?" she asked back melodramatically.

Zak laughed. "No, I just wonder if it still hurts. I would have expected that the priests would have tended to it by now."

"Soldiers wear the scars of cazzcalci for many days, sometimes all the way to Midwinter Deep," explained Vessi from across the table, and he pulled back his sleeve to show a tear in his forearm, of which he was obviously proud. "The oroks have such sharp teeth," he added with a dramatic sigh.

"It does not hurt," Azzudonna said quietly to Zak, leaning in close. "As long as you are careful when you kiss me."

The weapon master hesitated, caught off guard, and the aevendrow laughed and spun away.

Zak followed her departure until he turned enough to see Catti-brie staring at him with an impish little grin. He shrugged, having no answer to that.

"Fight beside me in cazzcalci next year, Zaknafein Do'Urden," Azzudonna called back, dancing out of the room, the others, except for Ilina and Galathae, following her.

The remaining six went back to the assembly together and took their seats. As soon as the room was filled and quiet, Galathae asked Jarlaxle to resume his tale, which he did with great energy. Catti-brie paid more attention now, for the mercenary was fast coming upon the part where her own story intersected.

Jarlaxle told it faithfully, spoke of adventures he and Entreri had shared in the distant Bloodstone Lands, and in the far, far south, tales that Catti-brie had not heard before. He burst with pride as he recounted the rebuilding of Gauntlgrym and of Luskan and the great changes along the northern reaches of the Sword Coast. His voice rose in triumph as he told of the heroic defeat of the demon lord De-mogorgon itself in the cavern of Menzoberranzan, and of how Drizzt had become the spear for an entire city. He spoke somberly of the more recent war throughout the lands about Luskan, and, to Catti-brie's sur-prise, he even told of the change of heart of House Baenre and the magical web of heresy the two great priestesses had woven to steal the driders from Lolth.

In that moment, Catti-brie feared that this whole setup of Cal-lidae might be a machination of Lolth to elicit exactly that story and admission from her companions.

But again, the fear passed, and the aevendrow continued to act and react properly, and as she considered Jarlaxle's brutal honesty here, she thought it a good thing. Jarlaxle was being less than his usual cau-tious self. He was putting it all on the line, a reflection, she thought, of his own desperation that this not be an illusion, or some fever-induced dream.

She thought it even a better thing when Mona Valrissa interrupted Jarlaxle on behalf of one of the representatives to ask a question that seemed to be on all their minds: What was this beast that he spoke of, this abomination he called a drider?

Catti-brie watched carefully the expressions of the members of the congress as Jarlaxle described the visceral horror of those beings, and she was glad of their disgust.

Sometimes, she thought, things really were just as they seemed.

By the time Jarlaxle finished, Mona Valrissa had to call a recess for some sleep, but they were all back together again very early the next day.

Zaknafein followed Jarlaxle, since so much of their tales over-lapped and Jarlaxle's remained so fresh in the thoughts.

Catti-brie had heard many of his stories before, but from the point of view of her husband, who had played so prominent a role in them.

He spoke of the not-so-little matter of his death and of Zin-carla and his second demise, explaining the time when he was dead by simply stating that he had no memory of it at all. And now he was returned, somehow, and glad he was, for he had met his new daughter, Catti-brie, and his beautiful half-drow, half-human granddaughter, now the joy of his life.

After another delightful meal with the same group as the previous night, Entreri began his story. Catti-brie tuned out a bit, focusing on her own life and what she intended to tell. But she was drawn back in almost immediately when she came to realize how open this always-guarded man was being. He spoke of things in his childhood, dark things that Catti-brie could not have imagined. He even truthfully recounted his first meeting with her, when he had taken her prisoner and dragged her across the land in pursuit of a halfling he had been tasked with kidnapping and bringing back to the far southland for the most extreme torture and execution.

He was so open that it made Catti-brie—and Jarlaxle, too, she believed from watching his reactions—wonder if there had been more spread on the persimmons than muskox cheese. Or perhaps the wine was stronger than they had believed.

But no, she realized when Entreri came to the part of his enwrapping in the magical cocoon of the one called Sharon, the one they believed to be the physical manifestation of the concept of conscience.

Artemis Entreri was telling the truth because he saw that as part of his penance.

And that truth coming from this man mesmerized Catti-brie. She thought it as wonderful as Callidae and the aevendrow. She had never been fond of Entreri, or even tolerant of him, until recently. There had been times when she had scolded Drizzt for not killing him!

But hearing him now somehow infused her with hope.

Unexpected hope, but not unwanted.

When her own turn came, Catti-brie started in Icewind Dale with stories of her adoptive father, who was now king of Gauntlgrym, and of Regis, and of her first meeting with Drizzt Do'Urden. So many adventures did she tell, and as she recited them, trying to be as brief and entertaining as she could, she found herself as amazed as any in the room at the sheer scope of her own life.

When she got to her death, she looked right at Galathae, and for this interlude in the life of Catti-brie, she took her time. For this was Iruladoon, a gift, so she truly believed, from the goddess Mielikki.

Galathae's eyes sparkled throughout the recounting, and on more than one occasion, Catti-brie noted them brimming with tears.

That moment more than any other except perhaps the miracle at cazzcalci convinced her that this was not some weird induced illusion, not a deception.

Indeed, indeed, sometimes things really were just as they seemed.

She went on to speak of her marriage to Drizzt and then burst out in a huge smile to tell of Briennelle Zaharina Do'Urden, her little girl, her greatest joy, and the smile became strained, and she teared up at the mere mention, only then fully realizing how badly she missed her family.

She looked again at Galathae when she finished speaking, the paladin offering her a sincere and approving nod.

The room was buzzing with chatter for some time before Galathae called it to order and turned the floor back to Mona Valrissa.

"We are most grateful again," she addressed the visitors. "The tales of the outside world remind us of our blessings here in Callidae. These insights are important, lest we take our bounties for granted. Wise were our ancestors.

"You express your desire to go and find Doum'wielle, and if this remains your chosen course, we will not stop you. Indeed, we will take you there—Doum'wielle was friend to Callidae, too, and fell with many of our people beside her. But beyond the entrance of the caverns of the uninhabited, you will travel alone. Our losses there earlier this year still hurt us dearly, and we, unlike you, understand that which lies within. We will try to persuade you to a different course until the time we leave you, although we find your loyalty and your cause just and powerful.

"You understand our conditions for taking you to this place. Should any or all of you somehow survive and escape that cursed place, your next journey must, on your word, be back to Callidae. Are we agreed?"

"Yes," they all replied, and Jarlaxle added, "Back here, where you will steal from me all thoughts of this place, the most wondrous memories of my long story."

"Where you will declare your choices," Mona Valrissa corrected him. "It seems clear to us that we already know Catti-brie's decision, for it is one easily made."

"But not without great lament," Catti-brie replied.

Mona Valrissa paused to acknowledge that with a look of appreciation and endearment. She continued, saying, "Then go and rest and prepare." She called the assembly to adjournment. "When you are ready to depart, simply ask and it will be done."

She raised her hands and clapped them together, and the assembled members of Callidae's congress began standing and shuffling about.

"Wait!" Jarlaxle called out loudly, surprising them all, particularly Galathae, who was coming over to escort the friends home.

"Wait, I beg," Jarlaxle continued. "There is something else I must tell you, and I have come to know that it should be here and now, and not when we bid you farewell."

His tone was not light, indeed sounded grave, and Mona Valrissa clapped her hands again three times sharply, reconvening the convocation. The members hustled back to their seats and the room quickly quieted.

"What are you doing?" Catti-brie asked Jarlaxle, but it was Zak who calmed her.

"Helping them, I think," said the weapon master.

Mona Valrissa nodded to Galathae, who told Jarlaxle to please continue.

"When we went to the cave, we found riddles," the rogue began. "The eggs, the polar worms. Why would slaadi and frost giants be caring for such a hatchery as that? Now, you supposed it to be a secret army of monsters that they could send against you, and perhaps you are right. But I think it might be something more."

He paused there and paced for a bit, clearly trying to sort out his thoughts.

"Everything is in balance about us," he continued. "This is true in the Underdark, but even more apparent here on the surface of Toril, with oceans and lakes, forests and fields. So, this glacier, Qadeej if you will, has stood for centuries uncounted, longer than your stories. Now you are speaking of its advance, taking Cattisola, and creeping toward the tunnel leading to Scellobel, correct?"

"We send teams out into the tunnel to cut it back, but yes, it is moving, slowly," Galathae replied.

"At its rate of advance it will be a hundred years or more before it comes near to Scellobel," Mona Valrissa explained. "It still has not fully taken Cattisola, but there is little of value there any longer."

"Your lifeblood is the hot springs that you call the River Callidae," Jarlaxle said. "Without it, you could not live here. You would have to abandon this place and find a new home."

"If the glacier continues its advance," said Mona Valrissa, seeming perturbed.

"If I'm correct, it will. I think the slaadi are doing it," Jarlaxle stated, and that began a hundred whispered remarks and exchanges throughout the assembly.

"The remorhazes," he went on, and he paused again, and Catti-brie could see him rewinding his thoughts to the background of his explanation. "Why do the hot springs flow here in the midst of Qadeej? Is it a deep volcano, perhaps, or a primordial, or great elemental god of fire? Did your people happen upon a godly struggle locked in stasis, where Qadeej and such a primordial of fire had fought to a standstill that leaves you with the streams of hot water that provide such life to Callidae?

"Perhaps. But I—but we—don't think so. In the abandoned Ulu-tiun town, Catti-brie reached through her ring and found no sensations of any such second beast. So possibly it is a volcano, far below, feeding the fire, melting the ice in these areas that the hot springs might flow.

"Or maybe it is something else. In the Underdark, there are vast chambers of huge crystals. We call them the breathless rooms, because—well, if you went in one, you would understand. I've seen only one, and from afar, and even from that great distance, I could feel the heat emanating from the place. To remain inside such a chamber would kill me, or you, or any of us."

"But not a remorhaz," Galathae put in, nodding.

"Do you recall what the infant worms were chewing in the hatchery?"

"Crystals," Galathae answered.

"Jarlaxle, what are you proposing here?" Mona Valrissa demanded.

"Take some miners and go through the tunnels to Cattisola," he explained. "Dig, and pray have many warriors looking over the miners, ready to do battle. I believe you will find vast chambers of crystals, and there on the edge of Qadeej's encroachment, you will find the work of the slaadi in the form of polar worms. They are unbalancing the land to allow the growth of Qadeej, a change that will drive the aevendrow and all the others from this place you call home. Kill their remorhazes and you will deal a great blow to the slaadi."

The assembly held perfectly quiet then, a decided hush, with the gathered representatives looking to each other, and ultimately toward Jarlaxle.

"Of course, I—we—cannot be certain," Jarlaxle finished. "But this is what I believe might well be happening, given what we saw in the strange hatchery."

Galathae moved to Mona Valrissa, the other inquisitors closing in for a private huddle.

"Jarlaxle, all of you, we are most grateful that you have shared these thoughts," Mona Valrissa said at length. "If there is nothing more, you are dismissed to prepare for your journey. The Temporal Convocation will remain in session until we have come to agreement on how to respond to these suspicions you have shared. Certainly, we will investigate."

"If your fears prove true, then Callidae owes you a great debt, my friends," Galathae added. She walked over, the other inquisitors beside her, and with Ilina, led the companions from the Siglig to prepare for their coming adventure.

CHAPTER 25

Through the Blizzard

The journey out of Callidae was quite different from the one that the friends had taken back to the hatchery. Accompanied by a contingent of nearly three score, mostly aevendrow but with a dozen Ulutiuns and a handful of kurit and oroks, they traveled from the lodging in Scellobel through Mona Chess and into the borough of Ardin, the Garden Borough of Callidae. All the way, a dull roaring sound continued far above them, the winter wind speaking loudly, and neither the stars nor the Merry Dancers could be seen as a ferocious storm filled the sky with blowing snow.

"We should come back here and remain for some time," Jarlaxle remarked to Catti-brie when he first looked upon Ardin, which was very different from either Scellobel or Mona Chess. Few large buildings could be seen here, and none rising more than a score of feet or so. Fields dominated the view, many speckled with huge and hairy bovine beasts, which the friends immediately realized were the muskox producers of that wonderful kurit cheese.

Catti-brie nodded, understanding the sentiment, although when the wind shifted in a swirl from the open night sky far above, the bits of snow that hit her came alongside a most terrible stench.

The muskox herds produced more than milk, clearly.

Even before that dose of reality, Catti-brie was nodding to be polite, and because this wasn't a discussion she now desired. Ever since she had told her story to the Temporal Convocation, the last parts of her address, ruminations on her family alone, had dominated her thoughts. She dearly missed her husband and daughter and couldn't wait to return to them, return to her life. Those many friends she had left behind, too—Wulfgar, Bruenor, Regis, Penelope, and all the others—beckoned to her. She had been eager to get out on the road for this mission both because of a sense of duty due to the notion that this quest might make a significant difference in the coming Menzoberranzan war, and because, simply, of her own desire for an adventure.

A vacation, of sorts, from the inevitable monotony of a peaceful and settled life.

Being here in this wonderful place had proven a great distraction, full of excitement. Yet still the pangs of homesickness were growing by the hour, only reinforcing to Catti-brie the blessings of her own life. If Drizzt and Brie were with her, she imagined she'd feel the same as Jarlaxle, and would stay here for months and learn and experience the uniqueness of Callidae. But they weren't here. Which meant that if not for Doum'wielle, if not for her responsibility to her friends, she would have accepted whatever conditions the Temporal Convocation had set for her, whatever ritual they used to blur her memories of this place, and recalled to the Ivy Mansion immediately following the assembly.

The party moved through the ways of Ardin, noting that there seemed to be proportionally more orcs and dwarves living in Ardin than they had seen in the other boroughs.

"They are wonderful with the oxen," Emilian told her when she asked about it. "Here and in B'shett, the kurit and the oroks have found lives more akin to that which they once knew and treasured. Now they have the best of their old traditions and customs with far fewer challenges and hardships. More of both peoples live in Scellobel than in Ardin, but that is mostly because Scellobel is where their ancestors, or even they, first came into Callidae, and it is easy to settle there."

"How many come in each year?" Catti-brie asked.

Emilian shrugged. "Sometimes none. Sometimes one or two are found out on the ice and brought here for aid. Sometimes, as with the Ulutiun village, a large group will come in all at once. Whatever the number, we have the room and welcome them as we welcomed you. This is the strength of Callidae." He flashed her a smile and a wink. "Long ago, the oroks showed us how to better ice the wine, freezing the grapes on the vine and stomping them while frozen to make it so much sweeter. And the kurit taught us all how to make the cheese." He pinched his cheek, which, like so many here, was a bit plumper and less angular than that of the average drow Catti-brie had known before this place. "I thank the kurit for this and the oroks for my better dancing."

Cattie-brie laughed.

"The oroks brought us the hagfish, too," he went on, "and the phlegm that has made our clothing and armor and many other items so much better. The kurit added to that orok work on our garments and fabrics, mixing the cured phlegm with the silk of the white spiders. You slept on a bed covered with that silk. Have you ever known a more comfortable sleep?"

She couldn't say she had. She wondered, though, given the additions these other cultures had brought to Callidae, why they were so determined to deny any thought of commerce with the south, as Jarlaxle had offered.

She dismissed that almost as soon as she thought of it, reminding herself of the many wars she had known in those southern lands. Up here, there was but one enemy, and from what she could tell, the skirmishes were few and far between. She thought of the hatchery they had found, though, and she hoped that the relative peace would continue for these friends she had discovered in Callidae.

A couple of hours of walking brought the group to the northeastern corner of Ardin and a great wooden door set between barracks of town guards. When it was unlocked and opened, they found a second portal only a short way in, similarly sealed, and then a third and then a fourth, finally opening into a tunnel set with a marker post that read TERAMARE.

"Land and sea?" Jarlaxle said aloud, not quite catching on.

"This marks the spot where there is no more land beneath your feet," Emilian explained. "Now we walk out upon the ice pack, and below that is the sea."

"That's not terrifying at all," Entreri remarked.

Emilian laughed at the sarcasm. "The ice pack is very thick here near the glacier, deeper than it is high. There is nothing to fear. You would have to bore down hundreds of feet to strike the water."

The magical illumination in here was not colorful, just simple lines of plain light cast under the ice at the base of the side walls. The corridor ran long and tight and fairly straight, dotted with side channels every so often. At one such intersection, they came upon a group of kurit and aevendrow loading a cart with blue ice.

"The mines," Emilian explained. "They are very deep, and the best of the blue ice comes from that flattened and most pressed ice over the water. Of course, you must know the exact places. Too near the sea, and it is just ice, and besides, a deep miner might break through, fall under, and be lost to the living world. The kurit know the secrets well. Most of their mines are in B'shett for the white ice and the lighter blues, but out here, there are rich blue sheets—you see?—which we all prize for their beauty and their strength."

Catti-brie and the others could only shake their heads in wonder.

"The blue ice can hold more powerful enchantments, too," he continued. "You have seen Galathae's sword, which might be the finest weapon in Callidae."

The tunnel continued a long way past the mines, with far fewer lights showing the way as it gradually climbed. The group camped right there in the tunnel on one relatively flat expanse, then started early after breakfast the next day.

Ilina spent some time with Catti-brie, telling her that they would be outside very soon and offering some tips on spells she might prepare. She explained that it would take them five days outside the tunnels to get to the caverns below the fortress, maybe more if the storm continued to rage.

"We'll be outside the glacier?" she asked.

"Oh yes, we would never allow tunnels to connect us anywhere near the slaadi, and never build tunnels large enough for frost giants."

"How will we shelter if not in the tunnels? We don't have mountain walls to protect us from the wind out here and it seems as if it's getting even colder."

"There are more rifts along the journey, but that is why so many Ulutiuns came along with us," Ilina said. "You will be amazed at their constructions."

Off they went, and less than two hours later, they came to a small chamber open to the sky, where the wind whistled a curious song and they were hemmed in on all sides by a wall of ice some fifty feet or more high on one side, and towering hundreds of feet above that all the rest of the way around.

Aevendrow immediately began fishing in a couple of the many bags and bundles they had brought along, taking out silken ropes and large grapnels, pitons, and spiked boots.

Catti-brie and the others went over to get a closer look.

"You will climb?" Jarlaxle asked.

"Yes, of course," said Emilian, "and set ropes up top so that the others may follow."

"Why not just use magic?"

"We prefer to keep all that we have in case of a desperate situation," Ilina answered.

"But this," Jarlaxle explained. He flicked his hands, bringing a dagger into each, then brought forth his innate drow magic and began floating, hand-climbing easily with the daggers.

"You are a wizard?" Emilian asked, seeming quite taken aback.

"He is drow," Zak answered before Jarlaxle, who was now floating back down. "As are you—you cannot levitate?"

The surrounding aevendrow stared at him as if they had no idea what he was talking about.

"Now, this is an interesting turn," Jarlaxle said, setting down beside them. "So it was the Faerzress all along, the barrier to the lower planes, which gave us this inner magic."

"Interesting indeed," Ilina remarked.

"Can you summon darkness? Or faerie fire?" Zak asked her.

"Of course! I am a priestess of—"

"I mean, without your divine magic," Zak clarified. "Simply because you are drow?"

She shook her head.

"And what else?" Emilian asked, rather sharply.

"Just those," Zak answered. "This is unexpected."

"And convenient, it would seem," Emilian said. "Do you think you might use these abilities to bring me up to the top of the wall?"

"The two of us could, certainly," Jarlaxle told him, and when Emilian had gathered the needed gear, they did just that, Jarlaxle and Zak levitating and dagger-walking up the wall. They repeated the trip several times, bringing others up with more ropes, while the kurit began pulling long planks from what were obviously bags of holding and assembling a large platform to secure the journey for all others.

At the top of that wall was a ledge that opened perhaps twice the height of the room on the other side, within a glacial rift. The wind was louder here, deafening almost, but it remained far above, and only occasional gusts whipped down. Still, it was no perch to be standing upon in a northern wind at all, for it was, of course, made of ice. So the aevendrow pulled a long, rolled carpet of hagfish mucus from another bag of holding and spread it about, providing a sticky and secure footing.

Clearly, it had been cut to specifically fit this spot.

"Take great care in your descent," Ilina told Catti-brie and Entreri as other aevendrow helped them into harnesses that would latch onto the ropes. "You won't fall even if you slip, but with the wind, you might bounce about the ice wall."

Rappelling down the other side of the ice wall was among the most terrifying and exhilarating experiences Catti-brie had ever known, akin to the first time she had used a spell of flying. Entreri, too, came down with an ear-to-ear smile, but the way he had so easily managed the rappel made Catti-brie realize that he was no neophyte at this activity.

"When have you ever climbed mountains?" Catti-brie asked him at the bottom.

"I made my way in Calimport by getting into the palaces in snea— let's say 'unconventional' ways," he answered with a wry grin.

"What do you think of all of this?" she asked him, looking around, and realizing that they had a couple of rare moments just to themselves. Jarlaxle and Zaknafein were helping the aevendrow shuttle supplies and no Callidaeans were near.

"All of what? They're prepared. They know the land and know how to survive well in it. It's impressive."

"No, that's not what I mean. What do you think of . . . them, the aevendrow? Of Callidae? Of their strange ways?"

He shook his head. "The aevendrow are what they seem."

"You knew that when you told them your tale, I expect."

"I knew it beyond a doubt when they saved Zak at cazzcalci," he answered. "That is why I dared to tell my tale. I think I knew it all along but was simply afraid to believe it."

Catti-brie could certainly understand that sentiment.

This chasm in the glacier went right and left out of sight in the dark night. The cloud cover hung very low in the sky, stealing the starlight, the moonlight, the curtains of green and purple. Too low, Catti-brie thought, for the storm clouds seemed to reach down right to the top of the glacier, and it took her a few moments to sort out that it wasn't just the clouds above, but a steady and unrelenting blizzard of snow up there. Through the gloom and blowing snow to the right came a high-pitched sound, like something in between a bark and a shriek. Soon after, many figures appeared, approaching fast. Orcs, the companions realized, a dozen, and each behind a sled pulled by what they presumed to be mukteff—but no, they realized as the teams drew close, these were larger, longer, and with four legs on each side. And snarling, yipping, and nipping at each other, fierce and barely tamed.

"What in the Nine Hells?" Jarlaxle said, rushing with Zak to join the two, Azzudonna close behind.

Entreri tensed at Catti-brie's side, so she grabbed his hand.

"We are not deceived," she insisted.

He relaxed a bit at least.

"The Burnooks," said Azzudonna.

"What is a Burnook?" Catti-brie asked.

"An arktos orok clan," she explained. "They are Callidaeans, but many of them spend most of their time outside the glacier. They are our eyes and ears out here, on this side of Qadeej. Fine friends."

She started forward, but paused and seemed to be considering something.

"The Burnooks were the ones who found Doum'wielle and brought her to us," Azzudonna added with a smile.

"Fine friends," Catti-brie agreed.

Galathae and a couple of other aevendrow, along with a pair of kurit, went out to speak to the orcs.

They returned, the orcs beside them, though they left the sleds and teams safely back from the group, snarling and yipping and showing nasty fangs.

"Not mukteff," a dwarf remarked as she walked by the four friends. "Ho hey, but ye might want to take care not to pet the little beasties."

"I can see that."

"Might've been mukteff once, lots of grandparents ago, at least on one side," said the diminutive fellow, a smiling chap with blue skin and tremendous white eyebrows, whose mouth seemed too wide for his face.

"What are they, then?"

"Arktos vorax," said the dwarf. "Vicious beasts that ye're not wantin' to meet absent their orok masters, I tell ye, hoi hoi. They eat what they can find, they do, 'cludin' each other."

Catti-brie hardly registered the words, caught by the accent of this kurit. She hadn't noticed it so strongly with Kanaq in Cascatte, but this dwarf rolled his words like a proper Battlehammer, though in the tongue of the aevendrow.

"Hoi hoi?" Jarlaxle echoed.

"What about it?"

"What's it mean?"

"Means hoi hoi, o' course."

The rogue started to reply, but just shook his head and let it go at that.

"The storm is blowing, but we should go anyway," Galathae told them all when she returned. "There's a sheltered nook a couple of miles on. We can get there, at least. If we wait for the storm to end, we might be here for a tenday."

"I'll get the runners," the dwarf said, and rushed off.

"You can ride on one of the sleds if you desire," Galathae explained. "Or you can try a pair of runners."

Before they could ask what a runner might be, the dwarf came hustling back, carrying a bundle of long, narrow planks turned up on one end and with straps near the middle.

"Skis," Catti-brie said.

The three others stared at her blankly.

"One of the Icewind Dale tribes uses them. You wear them as shoes and slide them along, using small spears to propel you."

"We are fortunate, for the wind will be at our backs," Galathae said. "You might need the poles to slow you more than to propel you. Come, then, if this is your choice. Alviss will fit you properly and help you learn to use them."

"We could just ride," Entreri said.

"On those?" Zak replied incredulously, pointing to a vorax team that was close to open warfare on one another, so it seemed.

"We have steeds," Entreri reminded him.

"Save them," Jarlaxle counseled. "Let us . . . slide."

"Ski," Alviss the inugaakalikurit corrected. "Ye got long legs. Ye'll do well, hoi hoi."

"Hoi hoi," Jarlaxle replied.

GOING OUT FROM THE RIFT TO THE OPEN ICE PACK SEEMED to Catti-brie like leaping into a fast-flowing, roaring river.

All sound was buried almost immediately under the howl of the wind, and the whipping snow, or ice crystals more likely, drummed against her back with such determination and frequency that she felt as if a swarm of large wasps was blindly flying into her.

"Stay close!" Galathae yelled, a most unnecessary order, for it was fairly obvious that if any got separated in this blinding tempest, they'd never find their way back. Catti-brie thought of using a light spell, but quickly realized that the aevendrow weren't doing that—Ilina, too, was a priestess of the domain of light, after all—for a reason.

Off they went at an easy pace at first, but as Galathae measured the steadiness of the foreigners, she urged the orok lead teams to go faster and faster still. It wasn't a long time—not more than a couple of hours, but enough that it left the friends thoroughly exhausted—before they pulled up into the sheltered area.

The Ulutiuns, all of whom had chosen to ride on the sleds, rushed into action, collecting their tools from the magical packs. The others began cutting blocks from the side of the glacier and sliding them into the intended campground.

The friends watched in amazement as the Ulutiuns and the oroks who had come with the sleds efficiently and expertly began constructing domed structures, and with all of the others supplying the building blocks, they soon had more than a dozen ready to go.

"Come on, then," Azzudonna told the friends, and she grabbed Zak by the hand and began dragging him toward one of the igloos. "This one's for you four, and I'll join if you'll have me. At least five to a shelter, Galathae commands!"

The wind went away when they crawled in, and Ilina and Emilian came in soon after, bearing large furs for bedding, along with some wood and stones. They placed the wood in a depression that had been dug in the middle of the chamber and Ilina lit it. Then, as the flames took hold, the aevendrow began stripping off their outer clothing.

Emilian prepared a fine supper of conjured blubber steak, and the seven sat around the circumference of the round room, enjoying each other's company.

A short while later, a shout alerted them to a visitor, and Alviss crawled into the igloo. He moved over to Catti-brie.

"Might I be troublin' yerself for a tale?" he asked.

"A tale?"

"Ye might've seen me at Temporal Convocation," he said.

"Alviss is a representative of B'shett," Ilina explained.

"Aye, and Boscaille'd've tied the war if that one hadn't started the magic!" the dwarf declared. "Though the magic was the better thing, I've to admit. Ne'er seen that before."

"What tale can I offer?" Catti-brie said to the cheery fellow.

"Any about yer da and that place—what'd ye call it??"

"Gauntlgrym?"

"Aye, and the other, the first one."

"Mithral Hall," she answered.

"Tell me, please," begged the dwarf. "Canno' hear too much about our kin to the south. Ne'er seen 'em, doubt I e'er will, but good to know they be there, ye see?"

"Hoi hoi," Catti-brie answered, and the dwarf roared with delight.

So she told him all about when she and her friends, well more than a century before, had found the long-lost Mithral Hall, and the shadow dragon Shimmergloom. She noticed Alviss's expression change rather dramatically when she started talking about the battles with the duergar, and she took care to minimize those parts of the story, realizing that she was making the friendly fellow rather uncomfortable.

"Shame in that," he said quietly when she finished.

"In what?"

"In them duergar going down into the deep Underdark," he explained. "Same as the drow elfs. Too low, too near the demons. Ruined 'em both for thousands o' years. Me own family's got duergar in the lines, so me grandyda told me."

Catti-brie couldn't help but glance at Zak and Jarlaxle at that reply, and they both had heard Alviss, she could tell.

"Ruined some, but not all of them," she assured Alviss.

"Ah, well, *a'aha'ile*," he said. "Ye mindin' if I put meself here for a sleep?"

Catti-brie looked at him in surprise. She was planning to ask what that greeting meant exactly, as this was the second time she had heard it, but the unexpected request buried that thought.

"Of course, good Alviss," Azzudonna answered before Catti-brie could get any clarification. "The more, the warmer."

"Hoi hoi," Alviss answered. He pulled off his heavy boots and wiggled his toes, then plopped down on his belly and buried his face in his folded arms right beside Catti-brie. Before she could even sort it all out, Alviss's snores filled the igloo.

She had to admit, it reminded her of home.

Smiling, wondering if Alviss's choice of his bed had been noticed by the others, Catti-brie glanced about in the low firelight. Her eyes widened, and her smile followed, when she noted Azzudonna snuggled comfortably with Zak, who seemed quite content indeed.

They started out the next day to great progress, for though the storm continued to rage, the wind had shifted and was now mostly blocked by the glacier. They went right past their next intended rest fissure, but turned back soon after, for the wind continued its shift, seeming like the path of the sun they had witnessed circling the top of the world.

Now the wind was at their backs as they retreated to the fissure, and in there set their camp.

And there they remained for several days, for they could not test those headwinds.

"It is just the way in the long night," Azzudonna said with a shrug, and if she or any of the other Callidaeans minded this unexpected delay, they did not show it. "So many things can happen, particularly out here on the ice cap," she told them, "and you simply must accept that and be prepared for it, and let the storm pass."

So they did. They rested in their igloos and they talked among themselves and with their new friends—and Azzudonna and Zak seemed to be great friends already, and lay beside each other every night.

Entreri and Jarlaxle spent most of the time with Emilian, Ilina, Vessi and Ayeeda, and Catti-brie had more than a few new friends of her own soon enough. She didn't even share an igloo with her companions from the south at this juncture, but rather with Alviss, a handful of other kurit, and even a pair of orcs, a husband and wife who told her that they were the ones who had found Doum'wielle wandering the ice cap—or more specifically, had found her in their own igloo, where she had crawled in, nearly dead.

Just like the kurit, they wanted to hear her tales more than tell their own, and at first, it was quite uncomfortable for Catti-brie. She thought of her arguments with Drizzt, and felt rather awkward now with this clear evidence of orcs who were worthy of her respect and friendship.

That epiphany led her to quiet and uncomfortable musing that followed her to sleep—questions about her goddess, about the actions of her life, about her perception of reality itself.

The next day, the storm still impassable, she remained with this group, and even told them of the conflicts in a land called the Silver Marches, of a war between dwarves and orcs that ended with the signing of the monumental Treaty of Garumn's Gorge.

And she told them honestly of how the treaty hadn't held, and war had come once more, to the fall of the Kingdom of Many-Arrows.

The orc couple seemed sad, but not too bothered. And the dwarves no less so in either case, with not a cheer among them for the victories of Mithral Hall.

"It is different up here," said Ninik Burnook, the female orc. "The land itself wants to kill you. You live because you have friends. You will need them and they will need you. You have no room for enemies."

"Except the slaadi and the giants?" Catti-brie asked.

"Only because they make themselves so," Ninik replied. "For those of us of Callidae, it is best to just avoid them. But sometimes we cannot."

"Like the fight where Doum'wielle was lost?"

"Yes," Ninik answered. "I drove one of the sled teams that brought the rescue teams to the caverns below the castle. We do not go near to that place often, of course, but we had to try to recover the captured kurit. We were hoping for a stealthy rescue; what the party that entered the caverns found instead was a great fight that cost many lives."

"Here's hopin' that yer Jarlaxle friend helped us sort out the riddle, eh?" Alviss remarked.

Catti-brie let it go at that, and asked for tales from her companions in the igloo. They were happy to provide many, particularly the orc couple, who were out on the ice cap most of the time and had some grand adventures indeed. Mostly in the summer, though, when they could find puddles and ponds of meltwater far from the glacier.

Ninik told of white whales coming up several at a time, poking their heads from the water simply to watch her and her husband. She told of a seal rookery, with thousands of baby seals waddling about and learning to swim.

It struck Catti-brie rather profoundly that while most of her stories were about battles and glory and generational conflict, those of the kurit and oroks were not.

The stories went on and on, and became more private discussions as one or another of the gathering drifted off, and even those gradually quieted, overcome by snores and heavy breathing as all fell asleep, Catti-brie doing so without the slightest reservation about her orc and dwarf companions.

The storm broke in the morning and the caravan set off once more, moving easily through the next days until one morning, soon after their breakfast and repacking, the friends were told that there was just one more journey to get to the caverns, a short one, and most of the team would not be going farther than this campground.

The aevendrow volunteers—Azzudonna, Emilian, Ilina, Vessi, Ayeeda, and Galathae—put on their skis and led the way. After only a couple of hours skiing along the side of the glacial wall, they turned down a narrow rift, and from there, into a tunnel to the right, one low and more fitting for a human or a drow than for a giant or a slaad. Any relief the four southerners might have gotten from that proved short-lived, though, for their aevendrow escort left the skis outside and entered the tunnel with weapons drawn and ready.

A short way in, they came upon a small chamber, which seemed a natural hollow and nothing that had been carved out and shaped. Galathae led them in.

"This is as far as we go," she told the companions. "One last time, I must ask you to reconsider. Your friend is lost, and if you go deeper into these chambers to find her, then I believe you are lost, too. You have a word of recall prepared for Callidae?"

"I do," Catti-brie assured her. "It will bring us to the signposts in Scellobel, near the inn."

"Keep it close in mind," the paladin advised. "When we return to Callidae, if you are not back there, then we will know that you have perished. I hope to see you. I do not wish the perils of this place for you, or for any. Follow the tunnel and stay to the right at any forks, and take no side passages left or right. When you come upon a huge chamber filled with pillars of ice, you will know that you have found the fall of Doum'wielle, and of so many others. I suspect you will not find her there, but if you do, it will not likely be the woman you once knew, but an overtaken. Do not feel any guilt when you destroy that monster, if you are able, for in that case, it is not Doum'wielle, and could not again be Doum'wielle."

"You've told us only a bit about these monsters, the cante and the n'divi, you call them," Artemis Entreri said brusquely. "Do you have any details to add? Perhaps like how we best fight them? What they look like? Anything?"

"There isn't much more to tell," Azzudonna answered before Galathae could reply. "The cante are empty as clear ice and flow like water. You don't see them until they are upon you. That is their secret."

"And they flow upon you, climbing up onto you, and encase you and freeze you and suffocate you," Galathae added. "Then their magic devours you, or melds with you—we cannot know because none have prevailed in a fight with them in any meaningful manner. No aevendrow has stood over a defeated cante, or wouldn't gain insights even if so because its corpse is no more than water. You can destroy them with weapons, with fire, with lightning, and likely a host of other magical spells, but that is not the problem. The problem is that they come upon you quickly, and overtake individuals before you realize you're under assault. Those victims become n'divi, the overtaken, not living, not dead. Not to be reasoned with, but only to be destroyed. In that event, you are left with the corpse of a friend."

"Use your fire, but take great care not to stir the wind god," Azzudonna added. "When we came here and fought, we awakened Qadeej."

Galathae looked to the warrior and nodded, her expression one of great pain and sorrow.

"We were fifty in number, fully armed and prepared for battle," the paladin added. "It was not a long fight. More than half were lost."

"But you didn't come back after them," Zak remarked.

"You should consider that truth alongside our pleas to you that you do not go back for Doum'wielle," Galathae replied. "We didn't come back because we had no choice but to accept the loss."

A long and uncomfortable silence hung in the air between them all.

"Might I have my whistle?" Jarlaxle asked, finally breaking the tension. "Not this one, for I see no mukteff about."

Galathae shook her head. "Your whistle remains in Callidae, and if you return to us, you will be given it under the agreed conditions. And if you do not return, it will be locked away in the Siglig, in the deep libraries where we keep magical items and books that we dare not use. I do hope you return to reclaim it."

"And in that case, perhaps refuse to take it back," Emilian added.

"We are leaving soon," Galathae said. "Are you sure you cannot be persuaded?"

"We are. Just as we are grateful that you brought us here," Cattibrie told her.

"I fear that you would not be if you truly understood that which awaits you," the paladin soberly replied. "Right at any forks—I recall three of them—and take no side passages and enter no side chambers."

She motioned at the tunnel beyond the room and let the friends go on their way.

Zak and Entreri took the lead, turning left at the tunnel and moving down a short distance, where Jarlaxle called for a pause and all four turned back to watch the departure of the aevendrow.

"You're sure about this?" Entreri asked.

"Of course I'm not," Jarlaxle answered. "But Doum'wielle would prove a great prize, and we might save ten thousand lives if we can rescue her. More, it is the right thing to do."

He nodded to Zak, who drew out Khazid'hea and handed it to Catti-brie.

She took it gingerly, held it loosely in her palm, and let her mind interact with the magic of the weapon. She opened her eyes only a moment later.

"I feel her. Very near." She paused. "I . . . think." She shook her head, for these sensations through Khazid'hea really weren't convincing her of much at all. She'd had no experiences with any magic akin to this until Jarlaxle had brought it to her attention, not even long before when she had wielded the sword. Nor had she heard of any such feelings with others when they used Khazid'hea. Still, she really couldn't be certain if the sword was telling her that Doum'wielle was alive or dead, or worse, if Doum'wielle had become one of these monsters Galathae had just warned of. The whole mission—as it ever had—seemed tenuous to her, at best.

She gave the sword back to Zak. "I have the word of recall at the ready, and I will be quick to use it," she promised.

"Not too quick," Jarlaxle said. "I have no desire to ski all the way from Callidae if we have to come back."

They started away, Catti-brie looking over her shoulder repeatedly the way they had come, where Azzudonna had lingered behind the other departing aevendrow and now stood staring at the companions. It was pretty obvious to Catti-brie that Azzudonna among all of their new friends was most anxious to see the return of the southerners.

Particularly Zaknafein.

With that cheery thought in mind, Catti-brie chased after her three companions.

CHAPTER 26

The Breath of Qadeej

J arlaxle pulled out a wand, very slim and of smooth metal. With it, he cast a dweomer upon himself allowing him to detect any magic in the area, while Catti-brie used her own divine powers to do likewise.

"You watch left, I'll focus on the right," he told her. "Let us hope these cante creatures are magical in nature, that we might discover them before they get too near."

"Move quickly," Catti-brie told Entreri and Zak. "The enchantments will not last long."

Down they went, but not as fast as they wanted, for the tunnel became quite slick. Entreri passed a side chamber and glanced in, but moved along as Galathae had instructed.

More side passages and chambers dotted the hallway, and again, with only cursory looks, the friends pressed on. Entreri came to another hole in the tunnel wall, this one rounded like an archway, and the chamber within curving and roughly oval, seeming almost as if this area had suddenly melted and flowed outward.

Entreri moved past.

"Hold!" said Catti-brie, coming behind him. She stared into the room, the hairs on the back of her neck tingling. She sensed something, or perhaps some movement had flickered in the corner of her eye.

She stood there crouched, staring, waiting.

Jarlaxle came beside her. "Magical and yet not?" he asked, and Catti-brie nodded, understanding his meaning completely.

Something was in there.

The floor undulated suddenly as if a wave had rolled through. And in its wake, a form arose, a single blunt watery pillar rearing like a cobra and swaying in a slow dance. It bubbled and rolled in on itself, and from there took shape, humanoid shape, except that it was completely of liquid.

"Cante. Uninhabited," whispered Jarlaxle.

Two more humanoids appeared.

Catti-brie waved her hands and three lines of fire shot forth, hitting one fully in the chest, clipping a second about the hip and taking one leg right off, and melting the head off the third.

The first diminished as it shed water, but came forward.

The second fell over onto the floor, dissolved into it, and came right back up again, leg reformed.

And the third continued its headless approach, until another head grew out of its collar.

Lightning flashed from Jarlaxle, hitting the first again, squarely. The bolt grounded on it, through it, leaving a spiderweb of cracks with bits falling away.

Zaknafein leaped in front, bringing forth his fiery whip.

Entreri tried to join him, but called out, suddenly stuck to the floor.

Catti-brie turned at his call, then looked on in horror as another monster climbed up his leg, giving him the sensation of sinking into a puddle. The watery creature's leading edge remained fluid, flowing upward, the liquid left behind froze solid.

Entreri whacked at the floor with Charon's Claw, breaking the ice all around. He grimaced and groaned in pain, and they could see the ice squeezing his leg.

A crack of Zaknafein's whip cut the floor just beside the trapped foot, then a second snap as Zak sorted out where the corridor ended and the cante began.

"The ones in the room!" Jarlaxle demanded, and another lightning bolt left his wand.

Catti-brie popped Taulmaril into her hands and began a line of arrows, aimed not at the humanoid-shaped ice monsters, but at the floor all about the entrance to the side chamber. Most just sparked into the ice, sending a small ball of electricity about and leaving cracks, but one caught yet another of the creatures flowing quietly, sneaking, out.

Entreri broke free of the icy grasp and attacked the spot with his red-bladed sword. He took up his jeweled dagger as he retreated and dug at the ice enwrapping his leg, but it was Zak's fiery whip that finished the job. The weapon master then turned on the one Catti-brie had struck with an arrow.

"Don't call to the Plane of Fire!" Catti-brie reminded him as the weapon master went into a wild dance, spinning and snapping the bullwhip, the weapon perfectly designed for fighting creatures made of ice, surely.

One humanoid-shaped monster got too near and Zak took its legs with a single, devastating crack of the whip. The torso bounced to the floor and began to dissolve, but an arrow of lightning shattered it.

Into the room Zak spun, battering everything in sight, floor, monster, walls, even taking down an icy stalactite.

"More!" Entreri called from farther along the corridor,

"Flee!" said Jarlaxle when he turned that way, and Catti-brie understood, following his gaze, for the whole corridor seemed alive with flowing forms, waves of elementals, water weirds, or whatever strange cross of the two these monsters might be.

But they couldn't flee, couldn't hope to get away from this liquid swarm.

"Cover!" Catti-brie called instead, and she threw her greatest fire spell, a tiny pea of flame flying away down the corridor.

She had no idea what the result might be, or how far back the fireball would expand in the confined space, but she was fairly certain whatever happened would be better than that which they now faced.

As soon as she let fly the spell, she shied away and lifted her cloak up over her head and shoulders, and the hot winds rolled over her, rolled over them all.

And then, as quickly as this encounter had begun, it ended, the air thick with mist and strangely quiet, save for a dripping sound. When it cleared, the friends, all shaken, skin red and warm, held the defensive posture for some time.

But the tunnel showed no further movement.

"We should leave," said Entreri, hopping all about, sword and dagger at the ready. He swept Charon's Claw around, dropping a wave of ash to the floor, thinking the contrast would show him any movement. "Now!"

"We are almost there," Jarlaxle argued.

"Cast your spell!" Entreri told Catti-brie.

She looked at him curiously for a moment, then came to understand. The human assassin had spent many days trapped in a magical cocoon, a memory that was clearly rattling him now.

"I have it ready," she assured him.

"I felt it. You didn't feel it. That thing. It wasn't just ice. It wasn't just *on* me. It was seeping into me, and it was telling me to let it."

"It was speaking to you?" Catti-brie asked.

Entreri shook his head. "Yes. No. I don't know." He blew out his breath, trying to steady himself. "All I know is that I don't want to feel that again. Ever."

"Doum'wielle is close," Jarlaxle insisted. "You felt it with Khazid'hea."

"You heard the warnings of Galathae and the others," Entreri argued. "It's not her. It's . . ." He looked back down the corridor, at the puddles on the floor and the rivulets on the walls, already freezing once more. "It's them."

"Give me the sword," Catti-brie told Zak, and he handed her Khazid'hea.

She fell right into it, dominating it, forcing it to consider the elf it had once controlled.

"She's not far at all," Catti-brie told the others. "I feel it."

"We have to look," Zaknafein said.

"Here they come again," Entreri warned.

"Do it," Jarlaxle told Zak, nodding at his whip. "And bring allies forth, Catti-brie. We have no choice."

"We could leave," Catti-brie reminded him, but Zak had already cracked his whip across, and this time it did tear a rift into the Plane of Fire, drawing a deep and dripping line in the air.

"Keep your spell of recall ready," Jarlaxle told her.

She didn't need that prompt. She did reach through the magic in her ring to the tear Zak had created and pull forth elementals—small ones, but many—then commanded them off down the tunnel, where they ran up against the approaching horde of cante in a steamy battle.

On they went. At Catti-brie's call, Zak opened another tear and more elementals came forth, leading the way. The companions followed Galathae's direction, staying right at the forks, and if they had any trouble locating the uninhabited, the small living fire elementals surely did not, seeking them out like aimed arrows, colliding with hissing embraces.

Whenever the flames went out, a crack of Zak's whip brought more in, and Catti-brie sent them running ahead.

Thus far, at least, Qadeej had not awakened.

GALATHAE KNEW THEY SHOULD BE LONG GONE FROM THIS place, but her arguments against Azzudonna and the others who wanted to linger had been half-hearted at best, for the paladin, too, wanted to see what these new friends from the southland might do. Galathae had led the group that had come here those months before. She had lost a score of aevendrow, Doum'wielle, and a trio of orcs.

That defeat had weighed on her, of course.

She knew her responsibilities here, and her orders were clear that they not risk any more Callidaeans. They were supposed to be on their skis and moving back for the previous rift, where the rest of the escort team waited.

But the sounds of lightning bolts had stopped them, and Az-zudonna had led the way back, cautiously, to the site of the first battle.

They could tell from the shards lying about the floor of the oval room, and from the smoothness of the corridor ahead—a glassy tableau that showed the melt of a fireball—that the southerners had fought a terrific battle here, and the mere fact that none of them were here, encased, showed they had won that fight.

"Perhaps they're right and Doum'wielle is alive," Azzudonna said when Galathae told them that they must depart. "Perhaps our lost friends are similarly so."

"They are overtaken," Galathae said. "We know that."

"*Do* we know that?" Emilian questioned. "The confusion of the battle was unlike anything we have yet seen."

"But the result was something we've seen all too often," Galathae reminded him.

"We'll stay safely back," Azzudonna promised.

When Galathae hesitated, the warrior started off down the corridor.

Galathae started to call out to her, to scold her and order her back.

But that last battle she had led in here, those losses . . .

"Just a bit further," she agreed. "But stay close and prepare to flee."

I'm not losing any more of those I lead, the paladin told herself.

THE TUNNEL OPENED AHEAD INTO A WIDER AREA, AND before the companions even reached that point, they knew that the chamber Galathae had described to them lay beyond. Catti-brie called to the few small fire sprites, moving them back behind the foursome to cover the tunnel, then motioned for Entreri and Zak to advance. They went in slowly, cautiously, and paused at the entrance to survey a most spectacular room.

It was as large as Cascatte, a huge chamber, roughly square, with a ceiling of ice far, far above, as distant as the ice wall directly across from the tunnel. To their right, the side wall was not far away, the chamber, predictably, as they were on the right-hand side of the glacier, opening to the left. It was not dark in here, the shimmering lights of the Merry Dancers coming in through a large circular hole in the middle of the wall far to the left—no, not a hole, Catti-brie thought, but possibly a thin sheet of translucent ice. Whether that was the case or not, there was an opening somewhere in here, for the wind moaned and sighed, the breath of a giant, the breath, perhaps, of Qadeej, a hollow and empty sound that gave the vast chamber a sensation of emptiness. A frozen waterfall loomed near the center of the opposite wall, almost as if put there to serve as a fast slide down from a long-running ledge some fifty feet from the ground. Perhaps there were tunnels at the back of that ledge, ready to bring a host of charging enemies in upon them.

The floor itself was broken, with varying sheets of frozen steps, or more appropriately, uneven and disjointed shelves. If the ice of a frozen lake had been cracked apart by undulating waves below, then flash frozen once more as the swells moved along, it would resemble this floor.

Dozens of stalagmites dotted much of the floor, particularly here near the tunnel entrance. Some loomed twice the height of a tall man.

The overtaken? Zaknafein's fingers asked, silently saying what they were all thinking. This had been the spot of the battle where Doum'wielle had fallen—or perhaps "fallen" was the wrong word, for if there were bodies encased in those stalagmites, they were likely standing upright.

But this was the site, from everything Galathae and Azzudonna had told them.

"The sword, Zak," Jarlaxle whispered, and he nodded toward Catti-brie when Zak looked back at him.

Zak handed her Khazid'hea and she immediately put it up before her, holding it loosely, letting it find Doum'wielle among the forms.

"There," Catti-brie said breathlessly only a moment later, now gripping the sword more tightly and stabbing it toward a stalagmite some thirty feet or so away, just a bit to the left in a cluster of several of the up-pointing icicles. "It is her!"

She gave Zak the sword back and they all strained their eyes in the dim light, trying to see if there were indeed discernable figures in those pillars.

Catti-brie took out her bow and called for an arrow from her magical quiver. She whispered to the arrow a command word to eliminate the lightning properties, then held her hand before the tip and looked to Jarlaxle.

"Light one," the drow rogue agreed.

Catti-brie stepped deeper into the tunnel and turned away, then placed a minor enchantment on the tip, a light spell. She set it to her bowstring as she turned about, leveled, pulled back just a bit, and let fly, the arrow speeding toward the nearest stalagmite and jabbing into the ice.

The companions gasped as one, for illuminated by the magical light, they could see the clear form of someone, likely an aevendrow, trapped within, arms raised up high before her as if trying futilely to defend herself.

"Are they going to animate and rise against us?" Entreri asked. "If not, do we try to break them all out, or just Doum'wielle?"

"Give the sword to Catti-brie," Jarlaxle told Zak. "Take us straight to Doum'wielle. If we can free her and she is indeed alive, we can then decide further."

"Stay close," Catti-brie told them as she took the sword. "I'll not hesitate to teleport us out of here, but I warn, the range of my spell is limited."

She took the point, following Khazid'hea's telepathic directions, with Entreri and Zak a step behind, flanking two steps left and right, and Jarlaxle in the middle behind them. The rogue cast a second spell of detect magic from his wand, as the first one had long since expired.

Catti-brie veered to the right, putting some distance between them and the magically lit stalagmite. She watched closely, as did the others, trying to see if there would be any movement at all from the figure trapped within.

They saw nothing, just the blurry form of an aevendrow in what seemed to be the last moments of her life.

Farther into the vast chamber they crept. Past more mounds, moving straight for the targeted one now.

"Zak, ready your whip," Jarlaxle warned. "We aren't alone."

With Doum'wielle's pillar clearly identified by then, Catti-brie turned back toward Zak and handed him Khazid'hea. She pulled out Taulmaril and set an arrow.

Not a moment too soon, for behind her and to the right, Zak lifted his whip and snapped it low against the floor, which shimmered beneath the blow as the approaching cante split apart.

"Here!" Entreri called from the other side, and Catti-brie reached through her ring to the tear Zak had created, but managed to glance back to the left to see Entreri dancing about, waving Charon's Claw down low, the red blade releasing walls of ash all about the floor.

"Clever," she heard Jarlaxle say as she brought forth dripping balls of living flame and commanded them forth to seek the monsters of water and ice.

Up came the horde of uninhabited, taking humanoid form, a veritable army of the cold monsters pressing in from all sides.

Up came Taulmaril in response, lightning arrows crashing through the monsters and flying on.

Up came Jarlaxle's giant conjured bird with a great squawk, running off wildly, wings flapping, pecking and stomping with its great talons.

Up came Zaknafein after rolling farther away from the group, buying himself the room he needed to fully work his whip. He did so in a fury then, snapping his wrist back and forth, cracking it against the ground before him over and over, shattering any monsters sneaking too near, icy shards and droplets flying.

And of course, more tears cut into the air to the Plane of Fire.

Catti-brie reached through them to bring in more elementals, as those she had already sent forth met with cante in a foggy crash of mutual destruction. She kept firing her bow, too, but they were being sorely pressed now, with monsters coming around every pillar, as if the entire floor of this vast cavern was rising up against them.

"We have to leave!" she cried.

"Too many," Entreri agreed. Catti-brie glanced that way to see the man and the diatryma rushing about, smashing their nearly translucent enemies. Entreri seemed cornered, though, and was too far away for her word of recall. If she cast it, he would be abandoned here.

A lightning blast from Jarlaxle bought Entreri a bit of room, albeit temporarily.

"Now, Jarlaxle!" Entreri yelled, rolling out between a pair of reaching uninhabited. He left something on the ground as he came to his feet, and Catti-brie understood just a moment later when a large, emaciated black stallion appeared, fire flowing from its mane and hooves and spouting from its nostrils with every angry snort.

Entreri leaped upon its back and sent it furiously bucking and spinning, every kick exploding an animated ice man, every stomp puddling the ground and sending flames and smoke flying all about.

An angry neighing from behind told Catti-brie that Jarlaxle had followed Entreri's lead.

But they had to get out of there, and now they were too far apart!

"Fight them! Fight them!" Jarlaxle yelled. Another lightning bolt shot forth, arcing past Zaknafein and skipping through a trio of cante. Cracked, they were easier to discern, and Zak put his whip to fast work, three quick strikes, three destroyed enemies.

Three out of legion.

Entreri and his mount went leaping and spinning, furiously kicking, up ahead of Catti-brie, though still to her left. Very near the stalagmite she had illuminated, the hellsteed bucked, spun, and double-kicked, exploding a cante—the nightmares seemed the perfect foils for such monsters!—and kicking right through it to smash into that mound of ice.

Entreri just kept moving past, not even watching, it seemed, as the stalagmite cracked and split, a slab falling off to the side.

"To Doum'wielle!" Jarlaxle commanded, but then came a second voice.

"Help me," pleaded the poor aevendrow caught within that mound. Battered, her skin blistered, she reached desperately toward the fighting four, trying to come to them. But as she was still frozen in place from the waist down, she just fell limply over the edge of the cracked pillar, her arms waving in the air pitifully, as if she were trying to swim to them.

Up ahead, Entreri pulled up his mount and looked back, eyes wide with shock.

For here came the next wave, and these were not uninhabited. They were the same size, and surely cloaked in ice, but with drow inside. Like ice-covered zombies, shambling and sliding.

Catti-brie gasped when she looked past Entreri, past the overtaken, to the ice waterfall halfway across the room. She blinked, trying to be sure of what she was seeing, and launched a silver-streaking arrow in that direction to light it up.

Dozens, scores, of n'divi poured down from that ledge above, sliding down the waterfall and coming on.

To the left and behind, the diatryma shrieked, and Catti-brie had barely glanced at it, barely registering that the bird was frozen to the ground, more ice forming all about its thrashing body even as it tried futilely to wing-beat and peck and shake free, before hearing a cry from Zak the other way.

He, too, was stuck to the ground, monsters swarming. He went into a whip-snapping frenzy, over and under with fury.

But they couldn't hold.

"Get to Doum'wielle!" Jarlaxle commanded, and he, too, went past Catti-brie on his hellsteed, kicking at anything that got too near.

Catti-brie looked past Zak, to the ledge along the wall opposite the tunnel, and there loomed a new threat, one that froze her in place in dread.

A slaad, perhaps, for it seemed a frog-like humanoid, but much larger than those they had encountered, giant-sized and dark-skinned, its eyes flaring with orange demonic flames, its mouth wide and full of pointy teeth, demonic flames behind it, too, making the monster's head look much like a gigantic jack-o'-lantern. It held a huge curving blade, jagged on both sides and looking as if it could cut the four of them in half with a single swipe.

"Come near!" Catti-brie ordered her friends. "Now!"

The giant leaped out from the ledge, bat wings unfolding behind it as it glided toward them. Were they leathery or were they flesh? Or were they simply smoke? Was all of this demon monster's form just smoke? Catti-brie could see its skeleton through the dark fog.

"Zaknafein!" she cried out, for it was swooping in from that side. She leveled Taulmaril, but then lowered it and lifted her unicorn pendant instead.

"Run!" she heard Jarlaxle yell then, and she knew he had seen it, too.

Catti-brie pressed the pendant, her holy symbol, to her lips and called to Mielikki, channeling the power of her goddess. The area around her lit up in a brilliant radiance, a divine light, biting at her enemies, melting them, diminishing them. The flying, smoking giant came into the radiance and recoiled, clearly stung, and Catti-brie dared hope, fleeting though it was. For her radiant light expired and the gray slaad behemoth remained.

They had to get out. Catti-brie knew they had to get out.

She glanced at Jarlaxle and Entreri, but they were too far away. So was Zak, but she thought she could get to him, so she leaped that way, ready to utter her word, ready to send herself and the weapon master back to Callidae.

She heard something, but in her head and not aloud, and thought it a name. As she sorted through the sound, she realized the truth of it, that it was the boastful announcement of a great being's arrival.

Ygorl!

Then a second word, a word she did not know, a word she could not unravel and could not decipher, and could not dismiss.

A word that stunned her and confused her and sent her staggering back several short steps.

In swooped the giant slaad, in came the blade, and then came a black flash and it was gone, leaving behind just a curl of dark smoke.

Zaknafein was yelling to her, but she could not hear. She could see the flashes of his whip, but could not reach out through her ring to call forth elementals.

She stumbled and turned and saw the great monster again, but

now all the way across the room, standing before the bright translucent circle letting in the light of the Merry Dancers.

All the way there, across the room.

A teleport?

But nothing made sense as that strange indecipherable word kept
repeating in her every thought, kept knocking her back and off balance.

She saw Jarlaxle upon his steed, kicking and spinning, destroying
another pillar with fiery hooves, an orc falling free to the floor and
trying weirdly and pitifully to rise, his limbs not quite answering the
call of his thoughts.

She saw Entreri similarly bucking his steed, ice flying, flames snorting and spouting with every breath and every slamming hoof.

And she saw, most of all, that giant silhouette before the huge ice
circle far away.

As if mesmerized, the stunned priestess watched the huge curving
blade lift, then suddenly sweep out and back, slamming the sheet of
ice, which broke apart and fell crashing from the wall.

And in came the wind, and even with her magical protection,
Catti-brie could feel the sudden bite of cold, and the sting of a hurricane of sleet, blasting through the vast chamber.

She couldn't remember her spells, couldn't remember her name.

She watched in horror a hail of ice pellets drive at Zak, then form
a small tornado swirling about him. He snapped his whip furiously for
a short moment, but then his arm wouldn't move as the ice grasped
him. The whip became a blade of flame sparking and hissing against
the unrelenting icy barrage.

A stalagmite of ice grew thick around him.

She saw Jarlaxle's hellsteed, riderless and leaping, and saw Jarlaxle
fall to the ground, then through the ground beneath the cyclone.

Farther on, Entreri's horse was spinning, spinning, lower and
lower, as a tornado formed about it. Spinning and spinning and then
it was not, for it and its rider became a stalagmite, and then the hellsteed vanished, and the mostly hollow mound crumbled, but reformed,
a lump of ice entombing the fallen Artemis Entreri.

And Jarlaxle's mount was gone, the rogue nowhere to be seen.

Finally, the stunning word let her go, and Catti-brie tried to lift her bow, for what else might she do? But it was useless, for she couldn't even see the far wall and the smoky slaad giant as the fury of the ice pellets pounded against her. She noted the poor aevendrow and the orc, still trying to rise, but caught again by the frozen tombs, and she heard the increasing roar of angry wind as the pellets began to spin tightly about her.

She dropped Taulmaril to the ground. She tried to remember her spells, her word of recall, to be out of there. But her face was encased and she couldn't utter a sound. She tried to cover, tried to break free of the frozen mask, tried to grab at anything that might help: her belt, an arrow, her pouch.

But she couldn't talk, couldn't cast, and then couldn't move as she, too, became a stalagmite.

So suddenly had it turned.

So suddenly had their plans shattered.

So suddenly had they lost.

Catti-brie wanted to call out, but she could not. She thought of her loss, of never seeing Drizzt or Brie again, of her foolishness in coming here, to the north and to this place, against the warnings of the aevendrow.

She wanted to see Callidae again, to walk its ways with her husband and their daughter.

But she would not.

She considered one other friend, but couldn't even utter her name.

Except . . . she didn't have to.

FLASHES KEPT THE AEVENDROW BAND MOVING FORWARD, slowly, slowly, inexorably pulled by their loyalty to these four strangers who had become such friends in so short a time.

They could hear the fury of the fight, the crackles of lightning and the snap of Zak's whip, a cacophony now fast diminishing.

Then the roar of the wind, thunderous and painful, and one both Galathae and Azzudonna had heard before.

Enough, we must be gone, Galathae's lifted hands silently screamed to them, and the paladin grabbed Vessi, who was closest to her, and tugged at him to turn back the other way. He resisted until far ahead, they saw a form, large and dark, rushing down the tunnel.

All the aevendrow turned and ran, even Azzudonna, who gave one last glance back for Zak, knowing in her heart that he had fallen.

The warrior wouldn't have outrun the pursuit in any case, but her hesitation had her at the back of the retreating line and so it was she who felt the heavy collision from behind, throwing her forward and down, rushing at the ground.

Enwrapped, shocked and overcome, she never even felt the impact.

EPILOGUE

She felt herself leaving her body, her spirit flying up through the glacial ice, up, up, into the air. She saw the lights of Callidae far ahead and below, and lamented the last beautiful glimpse of the home she so loved. She thought of her friends left behind. Thought of her fellow Biancorso soldiers, of the joys and the proud scars, of that last battle and the throw, one guided by pure determination and will—and that, too, seemed to her an out-of-body experience, much akin to this.

Then she was up among the Merry Dancers, shimmering in greens and purples and whites, and she felt as if her spirit was joining in that dance of exultation. The magic swirled and tingled and it was a beautiful thing to her, almost an explanation of cazzcalci's unexpected turn, of the power nearly fifty thousand voices had lent to that wounded southerner.

Her spirit lifted, higher and higher, up beyond the northern lights, flying fast for the moon and the stars.

Up and up. She saw the curve of Toril, then the whole of the globe, and still she flew, without tether, into the heavens, the Astral Plane.

Callidae was gone, to her great lament.

Her friends were gone.

Biancorso was gone.

She was sure that she had heard the last cheers of cazzcalci.

"IT WASN'T YOUR FAULT," ILINA TOLD GALATHAE AS THEY began donning their skis. "Don't be foolish. Azzudonna above all insisted that we follow them. Azzudonna alone hesitated in our retreat when the battle turned."

"And what was that?" Vessi asked. "It was no slaad, and no cante or n'divi."

"I think it was the great cat," Galathae admitted, but shaking her head, for it had happened so very fast and she had caught just a quick glimpse before they were gone. "Catti-brie's cat."

"Who was no enemy," said Ilina. "Is it possible that our Azzudonna . . . ?"

Her voice trailed off and she sniffled a bit, gathered up her poles, and pushed away.

The other four followed, quickly. They skied out of the rift and turned fast, keeping the glacial wall on their right as they sped along, not stopping at all until they came to the next real rift and the encampment where the rest of the expedition waited.

On Galathae's command, all of them—aevendrow, kurit, orok, and Ulutiun—broke camp immediately and rushed away.

She had lost the southerners.

Now she had lost Azzudonna.

She wasn't about to risk any more.

JARLAXLE SAT IN THE DARK AGAINST A MAGICAL WALL and beneath his great hat, which had turned into a huge, sturdy umbrella at his beckon, the handle set against the floor between his straightened legs. He could feel the weight pressing down upon it, the ice that had flown into this space behind him, the same ice that now encased his outstretched feet, and he could only hope that the umbrella would hold back the press.

Above him, the rumble of the wind gradually died away to nothingness, leaving behind a silence as profound as the darkness and as cold as the ice.

He wasn't quite sure what had happened. What was he to make of those magical cyclones, the likes of which he had never before seen or heard of?

All he knew was that his friends were gone and lost to him, and that he was alone in a hole, sealed in by a mound of hardening ice, and with hordes of formidable monsters outside.

This wasn't the way he had planned it.

Jarlaxle never liked when things went the way he hadn't planned.

EVERYTHING CAME AS FLASHES OF LIGHT AND SWIRLS OF darkness for Azzudonna, who felt as if she were swimming through the heavens, circling the world that had been her home, out of control of her movements and unsure if this was death or life or something in between.

She began to plummet, but was not afraid.

She came back into the sky of Toril, and it was light, not night, and below was a land blanketed in snow, with huge trees and towering mountains.

Then a town, a small town, set in a region of fields and forests, and a grand mansion built on a hill, overlooking all the other structures.

Down she went, plummeting for it, but she wasn't afraid, not until she neared the roof and kept going!

Right through, but without collision.

A spirit, insubstantial, and then not.

Azzudonna found herself sitting on a wooden floor in a small room with a closed door right before her and a giant black cat standing beside her.

Only then did she understand that it was Guenhwyvar, Catti-brie's cat, that had taken her on this ride, and that she certainly wasn't dead and wasn't a disembodied spirit—at least, not any longer.

Now she was just Azzudonna again, lost and unsure.

The great cat's ears went back and she gave a long, loud growl.

The aevendrow didn't know what to do.

The door burst open a few heartbeats later and a human woman appeared, her face going from an expression of surprise to one of abject shock.

She was older than Catti-brie, it seemed, with dark hair, and wearing a woolen dress and a colorful shawl.

Beside Azzudonna, Guenhwyvar faded away to nothingness.

Azzudonna didn't move. She heard talking in the hall, the voice of a man, but she couldn't understand the words.

"What is it, Penelope?"

About the Author

Thirty-four years ago, R. A. Salvatore created the character of Drizzt Do'Urden, the dark elf who has withstood the test of time to stand today as an icon in the fantasy genre. With his work in the Forgotten Realms, the Crimson Shadow, the DemonWars Saga, and other series, Salvatore has sold more than thirty million books worldwide and has appeared on the *New York Times* bestseller list more than two dozen times. He considers writing to be his personal journey, but still, he's quite pleased that so many are walking the road beside him! R. A. lives in Massachusetts with his wife, Diane, and their two dogs, Pikel and Dexter. He still plays softball for his team, Clan Battlehammer, and enjoys his weekly *DemonWars: Reformation* RPG. Salvatore can be found on Facebook at TheRealRASalvatore, on Twitter at @r_a_salvatore, and at RASalvaStore.com.